TANK
COMMANDER

TANK COMMANDER

A HISTORICAL NOVEL

"To be a good reporter writing about war, you have to write about the people. It's not about the tanks or the military strategy. It's always about the effect war has on civilians, on society, and how it disrupts and destroys lives."

Janine di Giovanni

Tank Commander puts you in the tank with its crew; from every page, you understand what war was like for our veterans."

CW2 Richard Fink, retired military

TANK COMMANDER ---- KAREN SCHUTTE

For further information contact Green Spring Publishing at www.karenschutte.com

Scripture quotations are taken from the King James Version of the Holy Bible. Permission, all rights reserved. Information/Maps permitted by 81st Tank Battalion, 5th Armored Division/Statute of Limitations Expired.

The opinions expressed by the author are not necessarily those of Green Spring Publishing, 3608 Green Spring Drive, Fort Collins, Colorado 80528

Copyright © 2016 by Karen Schutte. All rights reserved
ISBN for printed material: 978-0-9904095-9-5
ISBN for e-book: 978-0-9904096-0-1
Author's photograph by Skillman Photography, Fort Collins, Colorado
Historical WWII Cover photo, used under expiration of statute of limitations.
Cover Design by Thayne Sturdevant Graphic Designs
Interior Book Design by Elizabeth Klenda – Frontier Printing

**Watch for first novel in a new historical family saga series,
THE GERMAN YANKEE -- 2018**

Novels by Karen Schutte

Historical Fiction: The Family Saga Trilogy

THE TICKET – 2010

SEED OF THE VOLGA – 2013

FLESH ON THE BONE – 2014

'The Finale' - TANK COMMANDER – 2016

The German Yankee – 2018

This Novel is dedicated to:

Staff Sergeant/Chief Warrant Officer
Arnold W. Korell,

His wife, his family, all WWII and
Korean Conflict Veterans.

ACKNOWLEDGMENTS

This novel was inspired by actual family and historical events. It is deemed fiction because particular names and dates have been changed to protect the privacy of such. Certain characters and isolated circumstances of WWII and Korea exist only in this novel. Historical events are depicted as researched and as the once restricted daily log of my uncle's 81st Tank Battalion revealed. My purpose is to tell the story using my imagination to complete dialogue which is plausible. My research is amassed from numerous sources including authentic letters, diaries, and accounts from the era.

I am proud of my German/American heritage. At no time or point during the telling of this story did I intend to demean the Chinese, Japanese, or German people by the slang terms used. This is a novel from the American aspect of fighting a war in which they faced terrible, unexpected atrocities. I also endeavor to enlighten my readers of the plight of the German civilian as the war evolved and ended. Most found themselves at hopeless odds against the Nazi regime and faced certain death if they refused to participate. My German cousin, Siegfried Mell, shared the full account of the harsh and harrowing day-to-day struggles his family and most German civilians faced after the war.

As might be expected, this is a novel about war and contains numerous graphic scenes and profane language. Realistically, it is a known fact that when in the throes of battle, soldiers become verbally animated; they do not pause for proper adjectives when faced with death! For reference, I Googled common and frequent profanity used by soldiers in 1943 and used that as my guide. It was almost absurd to think of "tankers" looking through the periscope and upon seeing three formidable German Tiger Tanks descending on them, saying, "Oh my goodness, here come three Tiger tanks!"

Many people have contributed to the research of this book. First of all, I want to acknowledge my Greybull High School history teacher Roger Youtz. I loved every minute of his history classes. I'm eternally indebted to Rich Fink and, Karen Spragg, curators of the Lovell, Wyoming Museum and the Lovell's 300th Armored Field Artillery Battalion/National Guard, which was deployed to Korea in 1950. I spent an afternoon with several very knowledgeable and razor-sharp Korean veterans who generously shared their time and memories; Bob Baird, Kenneth Blackburn, Wes Meeker, as well as WWII veterans Robert Baird, Robert Doerr, William Fink, Elmer Gernant, John Gibler, and Meryl Gibson. Thank you!

It was a unique blessing to have had the opportunity to interview WWII veteran, Elmer 'Pete' Gernant, who passed away in February, 2015. I sat across the table from Pete on a snowy day in late November, 2014, and we talked. He served in General George Patton's 78th Lightning Infantry Division and was one of the first Americans who charged the Bridge at Remagen; crossing the Rhine River and onto German soil. Even though he was in failing health, his memory was not lacking. NOTE: I changed many of the names of the veterans whose stories I used in this book.

I want to give special acknowledgement to longtime personal friend Tom Davis, author of <u>GLIMPSES OF GREYBULL</u>. Tom holds a B.A. English/History degree from the University of Wyoming; member of the Wyoming State Historical Society; Big Horn County Historical Society, and serves as historical advisor for the Greybull Standard in NW Wyoming. Tom was intrigued when I conveyed my plans for <u>TANK COMMANDER</u> and leaped at the opportunity to do some preliminary tracking of Arnold's military service in Europe. He was instrumental in giving me a decent jump-start and I am deeply grateful for his contribution.

Certainly, there was undeniable information, honor, and yes---even some humor in the veteran's stories. My uncle's high school buddy and his best man Robert Doerr from Byron, Wyoming opened windows into my uncle's past, from their high school days to when he and Arnold were drafted and left Lovell for boot camp; they eventually went their separate ways to fight in Europe.

To Arnold's three children, my cousins Terrill Korell, Renee Wilson, and Arneen Korell---I owe my utmost gratitude for your eager willingness to provide crucial photos and documents that were beneficial in telling your father's story. The stack of information and photos (including duplicates) which Arneen provided was astounding and made such a difference in the authenticity of this story.

Having never been inside a Sherman tank, Brad Pitt's movie, "FURY" was a God's send to me. Through the story line and action of talented actors, I was able to experience being inside a Sherman tank as well as being part of unspeakable terror and horrors which occurred during battle. Having had that visual experience, I could, in turn, write about it. Thank you all!

As with the first three novels, my village came through with flying colors to read, edit, and propel me to the finish line for this fourth novel. The qualified editors/readers were: Ilse de Granda, born in Germany in 1938--German/English translator/editor, certified by ATA, chemistry degree from Flensburg Univ. with post grad. In neuroscience at John Carroll Univ., Ohio; Terrill Korell, BS Guidance Counselor/Psychology -- Retired High School teacher & family editor; CW2 Richard Fink, retired; Captain Jim Wong, USMC Vietnam; Charles Doggett, AIS, CSA, A/C USAF Korea- stationed at P-Y-Do radar site on the 38th parallel in the Yellow Sea; and Karen Boehler, VFW National Chaplin and veteran's editor.

Above all, I want to thank my husband, Mike, for coming to my aid time and time again with technical advice, editing, and encouragement. He is a proven, excellent, and trusted final editor of my manuscripts.

In retrospect, I want to thank my Uncle Arnold, for his service, for his sacrifice, for his bravery, endurance, and courage. As a child growing up, I never knew, I never understood, I never had any idea of what he went through, of what he saw, did, suffered, and the memories he endured for a lifetime. Now, because of my historical research, I get why he never offered to talk about the war and probably only a fraction of what he had to do to survive. Now I understand!

~~~~~~~

AUTHORS NOTE:

Beginning with THE TICKET, SEED OF THE VOLGA, and FLESH ON THE BONE, this fourth novel is the *finale* to my German maternal family trilogy. As with my other books, TANK COMMANDER is based on family--my Uncle Arnold's true story.

Arnold Korell/Kessel was born in Lovell, Wyoming, the only son of Jake and Raisa. He was the grandson of Karl and Katja Korell/Kessel and David and Sofie Schmidt/ Steiner, as well as brother of Beata/Beth.

I must admit it was unbelievably difficult at times to find the words to paint the picture of the horror and carnage that defines war. Certainly, I benefited from reading other war novels, but it was a horse of a different color when it came time to sit down and describe the pictures which evolved from my mind's eye. There were nights when sleep would not come to me because of the vivid atrocities of battle and suffering which my uncle undoubtedly experienced.

If you come away with anything after reading this novel, I hope it is a profound sense of debt and gratitude to all of those who don the uniform. Most military fight first to protect their buddies and themselves and secondly to protect their country. The novel begins with my uncle's tour of duty in WWII. As accurately as possible, this novel follows my uncle through tank training camp at Fort Knox, Kentucky, shipping out for Europe, and landing on Utah Beach on July 26th, 1944. Shortly thereafter, he was baptized by fire into the war and fighting for his life in Normandy, in WWII.

It was not possible to cover or describe every battle which occurred. My research was gathered from family stories, historical novels, the once stamped 'Restricted' daily log of the 81st Tank Battalion, museums much like the one we visited at Normandy, and finally, from interviews with living veterans.

Profound was the experience of visiting Normandy Beach. I stood on a high sea grass covered bluff overlooking Omaha Beach and looked down on the pristine white sand beaches that stretched as far as the eye could see. At my feet lay a gnarled and decaying wooden fence post still attached to snarled razor wire, a rusty reminder of what had been.

I stared at the scene that lay before me and could swear I heard it all. In my mind's eye, I saw the armada of hundreds of Higgins landing craft attempting to land on D-day or maneuver as close as possible to the beach. I saw those men fall and die, and others as they scrambled and struggled across the white sands. Those who reached and scaled the steep bluffs met a barrage of enemy firepower concealed in massive cement bunkers. Even after fifty years, the beach was pockmarked with holes as big as small houses where 1,400-pound high explosive (HE) rounds the battleships' 360 mm guns rained death and destruction on the enemy. Those great guns were aimed at the known camouflaged and reinforced concrete German batteries composed of 240 mm guns and Hitler's Zip machine gun nests. Some battleship shells hit dead on and some fell upon no special target still causing the enemy hours of terror and death. The deafening roar of exploding rounds was a crucial fear factor of the bombardment.

With every fiber of emotion in my body, I felt the utter horror and victories of that day course through me; my ears rang with imagined explosions and screams of the wounded and dying men. Of course, I was touched and impressed at that moment, but my tears didn't come until we toured the national cemetery. Visually witnessing acres upon acres of immaculate rows of pristine white crosses standing straight and silent was my moment of icy realization; each cross symbolized a cherished life lost on D-day. That's when tears of anger, sorrow, loss, and pride rolled unimpeded down my face.

Granted, many of you have read numerous books, seen movies, and other accounts of WWII and Korea, but it is my purpose and goal to take you with me as I reveal the personal experiences of my uncle. Of course, I didn't and don't know what went through his head, but I did know him well enough that I can certainly speculate. Fighting in a war was something they had to do; it was something that happened in their lifetime; it was something they had no control over but to fight to survive.

The war changed things for everyone because in some way we are/were all involved. I'm quite sure my uncle's life was never what it could have been without the haunting experiences of war. I know he did the best he could, coping with the horrific and plaguing memories of what was. Nobody ever really understood--- no one except those who shared similar memories and experiences.

As a country, as a people, it is our duty to try to understand or at best, appreciate what our military people go through-- the wounds and experiences they bring back. Simply put—I pray for world peace and understanding. *"Love one another, as He loved us!"*

~~~~~~

Everyone has a story, and I have tried my best to tell Arnold Kessel's story. He was a decorated member of the First Army, 5[1] Armored Division, 81st Tank Battalion, Company C, Combat Company B or CCB---Task Force Anderson. He was awarded six Bronze Stars; EAMF Theater Ribbon; Good Conduct Medal; and the Victory Medal.

The 5th Armored Tank Battalion shoulder patch is divided into three areas: red represents Field Artillery, blue represents Infantry, and yellow represents the Cavalry/Tank division. Superimposed are the tank tracks and the barrel of a tank's cannon. A bolt of red Lightning is overlaid, representing the speed of attack. The armored division's prominent number **5** appears in the peak of the patch representing the 5th Tank Division carried the apropos nickname of VooDoo! It was later known as, 'The Victory Division!'.

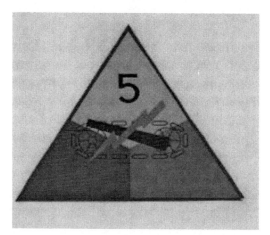

NOTE: Chief Warrant Officer Arnold Korell was later part of Wyoming National Guard – 300th Armored Field Artillery Battalion and was sent to Korea in 1950.

5th Armored Division Facts and Components:

Headquarters:
Headquarters Company, 5th Armored Division; Combat Command A (CCA), *Combat Command B (CCB), Headquarters, Reserve Command (CCR)
In order to be more effective, the Division was divided into three Combat Commands of equal strength. Combat Command B (CCB) was commanded by LTC John Cole and consisted of: the 81st Tank Battalion, 15th Armored Infantry Battalion and the 71st Armored Field Artillery Battalion. This CC was divided into two separate task forces---Task Force Anderson and Task Force Winternute – both named for their respective Commanders.

*Task Force Anderson: named after Battalion Commander, Lt. Colonel LeRoy H. Anderson.
B Co. 81st Tank Bn. --- married to B Co. 15th A.I. Bn.
C Co. 81st Tank Bn. --- married to C Co. 15th A.I. Bn.
Both B and C were married to Service Co. 81st Tank Bn., which supplied their units.

Armor: was 'married to' -------- Armored Infantry:
Armor	Armored Infantry
10th Tank Battalion	15th Armored Infantry Battalion
34th Tank Battalion	46th Armored Infantry Battalion
**81st Tank Battalion ----------	**47th Armored Infantry Battalion**

Division Artillery: Recon.
47th Armored Field Artillery Battalion.
85th Cavalry Reconnaissance Battalion, Mechanized
71st Armored Field Artillery Battalion
95th Armored Field Artillery Battalion

Engineers: 22nd Armored Engineer Battalion

Tank Destroyers:
628th Tank Destroyer Battalion (attached 2 August, 1944 – 18 December, 1944)

629th Tank Destroyer Battalion (attached 29 August, 1944 – 14
December, 1944)

Anti-aircraft Artillery: 387th AAA Automatic Weapons Battalion
(attached 1 August, 1944 – 25 March, 1945

The First Army, 5th Armored Division was briefly under General
Omar Bradley during combat at Normandy. Shortly after landing
in France, General George Patton was their leader. Shortly before
the Falaise Gap Battle, General Courtney Hodges was given the
command of the First Army, 5th Armored Division, and 81st Tank
Battalion. This army has a long list of FIRST accomplishments in
the European Theatre of War which include the following:
FIRST TO: LAND ON THE BEACHES OF NORMANDY ON
D-DAY
(81st Tank Battalion - CCB landed later in July 1944)
LED BREAK-OUT FROM NORMANDY AT ST. LO, France.
LIBERATED PARIS
FIRST TO CROSS THE SEINE RIVER
FIRST TO ENTER GERMAN SOIL & FIRST TO CROSS THE
SIEGFRIED LINE
FIRST TO CAPTURE MAJOR GERMAN CITIES
FIRST TO CROSS THE RHINE RIVER
LARGEST TOTAL CAPTURE OF GERMAN TROOPS BY A
U.S. FORCE
FIRST TO LINK UP WITH SOVIET FORCES
LARGEST U.S. FORCE UNDER SINGLE COMMAND IN
WWII (18 DIVISIONS)

NOTE: Even though the Fifth Armored Division accumulated this
extraordinary combat record, it was among the lowest in the
American military when it came to the casualty rate. This amazing
statistic was due in part to the speed and efficiency with which the
assigned missions were executed by its leaders, especially General
Lunsford Oliver and the men who fought with him. Patton's Ghost
Army, First Army Spearhead, or Ninth Army Spearhead – were all
anonymous tags which identified the Fifth Armored Division.

PROLOGUE

"Give sorrow words; the grief that does not speak knits up the over wrought heart and bids it break."
William Shakespeare, from Macbeth

Jagged, fiery bolts of lightning slashed the inky blackness of the summer night sky as deafening crashes of thunder rolled across the Yellowstone River valley, ricocheting off the million-year-old limestone rim-rock cliffs outlining the northern-most edge of Billings, Montana. Relentless cracks of lightning illuminated the night sky and exposed the form of a man standing alone at the large bay window of an unpretentious, cookie-cutter white house on Custer Avenue.

Icy sheets of wind-driven rain slammed against the plate glass window and slid unimpeded to soak into the ground below as the relentless storm battered the small house. The tall blond man who stood at the window wasn't old as years go, but through the window the image of his face was contorted with aging fear, pain, and anguish. With every crack of lightning and explosion of thunder, the man's face became a mirror of the inner torment and mental agony of unimaginable images he couldn't erase or forget, ever.

Oh, dear, God, I still can't get through a damn thunderstorm without it all coming back; those first horrific battles in Normandy—fighting like hell to get to the Falaise Gap. After all of that, we thought we had the Krauts on the run but then there was the dark bloody freezing hell of that Hurtgen Forest Battle. As if that wasn't enough, we went right into the endless Ardennes Forest at the edge of the Battle of the Bulge---those days of waiting in silent ambush for the German attack.

I tried to put it all behind me when I came home from Europe, but then there was Korea, where I damn near died again. There's nobody who understands except those guys who have been through what I have. How do I tell my family that a stupid thunderstorm or a firecracker scares the shit out of me and brings it all back in an instant? The reality of it is nobody really wants to take the time to try and listen or to help. All I get is lip service, sympathetic nods, and whispers behind my back. Everybody has hung us out to dry. They expect us to just forget it all and 'straighten up and fly right'. How do I explain what a living hell those two wars continue to be for me?

I don't feel no excitement or real joy in the life I have now---not as much as I should have anyways. It's like I'm still numb—going through the motions of living with this damn indifference about pretty much everything except my family, my wife and kids.

Blinding flashes and deafening cracks of lightning followed by rumbling explosions of thunder continued until the man put his face into his hands and sobbed. Wiping his eyes with his pajama sleeve, Arnold Kessel's face was a mirror of his haunting torment; his eyes were red and bloodshot. *Even crying doesn't erase the memories; it just releases them until the next time. The only sound that is missing outside this window is the slow, menacing grinding rattle of those monster German Panther and Tiger tanks as they inched closer and closer, coming in for the kill; there we sat in our insufficiently armored Shermans, waiting for them. It wasn't even a fair fight. It was all about the men inside of those rolling coffins and what we learned to do with what we had to fight with—it was kill or be killed. What a thrill it was to 'kill' a monster German Tiger Tank!*

Oh dear God---how many times was I reminded of the Bible story of the under-equipped and trained shepherd David, as he picked up his slingshot and a stone and went out to face the giant Goliath who stood waiting with his monster sword. The only thing we had on our side when we faced a German Tiger or Panther tank was the superior speed and maneuverability of our Sherman Tanks. We all knew they were built like a tin can compared to the German tanks. Every time we went into battle I was scared to death, like the rest of the tank crews, that ours would be the next one to take a direct hit and we would be roasted alive inside that metal tomb. We'd seen it happen too many times to our buddies. I can still smell the stench of blood, of death on a battlefield, of the gunfire, and the smell of cordite that clung to our clothes, our bodies, and sadly, our minds.

More tears came on their own triggered by unforgettable images and memories---the smell of death and the endless screams of dying men; of how their faces looked when they took a bullet, of seared flesh, of fresh blood, and the shrieks of those fellas the medics couldn't help or get to. *When in the hell am I going to forget all of that, when are the memories going to leave me in peace? I can't take it anymore. I feel like I am going crazy. Course, I guess that those of us who came back from hell on earth are all a little crazy because of it.*

I jump like a jackrabbit at the unexpected sound of a clap, a door slamming or just a surprise slap on the back. I've got a wife and two kids now; I've got a good job and even the all-American mortgage. They all tell me that I'm supposed to get on with my life, to just forget what happened over there, but nobody tells me how the hell to do that. Nobody wants to take the time to help us guys work through the hellish memories that haunt us, because frankly, they don't know how to make it go away, it's just that simple. I've seen shrinks and they each think they are the one who has the answers, but seriously, there are no set answers. There is no way to erase memories except, maybe death.

I was just a snot-nosed kid out of high school when I signed up to serve in Uncle Sam's Army. All of us guys were instant heroes back in our home town, back in Lovell, Wyoming. We were suddenly men going to war to protect freedom and our mothers. We had no idea in hell what lay ahead, what war was really like, what watching your buddy die in front of you was like. We just did what was expected and followed the lead like a bunch of stupid damn sheep. In boot camp and then in England, I thought I was a big deal, being in a tank battalion for General George Patton, "Old Blood and Guts" It didn't take us long to figure out where he got that label. All us guys, we went over there, to 'Hitler's Europe'—a bunch of wet-behind-the ears, innocent boys. Most of us younger guys thought we were invincible; we were fearless fools. I wouldn't call it courage at that point—it was gung-ho stupidity. I heard one officer call it audacity or some damn name. He said that sort of attitude really threw the Germans off balance and confused them. Yeah, right!

I do remember this --- in the heat of battle, fear seemed to leave most of us, especially when we saw a buddy fall. Then this blind red rage filled us and caused some of us to do stupid things. But I knew then and I know now --- fear never really left my side over there and it's still right here with me now. It's not courage that masks fear; it's how fast the situation is moving that causes you to not think, but to react.

Funny thing is that those of us who came back didn't have much audacity left at that point. We came back as damaged, war-wise men; nothing has ever been the same—nothing! One thing I know, during those first weeks in Normandy I felt a hell of a lot better after we were put under General Courtney Hodges and he let us sandbag and up-armor our tanks. Patton was too much by the book for me—all guts and glory, low on the common sense and outfittin' our tanks with sandbags or thicker armor! Hodges was a soldier's general—not Patton!

~~~~~~~

Arnold reached down and grabbed one of his smokes and put a match to it. Inhaling, he tried to relax and forget the storm. Suddenly he felt something pull at his pajama leg. Startled, he jumped to the side. Looking down through the dim illumination from the street light, he saw his eight-year-old son, Terrill. "Daddy, why are you standing alone in the dark? Did the storm wake you up? Did the rain get all over your face? Are you crying, Daddy?" The expression on his son's face only intensified the torment and anguish that had a death grip on Arnold's senses.

Arnold bent down, folding his arms protectively around his small son; he lifted him up into his arms and hugged his little body close. "No, son, I'm not afraid of the storm. It's just that when I hear a storm like this, it—well, it reminds me of the war, that's all. The big guns in the war sounded like the lightning and thunder." He kissed his son's soft face and rumpled his curly blond hair. "You get yourself back to bed now; you have swimming lessons tomorrow. I'm just going to finish smoking my cigarette and then I'll go back to bed, too. Don't worry yourself, I'm fine now. Go on, crawl back in your bed and go back to sleep."

Arnold watched as his son padded across the hardwood floor to his own room. More tears escaped from his bloodshot eyes as he thought of the innocence of his son, and he prayed his boy would never have to know what he knew. Arnold turned back to deal with the sound of the storm that raged outside the window and inside his relentlessly haunted and tormented soul.

Why do I keep having that same nightmare, the one where I went pure nuts in the Hurtgen Forest? It was when we came upon a whole squad of dead GIs who had been German prisoners and the Krauts had machine gunned them rather than move them through the forest. The next German infantry that came around that corner in those woods, I sure as hell raked them over and over and over with my .50 caliber machine gun. Even when they were dead, I kept shooting until Hans pulled me back inside the tank. I was shaking like a leaf and was completely out of it---didn't even remember doing it for a couple of days.

Maybe someday I'll forget and the nightmares will stop--- that will be the day I die!

PART ONE

LOVELL, WYOMING, 1943

"War seizes innocent boys and returns them as damaged men."
Author unknown

Chapter One

"THE LONG GOODBYE"

Arnold Kessel embraced his father. The young man could feel the work-hardened muscles tense and ripple through his old man's shirt as his father slapped him affectionately on the back, hugging him longer than was necessary or comfortable.

Holding on to Arnold's shoulders, Jake pushed him back so he could look him in the eyes. "You look real good son; that boot camp sure put some muscles on you and I expect they taught you all they can. Now it's up to you. Remember what I told you about picking your battles. Running from something you can't win is how you return the next day to kick some butt. Keep your head down, son. I love you! Oh and---don't take any wooden nickels!" Both men were tense, holding back their seething emotions. It had

only been an hour ago that Arnold stood at the bottom of his parent's wooden front steps for a last photo.

Taking a deep breath, Arnold gave a nervous loped-sided grin as he put his arms around his father. "I love you, too, Dad; always have, always will. I'll try my darnest to make you proud. I guess I'll see you in the funny papers." They had been there, at the station, waiting for the train from Billings, for the past half hour, but it seemed more like several hours. Arnold thought, *Man, you could cut the tension here with a butter knife.* He looked around the Lovell station platform at the twenty or so fellows in uniform who were saying goodbye to friends and family after their final furlough. *I wonder if it's as hard for the rest of the guys as it is for me to say goodbye. I figure we're all heading somewhere to fight; some are heading to the Pacific and others to the war over in Europe. One way or the other, I'm pretty damn sure each of us has considered that we might or might not be coming back to this sleepy little Wyoming town, to the people who have gathered to send us off in such a patriotic and rousing manner.*

Arnold glanced at his folks. *I can almost read their minds, especially Mom's. She's standing so stiff and still; I know she's wondering if she will ever see me again. I can see it in their faces—the fear and worry—even before I'm on the train. I'm glad that Beth and Jimmy and the rest of the family already said their goodbyes. It's getting damn hard to say that word and to deal with the emotion. I just want to get on that train and get out of here before I choke up or do some stupid thing in front of my pals.*

Finally the dreaded moment; it was time to kiss his mother goodbye. Arnold knew it wasn't going to be easy. *She already has tears in her eyes. Wish to hell she wouldn't do that, it's just the shits. Deep breath, boy, you are a tough soldier, now deep breath—just get it done!*

Raisa took a deep breath of her own and reaching up, she wrapped her arms around her only son. Not looking at his face, she whispered, "Arnold, your name stands for "strong like an eagle." Remember, God is with you and will protect you; we will be praying for you. Do what you have to do to come back to us, son. I will write to you and send you boxes as often as I can—let me know what you need. Come back to us, Arnold; we love you so much!" Her voice broke as she breathed in the soapy clean scent of him and ran her hand over the prickly blond growth of facial hair on his cheek. Raisa hoped she would remember the feel of her son's skin for as long as she had to.

Arnold could feel his mother's body begin to tremble and knew he had to make this goodbye quick. He kissed her damp rosy cheek and said, "I love you too, Mom. Take care of yourself while I'm gone, and don't forget how to make those chicken and dumplings!" He smiled nervously as he turned quickly toward the train, not wanting her or anyone else to see the tears welling up in his own eyes.

Out of the crowd, someone grabbed his arm, "Hey, soldier, can I have one last kiss before you get on that train?" Arnold dropped his duffle bag and pulled Norrie swiftly into his arms. He put everything he had into that last kiss. "Hey Sugar, I thought we had already said our goodbyes. I didn't expect you would take off work and come out here today, but I'm sure glad you did. That kiss will have to hold us both for a while. Write to me, will you? I am going to miss you, but you already know that, don't you? Just don't forget that you are my girl! Wait for me, Norrie, please wait for me."

Arnold bent, picked up his duffle bag and jumped onto the troop train that was beginning to move out. He turned to the left and hurried down the aisle until he found a window seat. Stowing his duffle bag overhead, he leaned out the open train window like all the other guys and waved goodbye to his parents, his girl, and his town. He waved until the train hit the east edge of Lovell and headed toward the Big Horn Mountains. It was then he settled back into his seat.

Most of the other soldiers were pretty quiet, trying to control their emotions and wrap their heads around what the future held. Oh sure, there were those big mouths who just wanted to start raising some hell and let everyone know how tough and gung ho they were to get over to Europe and start killing Krauts or to the Pacific and kill some Japs. Arnold thought, *Yeah, big tough guys. They are probably gonna be the first ones who turn tail, run and call for Mama when the bullets start flying. What lies ahead promises to be interesting, real interesting; we're all going into something that we know nothing about---war. None of us knows for sure what we will do when the shit hits the fan; I just hope I can hold myself together. First, I have to make it through tank school and learn everything I can about those babies!*

Arnold stared out the window, gazing at the familiar landscape, images that would have to last him for a while. *Hell, when the train pulled into the Lovell station today it was like some black smoking creature coming to devour us fellas. I'm glad for one thing: the sound of the engine and screeching of the iron wheels on the rails drowned out most of the audible crying and carrying on.*

Arnold took in a deep breath and let it out with a big sigh of relief that at last, the leaving ordeal was over. Looking out the train's window, he watched his old stomping grounds fade away. He thought about the series of events which gave birth to this very moment. Like when, the Selective Service Act was signed by the president, just three years ago on September 16, 1940. *I didn't know it then, but that little piece of history was going to have a big effect on my life. Sure, there was a serious threat of a war going on over in Europe again, but it seemed like one country or another was always at war over there and so hell, I didn't pay much attention. Besides, Dad said that President Teddy Roosevelt always said that we should "walk softly and carry a big stick!" Germany had these alliances with Italy, Japan, and Russia. So what was there to worry about?*

Just as soon as I hit the magic age of 18, me and four of my buddies walked down to the Lovell Selective Service office and registered for the draft like all the other guys. I remember how we laughed and kidded around; we felt like grown men for signing on that dotted line. We all knew I sure as hell wasn't going to go to college, so I guess like a lot of guys, I was ripe for picking. The Induction Officers asked us a few questions about date of birth and

Lovell Bulldogs - Arnold Korell # 99

general health, important stuff like that. I could tell they weren't too particular about what my answers were, what with the war getting worse and all. They gave us each an order and a registration serial number; that was our introduction to being a number in the service. They told us to go on back to school and that they would get in touch with us when the time came. In the fall of 1942, I was a senior in high school and frankly didn't think much about anything other than girls and basketball, but that was soon to change!

In May, the Lovell High School Class of 1943 accepted their diplomas. The next week Arnold had just finished playing a round of basketball with Bobby Doerr and a couple of his buddies when he headed home. He bounded up the back steps and into the kitchen, where his mother sat at the kitchen table. Not really noticing anything different, Arnold headed for the kitchen sink and turned the water on. Without bothering to get a glass from the cupboard, he bent over and put his mouth under the faucet.

"Arnold William Kessel, I have told you time and time again, NOT to do that. Just quit being so lazy and get a glass from the cupboard if you need a drink." Raisa gave him a swat with the dish towel accompanied with one of her withering looks and then returned to the kitchen chair and her coffee. She reached across the table and picked up an envelope; she handed the letter to her son. "Here, Arnold, this came in the mail today. I have to say I don't like the look of it."

Arnold reached for the letter and tore it open. A serious expression crossed his face. Taking a deep breath, he managed to say cheerfully, "Well, they didn't waste any time. It's from Uncle Sam, telling me to report for my physical." He laid the letter on the dining room table and then turning he picked up the black phone receiver and dialed a number. "Hello Bobby? Did you get your letter?" He paused a minute then said, "No, you dope, the one from Uncle Sam—the letter telling you to come down and sign the final papers for the draft. I suppose they'll tell us when we have to report for our physicals? Hey, I was thinking, maybe we should all go down together." Arnold cradled the phone in his right hand, listened again and replied, "Swell, I'll pick you up tomorrow around nine a.m., then we can swing by and grab Jim and Hank. Maybe, when we finish, we'll have time for a little "skirt patrol!" See ya tomorrow, Bobby. Bye."

Arnold glanced over at his mother, sitting cold stone silent at the kitchen table—she hadn't moved. He said, "Well Mom, tomorrow, June 7, 1943, is the big day. I guess you heard me talking to Bobby. We're going to go down to the induction center together and sign up—official like. We gotta get our physicals and stuff before going into active service. It'll probably be a couple of weeks. I'm not particularly looking forward to getting a physical—heard about that whole ordeal in the locker room! That should be a real experience seeing as how I don't like doctors to begin with. In the service, I hear they strip us all down and line everyone up like a conga line. Guess that makes it go faster. I just gotta suck it up and jump right in—forget the modesty you taught me."

Arnold didn't wait for his mother to reply, especially when he saw the stunned expression on her face. "When is supper gonna be ready? I think I might take me a short cat nap so I don't run out of gas tonight when I take my girl to the movie. Say, do you know what's playing anyway?"

Raisa rose from the table and took her empty cup to the kitchen sink. Rinsing her cup, she said, "Supper will be on the table at 5:30; that's when your Dad gets home from work." She turned and walked out the back door toward the garden.

Arnold watched her through the window and thought to himself, *Just as well, I know she's really upset and there's just no use hashing it over again. It is what it is, and that's that!*

~~~~~~~

As the train rumbled on down the track, a shiver of recollection ran down Arnold's back just thinking about that first physical. *We all left Lovell for Fort Warren[2], outta Cheyenne, WY. That's where we were inducted on June 22, 1943. Then they sent us different places for boot camp. They sent me and a bunch of the others down to Fort Carson, Colorado. The big brass told us to keep our draft notices with us at all times during the physical. Well, that was a tad difficult when we were all standing there with nothing but our skivvies on, and no pocket in sight! Some of them guys didn't have a self-conscious bone in their bodies. I have to admit I was just a little nervous about being almost naked in front of all those strangers and then the doctors. But it didn't take long for me to adjust. Hell, we were just a bunch of skinny kids with five or ten hairs on our chests. Besides, I'd played basketball for Lovell High and been in plenty of locker rooms with plenty of naked boys. Sure, sure, there were always a couple of dark-haired fellas with more than their share of hair and----!*

Man, I remember at boot camp and the first time I saw a guy with hair on his back. I never seen nothin' like that and I couldn't quit looking at him. The CO yelled at the top of his voice, "You green horns, now listen up, I'm only gonna tell you this once. Carry your clothes and draft notices with you at all times and line up behind that gate!" I seriously don't think those officers could talk in a normal voice. I got so used to being screamed at that it went in one ear and out the other.

When I laid my peepers on all of those docs, all seated in a row just waiting to poke and prod us, I got a shiver up my bare backside. We had to parade in front of them as they 'took a look-see' at everything we had and I mean outside and inside. There were a couple guys who didn't like a doc or anyone to touch their private places, but after we went through that physical, most of 'em had gotten over it. It was pretty humiliating, having to cough, and bend over and spread your cheeks. Gol damn, if that wasn't uncomfortable! My heart showed a few problems probably from the rickets and scarlet fever I had as a kid, but it wasn't enough that I got out of serving. When we lined up for the shots, there was a bunch of scuttlebutt about them doctors having square needles and all. They gave us shots (regular needles) for everything under the sun like small pox, tetanus, and typhoid fever. I guess they were getting pretty desperate for men and weren't exactly picky!

The troop train rumbled across a bridge as Arnold felt around in his jacket pocket for his cigarettes; his hand touched an envelope stuffed in next to his pack of Camels. Mystified, he pulled it out staring at the handwriting on the front. He could tell it was from Noreen. Arnold held it up to his nose and inhaled deeply getting a strong mental image of her and that Evening in Paris perfume she always wore. She was a great-looking dame, around 5'8" with a body that could stop a train. She wore her dark brown hair back in that U-shaped roll or whatever the heck they called that popular style—maybe it was called a pageboy? She was a swell dancer with the sexiest legs he had ever seen. Norrie had the softest baby-blue eyes, but they turned to stone if you got her mad! She wanted to go to school and become a nurse; that's what she really wanted to do after she saved up the money. She told me about her father dying a couple years before and how her mother was running a ladies clothing store where Norrie worked. Slowly Arnold tore the end from the envelope and pulled out the letter.

Hey Soldier,

I just wanted to tell you once more, what a swell time I had on our last date. There is so much that I am feeling, Arnold. I wanted to tell you last night, but I didn't want you to think I was some corny kid or that I was panicking just because you were leaving.

Every time I am with you, I feel swell. I've enclosed a picture your Mom took of us; I think we make a good couple, don't you? I feel something real special when you kiss me. It's hard to explain, and so I thought it would be easier to just say how I felt in a letter to you, rather than try to tell you last night and risk getting all weepy and stuff.

I am going to count the days until you come back home. Arnold, I will write you as often as I can, and you said you'd do the same. I know you have folks and all to write to and I also know you won't have a lot of time to be writing letters. I will be waiting and watching for even a post card from you. I have to tell you something, Arnold, something that I hope will make you want to come back to me. I'm pretty sure I have fallen in love with you. I have never felt this way about any other fella, and I have dated a lot. Just remember that I said it first: I LOVE YOU!! "I'll be Seeing You in All the old Familiar Places—I'll Be Looking At the Moon, but I'll Be Seeing, You!" For now, that's our song, soldier boy!

Sending Kisses and Dreams, Norrie

~~~~~~~

Arnold stared at the letter. He felt a warm flush from the top of his head to the tips of his toes. *I love you too Norrie, with all my heart. You are it for me; I'm sorry I didn't have the guts to tell you that last night. You will hear it in the first letter I write to you when I get to Fort Knox, I promise.*

Arnold gazed out the window as the train rumbled over the south-bound tracks; perhaps for the last time, he tried to memorize the all too familiar Wyoming landscape and memories of where he had grown up. *I remember when the folks farmed out here in Kane, at the foot of the Big Horn Mountains; and all those times Dad and I camped, hunted, and fished in those mountains. Those were special times Dad and I had together, real special. He's the one who taught me how to shoot a gun, that's one thing I didn't have to learn at boot camp; I'm a crack shot because of my Dad. I guess that's why I'm ranked as an expert marksman and they are sending me to Tank School down at Fort Knox.*

Moving to the other side of the train, Arnold found a window seat so he could look at the famous Sheep Mountain. *I remember when we were just a bunch of snot-nosed teenagers; me and a couple other guys climbed that there mountain. Man we could see all over the Big Horn Basin. That's really a weird thing how it comes right up out of the sagebrush-covered hills. Other than the Big Horn Mountains to the east and the Rockies to the west, Sheep Mountain is the highest point in the Big Horn Basin. We stood at the top of that mountain and beat our chests and yelled at the top of our lungs, and then the three of us sat down and slid half way down that soft dirt mountain on our butts. I always wondered why it's named Sheep Mountain. I never did hear where it got that name. Maybe at one time or another there was big horn sheep roaming on it.*

The train paralleled the scenic Greybull River as it cut through sheer red sandstone cliffs, north of Greybull. Arnold was feeling a little drowsy but didn't want to miss anything along the way. The train wound its way through the small eastside towns of the Big Horn Basin--Greybull, Basin, Worland, and Thermopolis--stopping at each station to pick up more soldiers on their way to either basic or extended training camps like he was going to. Arnold picked up his duffel bag and was searching for a pencil when he came across another small envelope. He pulled it out---a note from Mom! He read, *"Arnold, after you find this, read it and keep it someplace safe on you. Read it when you get down or need the words. "Be strong and courageous. Do not be terrified; do not be discouraged, for the Lord your God will be with you wherever you go." That's from Joshua, Chapter 9, verse one. I just wanted you to have it. I love you my son, Mom.*

Arnold tried to ignore the giant-sized lump in his throat---- *Mom, oh Mom, I hope you'll be okay!*

The train headed through the gazillion year-old stone walls of the winding Wind River Canyon and then angled east across flat grass-covered prairies dotted with non-descript sagebrush-rolling hills. They headed toward Casper, Glenrock, and Douglas then finally turned south toward Cheyenne. Arnold stared, mesmerized by the miles of empty plains that rolled by the train window. He began to think back about his basic training at [3]Ft. Carson---the initial training they called boot camp.

I remember the drill sergeants from Fort Carson stood at parade rest, feet spread, arms behind their backs, waiting for the next load of greenhorn victims to show up. We looked out the windows of the train; you couldn't miss those sergeants, just standing there, waiting for all us boys to haul our green butts off that train and onto the buses that would take us up to the base. From the minute we took a seat on those buses until we graduated, we had one or two of them sergeants in our faces, and I do mean in our faces yelling at us. I remember a couple of times the look on the Sgt.'s face struck me as funny, and I had to bite down hard on my tongue to stop from snickering. All that yelling didn't faze me much; I grew up with my Dad and his yelling.

Boot Camp---what an unforgettable experience that was! Each of us was assigned a space barely big enough for a cot and our footlockers. I think I had two nails to hang my hat and jacket on---it wasn't exactly a plush establishment, but then I wasn't used to much so it didn't bother me like it did some of the guys. That next morning after our big arrival at the base, they got us up at the crack of dawn and told us to haul our butts over to the general assembly building. That was the first day of the line, after line, after line. The first line was a barber line where we got our GI haircut! Then we were told to strip naked and carry our clothes with us. The next line was where we were issued our khaki's and basic training attire! Hell, I don't think any of those guys handing out the uniforms looked at sizes, because some big guy might have a small shirt and some small guy might have a large shirt. That's pretty much how that went until we started exchanging the clothes among ourselves until we got it right. It seemed to most of us guys that the sergeants and officers did their best to grind us into the ground. Oh, hell yes, we learned a lot, but I seriously doubt if that constant yelling did any of us any good. I had a feeling a couple of those guys even wet their pants more than once!

Man, I remember that second night in particular. I tried to get to sleep but kept hearing guys sniffling in the dark. I wanna say that it got better, but it didn't. Especially when they started working us out at the gym, then there were the two-mile runs, push-ups, sit-ups and a hundred other torture exercises they had on those charts. I was pretty damn glad I was half way fit from playing basketball and working on the farm. I didn't have it half as bad as some of those hot-house pansies.

There were lots of guys who got homesick or missed their girls; it was especially bad when we heard some of our hit music like, "You'll Never Know How Much I Love You" by Dick Hayes; another tear jerker was "Velvet Moon" by Harry James and that wailing horn of his. I've never been away from home for that long, but I toughed it out day by day. Those who graduated from boot camp were assigned to (AIT) Advanced Individual Training, like me----on to Fort Knox and tank training. I especially liked the war games that we played or participated in. I learned a lot from actually getting out there and pretending the enemy was behind every corner and rock. I had real quick reactions, and I could shoot straight from the git-go. I guess the CO noticed all that stuff.

Arnold came out of his day dream and stood up to get the blood running through his long legs. *Think I'll wander down to the smoking car and see what that's all about.* He opened the door to the specified car and walked into the haze created by a couple hundred fellows puffing on cigars or cigarettes. He bellied up to the bar and asked for a Coke. The guy next to him said, "Aren't you thirsty for something a little stronger than a Coke, soldier?" Arnold reached for the glass and took a gulp. "Hell, yes I am, but I don't have a fake ID!" The red-headed guy said, "Well, if you would like a brew, I'll buy you one." Arnold eagerly accepted. "Thanks buddy. I appreciate it and when I have myself a legit ID, I'll look you up and buy one for you." Arnold extended his hand, "My name is Arnold Kessel, what's your name, and where are you from?"

"They call me Cal, Cal Meyers and I'm from Butte, Montana. Where are you from and where are you headed, Arnold?" Arnold took a long slow pull from the beer and wiped the foam off on his sleeve. "It's nice to meet yah, Cal---I'm from down across the border, Lovell, Wyoming."

Arnold lit a cigarette then offered one to Cal. "Well, I am all done with my basic, and I'm headed down south to [4]Fort Knox and tank school. They tell us we will learn everything there is to know about a Sherman tank—even how to take it apart and put it back together. They are gonna teach us first hand just what those babies can and can't do, like how wide of a ditch can they cross and what happens when you get in deep water, you know--stuff like that. We're gonna learn how to handle the tanks in sand, mud, steep grades, and hedgerows-- whatever the hell those are. Anyway, how about you----where are you headed?"

Cal took a long slow draw from his glass, "That's a coincidence; I'm going to Ft. Knox, too—tank school. So I guess we'll likely run into each other again. You sound pretty gung ho about going to Fort Knox. What do you want to do when school is over, end up in a tank or fixing one? I hear say that some of them guys just can't handle being inside those babies—I have to admit that it looks like pretty damn close quarters. I suppose you get to know your tank mates intimately!"

Cal laughed, then took another long pull and continued, "I wanna be in a tank, and I'm hoping I get a medium tank; as far as I know, I think I like them the best. I don't want to be a tank mechanic, a radio operator, or those guys in maintenance whose job it is to clean out the tanks where guys have been blown to bits inside. No sirree, I want to be in the action—but I know for a fact I don't wanna be one of those 'dogfaces' –those poor guys that pack a rifle and walk everywhere they go-- in the infantry! I haven't decided yet if I want to be a gunner or a driver, but I'll bet you a buck I will know what I want to do after this training, not that we get a whole lot of choice!"

Arnold took a drag on his smoke and then finished off his beer. "That's about what I'm thinking. I wanna be inside that tank. I know some guys calling them rolling coffins and all, but I still want some iron around me when the bullets start flying! I'm sure I'll run into you again. Thanks for the beer, Cal. It was nice to meet you."

It was early evening when the troop train pulled in to 2Fort Warren, Wyoming's only military base, Arnold gathered his belongings. He and Cal, along with forty other guys, had their instructions to wait for another train that would take them south and then east to Fort Knox, Kentucky.

Arnold thought back a couple of months when he first saw Fort Warren. *This is where I was inducted and then assigned to go on to Fort Carson down in Colorado Springs for six weeks of basic Army training. Sure am glad they let me loose for a final furlough. It was great to see the folks and that gal of mine, even if it wasn't for very long. It was sure good to have Bobby and a few of the other guys I knew from Lovell with me at boot camp. They split us all up, according to what they thought we were best at. Bobby's off somewhere at a light armory school, probably gonna end up as a driver. Wouldn't that be something if he spent the war driving some general around in a jeep—that'd be just his good luck? We promised to keep in touch as much as we can. He's a swell guy— he's the one I'm gonna miss most of all. Wish we could have stuck together longer.*

Arnold found it difficult to contain his excitement about tank school—he constantly imagined about what it was going to be like. *I guess because I was a crack shot and already knew a bunch of stuff; the Big Brass decided I belonged inside a Sherman Tank. So, I'm on my way now, ready to learn all there was to learn about those there tanks and find out just what I can about the Germans. I guess it's a good thing that I speak a little German, maybe it will save my butt over there. I suppose they will have some classes that teach everyone some German or Japanese words. There are a few German words that us guys need to know—like Verboten (forbidden), Gefahr (danger), Minen (mine) and Panzer means tank.*

Arnold's head snapped up and his body automatically went rigid as he heard the all too familiar order, "ATTEN-TION!"

Colonel Jefferson addressed the group of soldiers standing at attention. "The troop train that is scheduled to take you boys to Fort Knox has been delayed. You will grab your duffel bags and march to barracks twenty-two where you will spend the night. Tomorrow at 0500 you will assemble outside the barracks and march to this station, where you will board train #421 to Kentucky.

"R—ight face, for--ward March!"

On the march to the barracks, Arnold recalled this basic training. *It sure as hell wasn't a cake walk, but I was in better shape than some of them guys. It was a pretty rough time for some fellas; I felt sorry for them, but they had to learn for themselves.* Arnold had known the big brass watched all the soldiers, all the time, trying to decide where each one would make the best fit. After making it through boot camp, he got his orders for extended training at tank camp down in, Fort Knox, Kentucky. *I guess when I get there, I'll find out which battalion and division I'll be in and who my commander will be and all that stuff. I'm not even sure how long this tank camp lasts until they send us to Europe. I'm kinda excited to travel and see what the world looks like and here's my chance. Man, I can't believe I am in the Army and headed for war. It all happened so fast, but here I am!*

That next morning they were up and on the troop train headed out of Cheyenne, Wyoming before the sun made its debut above the eastern horizon. Arnold grabbed a seat and settled in, hoping to catch a little more shuteye while they rattled across the southeastern part of Wyoming, headed toward the Nebraska border. He'd heard the night before that this train paralleled the North Platte River all the way to Omaha, Nebraska. At Omaha, they would turn south crossing the Missouri River then cut across the corner of Iowa. When they crossed the border into Missouri, they would head straight for St. Louis. Everywhere they stopped, they would hook another troop car on the back of the regular passenger train.

It took the troop train over two days to snake across Nebraska, part of Iowa, and then half the state of Missouri before they got to St. Louis. Arnold enjoyed looking out the window and watching as the landscape changed, going from brown and dry, to green and humid. At every town where the train stopped, there were always women and pretty young girls with baskets and paper sacks full of fresh baked goods and sandwiches. They eagerly handed them up to the soldiers who were hanging out the windows of the train. "Thank you boys, thank you for your service. Stay safe and come back to us, we'll be praying for you!"

When they pulled into the St. Louis train station, Arnold saw a few women with sacks of food for the soldiers on the train. The walls of the depot were plastered with recruitment and war bond posters, trying to entice more guys to sign up and help the war cause. People were eagerly moving all over the place like they had somewhere important to go. Arnold thought, *it's sure a different atmosphere with the general population now, than it was two or three years ago with the Great Depression still hanging over us. Now, it's almost like that terrible time never happened. People seem to have a purpose—they seem almost happy.*

Then Arnold eyes came to rest on something else he hadn't expected. There were a handful of obviously hostile, angry people marching and protesting. Arnold's eyes opened wide and a chill ran down his back when he noticed a man carrying a sign that read, "WAR CREATES NOTHING BUT VICTIMS".

Chapter Two

"FIRST THINGS FIRST"

Fort Knox, Kentucky—August 1st, 1943: The Armored Replacement Training Center Commander stood with legs spread, hands clasped behind his back as he waited to address the elite but green group of soldiers who eagerly awaited their orders and extended training. Arnold noticed that the general's 'by-the-book' expression didn't change; piercing eagle eyes stared straight ahead and his square jaws were clenched tight like a steel trap and he never smiled. They all knew the next time most of them would probably see their commanding general again would be at their graduation ceremony.

Arnold's eyes narrowed and his head cocked to the side as he scrutinized the man who stood ramrod straight up on the stage. *He's damn impressive, confident, all business. That general looks like he's been around the block a time or two. Those other guys up there must be the instructor staff; they look about as mean as my old man on a good day. It looks like I better toe the line and give them my utmost attention.*

Suddenly, the CG clicked his heals together, turned and marched unimpeded to where the podium stood. Pushing it aside, he stood directly in front of the crowd of fresh recruits.

"Welcome to Fort Knox, I am Major General Jack W. Heard. I am going to be your training camp commander. Gentlemen THIS, is the home of the United States Armored Vehicle Training Command and I'm telling you boys right now that we set the bar pretty damn high. You are going to learn how to jump over that bar then move at lightning speed, shoot straight, and go for the jugular. We are prepared to put you through seventeen weeks of the most intense armored training and maneuvers devised. Our intent is to find out just where you fit best and if you have what it takes to do the job. You have already filled out a preference sheet and that will be taken into consideration during your final assignment. The Component Commands are: 15th, 46th and 47th Armored Infantry Battalions; 10th, 34th, and 81st

Tank Battalions; and the 47th, 71st and 85th Armored Field Artillery Battalions."

"You are in your final stages of training for combat and we are not going to pussyfoot around. This special training is not going to be a cake walk! The Army thinks you boys are qualified and I intend to find out just how qualified you actually are! For those of you assigned to the tank division, you will learn all aspects of the new M-4 Sherman Tanks from driving them to polishing their behinds. We are going to train you in the cold, the rain, at dawn and at night--- in the mud, sand, and woods. The only thing we can't offer you here is snow and ice, which you will experience in Europe! You can believe that if we could get some snow down here, you would learn how to handle the vehicles in that as well. Mud in any shape or form is the greatest enemy of the tank or any tracked vehicle, and we have lots of mud just waiting for you soldiers. In fact, some of you will be digging mud out of yourselves for months to come!"

"You tank jockeys can wipe that smug smile off your face because the tank is not only a big target, it's an inviting target! We expect tanks to have tactical and mechanical problems every now and then and that's why you are going to not only know how to fight with them, but you will know how to fix em' when you can. Our tank design is above the mark compared to the Germans. Yeah, they have bigger, meaner, and uglier tanks, but our design is simpler and a hell-of-a-lot faster. For instance—the American breech block on a gun has seven parts compared to the German counterpart which has over fifty-five parts. Which one do you want to try and repair, under enemy fire?"

"Many of you are asking just where you are going to fit into the big picture. Well, we are going to be watching your every move as well as your scores on mechanics/maintenance, driving, loading, gunning, and the ability to lead. Before you walk onto the boat to cross the Atlantic, you will know just where we think you will best serve."

"Tanks work best as a team or a unit; they work best in open country; they prefer to fight at long range; they don't like walled in city streets, swamps, or wooded terrain; tanks like to work with infantry support and take care of the big problems letting infantry mop up. You will become [5]'married' to your tank, the crew, and the supporting infantry and artillery in your battalion. We have found that this new and unique arrangement produces tight working relationships and once you are assigned to a tank, infantry, and artillery command, you will be with them to the end."

"If a soldier experiences a preliminary reluctance or fear to complete an assignment or initiate a kill, he will be internally programed and encouraged to perform his duty for his team/his crew, without thinking first of himself. The psychology of war teaches that a soldier performs first for his initial team/crew/, then his company, and finally for himself."

"You will learn what the best defense is against mines and anti-tank guns as well as the most effective way of neutralizing them; for those of you who can't read between the lines or have trouble with big words---neutralizing means, blow the hell out of them. You will also learn all there is to learn about the enemy and how they fight, when they fight, and when they run. You will sleep in pup tents and eat field grub. You may be 'battle green' when you land in Europe, but you will be in shape, mentally and physically to take charge once the Kraut bullets start flying. We are going to pound you into a force to be reckoned with because our goal is BERLIN! We Americans and our Allies are going to stop the Germans because we have to, pure and simple! Did I just say we were going to stop the Germans? I stand corrected. We are going to beat the hell out of them, then chop them up like sauerkraut!"

As General Heard stepped back and saluted the forces, an inkling of a smile turned up the corners of his mouth. "Carry on, gentlemen!" A cheer went up from the 'green horns' as the general left the staging area and the attending officers took charge.

That evening after chow, Arnold took his free time and wrote a letter to his girl.

Fort Knox, Kentucky August 5, 1943
Dear Norrie,

I haven't had much free time to answer the letter you stuffed into my jacket at the train station in Lovell. We've been on the move, mostly riding the train. I've seen some pretty great looking country. There are huge farms, bigger rivers, and lots of trees and bugs back here. Can't say I am a fan of all this humidity.

We live in a pretty dry area back in Wyoming and I guess a guy doesn't pay much attention to that until it gets to the point where he's dripping wet all the time. They say it can get cold here but they rarely have snow so that's good.

Norrie that was a swell letter, I musta read it twelve times and it smelled like your perfume too. That's right I smelled your letter! I'm real glad you wrote it and it was a great surprise to me when I found it in my pocket. I have to tell you honey, that you are on my mind a lot and that could be dangerous cause I have to pay attention to this special training we are having here. We are going to learn how to shoot some pretty darn big guns next week. We are expected to learn everything there is about the guns and the vehicles we operate and that includes taking them apart and putting them back together. It's going to be pretty damn intensive and if I don't get around to writing that often, I hope you understand. It's not like I'm not thinking about you. I gotta pay attention to what they are teaching us so I can come back to you!

Seriously, I can't get you off my mind and I think about you especially every night before I go to sleep. I think I have fallen head over heels for you babe! I haven't known any other girl like you—you take the cake! I don't want to think about 'what if' too much because it might be a long war and thinking about a future together will make it longer. It's going to make a big difference if you write to me as often as possible. It's pretty tough when they have mail call and they don't call your name for a letter. Once in a while, I wouldn't mind a box of cookies that you baked with your own fingers either.

Norrie, please go out with your friends and have some fun when you can. I really don't expect you to sit home baking me cookies and writing to me every night. If you have a date, don't tell me, okay? That would be something I don't want to know unless you fall for another guy while I'm gone, then I want to know. I just don't expect you to sit home—you deserve to go to a few dances and have some fun once in a while. Let me know if you try that new dance---the bomb boogie! Holy Moley, it's been a long day and I am ready for the snore sack. I will fall asleep thinking of you baby!

I love you Norrie! Your soldier boy----Arnold

Arnold and his long time buddy from Lovell, Bob Doerr had lost track of each other over the last month. Arnold expected that Bob was in the First Army, but had no idea what division or platoon. *Maybe if we're lucky, we'll end up in the same outfit or run into each other along the way. I did hear say that they don't like to put good friends in the same company because it might be a distraction. But hell, like most of us, you make friends wherever you go, so that's pretty much beeswax.*

Privates Kessel and Meyers ended up in the same barracks. The first couple of nights Arnold and his new buddy Cal weren't the only fellas who lay in their beds, thinking and wondering what was down the road for them. The same thoughts and fears ran through each of their heads--- *what would these maneuvers and intense classes be like and will I be able to cut the mustard?* Once in a while, the wondering got the best of some of the guys.

As Arnold and Cal lay side by side on their army cots in the semi-darkness after lights out, Arnold said in a low voice, "Say, Cal, did you know that the state of Kentucky Highway Department wouldn't let the new Sherman M-4's on their highways because of those steel tracks. Hell, they cut those asphalt roads to shreds. Yeah, the maintenance guys had to change them over to rubber treads to move them across the roads to the bivouac areas or put down two by fours like a bridge. I guess some of the tanks broke that lumber all to hell."

Cal propped himself up on one beefy arm, "That sounds like a bunch of bushwa to me. What the hell do they expect to happen in a military tank camp? Anyway—there's hearsay that they are working on a new version of the M-4 tank that has some brand new type of Ford V-8 gasoline engine. That baby gets 1.4 miles to the gallon. We won't get to see one of those sweethearts in this place; I just hope they start shipping them overseas. Yep, those engines are gonna make our tanks more powerful, and they don't need as much maintenance or gas as them big-ass German tanks. Still wish they would come up with a diesel tank—from what I hear, those gasoline babies go up like a torch when they are hit! Some guys were joking that they call Sherman tanks, Ronsons after the cigarette lighter—you know *'lights up the first time, every time.'* Shit, that's scary stuff if you ask me. We can always hope they are improving that kinda thing every day."

Beaches of Normandy, France, 1944

Changing the subject, Cal said cheerfully, "Hey, in this one class I had, they were talking about some sort of freaky concrete or steel thing that the Krauts General Rommel came up with to stop our tanks and most any sort of vehicles, call em' 6Rommel's Hedgehogs. They are some sort of giant steel beamed 'jacks' that them Krauts buried all over them beaches over there; real nice of em', if you ask me. There are also reports of 15 foot poles just planted out in the meadows and fields of France to trip and crash the gliders landing there. Well, guess we'll see them soon enough! I say, on the positive side, we are gettn' in this war just in time my friend cause the big boys already worked out a bunch of the problems or at least they know about em'! We won't be going to Africa or Italy to fight—sounds like Patton is working his way north like a firestorm." Cal took a puff on his cigarette. "Hey, what did you think of the CG? He seemed like a pretty good guy, but I wouldn't want to cross him."

Arnold smiled to himself in the dim light of the barracks, "You got that right, he seemed OK to me too! Boy, I can't wait until we start maneuvers but I guess we'll have to sweat out the classes and all that book stuff first off. I think it is gonna be downright interestin' to learn everything they said they are going to teach us. Say, Cal—I never did ask if you had a girl back home. I've got a swell dame, her name's Norrie. I sure have some plans for us when I get back, if I get back in one piece."

Cal folded his arms under his head and stared up into the semi-darkness, "Ix-nay on the girlfriend thing. There was a gal I liked a lot, but she wanted to get all serious. She was a live wire, but I didn't want to get left holding the bag. I don't think she was all there—one of those screwy dames if ya know what I mean? I was scared to death I would knock her up and then be in a real kettle of fish. She always loved the one she was with, if ya get my drift. She had real nice gams though!"

~~~~~~~

In 7Quonset Hut number five, Private Arnold Kessel sat at a far table in what was known as the mess hall. On a Fort Knox letterhead he had scraped up, Private Kessel attempted to answer his Uncle Emil's letter. He and his uncle were only a couple years apart and had grown close over the years Arnold spent growing up around the Lovell area; his uncle Emil had taught him everything he knew! They were always fooling around and going to this dance and that dance, chasing the skirts from one end of the Big Horn Basin to the other. Emil had been deferred from service because he was the youngest son who was farming his parents' farm and was their sole means of support. He wasn't that happy about the deferment because he wanted to get in the action with his brothers and nephew. But as he liked to say, *someone has to take care of all these girls you guys left behind here in Lovell and Cowley!*

Fort Knox, Kentucky---August 25, 1943 *(original letter)
Dear Emil;

Well I finally, got your letter yesterday. Say just wait till sometime you want me to write you real bad. I'll just wait about a month and then write you and we'll see how you like it.

Well, for as the Army Emil, I like it swell at times and at other times it's the shits, because they have so many men and are poorly organized in some things. But the biggest part of it is all right. We have fired the .22 caliber and .30 caliber M.2. This last one is a honey of a gun. It holds eight rounds in one clip and its gas operated and air cooled. It throws the shells out by itself and throws another one back in the chamber. You can really shoot straight, if you adjust the sight just right.

There are three tiers of marksmanship: Expert – you hit 220 out of 250 marks. Sharpshooter – you hit 210 out of 250. Marksman – you hit 200 out of 250. If we can't even hit 200 targets we are disqualified as a rifleman. I'm not braggin' or nothin' but I am now an expert! That's right me, your nephew!

We've had eight hours of instruction on the .30 caliber machine gun; boy there are sure a lot of parts on that baby, but you have to learn every part and how to take it apart and put it back together.

Say Emil, one of the squad leaders just told me that I am going to be made a Lance Jack if I keep on the ball like I have been doing, 'not bad huh?'

Well Emil, as for taking girls out and having my way with them, that's way out of my head because after the army showed us their films about 'the girls'----well, boy it makes you sick for a week. I have been in Louisville about two times and don't like it at all. There are quite a few good-looking girls there and it's not hard to get acquainted with them and they dance just like they do in the good old west.

I gotta pass on this poem that's circulating around here— pretty much says it like it is. I don't know who wrote it, but I think you'll get a kick out of it:

"In the Army they call me 'private'. It is a misnomer. *(Whatever the hell that means)* I have been examined by 50 doctors and they haven't missed a blemish. I am not married and have no children. I have nothing in my past that has not been revealed. I am the only living thing that has less privacy than a goldfish. I sleep in a room with countless other men and eat with about 800 others. I take my baths with the entire detachment and wear a suit of the same material and cut as 5 million other men. I have to tell a doc when I kiss a pretty girl. I never have a single moment to myself and yet they---Call me a Private. What the Hell?"

Say Emil, how about writing me right away and I will do the same. I know you have more time than me and I answer all the letters I get as soon as I can. Well, write soon and be sure to tell all the guys-- hello!

Your nephew, Arnold

P.S. Hello Grandpa and Grandma; how are you feeling? I hope you are feeling good because I am feeling swell. How are the chickens growing? I bet they are laying eggs now. Well, goodbye from your 'GI' (government issued) grandson!

Arnold folded up his letter and sealed it in an envelope. He slipped it inside his khaki uniform and went in search of a mail drop. Just as he rounded the corner of the mess hall, he came face to face with his platoon's 90-day wonder –Lieutenant Kraft. Arnold snapped to attention. The heels of his feet clicked together as the toes of his shoes spread at 45 degrees. His right fist balled and then his hand began the upward movement past his waist as his hand went board straight with fingers tight against each other. Arnold's hand rested just above his eyebrow with the thumb touching his face, saluting the officer. The quick-stepping officer returned the salute; in a hurry, he dropped his arm releasing the private from his salute and moved on.

Arnold took a deep breath laughing to himself at the '90-day' wonder term the recruits had applied to the officers, especially lieutenants who had been put through a 90-day course in how to lead in combat. He continued through the muggy Kentucky afternoon to the mail drop. Suddenly he froze as the earth under his feet began to vibrate. He turned to the left as the strangulated screeching sound of metal on metal increased in volume until he could hardly hear himself breathe. The five Sherman tanks that were barreling toward him groaned and snarled as swirling dust rose in giant clouds from their churning steel tracks. Arnold stood, mesmerized as the tanks roared past. *I can't wait to get to the next level of my tank training and actually get inside one of those babies. The sheer power and presence is intimidating as hell. They are the real McCoy!*

After he mailed the letter to his uncle, he headed for the barracks. It was half way cool inside the wooden building as he walked down the aisle to his cot. Arnold removed his cap and laid it on the shelf above his bed. He unlaced his boots pulled them off, and stowed them under his cot. He stretched out on the taut surface. *I've gotta soak up all the comforts I can, because next week we are going to be out on maneuvers and sleeping in pup tents on the hard ground again. It's been great to know someone here. It wasn't two days after arrival that Cal Meyers and I ran into each other. I don't know about him though, he seems to get in a lot of trouble without really trying and I don't need trouble!*

Lying on his army-issued cot, Arnold turned the volume of his little portable radio on low volume and unconsciously hummed along with the Mills brothers' version of 'Paper Doll.' He thought of Norrie. He thought of holding her in his arms and how she smelled, especially when he buried his face in her mane of chestnut brown hair.

~~~~~~~

That first month of classroom training at Camp Knox was pretty much basic information about different vehicles in their division. They all needed to learn what each specialty weapon; each truck, jeep, tank destroyer, etc. was capable of. Through those weeks they learned the difference between a Landing Ship, Tank (LST); a Landing Craft, Tank (LCT) and Landing Craft Infantry-Large (LCI-L); Landing Craft Vehicle/Personnel (LCVP), and Amphibious Truck (DUKW) or 'Duck'.

They were all expected to memorize the Allied/American chain of command as well as the German chain of command. Arnold thought-- *Guess it's important to recognize particular names just in case we run into one of them. I'm pretty damn glad that General Eisenhower is heading up the whole Allied Army—he's one respected man. I don't know if I am looking forward to meeting or even seeing General Patton—guys call him 'ole blood and guts' and probably for a good reason. From what I hear, the scuttlebutt is that we might be under General Courtney Hodges. Don't know too much about him other than he started as an enlisted man and came up through the ranks. He's a straight shooter, one of those leaders who is actually concerned about his soldiers and he has one impressive record!*

Arnold especially liked this one instructor, Major Harris. He made learning easy and common sense. "Today, you boys are going to learn how to tell the difference-- on sight and profile, in day light and darkness--between an American paratrooper, British commando, and a Canadian infantryman, as well as every type of German soldier, SS troops, and all the rest of the enemy. In most cases, we want you shooting the right people. Because the Germans are Caucasian like us, they've come up with some pretty tricky situations like changing into our uniforms, speaking English, or whatever they have to do to infiltrate our lines. Our Division commanders will be changing the passwords--daily in some circumstances. If you ever happen on someone who doesn't know the password—shoot em! Well, on second thought—perhaps we might want to interrogate them first. We cannot be too careful. We do NOT want Germans infiltrating our lines and sending back information."

Everything changed on September 1st. That's when the big cheese started separating the men and assigning them where they would be most effective. Men who would be associated with the Sherman M3 and M4 tanks were in one Quonset Hut classroom and guys who were in tank destroyers and artillery vehicles that accompanied the tanks were in another class. That first day was a doozie! Arnold walked into the tank class room and took a seat to the side. He kept hearing, "Psssst, Pssst Kessel. Arnold looked over and about dropped his teeth—Cal was sitting there as proud as punch. He put his hand to the side of his mouth and mimed---"I made the cut—I'm in a tank!"

Arnold really got into the three-week class on tanks and accessories: DD amphibious tanks; crab flail mine exploder tanks; Rhinoceros hedgerow buster tanks; deep water fording kit for tanks; bulldozer blades; tank recovery vehicles; priest self-propelled 105 mm howitzer guns on tanks, and the Wolverine tank destroyer. THEN, it was time for his group to take an in depth class on German Tanks. Arnold told himself, *I guess it's important to know what's coming after you or at you so you know where their soft spots are. So far, I'd much rather deal with a Panther tank than one of those monster Tiger tanks.*

On September 10th, both Arnold and Cal sat in the general assembly called by the new division commander, General Oliver Lunsford. After several announcements, General Lunsford took the stage. "Gentlemen, as many of you know General Jack Heard has been issued new orders and I have been named as his replacement.

It is also with great pleasure that I welcome each of you 1,250 soldiers as part of the First Army, Fifth Armored Division, the Victory Division!" You will find out which battalion you are in, in the issued envelope. Welcome and I expect you all to make us proud!"

Both Cal and Arnold couldn't wait to tear into their envelopes and discover which tank battalion they were with. Before they opened their envelopes, Arnold laid a hand on Cal's shoulder and said, "At least we know we are both in the Fifth Armored Division, let's keep our fingers crossed we are in the same battalion." Arnold tore the end of his envelope off and pulled his orders out---81st Tank Battalion. "Cal, I got the 81st---CCB Combat Company B. What did you get?"

Cal looked up from his orders and managed to say, "81st---I'm in the 81st too---but, geez buddy, we are going to be different companies, they put me in CCC. Well, let's look on the bright side, we may not be in the same company, but we should be close by once we get over to Europe."

Arnold grinned, ear to ear as he replied, "That's swell Cal, just swell. I also heard some scuttle butt that once we arrive in Europe, we might be put in the U.S. replacement depot, you know the repple depples, that sounds like a kettle of fish if you ask me. I don't like that whole thing when different companies or battalions have the right to call us up as individuals or as companies to replace someone who got it—that would be the shits!"

Cal laughed and said, "Yeah—we'd be known as repple depples—like replacement deployment. I don't especially like those potatoes either, but I guess we don't need to worry about that until the time comes. Come on, let's go get some chow! How about us going into town this weekend---I feel like squeezing me some dames and maybe even tying one on! Which one comes first, doesn't matter one little bit!"

~~~~~~

Captain Otto Schutz taught the class on Germans tanks and as his students discovered, he was rightly suited. Captain Schutz had been a German tank commander before defecting to the United States four years ago. "Guten Morgen! I vill be your commandant/teacher of this class regarding zee German tanks and I vill be using many German terms vhich you must become familiar vith. The more German you understand, the better equipped you vill be! How many of you come from German backgrounds or homes and are now enrolled in German classes?"

Arnold raised his hand as did approximately one third of the class. The Captain replied, "YA, that is very gute. Now, we get down to it! The first tank ve vill study is zee Panther IV. This is zee vorkhorse of the German tank division. You may come in contact vith a few Panther III's but not too many I think."

PANTHER IV TANK

"You must read more and memorize about zee Panther IV Tank; this is probably the German tank you vill see most often. Zee Panther IV has a higher profile than zee Tiger Tank and has five large track wheels in the center of two large idler wheels which support the tracks---unlike our Shermans which have three sets of bogies attached to two small individual wheels. There are certain important characteristic specifications, and identifying marks on each tank. You vill learn all about these enemy tanks and also, how to kill them!"

The Panzer Tank Divisions you do not vant to come up against are the SS Divisions. They are skilled tank masters and do not like to take prisoners, vich slow them up! I assume I do not have to draw you a picture, YA?"

Captain Schutz continued, "After the Panther IV, THEN— Daimler-Benz came up with a new tank--30-35 tons and they vere up-gunned to a 75 or 88 mm L/70 with 79 rounds--- supported by one or two MG 34 machine guns---this is Zee Tiger Tank!

The main edge the Allied Forces have is, ve have four times as many tanks as the Germans do and ve vill need every one of them. Read and study it all again. You must know your enemy! Tomorrow there vill be exam—be ready! Dis--missed!"

Arnold stumbled out of the class room, his head buzzing with facts. *I know I have to really study the photos and characteristics of these tanks so I can identify one coming head on or a side view. Identification has to be instant; I get that!*

That next week, Arnold continually drilled himself on tanks. He learned that the newer version of a Panther Tank had a higher profile than the Tiger and a sharply sloping frontal armor that didn't protect the tracks as well as the Tiger's did. The Panther tank had a high velocity 75 mm gun wasn't that reliable--but when it worked, it was a better gun than the Tiger's 88 mm cannon.

THE TIGER TANK

Arnold read --- *The Tiger Tank is easily identifiable by the size, the massive boxed hull and short horizontal plate of frontal armor as well as the identifiable center, three rows of 'teeth'. It has four large frontal/exterior track wheels supported by three interior wheels. Beyond the boxy turret, the short area of frontal armor is normally about three to five inches thick making it virtually impregnable from our Sherman's fire power. The sides are a different story—only about an inch and half thick—*that was the vulnerable spot to aim for a killing shot. *The Tiger tank is one of Germany's largest and most powerful tanks but along with that power and weight came many unacceptable mechanical problems and maneuverability issues.*

Arnold thought, *and, what the hell were they thinking? Holy moley, they can't shoot that gun while moving! The tank and its gun are a beast, pure and simple—it's massive and not easily confused with another tank. This is one tank our Shermans should avoid unless we can get a Kester shot in! It would take four of our*

Shermans to take out one Tiger—we'd have to surround it and hope one of us gets that butt shot!

Over chow the next morning, Arnold plopped down beside Cal and began to shovel the things they called scrambled eggs down his throat. Between bites, he managed to get a few words in edgewise. "Say Cal—did you know that the Brits have a version of our Sherman Tank they call the Firefly. It looks a lot like our M4 on the outside except the gun barrel is about twice as long. Our Sherman has a 75mm gun and it's damn accurate, even when we are on the move. But that Firefly has a 17 pounder on it. Holy Shit—it's about the only British or American tank that has the capacity to take down a German Panther IV or even the Tiger Tank. Did you know that Tiger Tank weighs around 40 TON! Can you believe that? No wonder it has problems with maneuverability and besides that it sucks up the gasoline like there was no tomorrow!"

Arnold chased his scramble eggs with a pint of milk then said, "Did you know Cal that a Tiger tank can take out another tank over 1.2 miles away? That bit of news is not reassuring!"

Cal turned to Arnold and grinned, "Aww come on! That's a bunch of applesauce if I ever heard it! That's not possible!"

"Cal, seriously, that is what we learned yesterday. Those bastards can knock out a Sherman M4 from that far. What the hell chance do we have? I don't even know if I can see that far! Now that's just nuts." Arnold's body shook with silent giggles, "I guess it's back to that old saying---it's not the size that counts, it's what you can do with it!"

Cal dissolved into a fit of laughter, "I guess we will eventually find out, won't we?" Cal took a swig of his black coffee. "Okay Arnold, say it's [8]'balls to the wall', is there any sure way a M4 can destroy a Tiger or even a Panther?"

Arnold shrugged his shoulders, "All we gotta pray for is a lot of snow and mud because those Tigers are underpowered in the engine department and their massive tracks freeze up with mud and snow. Besides, most bridges can't handle forty tons and so the tank has to go through the water if it's not too deep. I guess early on, them Germans actually retro fitted those babies with some sort of snorkel that let them cross rivers up to thirteen feet deep. I'd love to see that!"

Cal finished up with his chocolate brownie or what the cooks called a brownie. "Well, none of it sounds all that easy and I guess we are going out on maneuvers in a week or so, you know--practice some moves. I read somewhere that an M4 can penetrate the upper frontal hull of one of them Tigers, if it gets close enough—like around 1700 feet or so."

Arnold quipped, "That's right as rain; the key there is IF we can get close enough. Maybe we can catch them sleeping and sneak up on them! That will be the day!"

Cal pushed his chair back and rose from the table, "Seriously Arnold, that there Tiger has so much thick-plated armor, our shells bounce right off like ping pong balls. So, like you said the trick is to get around them and put a round right up their ass! They don't have that much armor in the rear and that's their vulnerable spot! Kinda goofy, if you ask me, but it's nice to know just in case I ever run into to one. The other thing is---most German tanks can out turn our Sherman, which needs a 31 feet or a 9.5m area so it can turn a circle. A Panther IV can turn a circle in 5.92m." Cal slapped his friend on the back, "That there is something you might want to keep in mind if you ever mix it up with one of those babies!"

Arnold wiped his mouth on a paper napkin and put his utensils on his plate, "Personally Cal, I like the way that M4 Sherman handles. It might have a wider arc of turn, but we can make those turns faster than a Panther! Our Shermans have a pretty high profile, but those babies can scoot, did you know that they can go thirty miles an hour—we can outrun the German tanks? So I guess, we all have our good and bad points and I'm damn determined to learn every trick in the Sherman M4 book that I can. If I am gonna' be inside one, I want to know everything I can about my job, my machine, and the jobs of everyone in that tank. One of the things I like best is the difference in its tracks—the triple set of boggie wheels is pretty nifty!"

Cal turned on the bench to face his buddy, "Say, Arnold. How many times have you been in one of those M4s? Have you fired the gun yet?"

Sherman M4 Tank

Arnold swung his leg over the bench, "I've been in em'--- I wonder why they didn't make that turret bigger—it's a tight fit for sure. I even drove one the other day and that was a hoot, I'll tell ya that! Haven't fired the big 76 mm gun yet or even the Browning .50 caliber machine guns. I am itchin' to get my hands on them. Those machine guns can fire over 300 rounds a minute. They want us to do more learning in the class rooms first I guess. I'll let you know, for sure when I finally get my hands on one. What I did shoot the other day, was one of them burp guns, you know, the US M3 submachine gun. That pistol took the cake—sure would like to have one of them tucked in my belt. Well, 'don't take any wooden nickels', see around Cal!"

That night after chow, Arnold went to the library located in one of the Quonset Huts and settled in at a table. He hadn't written to his folks in a couple of weeks and it was time.

September 24th, 1943
Fort Knox, Kentucky
Dear Mom and Dad,

I have received about five letters from you and also thanks for the big box of cookies and bread. It sure didn't last long. I have to hide your boxes of goodies from my buddies or I wouldn't get much.

Things are going swell here—I'm learning a lot about all of the weapons, attack vehicles, and tanks. These officers don't miss a trick when it comes to teaching us stuff we need to know. I am definitely gonna be in a tank. Nice place to be when the bullets are flying. I've been inside a Sherman M4 and they are pretty roomy. They planned them out real well as there is a particular space for everything and everyone. There are five guys in a tank, you got the driver, a hull machine gunner who can also be the radio operator, the main gunner, the loader (big shells), and the tank commander.

Our Sherman tanks are pretty cool in the fact that they only need one driver and he doesn't steer it like a car but steers it with two levers or sticks—each stick controlling a left or right track— like Uncle Henry's drag line. When we push forward on both levers at the same time, the tank moves forward, if we pull back on one stick and push forward on another then it turns. To stop it we just pull back on both sticks, pretty simple. It's fun to run over hills and stuff with a tank—that old front end shoots up and then down like a roller coaster. They are amazing machines. Sometimes they put stuff in our way that we can't get over or through, like an anti- tank ditch. It's good to know what the limitations on this baby are and what it can do!

Arnold didn't mention anything about the fellas calling tanks 'rolling coffins' or anything that would get his Mom's panties all in a wad. He knew she was having a tough time of it and worrying herself sick! Besides, there was only so much he could tell his folks or any one for that matter. They had these censors reading mail to make sure nobody let out any military secrets! He learned in the next letter from home, that the censors had blacked out a couple of his comments.

Boy, I thought I was finished with the fitness stuff when I graduated from Boot Camp, but this camp is putting us through even more. I guess it's for our own good that we are in great shape. Our day begins with outdoor exercise---pull-ups; squat jumps; push-ups; sit-ups, and a 300-yard run! Depending on the LT's mood—he might make us do these outdoors even if it's raining etc. If there are too many squads out, then they march some of us inside to the gym and we do the required pull-ups, squat jumps, push-ups, setups, and an indoor shuttle run where we are running and hand off a puck to our team mate and he continues the race. We finish this off with a 60-second squat and thrust session. I have never been in this good of shape. Got some impressive biceps now,—for sure!

Arnold didn't tell his folks about the programs where they were made to grab bars and swing from one to the other over a deep open pit of something nasty like mud or barbed wire. Then they had to crawl on their bellies through mud, sand, rocks, and under more barbed wire. There was virtually no end to the number of field fitness exercises the sadistic instructors came up with.

How's that new job with Marathon going for you Dad? Sure glad you got on with that company. That's real security for you and Mom. I'm sorry that I just don't have the time to answer everyone's letters. Was wondering how that new Mercury is running? Did you pay $1,100 cash or are you buying it on time? What with gas at a whooping sixteen cents a gallon, you probably don't take it on long drives. I'd sure like to have enough money saved up when I get home to buy a car, but at $3 a day, I don't suppose I'll have the money for a new car unless this war lasts five years! Just joking MOM! They keep us pretty busy here. And, yes Mom, I am reading my Bible. I keep it tucked inside my jacket.

Love and Miss you all---Arnold

Feeling the familiar ache of homesickness, Arnold folded the letter and stuffed it in the addressed envelope. He licked the back of a two cent stamp and pasted it up in the right-hand corner, then tucked the letter in his jacket to mail later.

Arnold got a lot out of the class on German tanks and learning what they could and couldn't do; he passed his exam with flying colors. That next week was the beginning of an in depth study of the Sherman M4 tank. At 0600 hours sharp, on Monday morning, the tank candidates were seated and ready for the goods. Major Harris began, "This is where you boys are going to learn the rest of the story about the Sherman M4 tanks. You've already learned what the other tanks can do and NOW you are going to learn the whole bag of tricks your [9]Sherman M4's have. Of course, we hope all you have to do in your tank is to support your married Infantry, blow up buildings, and take out machine gun nests. However, we know for a fact that the Germans are going to throw everything they can at us including their [10]Panther IV and Tiger tanks."

"It's no dad-blame secret the Germans have us out gunned when it comes to tanks, but as I have said before, our Shermans are more dependable mechanics-wise, faster than hell, we get more bang for the buck when it comes to gas-o-line, and we have four times as many tanks as the Germans do! Our guys built these tanks simple and sturdy so you fellas have a better chance to repair something in the field, because these things break down now on a frequent basis. When something happens to those Germans tanks—the crews crawl out and head home!

We've now added thicker armor and given you a bigger gun to even up the odds a bit. The rest is up to you and the initiative, the guts, and courage you boys come up with when the cards are down! You will see snow over there and when that melts you will have mud. Your Sherman does a hell of a lot better in mud than those heavy Panzers or Tigers—you will pass plenty of them bogged down in the mud like a fat pig!"

Cal remarked offhandedly, "Yeah sure. Right now, I'm just worried I won't get this Kentucky mud out of 'special places' before winter sets in here." The next day they learned the specific duties and requirements of each member of a tank crew. Captain Michael Walters began. "The interior of a M4 Sherman tank is rather roomy and painted white to make it look bigger—that's called interior design! Now, it's not so roomy that you can have your own bed but there is plenty of room for each of the five tank crewmembers to carry out their assigned tasks! You will carry a full load of ammo plus a two-way radio, fire extinguishers, and have ample storage for food and clothing. You will physically go through situations where you will have to put out an internal tank

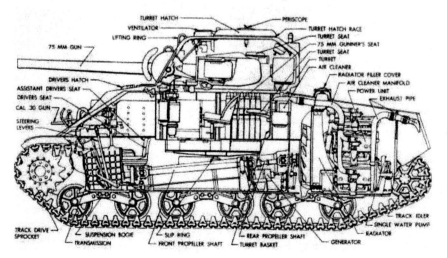

fire or take over for a wounded crew member. You will learn how to execute each other's responsibilities as well as learn how to repair everything on your tank that is feasible. We will also cover various methods of camouflaging your tank—for example white washing it in the event the battle takes place in deep snow and/or covering it with brush, tree limbs, etc. Your tank does not want to be seen until it is ready to be seen!"

"Inside your Sherman, everybody has a specific seat which is adjustable in height and forward/backward. Peripheral vision is not a problem for any of the crew--everybody has access to a periscope with a 360° traverse as well as vertical tilting---so you can have a good look at the enemy and terrain! The turret on a Sherman M4 is a work of wonder. It is cast of a one-piece fighting compartment which fits into a revolving rail. The tank cannon protrudes from the turret and is stabilized with gyro stabilization hydraulic system, making it possible to FIRE while the tank is in motion. This---is yet another advantage our tanks have over the German tanks which must be idle in order to fire their tank cannons accurately!"

The Captain smiled, "Have I mentioned that I love this Sherman M4 Tank? I call it our 'David' compared to the Germans' Goliath tanks! And—as many of you have learned, most German tanks break down frequently—like every thirty miles or so. Our Shermans have the capacity to run and run fast for 2,500 miles over normal terrain before needing normal maintenance in the garage or tank barracks. Now, that doesn't mean you run these suckers until they peter out on you—you take care of this machine as if your life depended on it, because gentlemen, it does!"

Rubbing his two hands together, the instructor continued. "There are also four escape hatches in your Sherman tank, two above the frontal glacis, one located in the revolving turret, and one just behind the driver's seat, on the floor of the tank." The captain took a sip from his glass of water and continued. "Beginning at the front of the tank: The driver sits on the left, at the front of the hull; it's his job to maneuver and drive the tank—that's all. He needs to know all there is to know about the tank's top speed, its acceleration, what sort of terrain it can and can't handle and at what speed. He needs to practice doing wheelies and cookies so he knows how the tank handles in a tight spot."

"The driver assistant sits on the right front side with his 30mm machine gun and he may also be in the back, acting as the radio operator. I am assuming you have all seen and worked with the mini-maps. These maps provide tactical advantage and battlefield awareness of situations—in other words, you can tell just where the good guys are. Radio operators send messages back and forth between tanks and command headquarters to call for backup air fire or infantry etc. All of you should be proficient in the operation of the two-way radio."

"Now, the gunner sits to the right of the tank's cannon and it's his job to sight in or take aim and then fire the cannon. He must be adept at knowing the aiming speed that the gun's sights will lock onto a target; he needs to know how fast or slow the turret is able to rotate or traverse and he must be highly proficient with the accuracy of his shot. Getting a kill with the first shot is preferable to taking four shots to take a target out."

"The cannon loader is the lucky guy who gets to handle each shell that is put into the cannon. He sits to the left, directly in front of the tank commander. Everybody has his spot and his assignment, so there's no arguing there! There are instances where the noise of battle is so intense that the tank commander has to use physical signals to the loader—like a kick or nudge to the right or left shoulder, arm, etc."

"The tank commander sits or stands at the rear of the turret area, just behind the loader so he is in close proximity to aid and instruct the loader. His main job is to spot the enemy and the better the spotter, the better the commander. You have to SEE the enemy first before you can hit him. It's the commander, who at a moment's notice must be able to fill the secondary role of gunner, driver, loader, radio operator. He must be a jack-of-all trades, while the driver just has to worry about driving the tank! My personal advice is when you are assigned to a tank crew, that you all take turns doing the other guys job, so if and when you get in a hot spot, you know what and how to keep your tank from being a target! One thing I will warn you about is the close proximity you fellas have to the ceiling. You'll find that out fast enough when you get bounced around in one."

"Gentlemen, in a nut shell—if you are a member of a tank CREW, you MUST have a high level of proficiency in every aspect of your assignment or position. The higher the level of your skill, the more proficient your crew will be—you must work as if you were ONE unit. You must be aware of how and when to carry out your assignment and do it with lightning speed." The captain walked to center stage, saluted and growled, "Dis—missed.

~~~~~~

For the next several weeks Arnold and Cal kept each other going, through some of the toughest training they had seen and half of that was during blackouts or at night. One day as they were up to their eye balls in mud and barbed wire, Arnold quipped, "Hell Cal, I guess if all this training doesn't kill us it'll make us stronger." Between being out in the field and taking specialty classes they didn't have time to think about home or the fields of war that lay ahead.

Arnold commented, "These breaks we get—looks to me like something is brewing, you know like an excuse to get everything in order for the start of another exercise. Why the hell do they always designate pre-dawn as the beginning of a maneuver? It would be nice to get some good long shut eye along the way!"

Cal ruffled Arnold's blond hair and replied, "That's not as bad as the forced night marches, black- out driving and finding our way over those damn pot-hole filled side roads through thick woods. I guess they are just trying to get us ready for Europe---that ain't gonna be no picnic! Some of the guys say the country is a lot like the states."

Arnold adjusted his military tie and said, "Have you noticed that they are really pushing proper communications and employment of the right weapon for a situation? I get it that they need to teach us how to bypass strongpoints of enemy resistance and roadblocks, but what I'm really looking forward to is the assembly of movement under cover of darkness and then launching a surprise attack. That should be balls-up!"

Cal added, "Hey---it all sounds like we'll be livin the life of Riley'! They talk about physical hardships like not having a toilet to take a shit in or clean water to wash up or even cook with. And, what in the hell is that meat crap they put in those tins—something

called Spam? I hope to hell they don't take that stuff over to
Europe. What I'm countin' on, is that it's just here, at the training
site to make us suffer more."

~~~~~~~

November 15, 1943 Fort Knox, Kentucky
Dear Norrie,

*How's my girl doing? Seen any good movies lately? They
showed one here on base the other night called, 'For Whom the
Bell Tolls' with Gary Cooper and Ingrid Bergman. That was sure
a good movie, have you seen it yet? Are you getting out much?
Hope you and your* girl friends *are having a little fun. I'd hate to
be stuck in a store selling dresses all day! I'm kidding—it's swell
that you have a job that pays you that well and keeps you busy.
Has my Mom bought any dresses from you lately? Did you get in
to the Nursing School in Bozeman?*

*My tank crew consists of our tank commander, Sgt. Mac
Darby; loader Pvt. Harold Wright (Reb); driver is Joe Carpuchi
from the Broncs, New York, assistant gunner is Pvt. Daniel Walton
(Danny Boy); and gunner Pfc. Arnold Kessel (Cowboy). I'm with a
swell bunch of guys and we get along fine. Don't have any*
[11]*goldbrickers or Mama's boys in our bunch. Harold is just a kid –
a real baby puss but he's got what it takes. Joe's got the craziest
accent you ever did hear and is kinda hard to understand
sometimes.*

*Our Tank Commander is a good guy—doesn't say much.
He's older than the rest of us. Most of the guys are between 17 and
21 like me. I'll probably turn twenty on the boat to Europe—at
least I won't be a teenager anymore once we land over there! I
want you to put your glad rags on and go out on the town, you
know –maybe even try that new dance, the jitterbug. Just don't let
any fella put his meat hooks on you or I may have to make a quick
trip home and sock him in the schnooz!!*

*I just heard another new song from Glenn Miller—
something about 'That Old Black Magic"! I can't listen to some
songs like "As Time Goes By' by Rudy Vallee-. I'm not trying to be
a wet blanket, truly, it's just that I think about you and miss you
terribly and I don't know when I will see you again. Well, my love,*

I'd better stop beating my gums and turn in. I will see you in my dreams!

    Love, Arnold

~~~~~~~~

    That night Cal and Arnold had their usual chat, just trying to catch up with what had happened during the day. Arnold stared up through the semi-darkness, "Well buddy, tomorrow is *the day* we start those final war games. I heard by the grapevine that there are three main hills that they are going to throw at us out there. Get this, they are named, Agony, Misery, and Heartbreak. Now, don't that just set your teeth on edge? By the way, how is your tank crew feeling about the maneuvers? It gives me the heebie jeebies if you want to know the truth, I'm just happy as a clam knowing that we aren't using real ammo this time. We've all made it through the [12]live fire exercise. I remember how scared I was when I pulled the pin on my first 'pineapple.' I couldn't get that grenade outta my hand fast enough. That was the first and probably not the last time I about had a little accident in my pants!"

Chapter Three

"BREWING UP"

By mid-November everyone and everything was ready and itchin' for the big games! Arnold quipped to Cal as they were standing in the chow line, "Now, we are getting down to the brass tacks. This is where we see if we've learned anything or are going to be banished to latrine duty for the duration!"

Battalion received orders to assemble for the first tactical maneuvers, approximately ten miles away in a specialty war-game arena. On November 17th, at precisely 0300 hours in the blackest part of the night, the training units of the Fifth Armored Division rolled out in the direction of Agony Hill. The arena was chopped up into three, four-day sequences of exercises/drills, with a couple of three-day periods for reorganization, maintenance, rest and regrouping movements. The fields were down right soggy from frequent rains during the past few days; mother nature was good enough to dump a rare light snow over the whole mess, just to make it even more miserable.

After the tanks, vehicles, and men finished tramping over the bivouac fields, it quickly turned into a mucky quagmire of misery and bitter cold; this delighted the officers to no end. This would be a perfect taste of the real thing-----no heated barracks here. The green soldiers learned quickly how to sleep in a pup tent and survive on C and K rations heated over a small stove or fire, if they were lucky. The mechanics had their work cut out for them keeping the tank's new V-type engines running with insoluble long-fiber grease and dead track blocks!

Arnold leaped onto the tank hull and then grabbing onto the holds, he hoisted himself up to the tank turret. Dropping down into the interior of the tank, he slid into the gunner's seat. Arnold and his four tank mates had gotten to know each other pretty well over the last month. It went without saying that when they were engaged in battle, they never called an officer by his rank; that would be giving the enemy a head's up on who their officers were.

Before the war games the tank commander Mac had a 'sit down' with his crew. "So fellas, let's think up some quick tag or nick names that we can use to shorten things up when we get in the thick of things. Is everyone alright with that? We want to stay away from names that might sound like a battle command, like 'Hank' might be mistaken for tank."

The crew thought it was a good idea and so they started coming up with some names that were acceptable to all. Their tank commander was--*Mac;* the gunner was (Arnold) *Cowboy* because he was from Wyoming; the loader was (Harold) *Butch*; and the driver was (Carpuchi) *Joe*---from the Bronx's; and the assistant gunner's real name was (Daniel Arthur), so he was happy with the new tag of *Danny Boy*. Some of the guys had painted a favorite name or decal on their tank cannon, but the boys in Sherman M4, #2736 hadn't come up with a suitable name---yet.

As expected, in the first day of maneuvers Cal and Arnold found themselves separated, they were in the same battalion but different companies. Arnold was in Combat Company B (CCB) and Cal was reassigned to CCC. Arnold had nailed the gunner position in his tank and Cal was the designated driver in his. Earlier that day, Arnold admitted, "Say Cal, I sure have the jitters. This is gonna be both fun and intimidating because you know the big cheese is gonna be watching us like a hawk." Arnold pointed to the 'crow's nests' where the camp commanders stood with their binoculars. "There they are, our eyes in the sky." With his second and third fingers, Arnold gave the V for Victory sign to Cal. "Good luck, and keep it on the road!"

Cal shot him a nervous grin and a, thumbs up, "And you try real hard to shoot straight, Cowboy! Hey, see you in the funny papers." Arnold laughed as he caught a glimpse of Cal walking toward his own tank, with his middle finger extended high in the air.

~~~~~~~~

As daylight broke, the tanks rolled down outrageously narrow, pothole-filled roads that wound around steep hills and through dense woods. Arnold thought, *I hope to hell Cal can keep his tank on the road, I just saw one slide off and sink in about two feet of mud.* Arnold had a good day---he hit all of his targets and was really getting the hang of being a gunner. *Something comes over me when I sight in that big gun and then hit the foot pedal to fire it! I'm getting so I can get the perimeters, sight in, aim and fire in a matter of seconds. Geez, I love seeing that target explode!*

That night Arnold lay in his sleeping bag on the cold ground, trying to ignore his chattering teeth, he thought about what he and Cal had talked about a few days ago. They had imagined what it might be like, being in battle. Cal had given Arnold a sharp elbow in the ribs and said, "Geez, don't even get me thinkin' about what it's gonna be like over there when those Germans start shootin' at us for real. I hear say that these maneuvers are supposed to give us an idea of what battle really sounds like and how fast things happen—so we don't shit our pants once we get in an actual scrap! I gotta tell you that I get pretty damn nervous as a tank driver, when all that infantry hanging so close to our tanks and those steel treads. I know they are just taking cover from incoming fire, but hell--what if we have to turn on-the-dime and actually roll over someone? That would be bushwa for sure."

Arnold didn't blink an eye as he remarked, "For cryin' out loud Cal, will ya dry up? You better straighten up and fly right and quit chasing yourself with all that hooey. But, to be on the up and up, I have to say that I'm pretty sure it's happened and will happen again. Those green dogfaces are just trying to stay out of the path of a bullet and that's why they use our tanks like that. If something happens, then it happens. It's up to them to watch for something that will make a tank driver turn sharply. Are you gonna need a [13]blue 88 to get to sleep tonight or do ya want me to sing you a lullaby?"

The next morning, dense damp fog hid the rising sun and held the cold dampness close to the frozen earth. The minute Arnold crawled outside his pup tent he felt the damp cold bite straight through to his bones. The air was filled with the ominous rumble of Sherman M4 tanks, tank destroyers, amphibious vehicles, artillery, and the muffled marching of over a thousand infantry. Game ON!

Nobody knew what their orders for the day would be until the pre-dawn hours when they met with their company commanders. Now, they all had their new orders and you could cut the tension and excitement with a knife. Every man and machine was like a race horse in the gate—ready to rumble!

They were divided up into two color battalions—Red and Green Armies. On this day, Arnold and Cal were in different 'enemy' groups. Arnold's group was the Green Army and Cal was with Red Army. Regardless, each tank battalion consisted of three companies of fourteen tanks each, adding up to forty-two tanks per battalion. The entire Fifth Armored Division had over 250 ready to roll tanks.

The 81st Tank Battalion's forty-two Sherman tanks consisted of three companies (A, B, & R companies) of fourteen tanks each. Arnold's tank was in CCB (Combat Command B); his tank rode second in their column of four tanks.

Arnold's group finally received the signal and everyone moved out under the cover of darkness. The surprise attack against the Red army was a go; they would be in place, precisely at dawn! Red army was just over the next hill, called *Agony*! Arnold could hear the anti-tank guns and a mine field being cleared up ahead. It was almost dawn, they had been on the move for over two hours when Arnold felt and heard the thud of anti-tank fire coming from a clearing just ahead. He bristled as Mac yelled, "Up ahead, two o'clock, in the woods—anti-tank fire. Get that one Cowboy!" The loader put in a blank powder shell as Arnold's eyes scanned the woods ahead, he sighted in the target. His body coiled with action as his foot pushed hard on the canon firing pedal. A slow grin crossed his face as he saw the puff of while powder indicating a 'hit'. He sighted in again and saw another flash of an enemy machine gun. Mac roared, "FIRE!"

The CCB tanks swung to the left, off road and headed across the clearing with machine guns blazing. Arnold knew this was just a game at this point, but it felt pretty damn real to him.

~~~~~~~

An hour later they were back in column formation and on the move. Suddenly the column halted and a Green jeep with a Colonel in it raced down the side of the road. Their orders came across the radio, "Coil – Coil until further notice." When the head or lead tanks of the column engaged in a battle or fire fight, the rest of the column would leave the road and pull back, off into areas where they would wait for the action to cool. If they needed reinforcements up ahead then they would get the order to move out and reinforce; this was known as [14]coiling. Arnold remembered, *this was one of the General Oliver's new tactics to keep a long column of military vehicles off the road—otherwise, all strung out in a straight line they were a perfect target for an enemy plane or chain reaction explosion.*

In an hour, they were back on the road; they had gone about a mile up a different road when reconnaissance spotted a column of Red army tanks. Sgt. Darby, called for the lead tank commander to radio in, "Enemy tanks dead ahead, looks like twelve of them." Looking through his gunner's slot in the Sherman, Arnold saw two of the Red army's CCC tanks leave the road in an effort to perhaps circle around to the back of the his Green tank column. Arnold couldn't believe his eyes as the two CCC tanks simply misjudged the angle of the embankment, and toppled down the steep incline. Both tanks came to rest against a clump of pine trees—stuck on their sides. Arnold honed in on the numbers on the tanks and began to laugh. One of the tanks was Cal's! Arnold couldn't help himself as his body shook with laughter. I'll be a monkey's uncle---b*oy, am I gonna give him grief about that! Kinda reminds me of a turtle on its back.*

The next two weeks flew by as the battalions fought up, down, over and around Agony, Misery, and Heartbreak Hills. They all learned a great deal about formations and battle plans, proper communications including map reading, control of units in a company, the use of road-blocks, how to bypass particular strongpoints of resistance. Each man learned about personal endurance of hardship in the field. These lessons would undoubtedly keep them alive in Europe or that's what the non-coms told them.

~~~~~~~~

By the first part of December 1943, The Fifth Armored Division, 81st Tank Battalion finished up with final war games at Fort Knox. Bivouacking close to Gordonsville, Tennessee, they spent several days preparing and maintaining their tanks and equipment for a vast movement to a new arena of training and preparedness. Back in the same unit, Arnold and Cal spent most of the next day helping to get their tanks and other vehicles loaded onto the flat cars at the train station to head north.

"Hey, Cal, do you know where we are going for sure? Arnold asked, "I just wondered what you have heard—I know they have used a place called Pine Camp, New York, but then other scuttlebutt is that we are headed for Indiantown Gap, Pennsylvania. Either way, we are going north and I imagine we'll be digging out some long underwear. They have plenty of snow up that far, you can bet your bottom dollar on that! HQ is just itching to get us in deep snow!"

Cal laughed rubbing the day's growth of whiskers on his freckled face and remarked, "All I heard is that it'll probably be New York. The tag on Pine Camp is that it has two seasons, winter and the Fourth of July!"

Pine Camp, New York: Arnold pulled the collar up on his army-issued overcoat and brushed the snow from his shoulders. He and Cal were walking back to their temporary barracks in a Quonset hut. "Well, Cal—here we sit in balmy New York—you can see the St. Lawrence River over there, someone said our major firing ranges are right on the shores of Lake Ontario. I bet this is pretty country in the summer—never seen so many trees. I'm just glad we are only here for a couple of weeks."

They were called to general assembly early the next morning. General Oliver addressed the men of the 5th Armored Division. "Gentlemen, Supreme Command Headquarters has issued new orders regarding the Fifth Armored Division. For now, it will be attached to the Second Army. You can expect numerous changes of attachments and orders over the next month as our Supreme Command figures out the big picture.

I will remain in my current status until further orders come through. General Omar Bradley has returned to Washington, D.C. to receive his command of the First and Second Armies. He will begin assembly of his staff and headquarters to prepare for invasion of Europe. That is all for now, we will continue to update your status as operations progress.

"Gentlemen, At Ease!"

Orders of highest priority were, to continue intensive training first with small arms—sighting and aiming were key objectives. Most of their firing was dry, no live ammo. The 'Louie's' wanted them to concentrate on proper firing position, sighting in their targets and practice squeezing the trigger so many times that it became a habitual reflex. Most of Arnold and Cal's training had to do with machine guns and tank cannons. Arnold was a crack shot.

"Hell, Arnold—where did you learn to shoot like that? Most of us guys had the same training as you did, but you don't miss, ever! Geez—do you know how that makes us feel?"

Arnold's ice blue eyes crinkled in the corners as a smile crossed his mouth and he continued to wipe off his machine gun. "I went hunting with my Dad all the time—been shooting all sorts of guns since I can't remember. I guess I learned young how to bracket a target and get it on the first shot." Arnold laughed, "Boy the Lt. is sure nuts about us not creeping up on a target too. He gave me all kinds of bushwa the other day—they want us to hit it from where they tell us. Most of these officers are by-the-book if you ask me! I wonder how that works for them when they get out in a real battle."

Arnold looked up in the sky, "What I am really looking forward to is--Wednesday when they fly those planes over us, with dragging targets, so we get to practice shooting at something moving in the sky. Hell, you couldn't pay me to fly one of those planes with some of these goofballs taking target practice at what the flyboys are towing! I would sure like to get my hands on one of those ack-ack guns. Those twin 40 mm babies can take down a plane real fast like. I've heard that they are pretty hard to handle tho."

Cal rubbed his cold hands together, "I'm getting' real anxious about driving my tank across one of those [15]bridgeheads them boys are going to set up across the river on Friday. I hope to hell they know what they're doing—I'm not eager to take a plunge into that icy river! I know for a fact that you'd never let me live that one down!"

Arnold stamped his army-issued boots and said, "This snow and cold is the shits! It reminds me of Wyoming--except the wind isn't blowing as bad. I guess they saved this choice bit of real estate for last—a little treat for us boys to get acquainted with driving tanks and all the rest of the stuff in snow and more mud when it melts. Boy, I shudder to think of what this is going to be like come spring! It's bad enough with the tank treads grinding up the snow and all."

Cal reached out and pulled Arnold back by the shoulder, "Hey, not to change the subject, but have you heard of those anti-tank dogs? Geez, what will they think of next. Our CO told us that if we spot a dog, especially like a German Shepard running toward our tank when we are over there---we are to mow it down. The Krauts are strapping explosives on them dogs and training them to jump onto our tanks---and baby, that's all she wrote!!"

Arnold stopped walking, "Holy moley, no shit? That's just damn right cruel. I guess our group will learn about that tomorrow. Do we do the same thing with dogs?"

Cal shook his head, "Ixnay! I guess at one time, there was some training of dogs to blow up other fortifications, but from what I hear the big cheese put the kibosh on that idea!" Cal opened the door of their Quonset hut barracks for Arnold, "Say, are you all packed up, I guess we head out at 0400 tomorrow?"

~~~~~~~

Indiantown Gap, PA. 14 January – 4 February, 1944:
The Port of Embarkation, that's what they call this place. At least we are done with the shots for malaria, typhoid, and those damn tetanus boosters. And—we have seen every gory movie they could come up with about personal infectious diseases. Hell, we even got new shoe laces for our boots; the boys at HQ spare no expense!

The camp settled into their routine. Cal and Arnold put in for weekend leave. "Hey Arnold, how about you and me headn' down to Harrisburg and catch a flick or I've heard they have a great canteen for us military guys. We might have us some fun— go on a skirt patrol. I wish to hell you were twenty-one, then we could have us some real fun. But shoot, we might get lucky and run into a friendly bartender who wouldn't mind selling a soldier a brew or two. What do ya say—wanna hitch a ride down to the city on Saturday?"

Early Saturday morning Arnold and Cal left the camp and headed for the highway. Arnold looked up and down the road, "doesn't look like there's much traffic, let's just start walkin'—at least we'll be getting someplace, until a ride comes along."

Cal pulled his army-issued coat up around his neck as the bitter Pennsylvania cold chewed right through. "They sure have a lot of woods in this part of the country, don't they; I think they get more snow than we do too. How does your tank run in the snow? I like it better than that damn mud—as you say, mud is the shits!" Cal turned at the sound of a motor, "Hey here comes a truck, stick your thumb out Arnold."

The old farmer didn't have any room inside the cab, "Howdy fellas, headin' into town are you? Sorry, I've got the family with me today, but you can hop on the back there if you don't mind."

Arnold smiled and replied, "Sure, sure—that'll work fine. I'm a country boy and it won't be my first ride in the back of a truck; it beats the heck out of walkin' all the way. Sure do appreciate it sir."

They hadn't gone a mile down the road when a luscious blonde in a late--model sedan pulled up behind the truck. She smiled and waved at the two soldiers and blew them a kiss before she signaled and passed them. Arnold balled up his fist and punched it into his other hand, "NOW---that would have been a better choice! We're just a couple of knuckleheads! You and me just don't have the best luck, do we?"

The farmer let them out about a block from the [16]USO canteen. "Now, you boys have yourself some fun but stay outta trouble. Those are nice girls in that dance hall—they'll give you a squeeze or two."

Arnold and Cal stopped by an inconspicuous little bar down the street from the USO. They took a seat up front, at a small table. A buxom cocktail waitress approached their table. "Hi ya fellas, out for a little fun are you? What can I get for you boys today?"

Cal ordered first, "I'll have a beer; anything you have on tap would be swell."

The endowed waitress looked long and hard at Arnold, "Do you want the same thing soldier?"

Arnold blushed and stammered, "Aww, s-s-sure, that'll be fine, just a beer."

The waitress, turned to walk to the bar but before she did she bent down and whispered in Arnold's ear, "I'm not gonna ask for your I.D. as long as you behave yourself—Capiech?"

Arnold turned and watched her hips sway as she walked away, "Say Cal, what does, 'Capiech' mean, anyway?"

Arnold and Cal had a couple more brews, paid their bill and started down the street to the USO Club. Cal pushed the doors open and the two of them wound their way through the smoke, noise, music, and people. Grabbing a couple of Cokes, they found a table near the dance floor and got comfortable. The band was great—started off with the G.I. Jive, a Louie Armstrong tune that had a great beat to it. Cal stood up, "Well, are you gonna ask somebody to dance or not? Come on Arnold, I know you've got a serious gal, but shoot—what is a little dancing gonna hurt. I bet ya the farm she is going to dances while you are gone. Come on will ya, lighten up a little!"

Cal tagged a lively brunette and in no time was hopping and jiving all over the place. Arnold took his time looking over the line of available girls. *It's kinda funny---it looks like everyone in here is desperate to have a good time and have it fast. The gals know the men are shipping out and pickings are gonna be slim and the guys are probably all wondering IF they are going to come back.* Arnold remembered what Cal said and he knew he had to get out there on that floor and have some fun, but his heart just wasn't into it—kinda felt like he was steppin' out on Norrie. Arnold turned as someone tapped him on the shoulder.

A petite redhead shot him her best smile as she said coyly, "I can tell you'd like to dance. You are keep a real good beat with your fingers on that countertop. I also have a feeling you have a girl back home, am I right?"

Arnold felt a bead of sweat run down his back, "Yes, and yes—you are right on both accounts. But I guess I am here and that music sounds great, so let's give it a try."

Arnold and Ruthie were into their second jitterbug when all of a sudden a fight broke out between a couple other soldiers. Arnold grabbed Ruthie's arm and protectively steered her away from the ruckus. Arnold said, "I guess that happens when you both want the same gal. They both probably had a little too much hooch under their belts too. I know you people don't have booze here, but most of us stopped off and grabbed a couple drinks before we hit the door here. It's just a way for us to relax and blow off some steam, if ya know what I mean." Ruthie nodded back in agreement as she thought, "Pretty mature for a kid, I hope like crazy, he makes it back!"

Back at their table, Arnold and Ruthie sat and talked about this and that for the next hour. She was a swell girl. Before he and Cal were ready to leave, Arnold pulled her into his arms and kissed her cheek. "Thanks for a swell night; this is probably my last night out on the town before we ship out and I really appreciate you dancing with me and well, just talking. Take care of yourself, Ruthie".

Ruth blew him a kiss, "You keep your head down when you get over there soldier boy. Thanks for the dances—you sure know how to shake a rug!"

~~~~~~~

Lying in bed that night, Arnold thought about the past five months and everything he had learned and gone through. *I don't get the thing about having to throw at least two live grenades before the CO signs off on each of us. That seems kinda nuts to me, but then I've met a few of the 'boys' around here and yeah, they probably shit their pants when they have to pull that pin.*

The next couple of weeks everyone was in a panic, getting ready for final orders. Check lists were marked off and letters written.

~~~~~~~

Indiantown Gap, PA.
January 22, 1944
Dear Mom and Dad,
We all got some time to write letters home before we ship out. Not quite sure when that will be, the big cheese likes keeping secrets around here. I'm not looking forward to getting on a big boat and going across an ocean, but then, I guess if the two of you

could do it at the ages of six and eight, then I should be able to do it too. Not too worried about getting seasick as I have an iron gut. I just remember all those carnival rides I went on and never once got sick.

I am really looking forward to seeing what Scotland and England look like. I just hope there will be parts of it left in place by the time we get over there, what with all the bombs the Germans are dropping. Mom, I know you are probably having a fit right now, but I tell you that they aren't putting us anywhere near London or where the Krauts are dropping the bombs, okay?

I am proud to tell you that I think I got top marks in all of my firing exercises as well as driving and leadership. I am hoping for a nice promotion to sergeant which would be a feather in my cap for sure.

I wanted to tell you about the inside of my tank and where we all sit. Pretty nifty! The driver and co-driver sit right up in the front on opposite sides of the transmission casing. The tank commander, loader and gunner (me) sit up back in the turret basket. That gun can turn a full circle. There's all sorts of storage and places to put things like our tank helmets when we aren't wearing them. We even have a wireless radio and four hatches where we leave the tank. It's pretty darn noisy inside one of those things—that's why we wear those helmets with the ear pads and radio over our ears.

Oh, forgot to tell you that I got married! RELAX—it just means we work with the same group of guys all the time. Like, our tank company is married to a specific infantry company. That way the tanks and soldiers can rely on each other, and it works well! Besides, the tanks have great fire power and are bullet-resistant, but that big machine doesn't maneuver as fast as a man can, and we can't see everything around us. While the foot soldier has great all-around vision of the field and can move real fast like, but they have trouble with bullets and can't usually blow up a building unless they have a Bazooka or something.

Our engineers have remade where the tanks' radio is—they cut a hole in the armor on the back side and welded on an armored box that holds our radio. Before, its position just wasn't good. Well, there's not too much more to say except don't worry about me. I know God is watching and sending his guardian angels to watch over me. I remember your advice Dad about not hesitating to turn and run if I have to—that way I get another chance. Thanks for all the boxes—I can't tell you how much that means as well as the letters. Keep em' coming! I will write when I can.

Love, your son, Arnold

P.S. Tell all of my grandparents, sister and everybody hello from me and give that little Karlie a big hug from her godfather!

~~~~~~

The morning of February 1st, Arnold opened the door to the mess hall and pushed inside. He saw Cal waving from up near the front and worked his way forward. "Hey Arnold, guess this is the big day where we find out which company is our final assignment and who our CO is. I am hoping we both get kicked a notch higher as far as pay levels. I sure would be happy with a Private First Class."

General Lunsford Oliver took the podium. "Good Morning Gentlemen! This is the day many of you have been waiting for. As you know we have reorganized the Fifth Armored Division's two tank regiments into five separate battalions. Two of those will be transferred out of this division with orders for another division. Our intent is to create a tighter force—streamlined if you will."

Both Cal and Arnold held their breaths, hoping they would not be split up again. Arnold looked over at his buddy as Cal crossed the fingers on both hands and flashed a big toothy grin.

General Oliver announced: "The combat commands and their commanders remaining with the 5th Armored are as follows: General Regnier with CCA; Colonel Cole with CCB; and Colonel Anderson with CCR. Lt. Col. Farrand is the new Chief of Staff. Combat Command C which will reattach to a new Division Battalion.

You will all receive an envelope with your detailed Fort Knox chronicle of performance and in some cases, your new promotion. Congratulations! By the way, we pack up and leave for Camp Kilmer, New Jersey, on Friday. This will be the last stop on American soil before we ship out on the Edmund B. Alexander. We will only stay at Camp Kilmer for four to five days before boarding. Final orders will be found in your packets. Good day—

Dis-MISSED!" Everyone snapped to attention as the general departed.

A spontaneous cheering rippled through the mess hall. Arnold and Cal gave each questioning looks. Arnold said, "That was a surprise. I wonder why they transferred to CCC to another division---something about streamlining I guess. Well, anyway we will still be together in England. Come on, let's get out of here and open our orders. I can't wait to see what kinda scores I got on that firing range and if I got a promotion or not."

Cal was happy as a clam with his promotion from private first class to Corporal. He, his original crew and tank had their final CCC re-assignment orders. Arnie on the other hand, was promoted from Corporal to Sergeant. He would remain with his tank and crew in Combat Command B. Arnold scrolled down the report, "Holy smokes Cal—it says here that I got top marks in all of my firing exercises as well as leadership. I didn't know that each tank might have two sergeants and two privates along with the tank commander who is usually a staff sergeant or higher. I'm still a gunner and that is fine with me—not ready to be a tank commander and stick my head out of that hatch with in-coming shells, if ya get my drift!"

The next few days were a blur of activity as everyone on base took part in preparing the tanks, halftracks, and anything else that had wheels on it for transportation, first to Camp Kilmer, then for transport to England. Arnold complained to Cal, "For hell sake, is there no end to the inspections, instructions, and final rosters? As if that isn't enough we have to put on our Mae West jacket and practice abandoning the ship and loading into life boats if there are enough to go around." Arnold snickered as he mentioned, "Remember, the Titanic!"

Cal gave Arnold a playful nudge as he grinned, "Yeah, there weren't enough life jackets or boats. Well, I am bringing a wig along just in case—you know they let the women on before anyone!"

Arnold snapped back, "Well I am sure, it will be a problem for you choosing which wig you will wear in the life boat!" The two friends pretended to face off and duke it out. Arnold headed for the door, I need a smoke and maybe I'll go down to the library and write to my girl, see ya later."

February 7, 1944
Camp Kilmer, New Jersey
Dear Norrie,

I love you, I love you, I love you and don't you forget it! We got our orders honey and we ship out shortly. I have to say I am keen on seeing England where your grandmother's family came from—it must be' jolly good'! Ha I just thought I would throw that in!

I don't think there is a spot left where they haven't given us a booster or some sort of shot to protect us. Frankly, I think I'd rather have the measles than a bullet. Oh well, happier things---I have been promoted meritoriously (you didn't know I knew such big words did ya?) to sergeant and remain as gunner in our tank. That makes three stripes on my shirt. I also get to stay with the guys I've trained with. That's swell news to me!

You'll get a kick out of this—based on my favorite songs— "Saturday Night is the Loneliest Night"—but "I'll Get By"—"Til Then"—but "It HAS to be You!" Those are great songs, huh? You know honey, sometimes I can't even stand to listen to the songs, especially the slow ones because my arms and heart just start to ache something awful, missing you!

"I'll See you in my Dreams"- Kid! I love you always---
Your Soldier Boy, Arnold

---

9 February, 1944: In the overseas holding area, the men again were ordered to wait and be ready a moment's notice to ship out. Arnold didn't like this part---being crammed into a building with orders to stand down and wait for the call to come.

Camp Kilmer's loud speaker interrupted the mid-morning lull with a shrieking squawk. "Now hear this, now hear this. Tomorrow, 9 February, 1944, The Fifth Armored Division will be attached to the Third Army and muster at 0300 hours. Each man will be responsible for his own duffel bag, weapon, and any other equipment necessary. Just as a reminder, any mention of any form of your troop movement is subject to court-martial offense. Good Luck and remember---You ARE the VICTORY Division! God Bless each and every one of you."

Chapter Four

"Over There"

Wednesday, February 10, 1944, Port of New York: Arnold and a few of the more curious G.I.s stood on the frigid upper deck of the ferry boat as it slipped through the icy waters, past the crowded skyscrapers of the famous Manhattan Island. The ferry was headed for the docks at Staten Island where the ships that would carry them across the Atlantic Ocean, were docked. Arnold handled leaving just fine until the Statue of Liberty appeared like an eerie sentry through the pre-dawn mist.

Suddenly, Arnold's heart pounded in his throat and his hands shook as he tried to light a Camel. *Well, son-of-a-bitch, I'm shaking like a little girl on her first date. Whatz that all about—I got the jitters?* Then it dawned on him. *I'm seeing the Statue of Liberty for the first time, at dawn, just like my father did thirty-seven years ago when he came into this country as a little boy. Only, now, I'm not coming to this country, I'm leaving it to fight against the country, the people of my ancestors--Germans. It's really happening. Up until now, I guess I was just going through the motions and the reality hadn't sunk in. Well, by damn, it's sinking in now.* Arnold privately lowered his head and momentarily closed his eyes as he said a prayer. *Please dear merciful God, keep me safe, keep me from harm and bring me back in one piece to live my life. If it is your will that I die over there, I ask one thing—when it happens, let it be quick. Please dear Lord, let my dying be quick. This I ask through Jesus' sake. Amen.*

Cal pushed his way through the crowd to stand beside his buddy as they pulled into the Staten Island docks. Both of them were completely dumbfounded as they gazed, silently at the massive convoy of ships that were loading cargo, troops, equipment, and food. Cal whistled, "Man oh man, there must be thirty ships waiting along this whole dock, as far as we can see. There's a carrier—holy shit those things are big—never saw anything so big in my life. Where are all the planes?"

Arnold grinned, "You bet they're big—just think of all the planes, bombs, and men it has to carry. Oh, and—the planes are never on a carrier when it's at dock. They will take off from a nearby airport and land on the ship when it's out in the ocean a ways. You know---just in case and all!" Arnold pointed about two city blocks ahead, looks like we are going to have several destroyers, a couple P.T. boats, and some other tubs to protect the precious cargo in these troop ships. Where is our boat? Have you spotted the [17]Edmund B. Alexander yet? I guess General Lunsford will be on our ship with us and Gen. Regnier will be on the British ship, Athlone Castle with the infantry."

Edmund B. Alexander –WWII troop ship, 1943

As they marched up the gangplank onto their ship, Arnold and Cal were impressed and reassured to see that it had been retrofitted with ten, 40mm cannons in five double mounts, fore and aft. They were surprised to see twenty-four, single barrel 20mm cannons in steel tub-mounts positioned along the upper deck along with another twenty or so smaller, specialty guns; they were armed to the teeth and ready to go. Arnold nudged Cal, "Well, blow me down. This tub is all decked out like the Queen Mary I guess before they could stuff us boys in these ships, they had to give em the once over in regard to some serious guns to take care of any possible enemy aircraft and U-boat attacks. Although I've heard that our Navy and Air Force have pretty much taken the U-boat problem out of the picture."

As they found the way to their assigned section of the boat, Arnold remarked, "Say Cal, did you hear about the Queen Mary troop ship slicing through some British destroyer—think it was the Curacao—just off the coast of Ireland when they were coming back for more troops. Yeah—that crazy nut pulled right in front of that massive Queen Mary and there was nothing anyone could do—it sliced the front end of that destroyer off like a hot knife through butter and set it on fire. They rescued about half the men from it before it went under the black sea. And—the damnest' thing is that the 'QM' kept right on going with a big gouge in the front stem. When it was in port here in New York, they welded and smacked her back together and sent her back across the pond."

Cal and Arnold reached the point where they had to split up. Arnold gave Cal a friendly slap on the back and quipped, "I'll see ya in the funny papers, don't do anything I wouldn't do." They parted company and each went with their assigned company.

Arnold made his way to the stern with the rest of CCB; they were located down on B deck, right above the 'mess deck.' He had discovered a map of the ship in his packet which helped him to find his designated canvas bunk or hammock; the bunks/hammocks were stacked four tiers high. Arnold thought to himself, "They've got us packed so tight in here it'll be hard to fart! He stored his gear and turned right around to head back up top. Arnold pushed his way through the throng of other soldiers looking for their 3 x 8 deluxe quarters!

The silhouette of the New York skyline stood out in relief as the night sky began to lighten with the glimmer of dawn. Arnold, found a spot on the rear second deck. He leaned against the cold iron railing and gazed at the disappearing image of America, of home. *I guess it's comforting to know that we are just one ship in one of the largest troop convoys that has crossed the Atlantic yet. We are quite a ways out already and as far as I can see, there are ships and more ships. It's a damn good thing that most of the U-boats have been destroyed and these troop convoys don't have to be so paranoid when crossing the pond. No more zig-zagging or blackout runs—just enormous conveys taking American men and equipment into battle. Watch out Krauts---here we come!*

Arnold took one more drag on his cigarette before tossing it over board.

"TENNN---HUT!"

Startled, Arnold spun around and snapped to attention, saluting as a Major stood not four feet from him. "Soldier, aren't you supposed to be down in your designated deck area? What the hell are you doing up here, or are you a general in disguise?" Not waiting for an answer, he spat, "I didn't think so. Now get yourself where you are supposed to be before I write you up! Contrary to your opinion, you DO NOT have free run of this ship. **Dis-Missed!**"

Feeling like a complete nincompoop, Arnold went back to his quarters; he looked at the narrow bunk set up and had visions of being on the bottom bunk with three guys above him being seasick. *By damn, I remember my bunk was right in the middle. I am going to see if somebody wants to trade with me. I'm pretty sure I'm not going to get seasick unless we hit some gigantic high seas along the way. I'm not taking a chance that some fella above me pukes down on me.*

After actually suggesting that a certain private, move to the lower bunk, Arnold climbed into his top bunk and lay on his back studying the closeness of the ceiling. *Whew—not much breathin' room but at least it won't puke or fart on me!* He inspected the construction of his bed. *These canvas bunks are suspended with chains on the outside corners; I wonder what happens if that chain breaks. That would be a good one. Looks like the cots fold up when someone isn't in them---pretty nifty, pret-ty nifty.* He checked out the map of the interior of the ship

Well first off, I better know what words mean what on this ship so I'm not late to chow. Looks here like the aft is the back and the forward is the front. That's easy enough—but stern also means the back and starboard or port also can mean right or left. Way to make it confusing for us land-locked guys. The keel is like the waist or middle of the ship---and that's where I am.

It looks here like they have a barber shop, the main dispensary, the mess offices, and Red area Headquarters at the aft part of the ship. In the middle or keel is the ship's hospital, the Blue Headquarters, sun deck, officer's lounge, main deck, A deck, B deck and below all that on the 6th level is the mess galley. Below *that are the D and E decks and below that is the enormous cargo area. Topside is strictly officer country, where us enlisted guys are not allowed! This is one big canoe.*

Oh, I see---at the stern is the chaplain's office and chapel; the white area headquarters, U.S. Adj., officer's barber shop, synagogue, the purser's office, the Provost Marshall's office, dental, and the Bridge. Looks like all in all there are six staircases, but hell---someone forgot the elevators! Ha I like the fact that there is open deck aft and starboard. I want to spend as much time outside as I can.

Arnold leaped down from his canvas bunk and wound his way through a group of guys spread out in the narrow aisles, already playing cards and throwing their money away. Arnold thought, *well, whatever keeps them busy and entertained I guess; I don't like losing my money like that. I was never a card player like my Dad—now there's a card player.* Trying to be friendly, he asked, "What are you boys playing today, anything new?"

One soldier looked up and remarked, "Nope, same old same old---'Up the Duck and Down the Cumberland.' You might find a Poker, Blackjack, Craps, Hi-Lo Seven game or 'Baseball' on up there. If you don't like the games, there's a Red Cross movie room you might like." Arnold got a kick out of the guys hanging over the edges of their bunks to get a bird's eye view of the game going on in the aisle. *It doesn't take much to entertain a bunch of guys!* A familiar face popped up out of the group of guys on the floor, Danny Boy, the assistant gunner from his tank. "Hey Arnold, come on and have a go at it—we can find some room for you. I got a feelin' I'm gonna make me a few bucks."

Arnold waved as he walked on, "No, you go on—Danny. Just don't take any wooden nickels. See ya later."

Just after sunset, Arnold found a secluded part of the deck and leaned back against the cold metal of the ship's bulkhead as he lit up another Camel. He thought about the fellas down below, gambling and yelling their fool heads off. *None of them guys seem to understand that they might not come back from where we are going--that they might die over there. That's the trouble with us young guys—dying isn't in our vocabularies—we all think we won't die, can't die yet! But, we can and you bet your boots that some of us will.*

Arnold leaned over the railing and peered down into the inky blackness of the ocean. Once in a while it caught a light from somewhere on the ship and the water shimmered and glistened back at him. Arnold moved with the rocking of the ship as it cut through the waves. He thought about what the ocean looked like during the day—there was so much of it that there seemed to be no end. It scares me a little, I've never seen this much water. *I had no idea how big these oceans were and that you actually couldn't see the shore from somewhere—kinda gives me the willies.* He took a final drag on his cigarette and flipped it over the side into the water; he pulled a replacement from his pocket and put a match to it.

Arnold tipped his head back and looked at the full moon tucked under a canopy of black; the night sky was lit with a million twinkling stars. He thought about God again and wondered why he allowed men to have wars—why men had to want something that wasn't theirs and to send other men to fight and die for it. Before he went back down to 'B' Deck, Arnold said another little prayer inside his head—a prayer for guidance and protection.

It didn't take the soldiers aboard the Alexander long to discovered that this was not the typical holiday cruise. The men were crammed in the boat like sardines; it was so congested they were only fed twice a day. Arnold learned fast that your number and time for chow depended on the deck and the company you were with. Men started lining up at 0600 hours and ended lining up at 2000 hours at night; yeah, that's right eight o'clock at night is when the kitchen shuts down. There was the constant clanking of mess kits as the soldiers filed through chow lines. The officers, of course, had their own dining room and hours. *I doubt they eat the same slop that we do either---no greasy pork chops for the big boys!*

~~~~~~~~~

February 11, 1943
Edmund B. Alexander
Dear Mom and Dad:
    Well, I'm on my way overseas now. Before we left, I was lucky to see the same Statue of Liberty that you saw as a 6-year old

when you came to this country. It was pretty darn amazing. We are on a remodeled ship called the Edmund B. Alexander and we are not alone. There are a bunch of ships going over with us, I can't tell you how many or anything because the censors will black it out. So far the food is the worst ever—even worse than boot camp. They have stuffed us on here like sardines. The belly of the ship and every available room or area has been converted to bunks. They have us stacked three or four high in what they call bunks, but what I call hammocks! A guy barely has room to slide into his bunk. I can't tell yet if I am going to have room to sleep on my side or even raise my head without hitting the ceiling. Looks like they are 12" – 18" apart---wowzer! I'm not sure how many soldiers are on here, but there must be thousands.

I don't think it's any secret that this bunch is on the way to England. I am looking forward to seeing the country after hearing Norrie's mother talk about it and all. Her family is English and so I know a little bit about it. I imagine we are going to see some bombed out cities and suffering people since they have been at war with Germany for a couple years. Don't know what headquarters has in store for all of us boys, but I am pretty sure we won't be sitting on our butts. So, anyway this Wyoming farm boy in on his way to see the sights in Europe. I sure hope I get to see Paris, France. Wouldn't that be something now?

I carry the small Bible with me everywhere I go—thanks for giving that to me, Mom. I know you are praying for me and believe you me, I am praying as well. I just have to go and do what I have to do and I know it's not going to be something I want to write home about or talk about a lot when I get home. Stay healthy and tell everyone Hi for me.

Your loving son, Arnold

~~~~~~~~~~

It took the huge convoy thirteen days to cross the Atlantic Ocean. It was slow going because of the large number of ships. The fourth day out, they hit a twenty knot gale and that tub gave them all quite a ride. Arnold chose to hang out any place but his sleeping quarters. *It smells like shit down there with all those guys puking their guts out and half of them don't make it to the head.*

Besides, I get to feeling too close down there with some of those guys literally hanging from the ceiling and the tight quarters— heard they have a big word for that feeling, umm—claustrophobic, I think. Well, anyways, that's what I feel and it's not a good feeling, like I can't breathe.

　　　　Arnold got caught up on his letter writing, practiced his German, and even read more manuals about Sherman tanks. He went to calisthenics when he could get in the gym and watched a few movies too. On Sunday he attended chapel. It wasn't Lutheran—just a protestant service, but it made him feel good to sing some of the songs and stuff. On Thursday, February 18th, Arnold woke with the realization that it was his 20th birthday. Standing in line for the showers, he thought, I think I'll get a hold of Cal and see if he's busy. *Maybe we could manage a beer or two. Well anyway, I'm not a teenager any more—it just feels right. Ya know this is the first birthday that I can remember when I never got a birthday cake. I did get a few cards before we sailed, but I miss those cakes Mom baked for me. Maybe she will send me one when I get to England.*

　　　　On the eleventh day, Arnold and Cal managed to meet up again, this time on the sun deck, where they got a chance to have a quiet conversation, catch some rays and have a smoke. They were both startled to hear a cheer go up as a plane circled above their ship. Arnold didn't know whether to get below or what until he heard one of the guys say, "Holy moley, that's one of those RAF Coastal Command patrol planes and it means we are getting close to the coast of Ireland. It will babysit us all the way in to the port in England." This was the part of the trip where the ship's crew was especially vigil because they were forced to slow their speed as they approached the muddy mouth of the Mersey River in England. If there were German planes in the area, the ships were an easy target when they were in the channel.

　　　　At this point, about half the troops were up top, craning their necks to catch a glimpse of their new temporary home, England. Cal spoke up, "I don't know what to expect as far as cities, I hearsay that even Liverpool has caught some German bombs. Great Britain has been at war for several years now and they've been taking a real pounding. I have to tell you that I'm not looking forward to those nightly air raids and hearing the screeching wail of the sirens when I'm trying to sleep. I guess once you hear the scream of one of those German bombs falling, you never forget it."

Arnold was quiet for a moment taking it all in then he replied, "Yeah, well Cal, we are in it now, that's for damn sure. This is what the books call 'the European theatre of war'. We are going to get used to the ever-present threat of bombs, shooting, and death for as long as it takes to kick some German butt back to Berlin. I got a feelin' we got ourselves in a fine kettle of fish here."

On their way back to their respective bunking areas, Arnold and Cal paused to give each other a slap on the back and a quick hug. "Good luck to you Cal, I hope to run into you, but we might be bivouacking in different places. Take care of yourself and keep your head down and for God's sake, keep that tank out of the ditch!"

Cal snapped back, "I'll keep mine on the road if you hit your damn targets with that pea shooter!"

Arnold practically slid down the iron ladder that led to B deck. He swallowed hard, trying to rid himself of the egg-size lump that was in his throat after saying goodbye to Cal. His baby blues filled with tears in spite of himself. *I hope to hell I see that boy again when this is all over, that would be swell.*

Contrary to when they usually deployed or went on maneuvers, the Fifth Armored Division arrived in Liverpool, England in the late afternoon, not the crack of dawn. Because of a bank of heavy fog, there wasn't much to see from the ship. Arnold quipped to the G.I. standing next to him, "So this is England. Can't see much of it, but I can smell it." The men lined up according to their orders, with their duffel bags on their shoulders, gas masks, their packs, weapons and special gear attached somewhere on them. Arnold even saw one G.I. with a small guitar hanging from his rucksack. In orderly fashion, they happily left the cramped quarters of the Edmund B. Alexander and filed off the ship and into waiting troop trains. Most of them noticed their wobbling legs. Someone laughed, "That's what they call sea legs!"

Arnold couldn't help but notice the number of matronly women with buckets and mops standing to the side on the dock. "What the hell are those women doing down here? I was expecting some pretty young English girls down here waiting with kisses and cookies and all that."

A voice from deep within the files remarked, "You knucklehead, they are here to clean up the mess we made on the ship before it turns around and heads back to New York to pick up another bunch of men ready to take a bullet!"

Chapter Five

TRURO

February 23, 1944. The large port in Liverpool, England, lay on the west coast at the mouth of the Mersey River. It was late in the day, yet the docks were like a seething creature with men running here and there, securing ships, unloading cargo---you name it. The decks of the arriving American troop ships were packed to the gills with men, eager for a first glimpse of Europe.

Sergeant Arnold Kessel knew he was lucky to find a place next to the railing on the second deck of the Edmund B. Alexander. When his group was called to disembark, he paused before walking down the gangplank and onto English soil. *Well forget about enthusiastic bands playing the Star-Spangled Banner or Yankee Doodle Dandy—Yee gods, there aren't this many people in the whole state of Wyoming. It's like a three-ring circus!* It was true, as troop ships from somewhere or another waited in long undulating ques for their turn to unload their cargo of impatient troops and equipment at any English dock, in preparation for the invasion of Europe.

Nobody knew for sure when the invasion was going to be, but you had to be an idiot not to know it was coming soon. Even the Germans knew it was coming, and most were certain the Allied Armies would land on the northwestern coast of France and General Patton would lead it. In reality, Gen. Patton was having a time out in England for slapping a shell-shocked soldier. Word was that, he was devastated not to be a part of the primary invasion but took his punishment like the true soldier he was. Patton hung on to the promise from Supreme Allied Commander Eisenhower, that (he) Patton would have the opportunity to lead the Third Army into battle on French soil, at some point.

Arnold settled into his seat on the train as they headed for the outskirts of Liverpool. He gazed at the rows of simple houses with colorful and unruly English flower gardens in the compact front yards. Most had little air raid shelters in the back yards and blackout curtains were pulled back to let the sun shine in. Soon the country side was hidden from view as the sun set to the west and a dense fog rolled in from the sea. Arnold's head nodded and then fell against the window as the rumble and sway of the train lulled him to sleep. He woke once or twice to briefly rub his stiff neck or when the train's high pitched whistle broke through the monotony. Most soldiers were sleeping and oblivious to the jagged flashes of white and red, lightning up the night sky to the southeast, over London.

The troop trains were heading one hundred and seventy miles to the south of England. Dawn was just breaking to the east when the first train rumbled into the English town of Swindon. The brakes locked and the iron wheels hissed and screeched as Arnold's train rolled to a stop.

Arnold looked at his orders for the umpteenth time. Combat Command B was to report to Ogbourne St. George. From the roster, it looked like Cal was going to be stationed at nearby Camp Obisedon. Most of the training camps were located in Wiltshire, England, and the men of the Fifth Division would be servicing the First Army troops as they readied for the invasion of France. It looked like the 81st and most of the Fifth Division would NOT be participating in the invasion.

I wonder why they left the 15th Armored Infantry in Swindon while the 85th Cavalry Squadron plus three of the artillery battalions are heading on down to Perham Downes Camp near Salisbury. All I know is that Colonel Cole made our reservations while he was coming over in the Queen Mary; I bet he had some nice digs on that luxury liner.

Area Map of where Allied Forces training camps were located.

First thing after unloading from his troop train, Arnold settled into his Quonset hut barracks and then in short order, the members of CCB marched in formation over to the mess hall. The cooks of the 3rd Armored Division had cooked up a nice hot breakfast for them. Arnold had a case of the shakes or shivers, he couldn't tell which. *It's not that cold here according to the thermometer, but it is damp and I guess that kind of cold goes right to the bone! I better get used to it because we're gonna be here for a while.*

That first night in Salisbury was a doozey! Arnold woke to the wail of air-raid sirens, intermittent spotlights scanning the inky night sky, and the sound of German bombers—flying low. He leaped from his Army-issued cot and ran for the nearest window; he pulled back the blackout shade and peered up at the night sky. The sky was a surreal revelation of black silhouetted Luftwaffe bombers, search lights, and exploding anti-aircraft flak. Eighty miles to the east the night sky was glowing red from bombs already dropped on London. Even that far away, they could hear or feel the impact of the bombs. The visuals were damn right daunting. Stunned, Arnold wasn't aware of anything else in the room but what he was seeing out the window. His fingers clutched the hem of the blackout shade as fear and realization of what was happening exploded in his mind.

Night Skies over England – 1943

Oh dear God---I am really here, this is really happening and people are dying right now, just eighty miles away. This is a nightmare. Actually, the nightmare was only beginning!

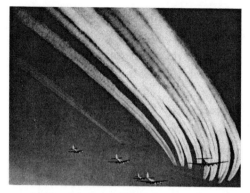

The next morning and every morning after that while they were in England, Arnold looked up in the skies and saw American planes on their way to make their own bombing runs over Germany. At a perpetual level, the British RAF flew at night and the Allied forces flew sortie after sortie during the day. The goal was to take out Germany's munitions, their factories, and destroy their cities along with their supplies and their will! They had all learned their lessons on audible and visible identification, between Luftwaffe, RAF, and Allied bombers in aircraft 101----- back in training at Fort Knox.

March 29th 1943: *"Now hear this - now hear this— General assembly - 0600 hours in the arena. All battalions, brigades, and divisions report."*

Arnold and his tank commander Mac rolled out of bed that morning to frost on the pumpkin. The floor of their Quonset hut was like a refrigerator and Arnold collapsed in a fit of laughter just watching Mac hot-foot it across the cold floor to the can. "You are a sight, man; I hope you make it to the 'john'!"

When Mac returned a few minutes later, Arnold was already dressed, "You'd better get a move on; we have to report for assembly in ten minutes. Do you have any idea what this is all about? Maybe we are gonna get our orders to still be part of the invasion! That would be sure be swell!"

As Mac jumped into his pants, he quipped, "Yeah swell---I don't think I want to be in that first group off those boats and get my ass shot off. Those first landing groups are gonna catch hell and worse! I'd much rather be in the mop-up group that lands later, think about it."

Seated at the assembly hall, the 81st Tank Division and several other groups were all ears. Major General Lunsford Oliver approached the podium and having second thoughts moved to center stage to be closer to the men standing at attention. "AT EASE! Men, it is with great humility and excitement that I accept my final assignment from First Army Commander, Gen. Omar Bradley. My new assignment is commanding general of the 5th Armored Division. We all realize that recently commands and attachments seem to have been on a rotating schedule but things are falling into place. We have been together for a while now and I couldn't be more pleased to be named as the Commander of the Fifth Armored Division."

General Oliver continued, "Now that we are settled down here in England, we are going to drill you men and introduce you to some new tactics devised for beach attack. I know you have all heard rumors regarding who is going to participate in the invasion. However, nobody at our level knows at this point, who exactly will be part of the invasion or when it will be. In the meantime, we will continue to prepare and prepare hard, this is no English picnic you are on here."

"TENN-HUTT!" Gen. Oliver clicked his heels, saluted and left the stage.

On the way back to their barracks, Mac said, "We know he's a good commander; there's something about him that I really like or maybe respect is a better word. I like having someone in command that we have a history with. We know from Fort Knox, that he's a soldier's officer---he cares about us and what we have to do."

~~~~~~~

Arnold still missed Cal, but he was bunking with his own tank crew and so it wasn't like he didn't know anyone. They had all been kept pretty busy with small unit training and drawing equipment/maintenance. Then, they received new orders stating that the Fifth Armored Division had been attached to the XX Corps (nicknamed the 'Ghost Corps'). Mac called his crew together that next morning. "I know I'm beginning to sound like a broken record, but they've moved us in the lineup again. I guess they are just trying to get a good fit for everyone involved. I sure wouldn't want that job, not with invasion on the horizon."

That night, with his arms folded under his head, Arnold lay back on his cot shooting the bull with his tank commander, Staff Sgt. Mac Darby. "Say Mac, what do you think about us having to learn all these regulations sent down by the ETO (European Theater of Operations)? Looks to me like they have a rule for about everything; I just wonder how that is going to pan out when we are actually over in France in an all-out battle. Seems to me, we won't have a hell of a lot of time to devote to fighting by the book, once we get in the middle of it and all! My way of thinking is that when the time comes, most of what we do will be knee-jerk reaction inspired by what we have learned."

Mac sat up on his cot and ran his fingers through his black curly hair. "Well, Cowboy, I'll say this, all that rule making keeps the officers busy, now don't it? I am thinkin' that when we are kickin' Kraut butt, if we do a good job, then we won't hear anything about by the book, unless Gen. Patton happens to drive by! If you hear or see him, you better have your shirt tucked in, your teeth brushed, and everything in its place and that includes hide the damn sand bags!"

Arnold chuckled, "You know, the last six weeks have been real interesting; I sure wasn't expectin' all this damp cold. It's the middle of March and I've got to wonder when spring time arrives here; I am ready for some sunshine on my back. I guess we are lucky though—no snow so far. I sure wish we had better food and more of it. I know headquarters got caught with their pants down as far as estimating how much food and supplies these troops would need." Arnold stood up and pulled the cover on his cot taunt. "I just think it's the shits when my orders call for me to stand by the garbage cans and make sure nobody throws any food away. I actually caught this one guy with his pockets full of some macaroni and cheese stuff he didn't like. Poor sap!"

Arnold ran a comb through his blond hair and pulled on his pants. "Have you been into Salisbury yet? How do those English women look to you? I heard they look just like our gals, but they don't sound the same and don't dress as flashy. That English accent is pretty hard to understand sometimes—and what the hell does 'blimey' mean anyway?"

Mac laughed as he tucked his shirt into his pants, "Yeah, I've been to Salisbury; had a tough time finding the way too. I get the feeling some of these locals don't particularly like us Yanks campin' here on their doorstep and all. Couple of the village guys purposely gave us the wrong directions into town. They are probably afraid we're gonna take their gals, which is probably true enough, right Cowboy?" Arnold laughed, "Well, I know you will give it the old American try for sure! I got me a girl back home and so I'm not interested in anyone over here."

Mac slapped Arnold on the back, "Come on now, you don't think she is sitting home every night do ya? You need to get out and kick up your heels a little---let a little steam off. Who knows when the next time will be that we get the chance to have some fun? Come on with the boys and me tomorrow—we have some time off comin'—you stay around here too long and moss is gonna start growing on your north side! Besides, we are going to London to have a look see---we hear it's pretty bad and it's something I think we need to see first-hand. It will help us when it comes time to start shooting some Germans---after we see what they are doing to London and all. Oh, and by the way, bring a bunch of chocolate, nylons, gum---all those giveaways. We are gonna see a lot of people who don't have that kind of stuff." Mac smiled as he added, "That includes all these lonely English dames. I think it's up to us Yanks to take their minds off their English boyfriends, don't you?"

Just as the sun began to rise to the east, that last Saturday morning in March, Mac, Butch, Danny Boy, Joe, and Cowboy packed up and headed to London on a one-day pass. They hitched a ride on a military service truck that was headed that way with a load of supplies.

They were surprised and awed at the stately beauty of some of the larger country homes. They just popped up out of nowhere—they were probably large land-owner's homes or country squires or something. As they crossed through the southern English country side, Arnold was curious about the humble cottages at the edge of the small villages, like the simple white-washed farmer's house with the prettiest bird-egg blue front door and matching shutters. The thing Arnold remembered later and also amazed him was that fact that the whole back side of the house was missing, but there wasn't even a bullet hole in the rest of the house. A geranium-filled flower box hung from the front window of a house by one end. He thought, *a bomb must have dropped close by and the explosion caused this damage.*

The closer they got to London the air became hazy with the smoke of fires still burning from last night's bombing raids. Arnold felt his body tense, not knowing what they would see once they got in the city. The truck slowed and started to pass another vehicle on the road. Arnold and the guys were in the back of the

truck and didn't see the other vehicle until they had passed by. At first there was silence, then realization hit them all—this was a cemetery load and it was probably a daily trek. It was happening all over the country.

The truck stopped at a cross roads of sorts, at the edge of London. The driver called back, "This is the end of the line for you yanks; I have to go a different direction now. Just follow this road into the city there. You might find your USO about a mile or two down this lane. Brace yourselves yanks, you probably ain't seen nothing like this before. Good day to ya!"

Mac and Arnold were in the lead as they headed east on the road. At the edge of the city, they noticed a group of people ahead. As they neared, they saw an enormous hole and the obvious devastation of where a bomb had hit just last night. Mac said, "Holy smokes look at the depth of that hole. It looks to me like those people are looking for survivors and anything that can still be had."

They approached one villager and Mac spoke first, "Good Morning Sir, we are just passing by on our way into London. Looks like you got hit pretty hard last night. Is there anything we can do for you?"

The man turned, his eyes were bloodshot, and his face covered with soot and grime, "As a matter of fact my lad, there is something you boys can do, you can get the hell over to Europe and beat those bloody Krauts into the bloody ground. I knows that your flyboys are doing their bloomin' best, just like our own, going out day and night with their planes full of bombs. Sooner or later, them Germans are gonna feel our vengeance. We're just doing what we can here—there's not much left. Those that lost their homes are welcome in our homes that are left and that's about all there is to it; we just got to keep a stiff upper lip and all!" The man turned away and rejoined his community as they sifted through the rubble.

Half numb with the shock of reality, Mac and his crew continued on down the road where dense rows of houses were built, joined at the hip to conserve heat and land they suspected. Arnold said, "How many bombs fell last night—they sure as hell made a mess of things. If they built their houses farther apart, it would be easier to control the fires. I mostly thought the Krauts were aiming to wipe out the industrial areas and not so much the neighborhoods, what the hell is wrong with them Germans? I don't understand the need to purposely kill civilians and destroy their homes and all."

Joe piped up and said, "They don't give a flying fart where they drop their bombs just as long as they hurt as many people and burn as much English property as they can—that's what they do—destroy and kill. Our planes are aiming for their industrial areas because that is where we are going to hurt their armies and supplies. Looks to me like they are in it for the killing and we are in the war to stop them from it."

Up ahead they saw a group of English servicemen and more civilians grouped around a destroyed structure. They were down on their hands and knees, methodically digging and throwing

 beams and carefully pulling stones out of a hole. Arnold moved forward, ready to give them a hand. "Mornin'---can we give you folks some help there? We're headin' into the USO and we'd sure not mind doin' something to help here if we can."

An older English corporal looked up at the American servicemen, "Mornin' to you Yanks, we got us a woman trapped down here, I think we are about to get her out. It's been a slow go of it—just a brick at a time. Don't want the whole thing to cave in on her, now do we? She's still alive and not hurt too badly, she just can't move herself out. Her wee lad is sittin' over on that there beam, been there since dawn, waiting for us to get his Mum out. You boys might cheer him up a bit before you go on into town."

All five of their heads turned to see a boy of about six sitting patiently on a broken roof beam. He wore an old brown coat, about three sizes too big and shoes the same. Kids were lucky to have clothes and even shoes that actually fit them during these hard times.

The minute Arnold laid eyes on the little tyke, his throat tightened and tears welled up in his eyes; he moved toward the boy. "Hey there little fella, what's your name?"

The little boy looked up at the group of American soldiers and replied, "You soldier boys talk funny—are you yanks now? Where you from? Me name is Charlie, Charlie White. And, what be your name?

Arnold squatted down beside the lad and put his hand on the boy's shoulder. "My name is Arnold—and yes we are yanks, we're from America. How long have you been sittin' here, waitin', Charlie?

CHARLIE

The little boy looked up at the soldier and said with a quivering voice, "I bean hare since I woke up over thar." He pointed to a stack of rubble. "Me Mum and me was on the run to the bomb shelter and that's all I 'member, til I woke up by me self, over on that bunch of rocks there. The soldier lads say they are gonna get my mum out of the hole, but it's been a long time she's been down there. I could hear her cryn' something fierce just this morning and I run and got the soldiers. They're good blokes, they are." Charlie thought a moment and looked up at the Americans, "Are you Yanks gonna kill Germans? Me Mum said you Yanks are good fair even tho you don't have good manners, like us English do."

Arnold sniffed his nose a couple of times and struggled to get his emotions under control. He reached in his pocket and brought out a chocolate bar and a box of K-rations. "That we are, we are here to help England beat the Germans too. I bet you're getting a little hungry, is that right, Charlie?"

Charlie's eyes glistened bright as he looked up at Arnold, "Blimey--right you are, I could do with a bit of glop (mixture of food). The soldiers gave me a cup of black strap (coffee) this mornin' and that's all I've had this day."

Arnold kneeled down and handed the K-ration and a chocolate bar to Charlie. The boy's eyes widened and a smile crept out of the corners of his mouth, "I say mate, what do ya have there? Are you gonna give that to me? Crackie!" He stood up on wobbly legs and reached for the offering.

Arnold noticed the boy wasn't well; he took him by the arm and sat him back down. "Here Charlie, you sit right there and have a little bite to eat while they are getting your Mother out. Did you get hurt when the bombs fell?

Between mouthfuls, Charlie managed to say, "Just a wee bump on me noggin is all; it hurts just a tad over here on my head. I'm a wee bit collywobbles (nauseated) and knacked (tired). I'll be okay, me Mum says I'm a stout lad, she does. Ms. Webbley said Mum and me could stay with her til Mum is feeling better. She's all I got left in this world and she's a real good Mum; that she is. I've got to have her back or else I'll end up as one of them orphans!"

Mac touched Arnold on the shoulder, "We best be getting on our way; those men said they would look after the boy."

Arnold put his arm around Charlie's thin shoulders and said, "You take good care of your Mum when she gets out of that hole now and maybe we'll see you around. Goodbye Charlie!"

~~~~~~~~

Mac and his tank crew spent the rest of the afternoon at the USO in London, having a bite to eat and they even danced with a couple of plump curly-headed English gals. Back out on the streets, everywhere they looked, it was the same. Rows and streets of destroyed homes and shops covered the beleaguered city. People were everywhere, digging around in the rubble to find what they could find, making a path through the rubble so they could walk, and searching for food and/or a place to sleep. The Underground and train station platforms were full of people staking out a place to lay their heads as well as a quick shelter from the falling bombs. It was a sight none of the men had ever witnessed and they knew in their hearts, that this was nothing compared to what lay ahead.

It was past dark when the five American soldiers started back for their camp. Back in his army-issued bed that night,

Arnold said a few prayers for Charlie and his Mom and all of the besieged people in London that he never saw, but knew were there. *They are a remarkable people and it's obvious they won't be beaten. How can you go through what they are going through night after night and still keep that stiff upper lip?*

~~~~~~~~

In early April, The Fifth Armored Division made preparations to begin their own field maneuvers and training for invasion. Then, General Oliver received new orders and everything changed. They were expected to completely re-vamp their previous assignment in order to manage the task force camps preparing for invasion. It was not definite but obvious that the invasion troops didn't include the Fifth Division. *"This is a slug in the jaw to our combat training,"* General Oliver explained to the men in each battalion. *"We now have a new job and the Fifth Armored will rise to the task. We will have our day of invasion but it won't be with the first wave."* They all realized that more changes in orders would come through as the invasion drew near.

American and Axis troops were scattered all over southwestern England from Torquay, to Plymouth, to the Truro region in the most western toe of the country. The men did their fair share of KP duties for the camps as well as worked on their equipment. Arnold soon discovered that each company was responsible for anywhere from four to six messes, and in one battalion alone, they came up with seventy-two pretty decent cooks.

The selected marshalling troops began invasion tactic training in vain. After he and Mac and the boys finished with KP duties one day, they stood and watched what the other troops were doing. They were impressed with the meticulous and calculating maneuvers; each man wondered if he would eventually be a part of something like that too.

Arnold said, "Mac, just look how they bring those big ships in and load up all that equipment and personnel and then go out into the channel, turn and attack. I guess we are getting a lesson just watching them. See how the infantry goes in first, followed by the amphibious tanks; the LST's and infantry crafts are followed by the engineers. Once they hit the beach, they go through their maneuvers and then they reassemble to do it all over again."

Arnold pointed out to the ocean, where a hundred yards out from shore, a mortar shell slammed into the water, followed by several more. "It looks like they are using some live fire—aimed well away from the ships; probably to give the guys the feeling and sound of what the actual Kraut shelling is going to sound like.

Mac affectionately slapped Arnold on the back, "Yeah, the top brass will run those boys over and over until they see what they want to see. Kinda helps em' work the kinks out. I got a feelin' that the invasion is gettin' close, the big brass aren't telling us nothin'!" Arnold's blue eyes glistened with excitement, "Say Mac, did you see that German reconnaissance plane that flew over here the other day? Some of our boys took some pot shots at it. Those Krauts wanted to get a better look at what we are doing over here. It looks to me like someone is getting itchy feet!"

Before they knew it, it was Sunday, May 28th, 1944. With summer fast approaching, Arnold soon discovered what they meant by the British double summer. The sun didn't set until almost 11 p.m.; they made the most of the longer days in which to prepare for the invasion.

Mac and his tank crew hit the sack around 10:30 that night. Arnold quipped, "Hell, I gotta cover my eyes to make it dark." Soon the sounds of sleep drifted through the barracks. Around two in the morning they awoke to a menacing rumbling growl of low-flying aircraft that vibrated through the hastily built Quonset hut barracks. Outside, the continuous flack fire sounded like a drummer practicing his beat on a snare drum. Arnold put his pillow over his head to block out the sound.

Long bluish beams of anti-aircraft lights flashed through the windows at a predictable pace, searching the night sky for the invading Luftwaffe bombers. Usually the sound of the bombers faded on their way to London, but not tonight! Arnold sat up in bed as the scream of diving bombers filled the night. Not stopping to grab anything, Arnold and the others ran for cover and weapons as wave after wave of bombs shrieked down from the black heavens.

When the all clear siren sounded, Arnold and the others surveyed the damage. They heard that CCB commander Col. Anderson's headquarters at the Livermead Hotel had been barely missed—bombs dropped on both sides never hitting the hotel. There were a few civilian homes and shops still smoldering. Farther up, they could see the boiling black smoke from a couple oil tanks and trucks that had been hit near Truro. Every able man ran up and down the streets, looking to see if they could be of help, pulling survivors out of the rubble and tugging fire hoses to put out the smaller fires.

JUNE 3, 1944: Assault troops began to gather in masse during that first week in June. Arnold quipped, "Boy, the pot is about to boil over---something is sure cooking. Looks like those troops will be boarding the ships any day now. Mac, did you see how many ships are in all of these ports around here. I think the practicing days are over; these boys are gettin' ready to do the deed and soon!

THE LANDING AT NORMANDY, FRANCE -- JUNE 6, 1944

Three days later, near daybreak, they all woke as an ominous, continuous heavy rumble rolled across the English Channel from France. It rattled the window panes and nerves of those left behind. Arnold and the rest of the boys in the Fifth Division saw that the assembled ships and troops were gone from English shores. It was [18]D-DAY! Everything that would float had left in the night; they waited while the battleships pounded the beaches and German fortifications in an effort to eliminate some of the enemy resistance and threat.

Arnold looked up and down the costal ports and there was not a ship or boat to be seen--- everybody was at the dance! That night after lights out, Arnold had to get something off his mind, "Say Mac, I've been wondering—where the heck is General Patton? I thought we'd see him and that ugly dog of his right here in the middle of things. But I've not heard a peep out of him since he slapped that private in that hospital, and that was months ago. Boy, that was something, he's damn lucky they didn't court martial him. They say that kid just had shell shock and was crying and Patton called him a coward and slapped him."

Mac propped himself up on one elbow, "The scuttlebutt is that he's here in England with the Third Army. They've kept to themselves around Kent and Sussex. I've heard the same gossip that he's going to lead an invasion of his own at Calais, France. I saw something the other day about another operation called [19]Operation Bodyguard. Believe me, he's around and we will hear about him eventually. I've got me a feeling that they have something more than D-Day planned. I guess we'll find out sooner or later what the plan is and when it's time for us to fit into it."

~~~~~~~~~

Now, it was their turn. The Fifth Division got their orders to attach to XXII Corps for maneuvers. They broke camp and headed back up to Swindon to retrieve their own equipment and *proceed to Salisbury Plain for preparation to go into battle.* The rest of the month of June, they practiced just as the first invasion troops had—loading into the ships and turning back to 'attack' the coast of England. Each day they grew stronger and more confident until they were like a well-oiled machine!

Arnold hated the most was the surprise maneuver! Sleeping soundly, the battalions awoke to the ear and nerve-splitting scream of an attack siren. Jumping from their warm beds, they suited up and ran to their tanks, half-tracks –whatever, and prepared to attack. By the fifth time this exercise took place, Arnold was a bit calmer but still pissed off that they had to train this way. "Hell Mac, I can see why they want us to do this—so we are ready at a moment's notice to fight. But it's really getting on my nerves, how about you?"

They waited and trained and trained some more-- until July 25th. Then, the top command opened the head gates for the FIFTH ARMORED DIVISION. Now was the time for their own invasion of France—time for their own glory.

Chapter Six

"The object of war is not to die for your country but to make the other bastard die for his!"

Lt. Col. George S. Patton

The First Army, Fifth Armored Division, 81st Tank Battalion and other infantry divisions loaded onto the waiting troop carriers and [20]LST's (Landing Ship, Tank). On July 22nd and 23rd they sailed out of the southern port of Southampton, England with orders to cross the English Channel and land on UTAH Beach, on the coast of Normandy, France.

The English Channel was particularly rough that day. Arnold felt reassured that he didn't get seasick on the ship coming over from America but today, he felt gorge rising in his throat every time the lighter troop ship crested a wave and then dropped into a shallow. *Man, this is the shits; I think I might have a case of the nerves as well as some sea sickness. I need to get out of this congested hole and get up top—get some fresh air. They've got us packed in here like sardines in a can and breathing that diesel exhaust doesn't help. But, he realized he had to ride it out!*

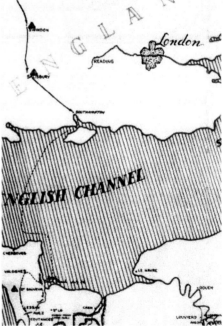

Major General Lunsford Oliver stood on the bridge of the LST as it headed out into the English Channel, bound for Utah Beach in Normandy. *Now, we get our chance to show what we can do. These men are 'straining at the gate' to fight—we want our*

piece of the pie and we will damn well take it. The Krauts will know The Victory Division has arrived!

The Landing: As they neared the beach, Arnold stayed up on deck with his tank crew as their LST negotiated its way around disabled, bombed out, and half-sunk remains of ships that never made it to the French beach.

Arnold's mind played with all sorts of scenarios as he surveyed the wrecked hulls of ships hung up on the shallow reefs of the ocean floor. His eyes nervously scanned the beaches to the north—Omaha, Juno, Gold, and Sword. As far as he could see the white sand beach was scattered with eerie forms of German Hedgehogs and burned out remains of tanks, half-tracks, and service trucks—just about anything that would have landed on D-Day. Arnold thought, *it looks to me like they are pushing most of the disabled equipment aside and making paths around them for now. I imagine that the tactical objective is to get these new waves of men and equipment ashore and fast, to beef up our invasion force and push the Krauts back to Germany!*

All tank crews were ordered into their respective tanks down inside the well deck, ready to splash. Even though they weren't in imminent danger, Arnold's throat still felt powder dry and he had butterflies in his stomach. The ship's captain was trying his best to get them as close to the beach as possible---a task most troop ships and LST boats weren't able to accomplish on D-Day with low tide and relentless incoming fire from the concrete German bunkers on the bluff.

As the ship bucked through the choppy surf, all sorts of thoughts spun through Arnold's head. *This landing is cake compared to our boys musta went through on D-Day. I wonder what those destroyers sounded like from this area when they fired round after round against the Germans, dug in on those cliffs.*

Arnold pointed to a massive LST that had moved as far up on the beach as it could.

"Mac, look at that over there—it just struck me as funny, looking at that LCT with its mouth open like it's puking up tanks and the rest of the equipment or getting ready to eat them! I think it's pretty nifty how they can carry the tanks up on deck and then when it comes time to put them on shore, they use them elevators to drop them down inside and drive them out the steerage mouth." Arnold rubbed his two hands together, "When do us boys get in our tank and drive it out?"

Mac looked over his shoulder, 'WE—don't take our tank out of the ship our driver does that job, alone!"

Later that morning, Mac, Cowboy, Danny Boy and Butch stood on the beach and watched with pride as their driver Joe Carpuchi guided their Sherman out of the mouth of the LST with precise skill. Once it was on the sand, Joe shifted to another gear as the motor strained and growled trying to get a foot hold in the soft sand. After the tank made it across the unstable sand and onto harder surface, it was time for the rest of the crew to mount their individual tanks and proceed to the rendezvous point.

As they walked to their tank, Danny Boy gave Arnold an elbow in the ribs, "Catch that---those are those Deep Wading kits on the back of that Sherman; they're meant to give the crew fresh air and take the exhaust out if and when a tank happens to get into deep water. They also might use something like that if a bridge is blown and they need to get across."

M4 Sherman with Deep Water Wings

"Those 30-ton babies DO NOT float unless they give them water wings! I guess they lost plenty of tanks in that deep water off-shore on D-Day. Damn—I am so thankful we weren't in that wave—it sounds like it was beyond hell and then some."

Danny Boy shook his head in wonder, "Now that is some engineering! Say, I wonder if we are going to get some of those dragon teeth on the front of our tank to cut through those damn French Hedgerows?"

German Bunker on Utah Beach - Normandy

Up ahead, they were halted. Joe shouted over the roar of the tank engine, "We have to stop here and let the engineers take the Deep Wading kits off those other tanks. In no time, they pulled ahead and climbed up the rise of the beach to where long blond

Bluff above Normandy Beach

seagrass covered the dunes. Arnold was looking out his gunner's slit when he caught sight of a bombed out German bunker, tucked into the bluff. "Holy shit, take a look at the size of that concrete bunker. Looks like our boys took care of that thing---and below it are some of those Hedgehogs — nasty looking things aren't they?

Arnold's eyes scanned the beach and the remains of a terrible battle. Suddenly his eyes stopped and fell on what remained, of a crooked, hastily-built roping razor, wire fence. *From the looks of it, those Krauts threw everything they had at our boys including coils of barbed wire. They didn't miss a trick! But, I know for damn certain, that we had a few tricks of our own for that invasion. It must have been pure hell.*

By that time the LST and troop ships had unloaded their men and equipment; most of them then turned to head back to England, for another load—all except for one troop ship that anchored off shore.

Arnold and the rest of the 81st Tank Battalion prepared to bivouac next to the bluff for the night. Mac and Arnold pitched their pup tent while Danny Boy and Joe built a small fire to heat their K-rations. Arnold pointed to the higher bluffs to the west, Say Mac. "According to my map, right up there is that village, Sainte-M'ere-'Eglise where our paratroopers landed on D-Day. The town was filled with trigger-happy Germans who mowed a lot of those boys down as they were dropping from the sky. I saw in the paper that one of our fellas got hung up on a church spire and the Krauts machine gunned him to death. Those paratroopers, who survived, cleaned the Heinies out of that town and then moved out to reinforce our troops landing on Utah and Omaha Beaches. I can't imagine jumping outta an airplane and floating down while Germans are shoot'n at ya, can you! That musta been pure bushwa!"

Mac hooked the last of the tent ropes to pegs in the ground and replied, "Yeah, that was a real bad scene, but those troopers are a special lot---not for me either!"

Thoughtfully, Arnold recalled a reporter's quote. "**They were just ordinary Americans doing extraordinary things!**" He sat down and opened his K-rations. *We gotta eat this junk tonight because they don't have a mess tent set up yet and I've got a funny feeling that this will be the case most of the time. It doesn't hold a candle to my Mom's cooking. I guess I'll have the blue box, that's the supper one.*

Cowboy tore opened the blue K-ration box and began sorting it out. *There's that Spam again, if that isn't the shits! I've got some biscuits, bouillon powder, powdered coffee, sugar cubes, some little packets of candy, Chesterfield cigarettes, and chewing gum. Arnold held the pack of cigarettes in his hand.* "Chesterfields? What the hell is wrong with Camels?" He reached for a wooden spoon and the can opener—*well isn't that convenient? And what is in this little packet---toilet paper? Now that's just damn considerate---this will be one time we don't have to use leaves or grass to wipe! And, just where do they expect us to do our business? Dig a hole in the sand like a cat?* Arnold laughed to himself half expecting that the others had the same reaction.

German POW's on their way to American POW Camps

"So guys", Arnold began, "are you ready to begin feasting on your K-rations?" Just then, there erupted all sorts of commotion reaching the ridge of the bluff as a line of German POW's crested the beach hill and headed down at a diagonal angle to the water's edge. They had their hands over their heads and were stumbling through the deep sand. Ten American's had their Browning automatics rifles aimed at the prisoners as they herded them toward a wire enclosure down the beach. "Well, look at that will ya---that's what I like to see—you bet your bottom dollar it is! Now, I know why that troop ship's anchored off shore like that. They are going to ship these Germans back to America, gonna get them clear outta this country! The war is over for them lucky dogs!"

Everyone in the area instinctively ducked as a squad of carrier-based Hellcat fighter planes roared low over their camp, headed for Normandy. Arnold looked up in the sky and wondered what that must feel like, to fly that fast.

~~~~~~~

Mac threw what looked like more orders on his cot. "Well I'll be damned! It's like the big cheese is playing some kind of a stupid chess game with us in the 81st Tank Battalion. We are attached to the Third Army --- again. You know what that means— we've got 'old blood and guts' for our commander. I've been thinking real strong, about giving our tank a name and putting it on the canon muzzle. But I guess that idea is 'is ixnay, as long as General Patton is in charge. If he finds something 'off' on any of his tanks there will be some royal ass chewing. There will be no alterations on any tank that is in his command and that includes sandbagging the front of them for extra protection." Mac was not to be consoled. "At least we still have General Oliver carrying the flag of the 5th Armored and Col. Dole is our Battalion commander! I've heard Gen. Patton is a great leader and all that, but he loves the press about as much as he loves a big battle. So brace yourselves, cause he is going to send us into the thick of it just so he can grab a headline."

Joe spoke up, "Hey, did they say where the rest of the First Army is?"

Mac replied, "Yeah, the main body of the 'First' is under General Omar Bradley along with several divisions under the Brits' General Montgomery. They all landed on D-Day and together they are pushing the Germans back off the beaches and through the bocage country. They are trying to give the Allied Forces room to land more men and equipment."

Arnold was silent for a moment then asked, "Say Mac, did you hear anything about some difficulty landing—and Kraut small arms fire along with bad weather off the coast here a while back, I think it was on July 24th ? Anyways, I heard that our guys called for air support to help em' out and our planes got screwed up and were firing on our own troops. They actually killed twenty-five men and like, wounded over 100. I guess some of them soldiers got so damn mad that they aimed their rifles and machine guns at our own planes."

A little smiled screwed up the corners of Mac's mouth as he replied, "Yeah, ya know I did hear something 'bout that and I don't blame 'em one damn bit. Course them pilots don't have an easy job either and I can see something like that happening. That's a crazy bit of luck!"

For the next week, the tank crews and personnel of the 81st Tank Battalion, Task Force Anderson -- CCA, CCB, and CCR attended to housekeeping duties as well as driving a deuce and a half (2 ½) ton trucks up and down the beach, transporting goods from ship to land storage areas. Cowboy and the other tankers watched ship, after ship, after ship, unloading supplies, equipment, and more troops to the area. It takes a lot of everything to supply an army and the beaches looked and sounded like a bee hive.

On the third day, the company Lieutenant or LT. approached Arnold and Danny. "I want you boys to drive that truck on that there road. About two miles out you will see some Red Cross tents, pull up and tell the MP that you are there to load and deliver wounded down to the hospital ship. Here's your pass, now get the lead out!"

Danny Boy and Cowboy hopped into their truck and drove up the beach road, cresting the bluff onto another area of the road that was all chewed up from the tank treads. They hadn't gone a half mile before Danny started bitching, "Don't know why the hell we have to play nursemaid to a bunch of gimps and mama's boys that get sent home now that they have a few 'million-dollar' wounds. That just gets my goat!"

Cowboy just ignored him and watched the mileage gauge; when it hit the two mile mark he lifted his head and saw five huge Red Cross field hospital tents and a couple of surgery Quonset huts. Right as rain, they were stopped by MP's; Arnold handed over their passes and drove to where the MP pointed. They hopped out of their truck and strolled nonchalantly up to the first tent flap.

Danny Boy stiffened as the odor of blood, antiseptic, and fear hit them square in the face. They hurried past the rows of beds, trying to block out the moans and cries of the wounded; they approached a man who looked like the doctor. He wore a long

apron over his fatigues which were once bleached white and now, were covered with old and fresh bloody stains along with other unidentifiable smears. The doctor had dark circles under his bloodshot eyes and he looked like he'd just pulled an all-nighter.

Cowboy saluted and spoke up, "Sgt. Kessel and Pfc. Brown, reporting, sir!"

The doctor wiped his brow as he pointed over at a group of wounded men, "At ease. You boys are to transport these wounded back to the beach and the hospital ship and the sooner you get the job done, the better—we need the space.

Carry on."

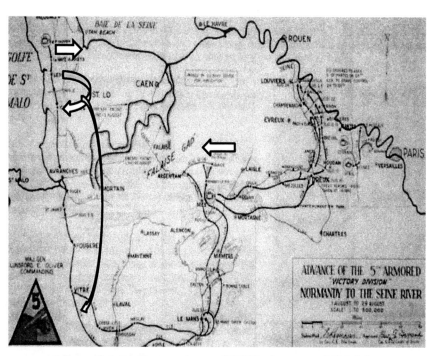

Map of Attack courtesy of Fifth Armored Division

[21]Operation Overlord

After landing at Utah Beach on Normandy Beach, the 81st Tank Battalion received their orders. They'd all heard bits and pieces of what had happened after our forces landed on D-Day, but now they got a bigger picture, in Technicolor.

After General Omar Bradley and the First Army had landed with the D-Day Invasion on the 6th of July, his army mounted an all-out attack against the dug-in German forces near Saint-Lo. Bradley's divisions broke through the Kraut defenses and as a result, nearly collapsed the majority of the German forces on the Western front. In essence, the German front line of defense was strongly attached to the northern beach of France just east of Caen and that line of defense snaked south across Normandy to Avranches, another costal town. Gen Bradley's forces along with British Gen. Montgomery and the Canadians successfully pushed the German line back and back until they were at a stalemate. Now, Germans forces were reinforced with men and equipment pulled in from the northeast and were fighting back with new vigor.

Chapter Seven

BAPTISM BY - 'FIRE'

"We can only highlight the military miracles performed by the men of the 5th Armored Division in their fighting drive to and into Germany. The countless deeds of individual heroism, the many inspiring examples of devotion to duty and the willing, cheerful spirit shown by all of you can never be written. It is in the hearts of your fighting companions---those men with whom you have shared the triumphs and despairs of this war—that your glory will be remembered forever."

Lunsford E. Oliver Major General,
Commander of 5th Armored Division
From "The Road to Germany" publication 1944-1945

The Breakout in Normandy: On the second of August, 1944, the First Army, 5th Armored Division received orders to beef up their division. General Omar Bradley passed the command of the First Army to General Courtney Hodges; Lieutenant General George Patton was activated the same day with command of the Third Army & the XV Corps. Gen. Omar Bradley was named as leader of the 12th Army Group as well as his role as Commander of the First and the Third Armies. Gen. Dwight Eisenhower was the Supreme Allied Commander over all Allied Forces.

The next thing they knew, [22]Operation Cobra was— striking! Gen. Omar Bradley's Twelfth Army continued to hammer away at the German front line of defense pushing them back and back. On August 1st, Patton and Hodges moved their massive armies out of Lessay to the far western edge of the German lines, and at top speed headed for Coutances. Thus began an unprecedented 300-mile exploitation and destruction of the German Seventh Army which gave birth to panic and they forces began to scatter in an attempt to survive. This was a first----for an armored division to rip through enemy lines and then proceed to move forward independently behind those lines.

Hodges and Patton's divisions headed due south at Patton's pace---top speed, because they were moving on treads and wheels, there was nobody on foot. The married infantry rode in halftracks, sometimes on the tanks, or in trucks! Over all, Patton and Hodges commanded over 140,000 men, seven divisions; it was a wonder how fast they actually moved and what those men did—they made history! Because of Gen. Hodges' original and brilliant idea of marrying (working exclusively) particular tank and infantry companies, the Fifth Armored Division initiated a new and highly effective warfare concept—of command and control, wreaking havoc on the enemy.

NOTE: *A division is made up of 10,000 – 20,000 men; a Brigade = 3000 – 5000 men; Battalion= 300 – 500 men; a company = 80 -250- men. A Division is made up of two brigades; 2 – 5 battalions in a brigade; 2 -6 companies in a battalion; 2 – 6 platoons in a company.* In the Fifth Armored Division alone, there were approximately 10,000 – 14,000 men—over 200 Sherman tanks and they were all moving in double time!

The men and equipment quickly fell into line, in the married formation preferred by General Oliver who remained commander of the 81st Tank Battalion. Col. John T. Cole led the fourteen tanks of Combat Command B (code Bravo) of the 81st Tank battalion. They were spaced between Col. Glenn H. Anderson's fourteen tanks of CCR (code Romeo) and Brig. Gen. Eugene A. Regnier's fourteen tanks from CCA (code Adam). Intermittent tanks took the lead to clear out scattered resistance for the infantry, and in other cases the infantry advanced with tank fire coming in behind them to take out large, centralized resistance.

~~~~~~~

Sgt. Arnold Kessel's gangly six foot frame fit snuggly in the gunner's seat to the right of the tank commander. In the left forward hull, Joe the driver was at the controls and was seated directly across from the assistant driver/gunner Danny Boy and his battle-ready machine gun. The loader, Reb sat in left-rear, behind the driver and directly across from Cowboy, the cannon gunner. The Commander Mac's seat was centered in the turret basket behind Cowboy and the cannon. Mac had close verbal and physical access to his loader and gunner—this arrangement worked like a charm when the fur started to fly. They had practiced long and hard for THIS and they were ready to roll!

Commander Mac sat high on his adjustable seat with his head sticking out of the turret hatch and his hand on the grip of the Browning M2HB machine gun. This first day, they were all sitting on pins and needles; they were loaded for bear and looking for Heinies! When they weren't in combat or expecting enemy fire, most tankers rode with their heads sticking out of their respective hatches. At the first sign of trouble or the commander's order, the tankers heads sunk into the tank and the hatches snapped shut, much like a turtle.

Arnold kept his eyes glued to the road; he scanned to the left and then the right, watching for something--anything out of the ordinary. They were all edgy this first day out, basically because Patton had told them, *"We are going to exploit those overconfident Krauts and the ones we don't kill are POWs; the ones that run-- we're going after them and we'll teach them one hell of a lesson. Monty (British General Bernard Montgomery)and his Canadian and Polish friends are playing hide and go seek with part of the 7th German Army, Army Group B, and the 5th Panzer Army. They are keeping those Krauts pretty damn busy between Mortain and Caen. In the meantime, we've got a little something up our own sleeve and time is critical. We are going to move and move fast, so hang on!"*

Joe admitted, "I feel like a cat on a hot tin roof, this is damn right nerve-wracking. I don't care if the big boys think that there aren't many Germans back here or not----the hair on the back of my neck is stickin' straight up. May God protect us!"

They rolled out of the small French village of Sauveur le Vic and at full speed, swept through Hayne du Puits and Lessay, unimpeded. It was virtually impossible for the infantry to keep up with Gen. Patton's pace, and so they would hitch a ride on the tanks, a truck—anything with wheels. At first threat of German ambush or fire they would hit the ground running.

That first night the convoy struck camp in a grassy field just to the south of Lessay. Maintenance crews were all over the tanks like flies on a dead dog—cleaning the sand out of the tracks and wheels, making sure they were battle ready. The guys worked all night welding saw-toothed cutters onto the fronts of several of the lead Shermans. Those saw tooth cutters were just another ingenious engineering feat a couple of regular sergeants came up with so their tanks could get through the damnable hedgerows.

Accommodations for the night were--pup tents and K-Rations. Before Arnold called it a day, he questioned, "At least we aren't sleeping on that sand; I think there were sand fleas in that stuff. Did any of you guys get bites and itchy when we was there?"

Danny quipped, "Nope, not me—they must just be attracted to your baby-soft butt!"

Mac pulled a short burning stick from the fire and lit his cigarette. "You know boys, I've been thinking about something—we gotta be more careful about smoking too close to our tank. I KNOW---I've seen some fellas climbing inside them with a cig' hanging outta their mouths, but I strongly suggest we don't take that chance. We can light up the minute we get out, agreed?" It was a suggestion most didn't pay any attention to because sometimes a fella just needed a smoke!

~~~~~~~~~

At 0500 hours on August 2nd, they broke camp and headed due south with staggered formations on parallel sunken country roads which bordered by waist-high rock walls and densely packed hedgerows. From the air, the advancing forked-formation army looked like a huge rolling battering ram. In the distance, through their periscopes they could see the next French village of Coutances. All morning they moved to the south and east of the Gulf De St. Ma-lo. It was obvious that Patton and Hodges' objective was for them to stay to the west of the undulating German front lines which lay between Mortain and Falaise, and just to the northwest of Caen, an important port city. Reconnaissance indicated there was a large mass of fortified Germans standing their ground, with Paris at its back. It was a continuous back and forth attacks and advances from one side, with the other countering the attack. Monty's boys kept ramming the eastern German lines hoping to break through.

Since D-Day, Allied forces had pushed the snake-like German line back from the St. Lo region and port of Caen. Now, the Allied Army had a massive surprise up their sleeves for the elite German armies—a major bombshell that required the Allies to first capture Avranches!

Suddenly Joe's voice rose in alarm, "Sarge, ther--there's a German tank cannon sticking out of that hedgerow ahead, to the right at one o'clock." The column had already slowed so everyone could have a good look.

 Mac replied to his driver, "Joe, you knucklehead, you never call me by my rank—never, you got that? I'll let it go this time, but NEVER again" Speaking over his wireless, the tank commander reminded his crew, "The other thing is, if we are ever alone and come upon an enemy tank that looks disabled, DO NOT assume there isn't someone inside. Why the hell do you suppose that officer was standing there with his finger on the trigger? And, those infantry over there with their M1918 BAR's (Browning Automatic Rifles) propped firmly against their hips are ready to fire while walking. There could still be Germans waiting inside, ready to take us out with their cannon or machine gun---or it could be booby-trapped. You got that? Never, I repeat—never, assume that what you see is--what is! The Germans have buried mines and wired everything they could with booby traps all over this country!" Mac shifted in his seat and then added, "And Gentlemen, if you hadn't guessed already, that there is a dead Tiger Tank, from what I can see of it!"

As the convoy moved along the French lane unimpeded, Arnold said, "So this is what they call bocage country. What the hell does that mean anyway?" Butch was the brain of the crew and immediately piped up, "Are you dense as wood or what? See all those hedgerows out there—the condensed mass of trees, bushes, and field rocks all lying in lines to divide these fields---they're also called bocages. I suppose, over the years it's like the French built a cage to keep their fields separate and their livestock confined. They started building them before they had such a thing as fences. They had lots of loose field rocks. Over the centuries, they built stone walls, stone barns, and stone houses from all that free building material."

Arnold looked through his gunner's slit again and replied, "Well, hell's bells—so hedgerow and bocage are the same damn thing. Never would have guessed that one. Those things are going to be 'the shits' to get through. I've already seen a few tanks with those saw-toothed cutters welded to the front bottom hull. I suppose that they just need one or two tanks outfitted with the cutters so the rest of us can go right through that stuff." Suddenly, out of nowhere, came the unmistakable clack clack of small arms fire, followed by the staccato chatter of machine gun bullets hitting the side of their tank.

Mac and the other tankers dropped like rocks into the protective cover of the tank, slamming their hatches shut behind them. Mac screamed---"Enemy fire, to the left, three o'clock. Reb-LOAD—Cowboy, it's yours- **FIRE at will!**"

Arnold's sighted the source of the enemy fire, and then quickly repeated the coordinates back to the spotter. *"Two - three snipers in trees, 200 feet left"*. Not knowing exactly where they were standing, he locked in and hit the floor trigger with his foot. Through his periscope he saw the explosion; he saw men and equipment fly in slow motion through the hot August morning. Stunned, he realized the smoking, gaping hole in the green hedgerow--was where the enemy had been. He had fired the shell which made that hole. They all watched as their married infantry advanced and swept over the area; he heard a few random shots before they got the go ahead signal from lead command. Suddenly it hit him that he had just taken lives, he had killed men he didn't even know. His face flushed and his hands began to shake. Cowboy waited another moment, pretending to study the canopy of trees and the destroyed underbrush. He leaned back and casually wiped the sweat from his forehead.

Mac reached over and slapped his gunner on the back, "Well done Cowboy, was that your first real kill? You were just baptized by fire Cowboy! Yessiree! Right as Rain!!"

Arnold was now as white as a sheet and beads of sweat gleamed on his cheeks. "Yeah, I guess it was, wasn't it? That was the shits man, I didn't even have time to think, I-I just reacted!" He took his leather tanker's cap off and ran his fingers back through his damp blond hair. "I think I can do this Mac, its survival mode from now on! Something just comes over you doesn't it?" Arnold was silent for a few minutes then said, "Say Mac, what happens to those bodies? Do they lie there until the Germans pick 'em up?"

Mac turned to Arnold, "Well, if they are lucky—yeah. If not then wild dogs, vultures and other creatures get a free meal! If these French don't start getting more to eat, they might help themselves as well."

Mac laughed as Arnold's lips pinched together tight and he busied himself with looking out his periscope.

Mac reached to his right and poked Arnold in the ribs, "About that shooting reflex, I guess for some it becomes a reaction, and then again it doesn't. You're probably one of the lucky ones—got quick reflexes—that's exactly the kind of gunner I want in this here tank, it'll probably save both of our asses in the end." Mac called out, "We've got ourselves a gunner, boys, right as rain we do! Hell, by the end of this week, you are going to be a first-rate specialist!"

With the English Channel and Normandy Beaches behind them, the Fifth Armored Division, XI Corps, and the Third Army headed due south. Passing through the previously bombed and burned out village of Coutances, they crossed the upper Seine River. So far, the advance tanks and formation had only met with light resistance from random pockets of fleeing Germans. Most infantry and armored companies figured that their elusive main objective lay ahead. Number UNO, was Avranches/Mortain and then they'd head for German headquarters at LeMans. After that, most of the soldiers didn't know where they would head, but it wasn't up to them.

Arnold's face grew serious as he listened to the wa-Woop, wa-Woop sound of tank fire up ahead and saw the low flying American bombers as they zeroed in on German forces holed up at Mortain. He questioned, "Say, Mac, can you hear that? Sounds like our planes are pounding the hell out of the Germans in Mortain. Are they that close to us? Why don't we turn to the north and take em' on? Why, are we movin' like a bat outta hell eastward, past all the action?"

Mac looked through his periscope at the road ahead. "We aren't turning north because we don't have orders to turn north. Those planes are keeping the Germans busy right now, giving us some cover to slip on past that extended German front line! I'm not sure what Bradley and Patton have in mind, but I can promise you, it's gonna be good! Well, that is good for us, bad for the Germans!" He laughed that unscrupulous laugh of his as he puckered his lips and spat a stream of tobacco juice on the floor.

Reb, remarked with disgust, "For Hell sake Mac—why don't you stop stinkin' up the joint! Get yourself a cup or something if you have to spit that shit, or better hey, just stop chewing!"

Mac reached to the left and flipped his loader's leather cap, "I suppose it's because it didn't want to swallow that crap and I don't have a cup—don't think they issued one with this rolling coffin."

Reb just stared straight ahead without saying any more. *What's the use in trying to talk sense into him? He acts like a slob*

and talks like a slob, so I guess that makes him a slob and that's that! Suddenly Cowboy exclaimed, "The CO musta called for air power cause there go six of our P47 Thunderbolts, headed over those hills toward Avranches. Looks to me like those flyboys are tryin' to lighten our load around Avranches. Those boys are damn good—sure take a lot of crap outta our day. They go right in there and stir up the pot—pull the covers off the bed---yes, sirree!" Arnold watched through his gunner's periscope as the fighters dropped low over the outskirts of the town and with wing machine guns blazing, they released their bombs. The ground shook and the air was filled with the scream of falling bombs followed by a rolling roar as they hit their targets. Suddenly an enormous fire ball **AVRANCHES, FRANCE** filled the sky followed by a thundering growl like a speeding freight train. They felt their tank shudder with the quaking of the ground as another ear-splitting rapid series of explosions filled the air. Cowboy exclaimed, "Son-of-a-bitch— they musta hit a fuel depot! Good shootin fellas!!" The heavy smoke from Avranches filled the air and seeped into the tank's ventilation system.

~~~~~~~~

Day Three: Patton's Third Army and friends rapidly advanced somewhat unimpeded toward Avranches breaking up into their standard pitchfork or staggered attack formation. They crossed the La See' River on a bridge the Germans didn't have time to blow up and within hours they had taken what was left of Avranches. Not wasting another precious minute on that town, they plummeted on to secure the small farming village of Ducey (Duce-a). They ate on the run, slept on the run, and all with precious little sleep. They lived on adrenaline and they were pretty damn proud of the fact that they had traveled 150 miles in three days!

Before they moved out that next morning, they all received the same field order, *"This advance is to be pursued with the utmost energy inasmuch as on its success may hinge the success of the whole campaign in western France. WE are destroying the rear guard of the German's Seventh Army and with that destruction we destroy Gen. Von Kluge's hopes of stopping the Allied Forces in Normandy. We know he was counting on the rear guard to protect his forces. We have just taken that equation out of the picture. Congratulations!"*

They had been sitting in convoy formation for twenty minutes when Arnold wriggled out of his gunner's seat and said to Mac, "I'm gonna take this opportunity to take a dump in that hedgerow over there. If I don't do it now, I WILL do my business in my pants inside this tank and I don't think you boys would appreciate that!"

Cowboy jumped from the tank hull and made his way around an anti-aircraft gun, then merged into the inner sanctum of the heavy irregular band of trees, brush, and rock. Hurriedly, he found a place between two large rocks and dropped his pants. He closed his eyes as relief flooded over him. When Arnold opened his eyes, he froze. He was looking directly into the blue eyes and ruddy face of a German infantryman who seemed to take great delight in having an American on the other end of his rifle, with his pants down.

Arnold's eyes frantically scanned the dark recesses of the brush, looking for more Germans. Locking eyes with the sole Kraut and in one slow deliberate motion, Arnold gradually straightened his legs, at the same time pulling his pants up. Never allowing his eyes to leave the German's face and gun, Cowboy slowly lifted his index finger to his lips in a gesture of silence and pointed to the road where his tank battalion sat. He whispered, "Nein! Bitte, geh'weg-geh'weg---leise, bitte! (please, go away, please)!"

The German's eyes caught the silhouettes of the massive assembly of American forces just paces away on the road. Reality registered as he slowly slid his finger from the trigger on his gun, hesitated, then eased back into the shadows of the trees. Without hesitation and barely breathing, Cowboy fastened his belt and high-tailed it out of the hedgerow in the direction of his tank!

Holy Shit—that guy coulda' shot me—and with my damn pants down. How would my Mother take that news? He clambered up the side of the Sherman and in seconds disappeared through the main hatch. Breathing hard, he slid into his seat and exhaled, sweat beaded his forehead.

Mac looked at Arnold with a quizzical smirk on his face, "Well, Cowboy was it that good?"

His skin slick with sweat, Cowboy looked up at Mac and said, "You have no idea. For a minute I didn't think I would come out of there alive."

Danny Boy turned and laughed, "What were you doing for that long, reading the funny papers?"

Cowboy gave a meaningful sharp slap to Danny's leather helmet, "No you nincompoop, it was the German with the rifle pointing at me that kept me away from you guys!"

Mac turned, "Are you telling me there was a German in that hedgerow and you didn't kill him?"

Cowboy wiped the sweat from his forehead, "That's about it Mac. I had my pants down and he had the drop on me. What was I supposed to do, pee on him? I was mainly concerned with getting out of there alive!"

Mac yelled at Danny, "Swing that damn machine gun around there and strafe that hedgerow, NOW, Damn IT!" Mac got on the radio, "Echo – 6 –Bravo---unknown number of Krauts in hedgerow, right. Suggest FA move in."

Cowboy watched through his periscope as two platoons of infantry rushed the hedgerows with guns drawn. Another group stood, feet planted as they propped their BAR 'machine guns' against their hips and sprayed a series of long bursts of fire into the hedgerow. Suddenly the air was filled with more rapid machine gun, rifle, and explosive grenade fire. In ten minutes the infantry re-emerged without prisoners and the Allied column continued on their way.

~~~~~~

Cowboy looked to the left and right at the small farms that dotted the French country side. *I wonder how these farmers feel about first the Germans coming through their farms and taking what they want, and now we are rolling over it as well. It's not like they have any say about anything—they just have to shut the hell up and take whatever comes. I wonder how they can make a living with all this hell breakin' loose around them. I've seen them out in their fields like it was just another day. I guess they have to try and get through in any way that is half normal. It's not like this is something new for the French. From what I've heard, after centuries of being in the middle of or at war, the civilians have learned to live their life as normally as possible, right along with the whole scenario. I'd hate to see my folks caught in the middle of something like this.*

Mac listened closely to a rash of orders coming over his headphones. Trying to shout over the continuous growling roar of the tank engines, he yelled, "Joe, pull this rig over into that farm yard up ahead, there---where you see those people. Do any of you jokers speak French?"

Joe geared down and wheeled the Sherman into the French farm yard. Arnold could see several cows lying on their sides and from the looks of it, they had been dead for a few days because they were all bloated and there was dried blood on their wounds.

Cowboy said, "What the hell happened here? Why are all those milk cows lying dead in the farmyard? It looks like some of our infantry are checking out the barn and other buildings to make sure it isn't an ambush or something like that. Are those French Resistance Fighters over there, talking to the farmer?"

Cowboy looked over at the farm house and noticed filmy lace curtain hanging out an open window and fluttering in the breeze. There was a heavyset, older, gray-haired woman standing in the doorway, clutching her apron to her mouth. Her compact bun had come loose and strands of gray hair clung to her damp neck. Arnold thought, *she looks like my grandmother. Shoot, they are just folks like us, living a simple life and now this!*

Joe spoke through the headphones, "Mac, I speak a little French, do you want me to jump out and see what happened?"

Mac said, "Yeah sure—go ahead and pull this rig off to the side and lets all get out and take a stretch, but draw your pistols just in case. Something bad happened here, real bad!"

Mac and Joe knelt down beside the farmer, "Do you speak Eng-lise-a or Fran-say?"

The farmer looked up at the American soldiers with a dirty, tear-stained face. "I speak only the wee Englise."

Joe put his hand on the farmer's back and spoke in French, "What happened here, why are your cows dead?"

"On c'est Dimanche (on Sunday), we were at church when the Germans came. When we return home, this is what we find. They took all of our chickens, eggs, and they killed my milk cows, they raped my daughter who was at home alone. I don't know what I will do now to feed my fam-il-y. At least they didn't burn our house. Are you Ame-ri-can? I pray you catch them and shoot them down like the dogs they are. We hate the Boches!!"

Mac went to the tank and pulled out five K-rations and handed them to the farmer. "Joe, tell him that I hope these help for today. Tell him we will try and find who did this and shoot them." Mac turned to the rest of the tankers, "Mount up!" Mac looked back as company reconnaissance men remained, speaking to the farmer, no doubt trying to get more information about German forces in the area.

As they walked back to their tank, Mac poked Arnold in the ribs, "What does Boche mean?"

Arnold laughed and replied, "It's a French word for 'cabbage head'. They have called the Germans that since WWI."

Mac snickered, "They got that right. Hey, how did you know that those cows were milk cows?"

Cowboy whirled around and pretended to take a punch at his commander, "cause, I'm a farm boy and we know the difference between a cow and a bull, and a milk cow and a meat cow! Those cows were Holstein milk cows—did you see the black and white hides and big udders? And don't you dare ask me what udders are, you knucklehead!"

Operation COBRA was striking like a lightning flash! Arnold thought, *Man oh man, it's only August 4th and we just swept through Avranches with little to no difficulty and now Patton is going to push all seven divisions over the bridge at Pontaubault. When that happens we will be out of Normandy and into Brittany with little to no opposition. Like a hot knife through—but-ter!*

~~~~~~

August 3, 1944: In order to divert German forces from the corridor in which Patton and Hodges were slipping through, the British Second Army purposely attacked the eastern flank, pulling the German reserves away from the corridor around Avranches. On the far southwestern flank, only nineteen miles from Avranches, the Germans still held Mortain and a vital road junction at Vire. The U.S. XV Corps advanced and fired on the disorganized German forces at Mortain, along the Falaise front. They were too busy fighting for their lives themselves to notice, Patton's Third Army and Hodges' First Army outflanking their southwestern most point at lightning speed. The XV captured Mortain and took the road at Vire (Veer), securing the western corridor for Patton and Hodges.

~~~~~~

Suddenly, anti-aircraft artillery erupted from the rear of the Third Army column. Mac's head was sticking out of the tank hatch when he heard the roar of enemy fighters coming in low. He spun around and identified the five Luftwaffe planes just before they dropped lower and headed straight for their column and the massive stone bridge at Pontaubault.

Beads of sweat dotted his forehead as Mac yelled, "Incoming Luftwaffe —to the left, the left ---12 o'clock high. Let's go, let's go!" He swung his .50 caliber machine gun toward the sky and began firing. Joe yelled, "Give em the whole nine yards, Mac!" The ack-ack chatter of the anti-aircraft guns echoed from the rock walls surrounding the village as the blue French sky erupted in bullets and smoke.

Joe immediately 'coiled' their tank—getting it out of the way. Inside the tank, the crew heard the infantry order to 'hit the dirt,' as the stutter of battalion machine guns began to fire on incoming enemy planes. With wing guns blazing, the planes made a low pass, strafing the Allied forces. Black puffs of smoke billowed from a direct hit on a recently vacated troop truck. Then they saw the planes turn and come back for a second strike. Mac was ready this time and took aim with his 50 caliber machine gun picking out one plane and following it all the way down.

They let loose with everything they had. In the heat of it all, Mac bellowed, "We need this damn bridge and those Krauts aren't gonna take it out." An anti-aircraft gun connected with one of the German planes as it dropped from the sky in a ball of flames before it could unload its bombs on the bridge. A third plane was coming in low, right over Mac's tank. It was the one Mac wanted. He spun the machine gun around and yanked hard on the trigger, hitting the pilot. "I got him, I saw his face and I know I hit the bastard!" They watched as the German plane did a nose dive into the woods; the ground shook with the impact of the plane and its bombs.

Just when things were looking grim, a cheer went up from the infantry on the ground as a squadron of Allied P-51 Mustangs bore down on the remaining enemy fighter planes. Cowboy and the rest of the tank crews opened their hatches and watched as last two enemy planes spiraled to the earth in a fiery decent. Cowboy said, "I'll be a monkey's uncle. Hell, that all happened so fast, I could hardly think. Our P-51s saved our butts today, for sure!"

The P 51 Mustangs tipped their wings as the ground forces waved their hats in 'thanks' and headed back to the east, leaving the bridge at Pontaubault intact! Everyone in the column exhaled as they high tailed it over the bridge and on down the road.

Four miles away, at Ducey they crossed the mouth of the slow-moving Selune River. As their tank splashed and rumbled across the shallow rock-filled river, Cowboy scanned the banks of the lazy stream. "Wow, this is beautiful, look at all the weeping willow trees and wild flowers growing here. Right here, there is no war, just 'mother nature' at her best. My mother loves weeping willows; oh, how she would love this place." He didn't let on to the others as a sharp pang of homesickness shot through him.

Mac snapped, "Knock it off Cowboy, you are supposed to be looking for Germans swinging from those willows, not thinkin' of your Mommy!" As the American forces neared Fougeres, they

THE CASTLE

were astonished to see a centuries-old French castle, obviously untouched. Mesmerized, Arnold said, "Mac, take a look at this thing. Is that what is referred to as a French castle? It looks like a city within a city. I wonder how old that thing is. And all built from stone. It doesn't look like the Germans bothered it."

Danny said, "The Germans probably used it as a headquarters when they came through here. Occupying castles is right up their alley and besides, they probably carted off all the paintings and valuable stuff when they left. I heard that's what they do."

Mac said, "Take a look to your left, that's the work of our flyboys—they damn near leveled this place. I'm glad they left that castle alone—it's a beaut!"

Day Six - Vitre: It was here that General Patton took about half the divisions and headed back toward the north along the Mayenne River, in the direction of Falaise. The order came down for Arnold's CCB to split from CCR. That night in camp, Mac studied their orders. "It looks here like they want us and about four other battalions to take the high ground to the east then turn south winding around to Cosse-Le-Viven over the Mayenne River then through Houssay. Problem is there's no bridge over the Mayenne River where they want us to cross, but the engineers are working on it now. I expect they will have a pontoon bridge ready for us by the time we get there. Mighty nice of them if I do say so!"

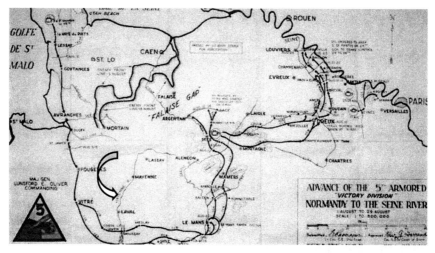

Photo - Map courtesy of the Fifth Armored Division

Mac read the orders a little further, then said, "this is a briefing: We've got orders to steer clear of Laval, it's a hotbed of Germans right now, and it's approximately ten miles to the north. CCR and CCA will continue in parallel formation to the south of us as we all drive for the target, LeMans. We will be in the attack pitchfork formation; CCB has the inside drive from the south, directly into the heart of the city; CCR drives in from the east and CCA swings around and hits them from the north. U.S. XV Corps artillery will be hitting the city from across the river—from the west. By the time we get to LeMans, we'll have another hundred miles under our belts! Good Work Men!"

Mac cleared his throat, "This is going to be a battle; we are going to be in the eye of the storm, right where we can do our best work! LeMans is the former location of the German 7th Army headquarters. Most of them have pulled out but it's still an important logistic area for them, so you know they aren't going to go gently into the night! We will bivouac at Meslay for a few hours to get our ducks in a row. At first light, we hit Le Mans with everything we have. They are sending in the P47 Thunderbolts first—they should take care of a few Krauts and their big guns for us! We are gonna sit tight until we hear from the 85th Cavalry Recon Squad. They are slipping south to check it out---take a look-see if there is any Kraut resistance between us and LeMans."

~~~~~~~~

Day Seven: Mac announced, "We've got a 'GO'—Move it out! The 85th had a short disagreement with some Heinies at Cosse-Le-Viven; they took out most of them and sent the rest of 'em hightailing it down the road with their arms over their head. Around noon, CCB rolled unimpeded through the French village of Cosse-Le-Viven. They were high on a bluff and could see the Mayenne River below them as it flowed from the north to the south of France. On the other side of the river, the village of Houssay lay silent, as if asleep.

Joe said, "They know we are coming, the civilians probably took to the hills to hide until this is over. I just hope we don't run into any German patrols from Laval before we get across that river." Joe continued to peer through his periscope as he drove the tank down the narrow hilly road. Suddenly he shouted, "Where the hell is our bridge? There's the damn river, there's the blown bridge, but where the hell are our engineers with that pontoon bridge?"

Mac looked through his periscope then popped up through the hatch to have a look see. In a moment, the men below heard Mac declare, "I'll be a monkey's uncle, our guys are there. They

were waiting in the woods with the pontoons—there they go, got the boats in the water and now they are dragging out the temporary steel tread ways. They will have it together by the time we get down this hill and are ready to cross."

Pontoon Bridge

Cowboy questioned, "Mac, what do they do with the bridge after we are across? Do they just leave it there or pack it up and take it to the next river that we have to cross?"

Reb piped up, "Seriously Cowboy, what the hell? Do you think we would leave it and make it easy for the Germans to follow us? Hell no, those boys dismantle it, load it up and take it to where we need another bridge!"

Reb wiped his nose on his sleeve, "Say, Mac—if you don't mind me saying so, I wish you wouldn't stick your head out of that hatch every ten seconds—one of these days you are gonna get it blown off! You are a damn big target for some German sniper, especially with that head of red hair you got!"

Once they crossed the river, Arnold said, "Mac, can you call maintenance to catch up to us tonight—I'd like them to take a look at our cannon. There's something not right with the sighting, and your turret isn't swinging like it should—what do you say?"

That evening as the army rebooted before the attack on LeMans, maintenance crews were on double duty, checking equipment, making repairs and adjustments on the spot, and taking care of replacements. They reworked a couple of things on tank #2736's turret ring as well as the cannon which was riding a bit off center. Cowboy quipped, "That probably happened when we mixed it up a bit back at Avranches."

Ammo was loaded to the ceiling, .30 bow bun ready trays were full, the .75 shells were re-stocked; all they had to do now was sit and wait inside or beside their tanks and equipment. Nobody was allowed to leave or spend any amount of time away from their column; they were all on a moment's notice to move out.

Mac said, "Just thought you boys would like to know that we have been on the right flank of the 749th Tank Battalion since we left Avranches. I say, the more the merrier, they are a good bunch!" He reached down under a shell box and pulled out a bottle of French wine, I suppose now is as good a time as any to pass this around, compliments of the French milk cow farmer!" Mac pulled the cork and smelled the wine, then put the bottle to his lips, tipped it back and then back again for good measure. "Damn, that is good stuff; I really hate to share it with a bunch of green tankers who don't know their wine! I think I am pulling rank here, if you ask me. Half of you aren't even old enough to drink!"

Joe grabbed the bottle, "What are you talking about? I'm Italian; I guess I know--good wine. Now, let's see if you know what you're talking about?" Joe took a couple of pulls from the brown bottle. "Yessiree---you do know what you are talking about Mac!"

Danny was the next to put his hands on the bottle, "Hey gee whil-likers, a wop doesn't get to have more than his share; its share and share alike." Joe was out of his seat, grabbed a handful of Danny's shirt and brought his fist around in a playful punch.

Arnold grabbed the bottle, lifted it to his own lips and took a couple of swallows. "Yeeow---that's a little rank—but, it gets better after the first swallow. I think I like it and no, I'm not old enough to drink, but I'm old enough to fight and die for my country, so that changes the rules in my book!"

Danny Boy smirked, "I'm with you all the way on that one Cowboy, and yes I am! I'm nineteen, but I got me a feeling I have more drinkin' experience than you do, so I'd say you have some catchin' up to do, even if you are half Kraut."

Cowboy grabbed the bottle and belted another one back, "Well, that's the shits. I guess I better get me a few more pulls off this bottle if I have some catchin' up to do—and for your information, I am full German, not a mutt like you!"

That brought everyone back to earth as they collapsed into a laughing fit. Reb reached for his share before it was gone as Cowboy said, "Actually guys what the hell does it matter who your relatives are or where you come from—we are all Americans and that's what we are all about. The day will probably come when you are glad that I can speak some German—just don't forget I said that!"

Reb wiped his mouth on his sleeve, "You're right, that was mighty good wine. Hey, Cowboy, can I ask you a question? Why don't you swear, I mean really swear with the f-word and stuff? All I ever hear you say is, it's the shits or damn---I did hear you say bastard once—but you never say God-damn it or stuff—what's with you? Are you one of them Bible thumpers?"

Cowboy flushed and turned to his left to face Reb, "It's pretty damn simple--I just don't believe in taking the Lord's name in vain. It's how I was brought up. Just doesn't feel right to me--- nothing's ever been that serious or bad that I used His name like that. Do you have a problem with that?" Arnold's blue eyes narrowed as he reached inside his shirt pocket and pulled out a small, thin copy of the New Testament. "And, for your information, I carry this with me everywhere I go---HE goes with me and if I was you, I'd be hoping HE'S going with your ass too! And another thing---why the hell do you have to be such a knucklehead all the time. Isn't there a serious bone in your skinny bag of bones?"

Now it was Reb's turn to flush, "Aw Cowboy, forget it; no need to get your panties all in a bunch. I was just josh-n' ya. 'Dawn sauth' where I comes from we have us some real honest to God, Bible thumpers, sures' hell do! Ever-body has their own way of sayn' what's on their mind I'm a guessin', no skin off my ass!"

Mac sat down in his seat after closing his hatch. "Okay, knock it off. Everyone try to catch 30 winks. Before you know it we'll be on the move, we have one big battle waitin' for us tomorrow. It'll be time to head out soon enough; and one more thing---if you ain't scared you're the only guy here who isn't. We just gotta do what we gotta do when the time comes." Mac saluted them and leaned back in his seat, took a deep breath and closed his eyelids.

Cowboy tried to relax, but he felt like he had three squirrels jumping around inside him and he knew he wasn't the only one. *I hope I won't chicken out or let my crewmates down, I'd rather take a bullet than let someone else do my job for me. Please God, be with me---be with my crewmates tomorrow. Lead us, protect us as only you can. This I ask through your son's name. Oh, uhh—and remember, if it's my time—make it quick. Amen.* It was a prayer he would repeat, if he had a chance, before every battle, and he never forgot to give thanks when he made it through.

Cowboy's blue eyes opened and burned as brightly as a pilot light. He'd always been kidded about his baby blues. But truth be known, he'd inherited his blue eyes from his grandfather Karl whose steel blue eyes could bore a hole, clean through to your soul! One had only to look deeply into Arnold's eyes to see that he too, had some of that steel in his blue eyes!

~~~~~~~

Around 2200 hours, a company of Germans from LeMans attempted to run the road block CCB had set up outside the city.

Tank 2736's crew woke to the sound of artillery fire and it was damn close!

Mac pulled his leather tankers helmet on, listened and then yelled, "ON ALERT---reports say we've got us a German 37 mm AT gun, four Mark IV tanks, and four light sedans trying to run our road block outside Meslay du Maine. Cowboy heard his commander reply with radio chatter, "Echo – 6- Bravo. Holding." Mac signed off and turned to his crew, "We are on standing down, on alert—the left flank of our TFA (Task Force Assembly) is taking care of it---it'll be over before it's started!" Mac listened to the report and said, "They took eight POW's and killed the rest! At ease, boys."

Mac and the crew kept their helmets on as they stretched out and tried to get some rest. "First thing tomorrow boys, we head out through Meslay-du-Maine—should be a piece of cake—just a sleepy little village. Then we get ready for the big Rumble!"

~~~~~~

At 0500 hours, the air was filled with the sound of Sherman tanks starting up, one after the other. The ground shook as the 35 ton vehicles growled, snarled, and clanked down the dirt road toward Meslay-du-Maine. Just as they entered the village, they came under an intense barrage of enemy sniper fire. Mac shouted, "The SOBs are everywhere—I thought they were supposed to clean these suckers outta here." They could all hear the quick stutter of small arms fire and the ping, ping, ping from rifle fire bouncing off their tank. FA had scattered and they were buttoned down until the tanks moved forward and cleared the area.

With the receiver pressed to his ears, Mac listened to convoy orders coming from the fourth tank where Col. Dole rode, "Burn em out! Bring those damn flame thrower tanks and throw some phosphorous shells in there on those Krauts. We have a more important mission today than to play footsie with these Jackass Germans. Burn every damn building to the ground – use the Gol-damn phosphorous shells and make sure the job gets done—it's time for hell's fire! Let's go, let's go!"

Arnold looked through this periscope at the village. His eyes skimmed over the manner in which the orderly stone houses were connected, how they stood tall, dark and dignified with their long narrow windows curtained and shuttered against the world and what was to come. Arnold knew those shutters were not going to keep out what they were going to throw at them.

Two hours later, the TFA was back on the road to Le Mans, moving forward toward their imminent mission. Behind them black smoke clouds rose like giant cauliflower thunder heads filling the blue French sky and blocking the light of the sun. The smoldering ruins of Meslay-du-Maine burned hot then smoldered well into the next day. In the Task Force columns, nobody was quite sure what lay ahead, only that they were bearing down on what promised to be one hell of a fight.

Chapter Eight

"LE MANS, FRANCE"

"He giveth power to the faint; and to them that have no might, he increaseth strength. Even the youths shall faint and be weary, and the young men shall literally fall. But they that wait upon the LORD shall renew their strength, they shall mount up with wings as eagles; they shall run, and not be weary and they shall walk, and not faint."

Isaiah 41: 29-31 KJV

Day Eight: You could cut the tension with a knife as the Infantry, Field artillery (FA), and tankers sat cooling their heels-- waiting, waiting, waiting for final orders. The August pre-dawn air hung heavy with humidity and it was even worse inside the tank. Arnold could smell the rank saltiness of his own sweat. Fact was, none of them smelled real good, probably because none of them had taken a real bath in over two weeks. They quickly learned how to take 'bird baths' using their helmets as wash basins. For now, how they smelled was the least of their worries.

The horizon was filled with the far away whine of three P-39 and a couple P-40 American Warhawk fighter planes. Suddenly they plunged screaming from the sky--their wing guns spitting tracers as they opened their bomb bays and dropped their bombs on designated German fortifications and artillery. The American Combat Command tank companies stiffened when they heard the unmistakable sound of German 88mm artillery as they thundered fire back at the Allied planes. The German 88mm was feared by infantry and tankers alike—it was the most effective enemy weapon in the war.

The tankers watched through their periscopes in awe as first the bombs and then artillery hit their targets with precision. The ground rocked with explosion after explosion and the air was filled with fire, smoke, dust, and the sound of exploding buildings. The planes left and mortars stopped---for a moment their world paused. Some of the soldiers felt panic, others felt elation, and the 'green' soldiers were simply numb with fear and realization of what had happened.

Mac's body stiffened as he listened to field orders come across his head set; finally he said, "Ok, here we go, keep us in line Joe, right behind the lead tank until I tell you to fan out with our infantry group! Danny Boy, you watch for any kind of fire directed at us, watch the buildings, the windows—Shit, you KNOW what to watch for. Cowboy, keep your eyes glued to that periscope and your foot ready. Reb---we're gonna see just how fast your chubby hands can load those .75mm shells. Good luck fellas, and for hell sake, shoot straight---First round kill, Cowboy!"

Mac opened the hatch and stuck his head out; he needed to see where they were going. His throat was powder-dry and his bowels churned before his finger found the trigger on his .50 caliber Browning machine gun and he settled in.

Arnold felt the tank lurch and groan, the treads of their Sherman clawing into the damp soil as they made their way down the steep bluff above the town of Le Mans. *I know we all want to do our job, but I don't think any of us are planning on dying doing what we get paid for. Get a damn grip on yourself, breathe, and think, just damn----THINK and react!* He could feel his heart pounding in his throat as sweat rolled down his back.

Moving with the prowess of a great cat, CCB descended the hill above Le Mans, the gem city on the Sarthe River. In the early morning light only a handful of city lights twinkled. It was a stroke of luck that all bridges were intact and August 8th promised to be clear and bright, the stage was sat and it was their time to seize the city of Le Mans. They sat tight as the P-47's came in low, orbiting on signal panels that pinpointed their objective. Orange puffs of Kraut flak pockmarked the pre-dawn sky; the captain called in from his Jeep for a counter-flak barrage of white smoke shells to mark the target for the planes. The Thunderbolts made a wide swoop and then one by one, dropped off, diving and dumping their loads on the target. Le Mans and everything around it reverberated from the tremendous explosions as the P47D Thunderbolts lifted off---mission accomplished. Now the rest was up to the boys on the ground!

~~~~~

Task Force Artillerymen were already busy spotting with their scopes, computing wind speed, temperature, and barrel elevation. Any coordinates that would affect hitting the target they shared with the tanks. The married infantry followed the tanks like a bunch of baby ducklings, taking cover alongside their protector; at the same time they acted as the tank's eyes and ears. Mac had the receiver pressed to his ears, ready to call in the targets as they appeared or infantry called them in. Joe followed the lead CCB tank to the edge of the city where the formation suddenly split in planned forked-attack formation. Fourteen tanks from CCB held to the far left while CCR's fourteen tanks took the center fork and blocked all roads south of Le Mans.

Smoke from the P-47 fighter planes lingered in the sky; task force artillery began to lay down their own barrage of direct fire on Le Mans, softening the enemy stronghold up even more. CCA sped northeast of the city intent on cutting the escape route to the Paris highway. On the outskirts, the Task Force Tanks paused to fire a volley of mortars on Le Mans. Mac explained to his crew—"the plan is to block the avenue of escape in order to trap the enemy as he attempts to leave the city. One thing we don't want is for the Germans to escape and regroup to fight again. We want and need to take them out, right here! Kill em' or take prisoners—none escape—we wrap them up RIGHT HERE!"

CCB tanks began to infiltrate and fan out, looking for the main streets into the city. Mac had the turret hatch open and was standing tall with his right index finger pressed firmly against the .50 caliber Browning machine gun trigger housing. Searching for the enemy, his eyes scanned first this way, then that. Without warning, they heard the rapid staccato of a machine gun and heard the bullets ricochet high off the hull of their tank--- ping, ping, ping, -- ping. Not waiting for a written invitation, infantry dove for cover in open doorways and beside stone walls. Mechanically, Mac tilted the muzzle of the .50 caliber Browning and let go with a steady barrage into a doorway about 40 yards ahead. A helmeted body and gun clattered into the cobblestone street.

All bloody hell broke loose as Cowboy heard more machine gun fire followed by the chatter of small arms fire. The battle scenario was accented with the intermittent thud of artillery. Joe wheeled the Sherman to the left at the next corner and they rolled along a debris-covered cobblestone street in the direction of the city center. Ten yards away a mortar shell slammed into an Amtrak and it erupted into bright red flames. Cowboy sighted in on where the flash had come from, the second story window of a building to the right. He called, "LOAD!" Reb stuck a 75mm shell into the cannon as Mac yelled, "FIRE"! Cowboy stepped on the firing pedal and the tank bucked with the force of the explosion. The building to the right took the blast, everything seemed to pause then the air was filled with raining debris as fire, smoke, and dust rose from the explosion. They were all a little jumpy because these confined city streets weren't a tank's favorite place to be. They inched down the restrictive narrow streets with infantry moving cautiously from doorway to doorway, some hung back bringing up the rear and following in the safety of the tanks.

The tank bucked and heaved over the rough surface of the street and the treads labored to find ground to propel it forward. Rifle fire was a constant---as the infantry scattered then advanced. "INCOMING!" Men dove for cover as a .88mm enemy shell hit and exploded in front of CCB's lead tank. Arnold watched as smoke began to pour from the tank hatches; the left track disengaged and crumpled at a grotesque angle in the street. The crew scrambled out of the four hatches as Mac yelled, "Cover those boys-----Joe—get us the hell out of here, it's gonna blow!"

Joe wheeled their tank into a side street just as the internal fire hit the ammo and their lead tank erupted into flames. Danny Boy exhaled and said, "Son-of-a-Bitch---we gotta find that gun. Over there Mac, it came from that barn to the right; the Krauts must have artillery or a Bazooka hid in that barn or whatever the hell that building is."

Mac stood higher in the turret hatch to get a better look at the barn, "Reb – 89mm shell, NOW." Reb grabbed the white phosphorous shell and slammed it into the cannon. Hearing the sound and sensing the presence of a shell in the cannon, Cowboy sighted in the target, hit the firing pedal and the cannon bucked in recoil. The barn was an instantaneous fire ball as four men ran screaming from the door, their bodies on fire. A rumbling WaWhaa—VOOM thundered from about two blocks away, followed by a billowing column of black smoke.

Cowboy kept his eyes on the periscope, his nerves were on edge and he jumped when a rapid rat-a-tat-a-tat of bullets hitting the tank, followed by the sound of rifle fire. He saw the muzzle blaze of a rifle from the roof of a nearby church, and then he saw it again as he swung the cannon and sighted in. FIRE! The entire building collapsed into a smoldering heap as Cowboy felt the dead weight of Mac's body slide like mud over his back, past the commander's seat to where it crumpled onto the floor of the tank.

Cowboy heard Reb, swear, "Damn it to hell, they got Mac. Who's gonna command our tank, we're in the middle of a God damn fight here." For a split second they were all in shock, and then Cowboy shouted at Joe, "I got it, I got it. Keep her going forward Joe, follow our infantry. Danny Boy you watch for trouble, keep your finger on that machine gun and Reb, keep a shell in that damn cannon chamber ready to fire until we are out of this mess. I'm senior officer here and I'll take command for now. I can do it---I will do it! Let's go!"

Cowboy reached up and slammed the turret hatch shut; then he reached over to check Mac's neck for a pulse. He could see where the bullet had hit their commander in the forehead and come out the back taking with it part of Mac's leather helmet, skull and brains. Arnold felt his stomach convulse and he forced back the puke. *No time to react, I gotta push Mac's body to the back, over here outta the way and then I have to get back to the cannon. I can run the tank from the gunner's seat for now. I know what to do, I just gotta do it!*

Tank Commander Kessel's head was reeling, his palms were sweating, and his brain tried to wrap itself around what had happened and what he had to do---survive! He scrambled back to his periscope and put on his headset. His heart was pounding in his throat as he heard the orders come through for the CCB to turn northwest and drive forward down the main street, toward the city square. Another mortar came in and then another exploded closer this time. "ADVANCE---Keep advancing!" It was like another soldier inhabited Arnold's body and mind now as he took complete command and control of the situation. He wasn't even aware he was doing certain things; he was numbly reacting--leading!

"Danny Boy, take that machine gun nest up front, take the damn thing out; Reb, give me an HE round--FIRE---FIRE

AGAIN." Arnold swung the turret/cannon around and sighted it in to fire at another concealed battery 300 yards to the left.

Commander Kessel gazed through his periscope at the carnage of dead and mangled horses, men and equipment that littered the streets. Joe turned this way and that weaving the tank through the street, up and over piles of brick, bodies, and debris--- always moving forward. Joe never knew for sure if he had run over a dead or partially dead body; he couldn't think about stuff like that, not now—not ever, if he was smart.

The tank commander watched as ten infantry fanned out to the right of their tank and six men on the left prepared to enter a building. *The heart of Le Mans is dead ahead. What's left of the 7th German Army headquarters is right up there in that square---just a couple minutes ahead.* Looking through the periscope, Cowboy saw the infantry on the left push into a large fortified building on the tails of a flame thrower. That's when he saw the flags flying from above the door---the flags of the 7th German Army.

Danny   screamed—"SNIPER-10   o'clock"—Cowboy watched as the bullets from Danny's machine gun peppered the window where he'd spotted the German sharp shooter. Suddenly, a form slumped forward out of the window; a rifle fell to the street below as body spilled out in rapid succession. He heard Danny yell, "I got the son-of-a-bitch---take that, you Kraut wiener!"

Commander Kessel tapped Danny Boy on the shoulder, "Good job, man—you nailed that SOB!"

Joe called out, "I can't see a damn thing the smoke is so thick, shall we sit here a minute and wait for it to clear? The last thing I want to do is drive us off in a shell hole. What do you want me to do, Cowboy?"

Arnold replied, "Get the hell out of this open courtyard; spin to the left—on the double, into that alley." Seconds after they left the square another 75 millimeter enemy shell exploded, leaving a hole the size of three cars. A Red Cross van filled with wounded men wove its way around the debris; they were full and heading back to the Red Cross field hospital.

He watched as infantry pressed in and flushed out twenty or more Germans out of the headquarters and into the square. The Krauts had their hands over their heads as other Americans disarmed them and roughly forced them to their knees. The

German soldiers called out to their captors. "UEBERGABE –
Uebergabe" (surrender).

After the smoke had settled and the Americans controlled
LeMans, they confiscated and destroyed an undetermined
assortment of German equipment and took 200 prisoners. As their
tank #2736 rolled past the POWs, Cowboy couldn't help but
contain his anger and wrath as he called down to the huddled
prisoners. "Uegergabe? Guten Tag Frauen. Das ist Der Ami
blitzkrieg, JA? (*Surrender? Good afternoon women. This is the
American soldier Blitzkrieg, Yes*). The German soldiers glared at
the American tank commander, daring to speak in their beloved
language. He added, "Auf Wiederschen – Achtung!" (Good bye –
watch out).

The Task Force crushed the German rear guard in LeMans.
An undetermined number of Germans slipped through their
fingers, running for their lives to the north to where the German 7th
Army was now dug in. The Allies had been successful in cutting
off the most obvious eastward escape route of the German 9th
Panzer division and attached *Kampfgruppe* of the 708
Infanteriedivision, in Normandy.

Leaving the smoldering ruins of Le Mans, the Task Force
wheeled back around to the north, toward Falaise. But, first things
first; it was fifty miles to the edge of the city of Argentan where
they hoped to squash another carefully preconceived German
escape route out of Normandy. That would secure the trap and stop
the mighty Seventh Army from escaping toward Germany.

Waiting for further orders, tank commander Kessel and his
crew waited in their tank. Joe turned to Arnold, "You did a great
job, Cowboy. That was crazy how you didn't blink an eye--you
just took over; you are definitely a clutch man. I can't believe that
Mac got it. What do we do with his body? We have to take it
somewhere and get some official order that you are promoted to
tank commander." A unified 'aye' went up from the three men left
in the crew.

Tank commander Kessel ran his hands back through his
matted blond hair, "Well, if that isn't the shits! I was just getting
used to being a gunner and now I'm in charge? Hell of a way to get
a promotion!" Arnold called for medics and before they arrived, he
and the crew cleaned Mac up the best they could. Arnold raised his

hand and said, "I'd like to say a few words over Mac before they come get him, if that's okay with you guys. He reached inside his shirt and withdrew his Bible from the inner pocket, he read, "*And God shall wipe away all tears from their eyes; and there shall be no more death, neither sorrow, nor crying, neither shall there be any more pain; for the former things are passed away.*"

Arnold swallowed hard, trying to get ahold of his emotions. "Mac was a gifted commander; hell, he was special in so many ways. He was loved, he was respected, and he will be missed. I, for one, am glad I knew him." Commander Kessel made the sign of the cross over Mac's body. "Rest in Peace, my friend."

Within the hour, Mortuary Affairs Battalion removed Mac's body. These were the boys who came in after a battle and took charge of the dead Americans. They often buried those killed in action in temporary cemeteries, often in the same country where they died. After the war, they were often moved and buried in a National Cemetery like the one at Normandy.

The commander of tank # 2736 watched as the Mortuary AB drove away with Mac's body inside. He felt his chest tighten and unexpected tears welled up in his eyes. *Damn, this is tough, losing Mac like we did and he's the first guy I knew who bought it. I didn't expect all this emotion---can't let the guys see me get all soft.* Commander Kessel shook it off best he could then he picked up the two-way radio. He put in a call in to his immediate commander, Col. Dole. "Echo – 6 Kessel Bravo. Echo – 6 Darby Bravo, KIA in LeMans. Mortuary Affairs called. Echo – 6-Kessel Bravo second echo CCB. Please confirm, roger and out."

The second call was to the tank garage. "CCB, two seven three sixer, Echo – 6 - Kessel Bravo. Request, repplet (replacement) tank, ASAP. Damaged engine in Le Mans; leaking oil/smoking. Please advise, Roger and out."

The 79th Infantry Division was left behind in Le Mans to mop up snipers and hidden nests of Germans. Arnold commanded, "Swing this baby north Joe, we are going to 'Aza-jaon-too'-- Argentan!" Within an hour, they halted long enough to exchange their damaged and depleted tank for a new M4 tank with a 76 mm gun; it was stocked to the gills with ammo. Once settled into their new tank, Cowboy and his crew headed on down the road to Ballon. First they had to cross the Orne River on a pontoon bridge.

Two engineer combat commands had sped ahead to start building the bridges for the Combat Commands of the 81st Battalion and all those attached Allied armies. By the time the battle-weary battalions, platoons, and squads were within a mile of the river, the bridge was up and running.

As tank commander Kessel and his crew sat in line waiting to cross the pontoon bridge over the Orne River, Arnold mentioned, "I've been thinking about something since Mac died— a name for our tank." There was dead silence. "Now that we aren't under Patton's command we can paint something on our tank, but I was thinking about the word WRATH! It's definitely something we all feel, especially since losing Mac. Anybody else have any good ideas---let's hear it."

Joe spoke up, "I like WRATH, also was thinking of Vengeance, but it's a long word. There are all kinds of emotions and words we could paint like: Sword, Hell, Fire, Annihilate, Destroyer, Death, but when it comes down to it, I think maybe the thing we are all feeling most right now---IS---Wrath. Wrath against the Germans and what they are doing; we want them to feel the fire and wrath from our cannon!"

Tank commander Kessel smiled as he said, "Well then, let's vote—all for 'Wrath' raise your hands. Okay then--first chance we get, we're paintin' that name on the gun. And ya know what else? I want to get our hands on some sand bags, logs, even find a welder to put some more armor on that front hull. If we run into Gen. Patton, then I will personally take the ass chewing. Meantime, we're gonna be as safe as we can be." An ornery grin curled the corners of his mouth as he added, "Besides, Patton is clear the hell over along the Mayenne River---doubt he will have time to survey our tank any time soon."

That afternoon, Joe and Danny got out the white paint and on the canon barrel of tank 2736 they irregularly painted the word WRATH. They painted it on the cannon for Mac.

Arnold told his crew, "Just to let you know, I've put in for a replacement gunner. He should meet up with us in Ballon, tomorrow!" Arnold looked out of the periscope then added, "CCA and CCR crossed the River Orne near Ballon; CCR swung around from the east side of the river and traversed the Orne River at

Marolles Les Broults. The French city of Se'es is next in our crosshairs."

Several companies paused for a day after leaving Ba-llon. Some crews were pretty banged up and more than a few men took a much needed dip in the shallows of the Orne River. As twilight faded gently into night, Cowboy stretched out on his tank's rear hull, smoking a cigarette and taking a break. *Geez—it feels good to be clean—that swim in the river was great. I can't believe that I am a tank commander. I wish it wasn't because Mac got himself killed---that doesn't feel good, but that's the way it is. I saw a lot of guys wounded and even some get killed yesterday—all in a day's work. I can't say it's getting easier, but it doesn't send me into a tail spin like it did at first. I think I am just getting numb and am operating in a forward motion mode. It's all crazier than hell, that's for sure. Now I gotta be a role model for this crew, who would have guessed that?*

CCR and the 106th Cavalry Group were assigned to patrol the east flank of the steel-tipped 5th Division as it rumbled north. CCB assembled and was preparing to roll out when a jeep pulled up. A short skinny Asian hopped out, he saluted and walked toward Cowboy. "Sgt. Kessel? I am Pvt. Hiro Nagasuki; I am your replacement gunner."

Arnold returned the salute; his knees locked as he starred dumfounded. Curious, Danny walked forward and as usual the first thing on his mind came outta his mouth, "Well son-of-bitch, Repple Depple must be getting low on replacements. We not only get a boot camp wonder, but they send us a Jap."

Pvt. Nagasuki bristled and his eyes narrowed, "I have Japanese heritage, but I AM an American. I was born in Portland, Oregon; the rest of my folks are cooling their heels in a retention camp somewhere in Wyoming. Where the hell are you from, the backwoods?"

Bobby backed off as Joe laughed and extended his hand, "Well now, how bout that! I'm an Italian American and I'm from New Jersey. All we really care about is if you can shoot straight? Welcome to 'Wrath'—the unofficial name of our tank."

Arnold slapped Hiro on the back and said, "Welcome, glad to have you on board. Where did you go to tank school? And, by the way, we all go by tag names in our tank, I'm Cowboy cause

I'm from Wyoming, and I think we'll call you Hero—okay with you? I got a feeling you are gonna be our hero!"

Hero accepted his new name and informed his crew that he had graduated from Fort Knox, top of his gunners' class. That's all they needed to hear!

"MOVE OUT!" Arnold responded to HQ orders that came over the two-way radio which was attached to his leather tankers helmet. He stood in the open hatch with his right hand gripping the machine gun as every unit in the convoy jumped forward.

Communication inside a tank was always 'iffy.' The crew could usually talk to each other via an intercom system. Even with the latest technology, at times the horrendous noise level inside the tank was so bad that they reverted back to physical signals of communication. Each tank was equipped with substantial antennae which allowed them to talk to each other and their married FA.

1944 – Leather Tanker's Helmet

Commander Kessel adjusted his goggles so he had a better view, "Boy, I can see why Mac liked riding up here—it's damn exciting and you get a bird's eye view of the 'big picture.' Arnold had studied the maps and couldn't stop thinking about the battle that lay ahead of them. At Argentan and Falaise, they would have the opportunity to trap the entire Seventh German army, if --- they played their cards right. Earlier in the week, General Bradley had briefed the Third and First Armies about the importance of the upcoming battles, ending with this declaration: *"This is an opportunity that comes to a commander not more than once in a century. We're about to destroy an entire hostile army and in turn, go all the way from here to the German border."*

The farther North they went, the stiffer the resistance was. There were pockets of aggressive Germans here and there—dug in and armed to the teeth. It was obvious to all that the Krauts resistance and fighting was becoming more intense and fanatical the closer they got to Falaise. The Germans might have been low on equipment and supplies, but their morale was pretty damn high. Arnold mentioned to his crew, "You know those Krauts are looking at our endless supply battalions and the sheer number of men we have over here, and I've got to believe that a few of them see the writing on the wall. Just take a look at the prisoners we take, most are young and inexperienced. Looks to me like Hitler sent his elite troops to the eastern front to try and beat the Russians. The Germans are running out of experienced and able soldiers here in France and they know it—and now, they know we know it!"

Joe, Danny Boy, and Reb were all perched head-high out of their hatches; they looked like 'heads' glued to the hull of the tank. Riding high in the turret, the tank commander could hear the fire fights breaking out to the front, the rear, and on both flanks. He was tense, and well he should be.

Groups of Infantry rode on the tanks as they sped north, some ran or walked along side, always using the tanks as cover from ambush; it wasn't always smart to be on a tank when there was active fire. The advancing American tank engines rumbled and belched black oily smoke as the steal treads chewed their way down the dirt roads of the French countryside. CCB, CCA, and CCR were fanned out, running in forked parallel routes with the 47th Armed Field Artillery and the 46th Armed Infantry assault guns; the 81 mm. mortars were ready to spit their fire at a moment's notice.

Reconnaissance radioed CCB: "*Alert, significant German resistance dead ahead after the sharp downhill turn in the road. Count three 88 guns, two dozen infantry and possible hidden tanks waiting in ambush.*"

Tank commander Kessel yelled at the infantry, "Enemy ahead, button up---infantry hit the road. One platoon come with us---stay to the rear and fan out!" Arnold slipped down in the turret and pulled the hatch shut. After adjusting his seat lower, he took battle position then spoke to his crew over the 2-way, "We've got trouble up ahead—Attack fork formation. We're gonna take that side road up ahead and swing to the right while CCA jumps to the left and CCR continues on the road. Watch for anything out of the ordinary, their tanks and artillery are probably camouflaged with heavy brush.

"Joe, knock her back to first gear and run low, take us on in, real easy-like, I want to try and crawl up behind them. Let's take a 'look see', what we have down this cow path." The road was narrow and the trees hung low and close onto the lane ahead; there was plenty of dense brush where a tank and/or artillery could pull in and hide, ready to ambush anything that came by on the main road.

They all heard the rapid hammering sounds and then the unmistakable chatter of a machine gun. The tank commander instructed, "Joe --- Danny—eagle eyes on that road, look for smashed foliage--tracks or anything that looks swept over. Easy does it" They moved---creeping around a corner and 'bingo'--dead ahead sat a [23]German Tiger Tank. It had pulled into the brush just enough to cover its front hull, so its gun and turret had a clear view of the road. However----its rear hull was sticking out into the lane.

A big smile covered Arnold's face as he whispered over the 2-way---"That's a bea-u-ti-ful sight. There's our Tiger just sitting there waiting for us to put one of our .76 shells up its keister. Reb---let's give him one of your special fire enemas! LOAD, Hero - FIRE!" The shell fired, hitting the Tiger directly in its vulnerable rear end! The tank lifted off the ground as the treads began to reverse. It was stuffed so tightly in the trees that its gun wasn't able to turn but it was backing out.

Arnold yelled, "Reb, AGAIN!" The Tiger burst into flames as the hatches opened and its crew began to bail. Arnold flipped open the Sherman's hatch and grabbed the .50 caliber Browning; together he and Danny Boy finished the tank crew before they hit the ground.

"Danny—hit that nest of Heinie infantry to the right." Danny's machine gun raked back and forth through the brush as German rifles flashed and fell silent. They heard bullets and then the unmistakable thump - thump reverberation of 88 shells as they fell on the CCR formation ahead on the road.

Arnold spun the turret around, watching in his periscope as a Panther roared out of the brush directly ahead of them. "Joe— LEFT---we've got their side! LOAD, FIRE, --AGAIN!" The first .76mm shell bounced off the Panther but the second shot hit right above the left rear wheel housing and into the engine. The Panther exploded in a ball of fire and Arnold yelled, "REVERSE, NOW! Let's GO!"

Arnold shouted above the inner noise, "Hero, see that 88mm artillery gun at 0200---hit that SOB!" The Sherman M4 rolled backward firing constantly as it swung around the corner. Joe spun the Sherman around and headed to the main road. All the time Danny Boy was firing his machine gun this way and that, raking the brush with bullets. Arnold unlatched the turret hatch and stuck his head back out just enough so he could get a better look. He could hear more fire power coming from their left up on the main road. In a matter of minutes, they rolled out of the trees and brush and onto what was the main road. They froze!

Joe exclaimed, "Holy, mother of God, Cowboy---did those Heinie's have a whole company hidden in those bushes? Look at that! The good news is we don't have any prisoners to deal with either!"

From the open turret, the tank commander surveyed the bloody carnage, bodies, and twisted forms of German artillery and tanks covered the area. He called down to his crew, "Just as well there aren't any PW's---we got no-wheres to put them and we have to stay on the move. Looks like a few of our FA (Infantry) took a couple of bullets or shrapnel; the medics are loading them up." A message came in over his 2-way from Col. Anderson, "Good job men. Re-assemble CCA, CCB, CCR & Infantry. MOVE OUT!"

Standing in the open hatch, Arnold wiped the sweat from his upper lip and put a light to a cigarette. His hands were shaking as he inhaled the smoke deeply and then exhaled with force. Over his 2-way, he said, "Nice job men—all in a day's work, all in a day's work! Did you notice the gun that Panther had on it—it was one of those 75mmKwK 42. That SOB coulda put a shell right through our 3-inch armor, especially with that freaky long cannon tube. Good thing we got the draw on him, nice of the Kraut tankers to show us their underbelly first, that made the kill easy."

The army made another forty miles that day before they bivouacked at the edge of a burned out village, near a small lake. The convoy circled the wagons for the night. Arnold and his crew pulled themselves out of their tank, stretched and rubbed sore muscles as they looked around. Danny said, "I think I am going to sleep under the tank tonight so I can stretch out. I am damn tired of trying to sleep in that tank. I'll put my bag down right under the floor hatch in case we have to leave, quick-like."

Infantry reconnaissance men conducted a thorough search of the perimeter of the lake and not finding any Krauts, gave the go ahead signal for anyone who wanted to take a swim. First thing Kessel wanted to do was get rid of his eight-day growth of beard, then he and his crew along with about fifty other road-weary men stripped down to their skivvies and dove into the cool water. After a few minutes, Arnold made for the shore and commented to Joe, "Damn that felt so good. Probably shoulda' wore my clothes in and washed them, but don't have any time to dry 'em. So, this will have to work. We all get to smelling about the same after a few days, especially since its summer and we're in those tight quarters. Ah well, all in a day's work!"

Arnold was on the ground, leaning against their tank, having a Camel when Danny walked up, patted his commander's freshly shaved face and said, "Smooth as a baby's butt. Mind if I join you?"

Arnold motioned for him to have a seat. As soon as Danny was settled and had put a light to his own cigarette, Arnold asked, "So, Danny Boy, tell me a little more about yourself. Are you married or got a girl? What's your story? We've never had much time to get to know you; you are pretty quiet for a gunner."

Danny looked off into the distance as his face clouded over and he inhaled the smoke from his cigarette. "Well, Cowboy, I don't say much because there's not much to tell. I got me no family—I was an only child and my folks were both killed in a car wreck when I was thirteen. My grandma raised me and she died when I was just outta high school. That's when I signed up—didn't have anything else to do, if you know what I mean."

Arnold sat for a moment, digesting what Danny had just said, "Hell, Danny, I had no idea. That's a hell of a tough way to have to grow up." He reached over, put his arm around Danny's shoulder and said, "But you have us boys from 'Wrath' now—we're your family and we watch out for each other, isn't that the truth?"

Danny dropped his head as his eyes misted over. His hand was shaking as he inhaled again before replying, "Yeah, I didn't have one of those milk and cookie childhoods, for damn sure. My Granny was a loving woman and took the best care of me she could, but it weren't easy for any of us. But, I made it through and here I am---and, I- I just want to tell you, Cowboy, that I couldn't be prouder than to serve with our tanker crew and have you as commander. To me, it's like the brothers I never had; I just want you to know I'll never forget you, no matter what."

"Hey Sarge, can I ask you a question? I don't want you to get the wrong idea about me, like I'm soft or anything. I ahhh,--will I ever get used to seeing the mangled bodies of men and horses just lying by the road or the smell of blood and dying mixed with the stink of carbonite? Do guys forget that or get used to that? Some days it really gets to me worse than other days; more and more I think I'm just getting numb to it all."

Arnold stared off into the darkness of the woods, thought a moment and then said, "Ya know Danny, I haven't been in this war very long. Our first tank commander was the first guy that got killed who I knew and I don't think I'll ever get over it. But, I'll tell you this, I think there are times when things happen that a fella doesn't know how to feel, or if you do feel—how long it should be. So maybe we'll get the point where so many bad things have happened that we'll just have to stop feeling or we'll go nuts. Do you know what I mean? I guess we just have to keep on and eventually we'll each figure it out."

Danny nodded his head in blank agreement, stubbed out his cigarette and made an excuse to leave.

Arnold sat finishing off his cigarette, thinking about what Danny had told him. *He's one hell of a kid. I would have never known that about him—he just doesn't let on at all. I sure do like and respect him for everything he's been through---he's a keeper that's for damn sure! I vowed I wouldn't let myself get too close to my men, but it's damn near impossible not to care. I think it's like they say—you fight for your life, your buddies, and then your country! Or maybe it's you fight for your buddies, then your life?*

Danny is just a kid, going through what we all do—learning to live with what we are doing.

~~~~~~~~~

Just like most other days, they were on the road before sunup the next morning. Grabbing a bite from his C-ration package, Arnold complained, "Holy smokes, I would give my left toe for a stack of flap jacks with butter and syrup and a cup of real coffee instead of this instant junk they give us." Without warning, an 88 shell landed about 100 yards in front of their tank. A ton or more of wet loamy earth exploded into the pre-dawn morning air. They could hear the clods of dirt shower down onto their tank. Stunned and before he could stop their Sherman M4, Joe drove off what had been the road and into the shell's crater. The front end of the Sherman dropped straight down into the massive hole, without hesitation and using forward momentum Joe instinctively stepped hard on the gas bringing the nose of the tank back up and out the other side of the deep trench.

Back on the road, Arnold quipped, "Well, now I'm glad I didn't have a whole plate of flapjacks and syrup on my lap when we took that little detour in the road. Instant coffee and biscuits are much easier to clean off! Thanks for the ride Joe----and just in case you were wondering---I AM awake now! We're damn lucky this bag of bolts didn't flip backward on us. All in a day's work boys, all in a day's work!"

Off in the distance they could see black smoke and hear a faint staccato rat-a-tat-tat from a machine gun. Arnold thought to himself, *it sounds sorta like when we were kids and would take a stick and drag it along a 'picket wire' fence.* He grinned as he thought of the playing cards they used to pin to their bicycle spoke, with one of Mom's clothes pins. *That made the best sound, ever!*

Chapter Nine

The Battle of Normandy–
'FALAISE POCKET'

"In war, you win or lose, live or die – and the difference is just an eyelash."

Gen. Douglas MacArthur

As so diligently planned, the noose formed around the German military force, growing tighter and tighter with each battle. Since liberating Le Mans, the 81st Tank Battalion pushed hard through daily moderate to heavy resistance then headed northward to Falaise. In Normandy, the Germans were dug in, surrounded with the British and Gen. Omar Bradley's armies constantly hitting them from the north. It now became apparent to the Seventh German Army that Generals Patton and Hodges had slipped past German lines to the west, and were now closing in from the south and the west to form a noose around them.

The Allied loop formed tightly around the combined forces of Group B, German 7th Army and Fifth Panzer Armies. Allied Forces had decimated the ranks of the XLVII Panzer Corps, 1 ½ SS Panzer Divisions and two Wehrmacht Panzer Divisions whose territory had extended all the way from Caen in the east, to Mortain (Mor-taa) in the west. From August 7th to 13th, the Germans resisted General Bradley's Twelfth Army, the U.S VII Corps, and British/Canadian forces. However, they continued to lose ground and slip back further to the west. Allied aircraft delivered a lethal daily pounding on the Germans, destroying nearly half of their tank force and thousands of infantry.

~~~~~~~~

Back in Berlin, the German commanders had tried in vain to reason with Hitler but he would not listen, he could only hear the voices in his own head — his command was supreme! In reality, the German generals feared there was little chance of Hitler's 'Operation Luttich' (an operation to regain the German line of defense to the west) succeeding. Their depleted armies were outflanked to the north, south, west, and east by the U.S. Fifth Armored Division, the 749ᵗʰ Armored Division, and the U.S. 90ᵗʰ Infantry Division. The Germans realized they had severely misjudged the tenacity and strength of the Allies and were about to be trapped in what is known as the Falaise (FA-leez) Pocket.

Sensing imminent defeat for days, maybe even weeks, the Germans now attempted to establish and maintain an emergency corridor of escape near the French village of Falaise, a narrow corridor flanked by the Eure and Seine Rivers. However, because of the micro-management of Adolf Hitler who denied Field Marshal Gunther von Kluge the request to withdraw when it was an option, now, vast numbers of the German army comprehended they were about to be trapped and they elected to flee in any manner possible.

~~~~~~~

August 11, 1944: From Le Mans to twenty miles south of Se'es, the 5ᵗʰ Armored Division met with considerable to momentary resistance from panicking and confused German forces that saw and felt the advancing wall of entrapment. Enroute to Sees, the Task Force groups of CCB & CCA along with their married FAs left a swath of destruction and carnage from Marolles northward. Enemy dead along with destroyed equipment littered the road; nothing moved in the burned out villages in the aftermath of the advancement of the Task Force, it was as if the life had been sucked out of them.

CCR was rolling in the same direction as the rest of the task force, holding the right flank about five miles parallel to the east. They circled the town of Mamers, then cutting back toward Se'es, they rendezvoused with CCA and CCB.

Riding high in the open turret hatch, Arnold looked down and spotted a mangy, half-starved black dog trotting alongside the tank. It had matted blood on it right front leg and was limping badly. Finally, it lay down beside the road and watched mournfully as the American forces rolled past, heading for their next battle.

Even after they were a mile down the road, Arnold thought about the dog, it was obvious that his days were numbered and the tanker silently wondered if that was some sort of omen—or not?

Tank commander Kessel frowned then smiled as he listened to his head set as he checked his battle maps. "Well boys, the big picture is this---we are going to bypass the Perseigne Forest and cross the Sarthe River on our way to Se'es. It looks like we're going to outpost this side of Sees for tank repair, fuel, and maintenance as well as some hot food. We get to spend one night there to get our ducks in a row and our equipment up to snuff in preparation for battle in Falaise!

Joe maneuvered the tank off road and into a tight spot indicated by an MP; he shifted to neutral and cut the engine. The silence after the continuous monotonous roar of the tank engine was as startling as a cold shower. The crew pulled their tanker caps off, scratched their heads, stood and made ready to get the hell off that tank and stretch out! Every tanker and infantry took advantage of the down time and spent that night washing, shaving, eating, and getting their equipment and fire power up to par. Maintenance patched up the oil leak in their Sherman, "this will have to hold you boys until those new Shermans with the Ford engines make it across lines and catch up with us. We hope to have them in a week or so and your task force will get the first 42 tanks, how about them apples?"

Most of the tankers tried sleeping outside on the ground where they could stretch out, but even inside their pup tents, the chiggers and mosquitos ate them alive. Back inside the tank, Arnold quipped "I'm saving my blood, in case I get shot---not lettin' those damn mosquitos have it all!"

August 12: Southwest of Falaise, Reconnaissance reported that Patton's Third Army was pressing through the heart of Brittany toward Falaise at top speed. They had captured Alencon, forcing part of von Kluge's army to commit and fight, pulling them away from a combined counter-attack to the east. The Divisions were forging a mighty and deadly steel snare around the Germans.

On the morning of the 12th their orders commanded the task force to split up again on the outskirts of Sees. CCB of the 81st Tank Battalion took the east approach skirting the Orne River. CCR took the eastern flank toward the village of Gace'.

For thirty-five miles CCB advanced from the south and continued to smashed pockets of the German rear guard. They took their battle positions on the edge of Argentan and waited for further orders.

Tank Commander Kessel reported back to his crew, "Here's the deal, CCA and the 47th FA will take the lead attacking from the east moving through a series of villages. We follow behind along with Company C of the 46th who is going to mop up. After we take our main objective of Argentan, CCR and CCA split toward Gace."

The Task Force rolled through what was left of Sees with minimum trouble, liberating it by mid-morning with help from a squadron of American P-47 fighter planes that pounded the heck out of the village at dawn. It was obvious the Germans were jumping ship like a bunch of rats; they were on the move, and most weren't interested in stopping to fight it out. The majority of their equipment including tanks was left behind, especially after they ran out of fuel. If time allowed, the Krauts destroyed their abandoned tanks and artillery, but their main objective was to save their own skins and escape to the east where they could hook up with what was left of the 7th Army.

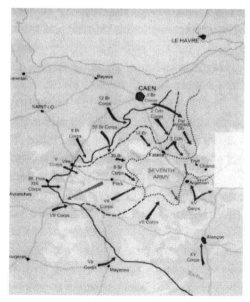

FALISE GAP MAP

Staying to the rear, CCB followed orders and took the river line. They encountered heavy anti-tank and artillery resistance and encountered their first minefield. Tank #2736 wound its way around a knocked-out German Tiger tank; no one said a word as they looked at the charred wreckage.

For the last two days they watched American bombers and fighter planes wreak havoc smashing away at the German armor and forces.

The sky to the north was filled with heavy smoke as explosion after explosion reverberated through the heavy air. Cowboy used his two-way to communicate with his crew. "Two attack forces of CCR just blocked the main highway crossroads south of Le Pin au Haras and Gace'. We got em, we got those Kraut bastards!!"

~~~~~~~~

August 13: BY midnight August 12th, they were on the outskirts of Argentan where they paused to let artillery and the Allied planes rip a hole in the meager German defenses. The sky above Argentan lit up like the Fourth of July.

August 14: The fifth Armored Division was coiled and ready for battle. Commander Kessel stood in the hatch and smoked a cigarette; he had his leather tanker's helmet on, waiting for imminent orders to attack Falaise. Arnold's body stiffened as he listened intently to the words coming from head set. The blood left his face and his fist clenched the grip of the Browning machine gun. He reached up and grabbing the cigarette out of his mouth and flicked it viciously into the road.

Seething with mounting anger, Arnold dropped through the hatch and spilled into his seat. Ripping his leather tanker helmet off, he addressed his wide-eyed crew, "Well if that isn't the shits—we are pulling out of Falaise. Gen. Bradley has over-ruled Patton's idea of pushing north. Damn IT! Now, Bradley wants us to concentrate on operations in another direction. Of all the gol damn stupid things! We were 'that' close to taking the entire German Seventh Army outta the picture if they'd let us advance. WE are the ones who snapped that lower jaw of the pocket shut— CCR has blocked the main highway junctions at Gace' and to the south of La Pin; east of Argentan, the 2nd French Armored Division cut the highway from the west. The 85th is out posting Courtomer and Moulins-la-Marche with patrols northeast to L'Aigle. We've got 'em, right there, right now!"

"We could have taken half the German army as prisoner, if they'd let us push in there. Now, we sit on our asses and watch the Krauts run for the Seine. I don't get it; it makes no sense to me--- what the hell? Now, we have orders to retreat and try to stop the remaining Heinies as they come through that pocket between the

Orne and the Seine Rivers. THAT's where they are coming through, it's as plain as day. Well, by damn---THAT's where we'll be then. Let's Go!"

Hero hit the side of the tank with his open palm, "That's just plain stupid, it's like the top brass is giving the Germans another chance to go home. We could end the whole damn war right here at Falaise; I know we could; only they won't let us! That's just pure Bushwa!"

Feeling disappointed and frustrated, Arnold pulled his helmet back on and stood up out of the turret hatch as the other tanks, equipment, and infantry regrouped and made ready to roll out, back down the same road they'd come in on. Nobody was happy with the order. The tankers watched Arnold raise his arm in the air and circle it then point east before dropping it to his side. "MOVE OUT!" He rode up top for a few miles, trying to cool off because he was damn mad and he didn't feel like taking it out on his crew.

After turning over the defeated Argentan-Gace positions to the 90th Infantry Division, the Fifth Armored Division made their way back to Sees. CCB had a quick skirmish with a platoon of fleeing Germans just outside of Argentan but other than that, it was smooth rolling. Arnold remarked, "It's pretty damn obvious they are high-tailing it outta town and don't want to take time to mix it up. RUN Kraut RUN!"

That evening they pulled into their designated outpost. The crew peered through their periscopes, astounded at the mass chaos and entanglement of men and machines. The once grassy area next to a lush French forest, was transformed into muddy mire by the treads of the tanks, Amtraks, and general pandemonium of thousands of hungry, tired, and pissed off men. They rolled past several small groups of soldiers huddled around intimate cooking fires, warming their K-rations, shooting the bull; some were even sharing a bottle of some sort.

August 15: It was a sore fact that the lower jaw of the Falaise trap and the Germans' escape route back to the border had momentarily snapped shut. Fifty thousand Germans were still trapped and were now POWs. But that didn't soften the bad taste in most men's mouths that over 100,000 Krauts had escaped through the Falaise Pocket with only their lives and without most of their equipment. Arnold looked around, surveying the carnage. *This is just like the damn Krauts; they always use, work to death, and then leave the dead horses. That's one of the things I hate them for, how they treat their horses after the poor bastards gave them everything they asked and more.*

American artillery, bombers and fighter planes continued to have a field day creating havoc and pursuing the once invincible German Seventh Army in its desperate struggle to escape backward, through the trap. Some divisions reporting back to HQ said it was like a 'turkey shoot'! Nineteen German divisions were stampeding through the pocket in their frantic attempt to escape the trap, not pausing to even shoot back or fight. The only thing on their minds was – escape. The Fifth Division pursued the enemy like 'ugly on ape'---according to their plan they began inflicting heavy casualties and smashing German armor all the way to the Seine River.

On 18 August the U. S. First Army was ordered to form the southern arm of the encirclement. By nightfall on 21 August, the escape pocket had been sealed with over 50,000 Germans trapped inside. Sometime during the night of 30 August, the last remnants of German Army Group B slipped through the line and escaped over the Seine. Operation Overlord had ended.

The Fifth Armored Division struck up a new battle cry "On to the Seine!"

Chapter Ten

"ON TO THE SEINE"

"War does not determine who is right, only who is left."
Bertrand Russell

As the 81st Tank Battalion/Infantry raced to the east of Sees, France, CCB tank commander Kessel reviewed his orders with trepidation. The 'big brass' was depending on the tank and married infantry to capitalize on their proven working relationship, along with the unexpected speed and power of movement. Their mission was to cut off the Kraut armies, the members of the rear guard of the elite German forces which had slipped the noose.

Tank commander Kessel announced to his crew, "Well boys, as luck would have it, CCB has earned an outstanding reputation, we've been ordered to take Dreux and the Eure River crossing. They want us to cut the town off from the north and in our spare time, protect the 5th Division's flank. CCA is taking our northern flank towards the city while we will take the southern wing through Mortagne and sweep back around to the north. We will both fork into attack mode once we reach the edge of city; CCA will hold back if we need reinforcements. After we get the job done, we are supposed to continue north through Houdan and Gaillon. As of now, we are set to punch north to Louviers." Arnold cleared his throat, "That's all I've got for now. We've got to be on our toes watching for pockets of fanatical Krauts who will pull anything to get the hell out of here!"

August 16: CCB commander, LTC Cole rode in the third tank of the married formation of tanks and infantry as they dashed toward the city of Dreux. They covered almost a hundred miles that first day without any enemy action.

Joe called out over the wireless, "We've got thick woods to the right, looks like a good hiding place to me. Heads up - Alert!" Arnold dropped back down his hatch and, reaching up, he slammed it shut. Taking his seat, he peered through the periscope just as the forward Infantry rifle platoon was pushed back with enemy rifle fire. CCB orders came in and Commander Kessel reported, "We're going to reorganize, reverse—reverse--Coil! We'll wait here for artillery to knock the shit out of that pocket up ahead. When I call for FIRE—we'll move forward at top speed, firing our cannon and machine guns as we roll. We're gonna let them know they messed with the wrong damn unit! When we go--Reb, you keep throwing those shells in the gun and, Hero, fire that S.O.B. at will. Danny Boy I'm countin' on you to give 'em the whole nine yards with that machine gun, you are our eyes. Joe keep it on the road, just keep it moving straight on the damn road!"

For five minutes, artillery knocked the hell out of the woods then Arnold called, "Forward and FIRE!" The tank bucked with each firing of the cannon as they moved like gang busters toward the fortified pocket of Germans. Infantry fanned out as artillery continued to drop rounds deeper into the woods; they could hear the chat-chat-a-a-chat from automatic fire. When it was all said and done, fourteen CCB tanks destroyed three acres of woods and the Germans in them as they pushed on toward Dreux. Infantry remained behind and penetrated deeper to ensure the source of enemy fire had been annihilated.

Commander Kessel listened to a report coming over his headset. "Halt, dead ahead, we've got a situation coming out of Dreux. Major Giorlando reports a German medic just brought him word that there are over 600 Germans in the city, ready to surrender." Lieutenant Colonel (LTC) Cole replied, "We'll give 'em a ½ hour to show themselves, THEN we are coming in!"

Cowboy smiled, "Don't think the Krauts are going to surrender, they are just buying time and figuring out how to escape."

The half hour came and went----nothing happened. The task force entered the city and fanned out down the main streets. "Shelling reported to the west," Arnold relayed incoming information to his crew. "The infantry has located the enemy near a cemetery; artillery is dropping their calling card, and then we will go in. Hells bells, so much for the medic's message; we are done pussyfooting around-- let em have it boys, FIRE!"

As CCB and its infantry rolled out of the city of Dreux, the French flag was flying from a church tower and they took no prisoners! They joined up with CCA and CCR as the task force

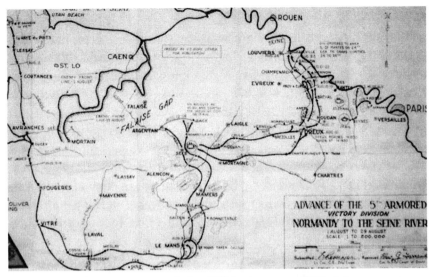

Map courtesy of the Fifth Armored Division

turned north to inflict as much misery on the fleeing remnants of the Seventh Army as they scattered like ducks toward the Seine River.

Arnold said, "Boys, did you know that we are only fifty miles from gay Par-ee. Sure hope we get to see that city, that would be something, wouldn't it? Good job today fellas—all in a day's work!"

Joe asked, "Where are we headed now Cowboy?"

Arnold frowned as he looked at his map, 'The high ground at Heudebouville---it's close to where the Seine and Eure Rivers meet. Artillery is going to hammer all possible river crossings as we move north. We're instructed to take our time and scour this eastern flank.

On **August 19th**, Cowboy gave his crew the latest dope from HQ. "CCR has seized the high ground to the west of Anet'. They ran into an artillery-supported German infantry battalion which they bloody well smashed!" Arnold laughed, "I'm beginning to sound like some of those bloody Brits, gotta watch that or Monty might hear about it and want us to attach to his group."

August 20: Arnold reported, "Col. Cole just reported reconnaissance patrols discovered the Krauts have fled the city; no fight left there—it's clean.

CCA and CCB joined forces with the 79th Infantry Division at Vernon." Arnold looked out over the top of the turret hatch and noticed the American forces shadowing them. He said, "It's good to have the 79th back with us, we've known those boys since Fort Knox. We made history today, men. You got that right; our task force is among the first Allied troops to reach the Seine River. All in a day's work for us, isn't that right? Right as Rain, I got no pain!"

August 21: "CCA is mixing it up real good ahead of us at Douains and La Heuniere. They've called in for air support, artillery, and TD's to zero in on the Krauts up there at that sharp turn in the road." Arnold listened to his head set for a moment then said, "Son-of-a-gun, I'm getting all sorts of reports from reconnaissance that all hell is breaking loose in the area where CCA is---sounds like the Heinies are putting up a fight. Our advance guard has turned around to support the main body, and they are attaching from the south and the north. Son-of-a Gun— looks like the FA are taking out all German resistance found in La Heuniere. Sure is nice of those guys to clear that side of the road for us! It musta been one rough SOB, I'm getting reports saying that the 46th Infantry had four different commanders before the day ended!"

August 22: With CCB bringing up the far side of the advancing column, the day began much like yesterday until they neared La Chapelle. Tank commander Kessel called out, "Just got word that we might get some resistance from those woods ahead. Let's go in! Joe, take us to the right and hold until we see what the infantry finds." A hell-bent-for leather fire fight broke loose about 300 yards directly ahead as their married infantry dove for cover.

Joe wheeled the tank and Hero zeroed in on an area where several flashes had come from the roadside brush. "FIRE— AGAIN---AGAIN!" Arnold looked through the periscope as infantry advanced and cleaned out what was left of the Heinie's. He announced proudly, "We got us about twenty dead Krauts on that one! Good work!"

Arnold screamed from the open hatch, "Twelve o'clock, eight Messerschmitts, coming in!" Arnold crouched down and whipped the 50 cal. Browning machine gun around, aimed, and fired continuously as the Messerschmitts dropped from the blue sky and launched fire from their wings. Suddenly one plane erupted in flames and screamed as it spiraled to the ground where it exploded in a fiery ball. "Good work, Cow-boy, WAY to GO!" Joe called over the two-way.

Arnold was shaking like a leaf, "Damn, do you think it was my machine gun that brought him down?" Reb replied, "No doubt about that Cowboy, no doubt at all! It's just all in a day's work, right?"

CCB and their married infantry had rolled, maybe four hundred yards down the road when behind them they heard tank fire. Arnold yelled, "It's dug in—those woods to the left—they got that thing camouflaged; the bastards let us go by and then hit the next column." Arnold stared intently through his periscope and yelled, "JOE, wheel LEFT!"

Destroyed Panther Tank

"Hero--- FIRE-----FIRE! Keep the son-of-a-bitch pinned in that damn brush until anti- tank fire can get to it."

Danny called out, "Cowboy, take a look to the right---there's Krauts in those damn grain shocks out there in that open field. Watch and you see 'em run from one to the other."

Commander Kessel grabbed the field phone to alert Infantry, "Echo - 6 - Bravo. We've got probably twenty Krauts hiding inside grain shocks – field to right. Suggest flame throwers. Take 'em out, call for support if you need us."

Arnold went back to his two-way to call HQ. "Echo - 6 – Bravo -- four Panthers moving across open field. We've got Kraut SS infantry hiding in grain shocks. Need air and artillery support, stat." He paused and then dumfounded, yelled, "There's two more Panthers coming up over that hill, let's go!" Back on the tank to tank two-way, Arnold called it in, "Echo- 6 - Bravo. Six Panthers advancing in grain field to right – column swing. Mortars, Bazookas—throw everything we have at them. Need, AIR Support-----NOW!"

Four P40 War hawks screamed down from the sky, wing guns blazing as they dropped their bombs on two of the tanks along with a series of phosphorous bombs. The dry wheat field and the standing shocks of grain erupted into a field of flame and death. Infantry bazookas took out the rest of the trouble. They could only watch as the supreme SS infantry ran from their fox holes under the grain shocks—their bodies like moving, screaming torches.

Arnold called out to his battalion tanks, "Support CCR infantry---they are going in to clean up the grain shocks. We'll protect the left flank!" CCR tanks advanced with their married infantry cleaning up behind. Actually, there wasn't much to clean up, just a smoldering mass of flesh, steel, and burned grain stubble.

The next morning as they were moving down the road toward Louviers, Arnold announced, "Just thought you boys would like to know, that little skirmish we had yesterday took out over 200 SS infantrymen who were dug in their fox holes underneath those grain shocks. NO prisoners! We mixed it up pretty well. We didn't take any wooden nickels, that's for damn sure. We lost four medium and one light tank as well as one light tank damaged, along with five infantry casualties and a handful of wounded. All in a day's work, good job, boys!" Arnold added, "We are moving six miles south and east of Mantes to outpost for intensive maintenance."

Joe complained, "Why the hell don't these fleeing 'Frenchie's get off of the damn road when there are Kraut planes or artillery coming in? They act like they are just out for a Sunday stroll. Besides, most of 'em don't even give us enough room to get by to go fight for their country. I hope to hell I don't run over one of them people!"

Danny Boy commented, "At least they like us being in their country. I kinda like it when a pretty French girl blows a kiss my way. Makes me want to run over and collect, if you know what I mean!"

Joe gave Danny a playful punch on the arm. "You wouldn't know what to do with one of them French women. They are out of your league. Hell, you are still wet behind the ears! If the situation comes up, I'll be a friend and take care of it for you! Sure as hell will—right as rain!"

~~~~~~~~

August 24: Tank Commander Arnold Kessel stood alert, his six-foot frame looming out of the M4 Sherman's open turret hatch, staring at the mighty River Seine. After the tension of the past week of bitter fighting, cleaning up, and pursuing fleeing German forces through the Seine River Gap, Arnold inhaled deeply and shuddered as his body relaxed. He was lost in his own emotions and thoughts, hypnotized by the calming sensual movement of the waters of the famous French river. *We fought so hard to reach this river, to stop the Germans, and all that time, this water flowed as it did yesterday, as it did last year, even a hundred years ago. Some things change in a second and some things never change. Two weeks ago when we landed at Utah Beach I was a boy. I didn't know it then, but I was. Now, I've changed. I have seen and I have done things in those two weeks that have changed me forever, things I never dreamed of doing and seeing.*

Arnold's blue eyes, misted over with emotional tears as he lifted them to the canopy of the trees along the banks of the slowly flowing river. Trying to get control of himself before his crew noticed, he inhaled deeply, filling his lungs with the cool morning air. *I will never be the boy that I was; I will never think or act as I did. Seeing war, participating in war, killing---that, does something to a man. I'm not sure what it is, but it weighs heavy on my mind, my heart, and my soul. I only hope that my Lord can forgive my sins! I know in my heart that I do what I do because I have to, I am following orders. This is war and I am fighting for my crew, myself, and my country.*

Earlier in the day, the XV Corps secured a bridgehead east of the Seine at Mantes which cut off any remaining German armor and became the grave of numerous German foot soldiers, much to the delight of Gen. Patton. Tank commander Kessel received the following message over his two-way radio, The Fifth Armored Battalion received the following commendation from XV Corps, addressed to Gen. Lunsford Oliver: *"I desire personally to thank you and every member of your command for the splendid accomplishment of every task assigned. Your achievement as a first class fighting division is playing a large part in the liquidation of the German Army which is our eventual goal."* General George Patton.

Arnold smiled with satisfaction and said to his crew, "So, what do you think of them apples? We got us a genuine 'thank you very much' from the XV Corps and old blood and guts himself. That's pretty damn snappy if you ask me. I just want to add to that – I am proud to be your tank leader, damn proud. You are one hell of a crew and together we made a difference!"

Joe raised an imaginary glass and said, "And you, commander, are one hell of a tanker!"

~~~~~~~~~

"Breathe, boys, breathe---we got us a bit of a maintenance lull and CCB is getting fourteen new Ford tanks!" Arnold was as excited as a kid at Christmas. They'd all heard that these new [24]Ford-motor tanks were supposed to be the cat's meow! It was true that CCB got fourteen new tanks, while the other boys in the task force just got new motors! Either way, those new motors were supposed to be way better than the Continental radial engine they had before!

Joe chipped in, "I can't wait to see what these babies can do." He turned to Danny, "What do you think Danny Boy? You never say too much, but you do a hell of a job with that machine gun---that you do!"

New Sherman M4 tanks with Ford Engines

Arnold said, "Oh by the way, a couple promises of improvement to our situation from our battalion commander, LTC Anderson. They have put in for a 250 gallon water trailer that sticks with us at all time so we don't run out of water on the road. CCB will continue to attach to a QM fuel truck platoon; that way they will keep everyone from running on empty during these bent for hell endurance races to a battle! They are also asking the Big Brass what the hell we're supposed to do with the POWs when we are in a big battle. They are a pain in the ass—here we are trying to fight and kill the enemy on one side of the road, and molly coddle their captured keisters on the other side."

"They've got to come up with something better than pulling our guys off line to babysit the Kraut POWs. The other thing headquarters has to address is the fact that the enemy is constantly harassing our supply trains and because of that, we have to use a couple light tanks to chase them the hell away from our food and fuel! They remind me of a bunch of hungry damn vultures."

Tank commander Kessel lifted his finger in gesture for just a minute, "Allied Headquarters reports at this moment, all four Allied armies involved in the Normandy campaign are on the River Seine. That would be the 2nd British, 1st Canadian, Patton's Third Army, and our own First Army! Here are some stats you are gonna like. When the 'party' was over in that Falaise pocket we created, approximately 80,000 – 100,000 German troops were trapped—of whom 10,000 – 15,000 were killed. They estimate 40,000 – 50,000 were taken prisoner and the other 20,000 – 50,000 Krauts escaped to fight again! And, get this---the mighty 12th SS-Panzer Division came in the battle with 20,000 men and 150 tanks. After we got done kickin' their ass, they had less than 300 men and 10 tanks! Now—how is that for a day's work?"

Arnold took a long drink of water from his canteen and continued, "And, we know this for a fact, because we were doing some of that kickin and, we were also hot on the trail of those escaping Krauts when they tried to cross the Seine River. Those Heinies were in such a damn hurry that they left behind most of their equipment including 500 Panther tanks, which is good news for us. What fries my left toe is that they tried to destroy or at least mess up the ones they had time for, but other than that—we got us some second-hand German equipment for when we want to infiltrate their lines and play dress up!

Arnold started to sign off and then paused and said, "Oh, I almost forgot to tell you the good news. We are re-attached to the First Army now, so we don't have to worry about running into Gen. Patton because he is no longer our commander. Have you boys checked out the design of this new Sherman Tank? It has thicker armor in the front, but I'd still like a little more insurance, so we'll throw some sand bags on it too—what do you boys say?"

Commander Kessel rode in the open turret hatch as they proceeded on the pock-marked road to Paris. He couldn't help but look at the faces and body language of the refugees that flooded the road out  of Paris. If they were lucky, most had a horse-drawn cart carrying their worldly goods, some were on bicycles, some pulled little wagons with all their possessions, and some were just walking. Most had that same blank expression in their eyes but when they saw the American tanks and infantry, many of them raised their arms in victory and cheered the Allied forces.

Arnold noticed that the infantry kept trying to explain to the French people that when the German planes came in low to strafe the road, that they should not get close to a tank or any vehicle that held gasoline. It was just something that a soldier knew and a fearful civilian did not.

After five days of much needed equipment maintenance, some decent hot food other than K-rations and a few uninterrupted nights' sleep, they were on the road again, but this time their destination was----PARIS! Not everybody in the Division got orders to ride through the city of lights, so the boys in CCB knew they were lucky when their orders put them on track as part of the Allied Forces who would be in the victory parade through part of the city.

Specific units of the Fifth Armored arrived on the outskirts of Paris and according to orders from HQ, they waited patiently in the wings while French General DeGaule led the 2nd French Armored Division in a victorious parade, taking all the credit for the liberation of Paris. Before they joined in the victory parade, the entire task force received a special commendation.

Subject: Commendation.
TO: Officers and Enlisted Men of the XV Corps and attachments.
 1. *It is with extreme pride that I publish to you the following commendation of the Army Commander on the historic movement of the XV Corps around the German Armies in Northern France during which the Corps advanced against resistance a distance of approximately 180 miles in nine days and stopped only because of orders from a higher authority,"*
 2. *Please accept for yourself and transmit to the officers and men of your command my sincere appreciation and commendation for the masterly manner in which the Corps has pressed relentlessly forward, executed difficult changes of direction, and taken calculated risks with the utmost daring. The whole performance on the part of you, your officers, and men has been very superior!"*

3. *"You have done a fine job. You have whipped the German wherever you have met him. You have strewn the country-side with the wreckage of his equipment. You have captured thousands of prisoners. With the experience gained in this campaign you will handle whatever lies ahead of you with confidence and ease. My heart-felt thanks and best wishes to you all."*
Signed:
Wade H. Haislip, Major General, U. S. Army, Commanding

**Fifth Armored – 81ˢᵗ Tank Battalion
in Paris Liberation parade**

After receiving the commendation, Arnold addressed his tank crew. "Fellas, I just want to say that I couldn't be prouder of you and your action during battle. We are not only one hell of a crew, we are the best and that's what this commendation endorses. I am thinking there will be some Bronze Stars awarded for this! May God continue to be with us! It's all in a day's work, isn't that right? Thanks fellas!"

30 Aug. 1944-Paris, France: As a part of the V Corps Fifth Armored Division, Commander Kessel and his tank crew passed over the Seine River and waited on the outskirts of Paris. The city had been liberated five days earlier, but the rejoicing continued as the French tri-colored flags gently stirred in the summer breeze. The Americans hung back, giving the French military their moment of glory.

When it was their turn, Tank Commander Kessel stood proud and tall in the Sherman's hatch while jubilant infantry rode on the flanks of the American tanks, collecting flowers and kisses from thankful French women. Proudly, they made their way down the famous broad avenue of Champs Elysees and through the Arc de Triomphe. Jubilant and colorful French countrymen and women filled the sidewalks; they cheered and waved their flags as the 81st Tank Battalion tanks rumbled past. It was especially fun when the column would pause—then the jubilant crowd would press forward. The French people seemed grateful to have the opportunity to personally greet the Victory Division and it was a moment in time for the men of the Fifth Armored Division!

CCB didn't spend any time in the City of Lights other than driving through the streets. After the fanfare, they made their way to the edge of Paris where they were scheduled to attach to Gen. Courtney Hodges' First Army and rendezvous with Gen. Patton's Third army.

CCB tanks were in formation on the left side of the advancing columns as they rumbled at top speed through the French countryside, Arnold commented to his crew, "Well boys, we've seen Gay Parr-ie and I hope to hell you didn't blink! I have to say I still can't believe it. It was the cat's meow if you ask me--- man all those swell lookin' dames were sure easy on the eyes."

Keeping his eyes on the road, Joe quipped, "Yeah, it was pretty swell. I just hope that isn't our last 'hurrah'."

Commander Kessel replied, "Well, I think we all knew that our little parade through Paris was no sightseeing trip. We've got our orders now to high tail it to Conde, Belgian, and the brass wants us there by the 2nd. That means boys, we have over 130 miles to travel in three days and we are going to be catching up to plenty of pockets of German rear guards who are probably gonna want to fight. We'll have to be on the watch for ambushes and anything that looks like a mine field. Our reconnaissance has its work cut it for it and those [25]Piper Cubs will be our eyes up ahead."

Butch interrupted the conversation, "Say, Cowboy, I'm just curious--do you know who is leading our armored column on this race to Conde?"

Commander Kessel smiled and winked at Butch, "We have none other than our own Gen. Lunsford Oliver leading our column in an unarmored Peep (Jeep), so we gotta mind our P's and Q's; we are in good hands! Only a couple of hours ago, LTC Fay with an infantry platoon from the 5th Armored took a bullet at Rully. Those boys in CCR are running about five miles parallel to us and he was over there with them in an armored car when he was killed by a sniper. So we gotta be on the lookout every damn minute!"

Danny shook his head in disbelief then said, "I don't have a good feeling about what we are heading into. The closer we get to the fatherland, them Germans are gonna be like nests of angry wasps. We are heading straight into hell and you know it! You'd better brush up on your Kraut words Cowboy—I got me a feeling we're gonna need it."

Chapter Eleven

"LUXEMBOURG"

"The Fifth Armored Division was the first Allied force to set foot on German soil in 1944."

Outside of Paris, on the morning of 1 Sept. 1944, **the Fifth Armored Division, First Army** attached and was deemed the spearhead for V Corps. Their immediate orders were initiated by a 130-mile lightning push across France toward the Belgian border. The heavily armored and mobile divisions of the V Corps were picture perfect in their preferred pitchfork attack formation. Slowly approaching the Compiegne Forest, their armored columns coiled and cautiously wound their way through heavy growths of tall pines and thick clumps of deciduous trees. Every eye was pealed for snipers, ambushes, and all-out German attacks.

As CCB inched their way through the dense forest, Arnold couldn't help but think of the pine woods in the Big Horn Mountains of Wyoming. The leaves were just beginning to turn color and the pungent smell of Pine coupled with the heat of late summer filled the air. That first night in the forest they erected their pup tents and many felt like they were actually camping in the woods. Arnold exclaimed, "Now, this is what I call living! Man, there's nothing I like better than being around a campfire out in the pine woods—it's just swell." He looked over at Danny who was trying to get comfortable. "So, Danny Boy, is this your first time?" Danny blushed and just looked at his commander. Arnold laughed and rephrased his question, "I mean, Danny, is this your first time camping in the woods?"

Danny smiled and snuggled down deep into his sleeping bag, "It sure is. Do they have bears around here?"

The next morning they were up and back on the road before the sun. It was just turning light when suddenly, what looked like a French national came running down the road, yelling "La Boche, la Boche". He was pointing ahead of their column. Arnold hollered over the growl of the tank treads, "He's saying there are Germans up there, Germans!"

Joe jumped down from the tank and speaking a few words of French, discovered that there were nine Germans in the woods ahead and they wanted to surrender. Arnold radioed in to Col. Anderson who sped up in a jeep. "We have to be careful, it could be a trap. Send the Frenchman up with five infantry in cover of a tank and take a look see!" The first tank and two teams of Infantry began to inch their way up the road to where the Frenchman pointed.

The column continued up the road in force, just behind the investigating team. First one German, than three came out of the woods. "Hande hoch, hoch---wir kommen raus." (Hands up, up, we are coming out.)They put their hands in the air and pointed back at the woods, indicating there were more. Reb remarked, "Hell, that Frenchman couldn't count---look, there are forty Germans prisoners marching back to the rear of our column. In my book, that's forty less to shoot at us or lay road mines unless they already buried them and now they want to get the heck outta Dodge!"

~~~~~~~~

That next morning, General Oliver, his aide-de-camp Capt. Davidson, his driver, and his guard were riding point for the column. They were about half way through the Compiegne Forest when the column came to a high arching bridge spanning a canal up ahead. General Oliver was enjoying the quiet pristine surrounding as they crossed the bridge, when suddenly he spotted a poorly camouflaged German anti-tank gun, aimed directly at the heart of the bridge.

Gen. Oliver grabbed his driver's shoulder and directed, "Ben, get this worthless Jeep across this bridge and off the road and over there, behind that woodsman's house – fast!"

Oliver radioed back to the lead tank in the column, "We've got us a German anti-tank gun in that brush to the left of the bridge—looks like it's aimed at the bridge and waiting for the first tank that crosses it."

The lead tank commander flung open the turret hatch and with his binoculars, spotted the camouflaged anti-tank gun. The problem was he couldn't tell if it was manned.

Standing at the edge of the woods, Gen. Oliver raised his hand and in a wiper motion he crossed his forearms for the signal to take the Germans out.

The first and second CCB tanks moved forward and sighted in on the German gun and the surrounding area with their cannons and machine guns as their married infantry fanned out in the cover of the woods. The Sherman's turret swung to the left and sighted in on the target as the tank commander shouted, "FIRE! The sound of machine gun fire filled the woods as the tank commander grabbed his .50 caliber machine gun on the turret and proceeded to insure that no more Germans were lying in wait for them to cross the bridge.

The next day the army column was within twenty miles of Conde. It was close to sundown when Kessel's tank 2736 just nicked a road mine with the right front tread. The blast rocked the Sherman tank and scared the shit out of everyone inside, but the only damage was a mangled boggie wheel and a dislodged tread. The maintenance depot was Johnny on the spot with a replacement tank and off they went. "All in a day's work," Arnold remarked to his crew.

Reb replied, "Ya know, Cowboy, I'm getting a little sick of hearing you say 'it's all in a day's work'---where the hell did that come from, anyway?"

A smile crawled up the corners of Arnold's mouth as he replied, "That's my attempt at a little humor or to lighten the load, sorry if it annoys you, Reb. That is just something my Dad always said to let us know that shit happens and we should just keep truckin'---that's all!"

The V Corps crossed three substantial rivers, the Alse, the Aisne, and then the Somme before reaching the Belgian border at Conde around midnight, on **2 September**.

NOTE: *The Fifth Armored was one of the first divisions to enter Belgian, beginning a long list of historic firsts on their drive eastward to Berlin!*

After numerous small skirmishes with the German rear guard along the road from Paris, the 5th Armored collected over

500 prisoners and destroyed the majority of captured Kraut equipment in the process. That is, except for the 70 two-horse teams that pulled various military wagons and guns, along with a handful of riding horses previously used by German officers.

The Battalion circled the wagons for the night. The tankers jumped off their tanks to stretch their legs, others to attend to nature calls bivouacking for the night, everyone hoped to catch some rest before they hit the road in the morning. As the crew of WRATH was settling in, Joe said, "Cowboy, do you think now that we are up here in Conde, that we might get a couple days of R&R (rest and relaxation)? That would sure be swell." Arnold laughed as he pulled his coat over his head, "Dream on, Joe, they've got us on the move to somewhere and it's not R & R. I haven't heard anything to tell me just what or where we are going but something is brewing that's for damn sure. I guess we'll hear when the brass is ready to clue us in. Until then we try to catch forty winks and wait. "

Danny Boy complained, "Sleeping in this tank is getting to be a habit and when are we going to dine on real food again? I'm sure getting sick and tired of theses damn K Rations. Besides that, I don't even remember the last time I used or saw real toilet paper."

Joe chimed in, "Well you have to realize that when we are moving this fast, the supply and kitchen service battalions can't keep up and get set up like normal before we are off and running again."

Just after the sun rose in all its glory to the east of Conde, Arnold strolled down to where they had tied the captured German riding horses. He spotted a magnificent black stallion with dried blood on its left hip. He couldn't resist walking over to it. Standing completely still, Arnold let the horse get used to him before offering it the hand of grass he had pulled up. The stallion shied to the right and tossed his head as Arnold reached up to stroke his mane. *There's something really sad in this horse's eyes. I bet he's been through hell with bullets flying and explosions all around him. I guess we have something in common—him and me.* Arnold gently slid his hand across the horses back until he reached the dried blood. Working his hand over the haunch, he discovered there was no wound—nothing but someone, some other unfortunate's dried blood. He said in a low voice, "It's okay boy we're going to turn you over to some Belgian farmers. You don't have to be a German army horse any more---just green pastures and nice fat mares for you. Good Boy!"

Arnold's eyes suddenly misted over with tears, thinking about all the horses blown to pieces or maimed and left to die in agony beside the roads from Normandy to Conde. The Germans were not kind to their horses, and when a horse took a bullet or a shell, the Krauts pushed the animals aside like so much disposable rubbish. Arnold thought about the horses he had ridden and worked with as a kid on the farm back in Wyoming. He loved horses and it broke his heart—that they too were forced to endure the horrors of war. A fleeting question crept into his mind. He wondered if he would make it through the war and ever see the rolling sagebrush covered hills of Wyoming again.

~~~~~~~

Sept. 4th: Tank commander Kessel called out to his crew, "We've got new orders. The Victory Division is heading back to the Meuse River. We are to cross the Meuse River at Sedan & Charleville; our new target assignment is the liberation of Luxembourg. And we are to make it snappy; we've got over 100 miles to go before we rest!"

Danny bitterly remarked, "Us, get to rest? That will be the day. We are going straight into the jaws of the German army, and if we don't jump first, they are going to chop us up like sauerkraut. We all know they aren't going to keep running forever—we all know that, it's not what they are about. Pretty soon, damn soon—they are going to mass together and come back at us with a vengeance. That's pure common sense, they like to fight!" As the column headed back down the road, tank commander Kessel listened to the crew grumble and complain, "Hey boys—remember it's all in a day's work and some days are longer than others. Heads up---let's go!" A mile up the road CCB ran into a nest of Germans. It was a brief skirmish with the Heinies coming out on the short end of the stick.

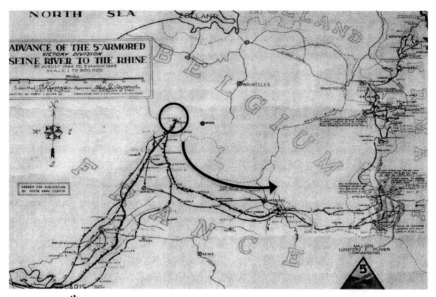

The 5th Armored/CCB route: Paris to Conde, France, to Luxembourg, to Wallendorf, Germany

Tank commander Kessel reported to HQ. "Echo – 6-Bravo: Encountered enemy at 1300 hours: Small unit, disorganized, poorly equipped and confused: Not interested in fighting: Transported 21 POWs to rear guard: Over and OUT."

~~~~~~~~

They were traveling on a different French road from the one they had been on to Conde. The Division raced southeast of where they had traveled only days before. The column stayed to the west of the Belgian border until they hit the village of Vise, then they angled due east, advancing over 100 miles in less than eight hours. They had minimum contact with the enemy, mostly running into a few road blocks and blown bridges.

As a result of their lightning-pace drive to Sedan, France, the 5th Division and all attached armies came face to face with a new dilemma---fuel shortages. They had moved so fast their normal fuel supply convoys couldn't keep up. They pulled off the road just before noon and bivouacked for a couple of hours for minor maintenance issues. Commander Kessel pulled himself up through the open turret and hopped off the tank. He walked over to where a few of the other tankers were shooting the bull. Arnold said, "What's up? Why are we stopping, I thought the brass was hell bent for leather to get to Sedan?"

The tank commander from the 81st CCR laughed and said, "Well sure, that was the plan, but tanks can't run on fumes—we're waiting for our fuel trucks to catch up with us. I heard that the 749th Tank Battalion, who is acting as rear guard on this trek was sittin' back there on the road—ran their tanks dry. Along comes Patton and asks, "Why the hell, are all these tanks stopped?" Some smartass tanker spoke up and said, "Well, General Patton, tanks won't run without gas." I guess Patton let go with a few choice words of expression and hopped in his jeep with his ugly white bull terrier and disappeared back down the road in a cloud of dust. Those tankers said that within the hour, Patton was back with three fuel trucks in tow!"

Arnold questioned, "Where did the fuel trucks come from so damn quick?"

The tanker answered, "Good question. The QT is that Patton actually hijacked a column of fuel supply trucks. That guy will do anything to get his way—hell, somebody said that he also told his men to change the patches on their uniforms to get into the fuel depots and get extra allotments of fuel!" The tanker wiped his mouth and added, "They broke the mold after they made that SOB---there's one way to do something—Patton's way. But you know what, he gets it done and on time or before--or there is hell to pay! He's just damn unpredictable and that is exactly why the Krauts fear him and admire him, from what I hear."

After a few hours, their own fuel trucks caught up with them, the tanks and other equipment were refueled and they were off like gangbusters.

Before dawn, the engineers of CCR raced ahead of the column to the outskirts of Charleville where their orders were to locate the Meuse River crossing. Not waiting for daylight, they began their search, to their delight they found a partially destroyed dam. They activated their plan where, with adequate cover from HQ Company's assault guns, mortars, and the trusty canons of the 10th Tank Battalion and the 196 attached infantry, CCB and CCA tanks as well as the 47th Infantry might easily cross the river.

Sept. 5: Once CCB and CCA along with married infantry were across the Meuse, they were able to take out heavy enemy rifle and machine gun fire from Germans who were dug in on a 50-foot cliff overlooking their positions. By 1200 hours they took the cliff and four hours later, the rest of the battalion was crossing the Meuse River on a 192-foot Treadway bridge.

Arriving at Sedan on late 5 September, CCB crossed the tip of the southern Belgian border and took the northern fork moving from Sedan to Kopstal, Luxembourg. The tank task force of CCR and CCA stayed to the south and prepared to liberate Luxembourg City on Sept. 10th.

At the same time, CCB acted on much different orders as they headed straight for the German border. Meeting with only light unprotected road blocks and no mine fields, they pushed forward. With housekeeping duties out of the way, CCB column proceeded at top speed to an assembly area just to the north of Diekirch, Luxembourg.

Riding in the second tank, Commander Kessel spotted trouble ahead as he called out, "Looks like we've got us a Kraut 20mm Flak/anti-aircraft gun and two high-velocity, 75mm AT guns up ahead in that grove of trees to the right."

Arnold got on the two-way and then radioed their married infantry to alert them to the problem. The infantry fanned out as 'Wrath' and four other Shermans moved up to take care of any big problems while their infantry took care of sweeping the area and mopping up. Commander Kessel said, "Reb, we've got orders to blow all of that Nazi equipment to 'kingdom come'. Burn it!" The Allied forces destroyed the equipment, took four prisoners, and counted twelve dead."

Later Arnold and a couple other CCB tank commanders walked the battle ground and surveyed the carnage. Commander Kessel remarked, "Well boys –looks like we did some work today—took damn good care of those Krauts. I wish to hell the Mortuary Battalion would move up faster and get those bodies out of here. I hate looking at their faces---gives me nightmares. Have you noticed how young some of those Germans look? I bet they're 15 or 16 years old---that's the shits. Looks to me like Herr Hitler is running out of fighting men and he's bringing up the young boys to fight. Good thing for us, not for them cause these kids don't know how to fight, they just get killed."

Sept. 10: Tank commander Kessel noticed on the orders and regional maps that his old friend Cal Meyer's tank battalion, CCA had been paralleling his CCB Task Force all along from Brussels. They had also driven eastward through the capital of Luxembourg and reported some significant resistance. Arnold continued to read the daily log/report. *A second concentration from the 47th and 400th FA Battalions along with CCA cleared the woods north of Hamm and pushed on to the east.* Arnold blinked, rubbed his eyes and read the next sentence again. *Well concealed German anti-tank guns knocked out CCA's first four tanks while a Tiger tank opened fire on the married infantry. Battalion reported four tanks, two half-tracks, and two anti-tank guns destroyed in the battle. Twelve wounded and nine dead.*

The blood left Arnold face as he read 'nine dead'. He grabbed his two-way phone and without hesitation, called headquarters. "Echo 6 - Romeo (Col. Anderson), Echo 6 - Bravo." Arnold waited a few minutes and then Colonel Anderson picked up. For a second or two, Arnold couldn't make himself ask the question, "Colonel, Sir--sorry to bother you, but do you have a list of CCA's dead, in ahhh, those four tanks that were knocked out yesterday?" Arnold listened for a minute, then asked, "Is, is Sgt. Cal Meyers on that list, sir?"

"That's affirmative Commander!"

Commander Kessel's jaw was clenched as he struggled with some excuse, any excuse to get out of his tank. "Say Joe, ahhh you hold everything together, we are just sitting here for another half hour or so. There is something I have to check on, be right back." Not waiting for any reply, Arnold pulled himself up through the turret hatch and jumped down from the tank. He half ran, half walked, not really knowing where he was going. *I need some time alone, to get this through my head. SHIT! It's the damn SHITS! I didn't even get to say goodbye or nothin'! Dammit---Damn that Nazi pig who fired on Cal's tank. Ohhh Cal—it wasn't supposed to end like this!*

Nick Eastin, one of the other tankers called out to Arnold as he noticed him wandering around the bivouac area, "Hey, Cowboy, where are you off to? Aren't we on alert?"

Arnold just waved him off and kept going. He felt numb—a feeling he was becoming pretty used to. *I guess it's called survival—a way to keep going when you see and experience what we do, day after day. But, with Cal, now—with Cal, it's a different story. He was my friend, we had us some times together, and to get it through my head that he's dead is, ahhh shit it's so hard! Why did he die and I still breathe?"*

Sept. 11: In the vicinity of Obereisenbach, CCB moved to the high ground, inching closer to the Siegfried Line and the German Rhine River. Arnold had buried Cal's death somewhere in the recesses of his mind as he needed to function. Steely-eyed, Commander Kessel announced, "Boys, our orders are to play a little cat and mouse with the Germans—irritate the hell of them and try to keep them occupied to give the Third Army more room to cross into Germany down river, near Aachen. They want us to pull off a large-scale diversion, you know,—test the enemy's strength by drawing a big German force into a fight. We're also supposed to stop any reinforcements getting through to the Krauts holed up south of us. Sounds like a damn picnic if you ask me."

Commander Kessel motioned for quiet from his crew as he listened closely to his two-way; suddenly he looked up and let out a whoop. "Boys, we're gonna celebrate as soon as we can. Up to the north around Stolzenberg, our 81's Tank Battalion reconnaissance patrols have done it--they crossed the German border this morning! They are the first Americans to step foot on German soil! That's damn good news if you ask me!" A cheer went up and echoed throughout the entire assembly area as each unit of the battalion got the news. Another FIRST for the 5th Armored Division!

Sept. 13: The sun was just clearing the ridge behind them when CCB woke to a concentrated barrage of direct fire into German locations from the 10th Tank Battalion and assault guns of the 47th Infantry. Commander Kessel opened his turret hatch and watched for a few minutes, "Will you get a load of that. Those Krauts aren't even interested in returning fire and that's a good thing for us." He listened intently to his two-way. The crew was watching his facial expression and they knew something really big was coming through the line, but they had no idea what it might be. Cowboy turned and addressed his crew. "Tomorrow is our day---tomorrow CCB crosses the Rhine!" Cheers went up as Joe, Danny Boy, Hero, and Reb all congratulated each other and their commander. This deed would put them on the map; they would be getting into the thick of it now.

Sept. 14: Arnold peered through his periscope, surveying the fog-shrouded river bank and surrounding area. It was thrilling to actually watch CCB and CCR's attached infantry cross the

Siegfried Line, walking through the destroyed dragon's teeth and hedgehog steel girders which were meant to stop Allied tanks and armored vehicles. Waiting until he got the word to move out, Arnold remarked to his crew, "This is a damn proud moment for the 5th Armored Division—to be the first across the Siegfried Line and onto German soil. I don't know what we are going to run into on the other side and neither does the top brass. From what I get, we are going over for a look see and report back, if we're still in one piece." He winked and held up his right hand to tap the top of his leather helmet in a visual Move Out gesture.

CCB and CCR from the Fifth Armored Division penetrated the sacred [27]Siegfried Line at Wallendorf, going for the high ground of Hill 407. Both task forces noticed an increase in German tank and artillery resistance once they crossed onto German soil.

Commander Kessel reported, "Our married infantry is working its way up the hill, slogging their way through the last of the occupied pillboxes with small arms fire, flame throwers, and grenades. They will let us know if they need us to move forward and blast the Krauts out of their fortifications. We have orders to follow them up Hill 407 when summoned. It looks like CCR engineers are going to have to demolish the rest of those pillboxes with 400-pound explosives. How much concrete did those Krauts pour into those things? They are damn near shell proof!"

Hans asked, "Why don't we just kill the Krauts inside of them and move on up the hill? Why waste time and ammo blowing the damn things up?"

Cowboy replied, "Because, Hans, the Germans will return and resume residency as soon as we move out—right as rain. That's just what the SOBs do---infiltrate back in. So we have to make sure they don't have a residence left once we are done with the area. We've already taken over 240 prisoners and killed about that many to boot."

That night they bedded down inside their tank, trying to get as comfortable as possible. Commander Kessel told his crew, "Boys, we have orders to hold this position the best we can until September 20th or, if and when orders change As you know, our mission is to attempt to draw the enemy reserves to our position, like a bee to honey---and away from other significant battles and crossings on the Rhine."

Once across the Siegfried Line at Wallendorf, CCB kept moving forward, moving into Germany as far as the village of Hommerdingen. CCR stayed on Hill 407. It was a daily task to rout the enemy out of their fortified positions; they were like a bad dream---kept coming back and back. CCR established defensive positions around the semi-deserted villages of Halsdorf, Stocken, and Ettlingen.

After the 81st went across the border, Joe remarked, "Well, it looks like we are in it now. Where in the hell are the famous SS troops? What are they up to?

Part of CCB infantry remained in a bivouac area while the other half went out on patrol. They took turns because the troops and tanks that stayed behind took almost continual artillery fire from German 8 cm to 15cm shells. Concealed enemy fire came from every which way—they never knew where it would come from next. Artillery fell incessantly like unwanted rain.

Commander Kessel issued orders the next morning. "Today is our turn to go to the woods and take more of those damn pillboxes out—the ones where the Krauts are dug in. We're gonna have assault gun and mortar support while we are on our seek and destroy!"

Danny Boy called out, "Cowboy, there is a lot of fire coming from those two little villages up ahead, what are they—Neidersgegen and Ammeldingen? That's what this here map says. Anyways—what do you think about calling in some artillery or tank-destroyers to give 'em some grief?"

Arnold replied, "Good spotting Danny Boy—I'm calling that in right now."

Five Sherman tanks creaked and groaned down the wooded road toward the two villages; Cowboy, Danny, and PT were all operating out of open hatches so they'd have a wider area of vision. Suddenly their married infantry scattered and hit the ground—"INCOMING"! The three tankers dropped into the tank just as earth and trees exploded. A shell hit about 50 yards to the left of Tank # 2736. Joe didn't need to be told, he wheeled the tank to the right and Cowboy swung the cannon to face in the direction of the fire.

Commander Kessel shouted, "Coil back into that grove of trees while Infantry scouts the area and lets us know if we can help."

It didn't take long for the call to come. Cowboy listened to the two-way then reported, "Okay Joe, move up, nice and slow. Everybody stay inside the tank—lock those hatches! Infantry found a couple of concealed pillboxes next to that barn up ahead and two or three more in haystacks near the first village. Let's go give me a ride skyward! Danny you watch for any additional enemy fire—let me know what you see."

Reb put a phosphorous shell into the cannon, while Hero the gunner, watched intently through his periscope, ready to fire in an instant. An explosion, 'Whaa-VOOM' rocked their tank.

Commander Kessel said, "Easy does it, easy now."

Suddenly Danny Boy called out, "There, at 3 o'clock, between that outhouse and tree,"

Cowboy yelled, "Sight it in Hero, ready? FIRE. Reb, give us an HE – FIRE!"

Danny Boy yelled, "To the left—300 yards, haystack!"

Cowboy shouted, "Reb—Phosphorous—burn the hell out of those SOB's."

Hero sighted in and hit the firing pedal—the haystack erupted in a ball of flames as four Germans ran from it, their bodies blazing. Danny turned the machine gun on them and put them out of their agony. At the end of the day, the group of CCB tanks and married infantry destroyed five smaller pillboxes and took 25 prisoners.

That night back at bivouac, Hero said to Cowboy, "You know those prisoners our infantry took today? Well, this dogface told me that the Krauts told an interpreter there are lots more of them who want to surrender if we promise not to shoot them. They also asked the interpreter if us tankers weren't scared, being inside one of these Tommy cookers. That's what the Krauts call our Sherman tanks. How do ya like those potatoes?"

Joe responded, "Hell, it ain't us they need to worry about if they surrender, it's some of their own fanatical soldiers. Did you hear about those fifty prisoners that CCR took the other day — before our guys could get the Krauts rounded up, their own people hid in the woods and mowed em down. And, for the record, we do just fine in our Tommy Cookers at least we aren't on the receiving end of their bullets."

19 September: The 81st Task Force Anderson[26] along with Task Force Gray covered the withdrawal of CCR back across the border. For the time being, CCB and Combat Command Headquarters tanks along with their married infantry were the only forces left behind on German soil. That next day was pure hell as the remaining Allied Forces took heavy enemy fire and lost six tanks and three halftracks; their causalities were growing and it looked like they were stuck.

Commander Kessel listened to the radio, "Okay boys, head out, we are pulling into a tight defensive position on top of that hill over there between Niedersgegen and Ammeldingen, the one they call Hill 375."

With the turret hatch shut and locked, they rolled out for Hill 375. Cowboy watched through his periscope as every tank, prepared mortar, artillery, and tank destroyer headed for the hill, along with the infantrymen and engineers. Everyone pitched in to dig a defensive cordon around the perimeter of the hill in anticipation of a night attack, or worse yet, an infiltration of numerous Germans who might move up in mass.

No one had a good night's sleep that night---a copious number of guards were posted and periodically relieved throughout the night; there was no attack that night. Those who slept woke at daybreak to a heavy fog with little to no visibility.

Joe looked out through his periscope, "Hell, you couldn't see your hand in front of your face in this pea soup—it's worse than England."

Cowboy had slept with his two-way on and now, eyes wide and face pale, he screamed, "ATTACK—Kraut SS infantry from the south and east. Joe reverse, position cannon left. Danny and Hero-----sighted in on anything that moves beyond the perimeter, automatic FIRE."

Cowboy shouted into the radio, "CCB and Headquarters Company are taking the brunt of this one. The damn Heinie's have been shelling us non-stop. Our infantry boys tried to advance but now have pulled back and have lit fires all around the perimeter; they're staying put in their foxholes."

Arnold instructed his tankers again, "Shoot anything that moves out there because it ain't one of ours!" All that night they roused from a semi-sleep by an occasional explosion or sound of a lone rifle and/or cannon shot.

When the fog lifted, they were relieved to discover the Germans had been held off; forty of them lay dead. For the rest of that day, the Allies received enemy mortar fire from the East, South and Northeast as well as some high velocity rocket fire, mostly from the South. They couldn't even scratch--they were pinned down and they knew it!

After being inside the tank for the last 36 hours straight, Danny Boy complained. "Hell, we can't even get out of this thing to take a pee. I guess we have to be glad we have a floor hatch to do our business in; how----ever, there is no way I'm hanging my butt over that hole! I'll hold it until my eyes turn brown!"

Cowboy laughed and slapped him on the back, "Cheer up Danny Boy—be thankful we are inside this tin can and not out in one of those damn cold foxholes! I got a feeling winter is coming early this year."

Cowboy watched as infantry regrouped in the daylight and fanned out to clear the Germans out of the woods. "Hell, those poor saps just get the Henie's out of those woods when they slither back in and our boys have to go back out after them. Those Krauts are persistent bastards; I'll say that for them!"

That afternoon, just after the crew finished a scrumptious meal of K-rations, all hell broke loose. The entire hill rocked with an explosion. Reb shouted, "What the hell? That sounded like a railway gun! That's shit for the birds--we need to get that thing taken out. The fog has lifted---it's cleared up, what about some damn air support in here to help us out just a tad?"

As if delivered upon request, they heard the low whine of P-47 Thunderbolts and subsequent sound of bombs dropping on enemy positions. Explosion after explosion rocketed through the woods and over Hill 375. Danny Boy smiled that toothy wide grin of his as he exclaimed, "Hell, Reb, ask and ye shall receive. What—do you have a direct line with the planes or the 'Man' upstairs?" They watched through their periscopes as fighter planes viciously attacked the Kraut defenses. Danny commented, "Holy shit, those Jugs have to be coming in only 100 yards out—kinda getting up close and personal, don't ya think? Just hope to hell they don't mistake us for the Krauts!"

Joe quipped, "Well Danny Boy, they are doing what they do best—look at all the Heinie equipment burning and nobody is shooting at us right now, either. If any of those Krauts are left, they are probably high-tailing it back to their pillboxes." Joe looked through the periscope again. "I feel half blind inside this tin can--- wish to hell we could see around us more, makes me squirrely! Hey, does anybody else think that these German soldiers we are seeing now seem disorganized and messed up? For sure, there are plenty of them, and they must have some leaders with some brains, but these troops just seem to be charging with no plan--not properly field trained. They don't compare with the Krauts we ran up against in Normandy—those boys were SS troops."

Danny replied, "Yeah—most of these dummkopfs can't even shoot straight. Not to change the subject, but this fight on Hill 375 has been about as bad as the one CCR had between Paris and Conde—you know, the one around Remy. Remember when headquarters ordered them to move through enemy territory at night? Hell, those Krauts used flares, mortars, bazookas— everything they had on our boys and they took it in the shorts. That night-fighting is useless plus it gives me the heebie jeebies! I wish to hell we would get out of here and back across the border."

Joe shot back, "You got that right. I'm ready to get out of Germany and the sooner the better."

Arnold switched on the auxiliary generator, the Homelite[28] or Little Joe as the tankers called it. Immediately Reb started bitching, "Gol damn it, do you have to turn that thing on again? I hate the smell and like we needed more noise in this tin can—I'm gonna be deaf if and when I ever get back home."

Commander Kessel replied, "Yeah, it's time to turn it back on-- we need to back our battery up. We won't need it for long and the good news is boys---we just got orders to head back towards the border and the crossing at Wallendorf tomorrow! They are sending up a couple of reinforcement patrols to get us off this damn hill."

Shortly before dawn, the patrols consisting of Task Force tanks and infantry reached CCB. At 2100 hours on 21 Sept., CCB and CCB Task Force began to move back down the hill through the corridor Task Force Anderson had cleared. They encountered light small-arms fire and sporadic artillery fire until they began to cross the Roer River at Wallendorf. Commander Kessel's Tank #2736 was second in the column as they moved in formation, fording the river.

Colonel Cole from CCR stood knee deep in the river guiding the entire command across. The tankers had been told to watch out for any deep holes in the crossing. The tankers were in such a hurry to get across that most of them didn't recognize the colonel. The tanker in front of the WRATH called out to the officer in the river, "Hey buddy, where's that deep hole?"

Col. Cole responded, "Hell, I don't know!"

Not realizing who he was talking to, the disgusted tanker yelled back, "Well, you're' a hell of a road guide!"

Commander Kessel has just guided his tank across the river when suddenly enemy fire began to rain down on them from the woods back behind them. The column was moving as fast as they could. Suddenly, behind them, FA and infantry spotted four Tiger tanks on the German side of the river. The FA (field artillery) began firing on the Germans trying to distract them from the vulnerable tanks in the middle of the river. The Germans continued to pepper the retreating Task Force column with artillery.

Danny Boy was using his machine gun to return small arms fire along the Roer River bank, "Take that you SOBs---we got more where that came from. You are not gonna stop us from headin' back—we deserve some long R & R! Let's get across this damn river; make is snappy, Ladies!" For good measure, he strafed the area where the flashes of gunfire came from the woods. The Germans launched flares that lit up the inky pre-dawn sky lit up like the Fourth of July.

As he often did, commander Kessel opened the turret hatch to stick his head out just enough to get a good 'bead' on the enemy tanks. Kneeling on the chair, he called for a calculated strike. "Hero swing that cannon 45 degrees to the right and give that Kraut Tiger over there some grief with a damn HE shell, aim low for his treads. FIRE! FIRE again!"

Without warning, in a split second, an incinerating roar filled their world; sight and sound ceased to exist as everything shuttered and went white hot. It was as though the last molecules of oxygen were sucked from the Tank Commander's lungs. Arnold was semi-conscious of being pulled against his will through a sucking vacuum, out of the hatch. There was no other sense but an all-consuming reverberation of the bellowing growl which devoured him as he was ejected through the open turret hatch like a rag doll. The white hot light swallowed him whole, followed by absolute, blessed darkness and silence. Later he would remember the odd sensation of being carried through the woods on his back with the fluttering leaves silhouetted against the morning sky. Then, everything went black as tank Commander Kessel was swallowed up in a swirling, inky vortex.

Chapter Twelve

"THE HELL OF IT ALL"

"War will end when enough people die."

Lovell, Wyoming – 3 October, 1944: Jake Kessel hurried across the living room to answer the insistent knock on the front door. When he opened it, he froze. After closing the front door, he paused, took a deep breath and walked slowly back toward the kitchen where Raisa was washing the breakfast dishes. She turned when she heard him come into the room and asked, "Who was that at the front door just now?" The words no sooner were out of her mouth when her brain registered the look on Jake's face, and then her eyes fell on the manila envelope in his hand. It was a telegram.

Jake caught her as her knees buckled. "Here Raisa, let me help you to the table, sit down and I'll read the telegram." Jake sat down across from Raisa as he unfolded the official notification.

October 1944 ---Western Union Telegram
Mr. and Mrs. Jacob Kessel:
*   Regret to inform, your son, S/Sgt. Arnold Kessel was wounded in action five days ago in the performance of service to his country. For national security, we cannot divulge further information at this time. He is in a hospital in Paris recovering from wounds.*
*   The Adjutant General*

"Raisa, Arnold is alive! He's in a hospital in Paris. It doesn't sound like his wounds are serious because they expect him to recover. He's safe and alive---that's all we know right now and for that we are thankful." Jake pulled Raisa to her feet and held her as they cried together with relief----their son was alive.

~~~~~~~~~

Paris, France----10 October, 1944; 108ᵗʰ General Hospital: Trauma ward head nurse, Carol Bentley was making her nightly rounds of the trauma area of the ICU ward in the Paris Field Hospital. These men were the long-term cases they couldn't handle in the emergency triages on the front line. She stood at the foot of S/Sgt. Arnold Kessel's bed and examined the information on his daily chart. A frown crossed her brow as she looked at the night nurse's notes. Carol replaced the clip board on the hook at the foot of SSG Kessel's bed and walked around to stand at the bedside. She watched him for a moment, noting the normal rhythmic pace of his chest rising and falling and how his closed eyelids fluttered but did not open. She reached down and seizing his wrist, she felt his pulse. *All his vitals are good and improving, his concussion and other minor physical wounds from the blast have healed but he hasn't woken. It's almost like he doesn't want to. It's like he knows what happened and he is willing himself to stay in the oblivious peace of sleep. We always wonder if the semi-conscious can hear and IF Sgt. Kessel can hear he already knows what happened—even more reason for him to elect to stay where he is. He is going to need a lot of time and help emotionally, to handle everything that happened.*

Nurse Bentley began to gently massage Sgt. Kessel's palm and wrist and then grasp tightly his hand as if to shake it. She spoke softly but urgently, "Sgt. Kessel, you are in a hospital. Sgt. Kessel, can you open your eyes? Please squeeze my hand if you can hear me." She waited for a response and then tried again and again as she had for the past three days; she was beginning to wonder if he would ever wake up. On the fourth day, she was going through her routine, a little more forceful this time. "Sgt. Kessel, I want you to open your eyes. Look at me! You have to try to open your eyes. I'm right here beside you. You are in a hospital in Paris, you've been wounded. Arnold, open--open your eyes."

Somewhere deep in the healing mental fog, Arnold was semi-conscious of a garbled sound, a sound that seemed to be coming from far off or like it was underwater. The sound rolled around in his ears, bouncing off his damaged ear drums, trying to connect to his bruised brain. It became louder and louder until he slowly opened his eyes. Startled by his surroundings, the sergeant's body jerked and went rigid with obvious alarm.

Nurse Bentley laid her open palm on the patient's cheek and spoke softly, "Sgt. Kessel, it's okay, you're okay. Please relax and just breathe for me, I'm right here, I won't leave you. My name is Carol---I'm right here. Don't close your eyes---stay with me, look at me."

Arnold tried to focus on the blurred face, on the soft chocolate brown eyes, focus on the sweet, compassionate voice. He blinked his eyes several times, trying to clear his vision as his hearing gradually became less garbled and his eyesight sharpened. Tears rolled from his ice-blue eyes and over his prominent Germanic cheek bones. He couldn't understand why he was crying, nothing made sense. His mind was flooded with questions-- - *What am I doing in a hospital? Where am I? Where is my crew, my boys, my tank? What the hell happened?"*

Nurse Bentley instinctively knew what was happening to Sgt. Kessel now that he was awake---questions. She called for a nurse's aide who was nearby, "Martha, please hurry and find Dr. Renee Markham, tell her that Sgt. Kessel is awake and I think she should be here, he is going to need her."

Chief Psychologist Renee Markham was one of the most respected English psychologists practicing in Paris and they were lucky to have her at this particular hospital. Her renowned specialty was working with battle trauma. It was her job to help soldiers cope with horrific circumstances and hopefully to heal enough to return them to the war. She had been watching this case and knew she would have her work cut out for her. If and when he woke, Sgt. Arnold Kessel had a very steep mountain to climb if he was going to leave the shocking circumstances of what had happened behind, at least for now. She was fully aware that his experience most probably would never leave the recesses of his mind, how could it? All she could do was to try and help him understand, to accept it all and to work through it.

Dr. Markham pushed back from her desk; she walked out of her office and briskly down the corridor toward the trauma ward. Upon entering, she saw head nurse Carol Bentley standing beside Sgt. Kessel, holding his hand and speaking softly to him. Carol turned when she saw Dr. Markham and stepped toward her with hand out, "Oh thank you for coming so quickly. He is awake and coming around nicely. His vitals are all good; his hearing is around 80% and improving. His minor physical wounds have healed over the past two weeks and now we have his emotional wounds to deal with. He hasn't asked about the crew yet. I wanted you to be here with him when that happens. I have other rounds to make so I'll leave you now, unless you want me to stay."

Renee Markham took Nurse Bentley's place beside the bed as she reached for Sgt. Kessel's hand. She did a quick mental evaluation of him---tall, blond, intelligent icy blue eyes, strong lean body—he was a very good looking man on the outside. Her job was to help fix the inside of his mind—they would get to that after she answered his questions and explained why he was here. She said a silent prayer, *Please dear God, help me to help this man make his way through understanding and accepting what has happened. Help me to find the healing words.*

Sgt. Kessel studied the woman standing next to his bed as he attempted to speak for the first time in weeks, "Wa-where is n-n-nurse?"

Dr. Markham replied, "Sgt. Kessel, nurse Bentley had other patients to look after and she asked me to sit with you, I'm Dr. Renee Markham, chief of psychology. You've been asleep for over a week and we are quite happy to see you open your eyes. How do you feel?"

Arnold looked up at the doctor, a million questions coursing through his mind as he reached to swipe the tears from his cheeks. "I c-can't think too good, every-thing blurry, can't r-remember much." He straightened up and his eyes widened, "You're a doctor---of psychology? Isn't that something to do with the head, with mental problems? What the hell is going on?"

Dr. Markham moved closer as she picked up his hand and held it in hers. "May I call you Arnold?" Her patient nodded his head, and she continued, "Arnold, I am here to help you remember what happened. But I think before we talk, I want you moved to a private room where we can have time alone to work through your recovery. I'll be back to see you in a couple of hours when you are settled in your new room. Try to lie back, relax and rest assured that I will be working very closely with you. You are going to be fine, Arnold, just fine!" Dr. Markham injected a mild sedative into the arm of her patient before she left the ward

Arnold watched Dr. Markham walk confidently from the intensive ward and out the door. He lay back on his pillow and stared out the window across from his bed. *Why am I here? What happened? Where is my crew? I have so many questions and no answers. Nobody is telling me anything. If only I could remember, I just need to remember. Sleepy, feeling sleepy.*

Arnold closed his eyes and fell into a fitful sleep. Images walked in and out of a fog. He saw it again, a beautiful brunette in a print dress, standing under a large willow tree. *Who was it? There was an older man with a bald head and woman with an apron tied around her waist; the little toddler with blond curly hair; the tall dark headed man on a tractor. A team of guys were playing basketball and they called themselves the Bulldogs. Danny Boy---who is Danny Boy? A Tiger tank, the treads growling and clanking; kept coming and coming---the white flash and then falling down, down, down.*

Arnold sat up, sweat bathed his body. He shook his head and called for the nurse. Two nurses rushed over to his bed and settled him back down. "Sgt. Kessel, we just received orders to move you to a private room. We are going to move you in the bed, so hang on, here we go now."

~~~~~~~~~

Two hours later, Arnold was adjusting to his new room. He had asked to get out of bed, but the nurse said they would need a doctor's order for him to do that. So Arnold lay back and closed his eyes for what seemed like only a moment when suddenly he felt a soft hand on his wrist. Arnold's ice-blue eyes opened and he looked into the attractive face of forty-year old Dr. Renee Markham.

"Well, Arnold, how do you like this room? I must say you have a wonderful view of the Eiffel Tower in the distance. Have you been in Paris before?"

Arnold asked for the head of bed to be cranked up to a sitting position. He looked out the window as he thought for a moment, and then replied, "Yeah, after Normandy and the Falaise Gap, our Combat Command 'B' – we got to parade through Paris in our tanks. We didn't get to stop but that was a bit of fun, for sure. At least we got to see a few of the famous sights."

Dr. Markham continued asking Arnold questions, moving him along the route of battles until they crossed into Germany as a reconnaissance task force. She noticed that every time the word 'tank' came into play, Arnold began to move around in his bed and she suspected he was having some unconscious flash backs. She moved closer to the bed, waiting for the crucial questions that lurked just under the surface.

Arnold didn't understand why the doctor's questions and her talking to him was upsetting; he couldn't put two and two together, until she asked him about his tank---Wrath. Arnold's face reflected what had just registered in his mind. "Where is my crew? What happened to my tanker boys?" Arnold paused as images flashed through his mind. "There was a Tiger tank across the river, it was firing at us and Danny Boy was yelling and swearing at the Germans. Joe was driving like hell, zigzagging--trying to get us out of the river, out of range while Reb was loading a shell. Hero was sighting in on the area. I opened the turret hatch to get a better location of the Tigers firing at us. I'd just stuck my head out---- then, nothing!"

Arnold stopped, his face was white as the sheet, sweat beaded up on his forehead. Dr. Markham stood beside the bed and placed her hand on Arnold's shoulder, "Easy now commander, easy. It's coming back, isn't it? Just take it easy, this is going to be rough but I am here---it's my job to get you through this."

Arnold looked up at the doctor, "Doc, where are my men? Where is my tanker crew? I remember an explosion—my ears, all so loud, oh my ears. I felt like I was being squeezed in a giant fist, an-and I was flying and then nothing. I remember nothing more until I woke up here. WHERE are my damn men? Tell me, NOW!"

Dr. Markham looked out the window, then back at Arnold, "Sgt. Kessel, I think you know the answer to that question. They are gone; they didn't make it out of the tank, it exploded and burned. You---the explosion blew you out of the open turret hatch, and you've been unconscious for over a week. You had some minor wounds but nothing broken. A field ambulance transported you here to Paris."

Arnold put his face in his hands and began to sob loudly. Dr. Markham called for a sedative. She sat on the bed as she injected him with the tranquilizer, then put her arms around him, holding him, "Arnold, it was over in seconds, they didn't suffer. The explosion killed them instantly before the tank burned. They never knew what hit them."

Hearing the words again, 'the tank burned,' was too much as realization hit him, hard. Arnold pushed the doctor aside and tried to get out of bed. He was wild with grief and disbelief. "NO, NO, NO, you are lying. My boys, my crew can't be dead. I can't believe that---that's the shits, the damn shits! We were so good together, we were a technical machine—the five of us have been through so much. Why did they die and not me? Why the hell didn't I die too?"

Dr. Markham watched her patient begin to relax as the sedative slowly took effect. "Arnold, I see here that you are a Christian, a Lutheran, and you were carrying a small Bible. None of us can understand or explain why one person lives and another dies, even when it's someone right next to you, even when it's someone you care about and love. I am quite sure that you are asking yourself 'how' you are going to have the courage to go back out there, to climb inside another tank with another tank crew and do it all over again. I want you to think about Isaiah 6:8. Are you familiar with the verse? It goes like this: "And the Lord said, "Whom shall I send?" The answer came from the crowd---'Here I am Lord, send me, send me."

Dr. Markham didn't wait for her patient to respond, but added, "Arnold, I want you to lean on your faith in God, he isn't through with you yet. He obviously has other plans for your life; you are alive for a reason---which shall be made clear to you some day. Some believe that we really don't have choices in life, that we don't control any of it, that it's all pre-scripted. None of us know when it will be our time, even me. You and your crew were obviously in the middle of a war, a terrible battle, and the odds were much higher than if I were to drive down the streets of Paris to my apartment. But the end of our lives can come quickly, and often it's when we least expect it." The doctor thought about Arnold's chart, "I noticed from your chart that when you were beginning to wake up, you would say over and over, 'make it quick, that's all I ask make it quick'. Do you know what you were referring to?"

Arnold looked up at the doctor through sleepy tearful eyes, "Yeah Doc, that's my one constant prayer to God---that if he can't protect me, and my number is up, to make it quick! That blast was damn quick, but he didn't take me, he took my boys!" His eyelids closed over his blue eyes and his head gently fell to the side as the sedative took effect.

Dr. Renee Markham rose from the bed, instructing the nurses to monitor Staff Sgt. Kessel and when he woke, to notify her immediately. She knew her job was not finished; they had only just begun the journey. He realized now, what had happened, hopefully next would come acceptance and recovery from the horrific ordeal he had experienced. She knew only too well that now it was up to her and her patient to continue to work through it all.

~~~~~~~~

1 week later: Arnold stood, looking out of the hospital window as the fall storm blew the withering red and gold leaves from the perfect rows of stately Linden trees as icy rain drops splashed against the windows. *Thanks to the daily therapy sessions with Dr. Markham, I feel like I'm getting a handle on my feelings and dealing with what happened. But, dear God, please help me, I still can't wrap my head around the fact that Joe, Reb, Hero, and Danny Boy are all gone. Now, Headquarters wants me to go back out there, to take on another tank, another crew and continue on because it's war. Sometimes I feel like I am going nuts, like this is all a bushwa dream, and then I wake up and it's not a dream—it's my damn life and I don't have a choice.*

Arnold sat down at one of the desks in the patient's lounge and took out some paper and a pen. *I guess I better write my folks before I head back to the front.*

Paris, France
October 20, 1944
Dear Mom and Dad,

Thanks for all of your prayers as well as the letters and cards you and the family sent to me while I've been in the hospital. I am doing much better now, thanks to the doctors and all. It was a rough go for a while, but I have an understanding of it all now and am ready to 'get back on the horse'---just like you always taught me, Dad.

I have my orders and I leave tomorrow for eastern France where I will be given a new Ford Sherman tank and a new crew. HQ is giving us a week or two to train together and I hope that will be enough. I also hope I don't get so attached to these guys as I did with the others. It's just that when you work with the same fellas every day for several months, you get pretty comfortable with each other. This hospital and the staff have been terrific and they got me patched up pretty darn good. This one doctor is a psychologist. Dr. Renee Markham is English, like Norrie's family. She really helped me sort through my feelings and anger---a big help.

Oh--- my Combat Command commander LTC. LeRoy Anderson took the time to pay me a visit in the hospital. He was swell; he told me that all the fellas—the other tankers and our married infantry missed me; they wished me well and want me to hurry to get back and hook up with them. He presented me with another [29]Bronze Star for the battle around Wallendorf, Germany. I'll never understand awards for being in battle and shooting someone. It's just not like in school, when you did well and the teacher gave us gold stars. This 2nd Bronze Star goes in the bottom of my duffel with the other one.

Well, I don't have much more to say except that I love and miss you all and we are all hoping and praying that this damn war will be over soon and us boys can come home. You haven't forgotten how to cook, have you, Mom? Keep an eye out for my girl—she's pretty special to me.

Your loving son, Arnold

Arnold purposely omitted the details of being blown out of his tank and the fact that all of his crew perished except himself. *Mom and Dad don't need to know that, they will only worry more. Someday, maybe I will tell them. Right now I want to forget about that day. Right---I'll forget about that when hell freezes over!*

Commander Kessel stood in front of the mirror, adjusting his tie and new uniform. He'd lost more weight from lying in a hospital bed for two weeks. He was startled when Dr. Markham walked into the room. "My, oh my, don't you look handsome in your new uniform. How does it feel?"

Arnold turned and looked at his doctor, "Feels about the same as before except it's looser! I guess I'll have to eat more mashed potatoes and gravy, get my weight back up there. Say, Doc—I know you aren't supposed to fraternize with your patients, but when I walk out that door, I won't be your patient any longer and I have one more night in Paris before I hop a truck back to the front. I was wondering, ahhh---since it's my last night and all, would you have dinner with me?"

"Before you say no, I just want to add that I have a serious girl back home, but I would like to thank you for all you did for me by buying you dinner. The other part is that I'm in Paris, France – the city of lights--and taking you out to dinner would mean a heck of a lot to me. How about it, dinner---just you and me? Dr. Renee Markham smiled as she reached out and touched her patients shoulder. "I was never one to pass up a free meal with a handsome man. Would you like me to choose a quiet, very French restaurant? I could be ready around 8 p.m. after rounds---does that work for you? There's a special little restaurant on the rue de Lappe, a favorite of mine, where we could have a nice glass of wine, quiet conversation, and some great French food." She began to walk away, then turned, "Oh, and it's my treat!"

~~~~~~~~~

Arnold rode reluctantly in the back of a transport truck along with other soldiers who had been released from hospitals and were heading back to the front. He felt guilty that he had no visible wounds like some of the guys did; he carried most of his wounds inside where nobody could see them—but he felt their presence every damn day and he knew he always would.

November 1, 1944: The troop transport dropped Arnold and a couple other soldiers off as close as possible to their bivouac area near the German-Luxembourg border, northwest of Wallendorf, Germany.

The first night back, he bunked in a Quonset hut knowing that would probably be the last bed he would sleep in for a while if the battalion was moving out. After chow the next morning, he reported for duty and Col. Anderson introduced him to his new tank and its crew.

Col. Anderson said, "Commander Kessel, this is your tank #2736---it's the same number as your previous tank. You and your crew are welcome to give it a name if you so choose. Now, I'd like to introduce you to four guys who are going to be your new tank mates."

Arnold felt his stomach convulse and he struggled to breathe. *Dear God, don't let me puke now---not in front of my new crew. Give me strength to handle it like a man, like a soldier!*

Col. Anderson pointed to the four soldiers, "This chap is your driver, Sgt. Peter Thomas; over here is your assistant driver, Miguel Meste; then your loader, Robert Reilly; and finally your gunner, Hans Schmidt!" Each man stepped forward and shook Arnold's hand; Arnold looked each one in the eye, mentally sizing each up. He felt numb, like he was going through the motions. He hoped he wasn't coming across as a head case to his crew. He was well aware they were all watching him like a bunch of hawks.

Col. Anderson said, "Just for your information, Commander Kessel, you don't have a totally green crew as would be expected this late into the war. P.T. and Hans have seen plenty of action and have transferred from other tanks--they are well experienced. As far as the other two men, well, I'll just say that you have your work cut out for you. I'll let you boys get acquainted with each other and your tank. I expect you'll be wantin' to take it out and run through a few field exercises before we get in the mix again. From the looks of things, our Task Force is going to be stuck right here on the border since being relieved by an Infantry Battalion. Don't expect much action for a couple of weeks at least. At Ease!"

Once Commander Kessel and his new crew were settled in their Sherman tank, Arnold said, "It's up for a vote, but I like to have an easy go-to name for myself and for each of my crew. It's pretty important not to have any names that might be confused with something else when we are in the middle of a battle and the fur is flying. For instance the last name Meyer might sound like

FIRE when we have jumped in a battle. I'm known as Cowboy because I'm from Wyoming. So, let's go around and you tell me what tag name you want to be called by our crew.

Peter Thomas spoke first, "Why don't ya all call me by my initials, PT."

Miguel raised his hand and said, "My friends call me Miggie, so that would work for me, Cowboy!"

Robert gave a half smile as he said, "I'll respond to just plain Bobby."

Cowboy looked at Hans Schmidt. "I would guess you have German background like I do, am I right Hans? Sprechen Sie Deutsch? What would you like us boys to call you?"

Hans' eyes lit up as he replied, "Ein wenig Deutsch – just a little German, enough to get me in trouble, or at least, to know what the Krauts are saying about us. I was born in Madison, Wisconsin, and my folks spoke German when I was a kid so I picked some up along the way. You all can call me Hans, if that works? Are your folks German too, Cowboy?"

Arnold laughed as the crew relaxed. "Ja—Ja--Das ist gute, Hans – Ich bin Deutsch (*I am German*), in fact, my mother's maiden name was Schmidt---we might be related! So, boys, the other thing---do you want to name our tank—you know give it a special name? How do you boys feel about that?"

Arnold paused, then thought again, "Oh yeah, also--you might as well know that I, personally don't take the name of the Lord in vain. I swear plenty, but in case you might wonder about why I don't use certain words—that's the reason. I know every once in a while something might slip—like when the shit hits the fan, if you know what I mean. I'm not telling you tankers what you can and can't say—I'm just saying what I don't say."

Jack spoke up, "Hell Cowboy, no skin off my butt; I appreciate you tellin us tho. I have a suggestion for a tank name, what about Avenger?"

Miggie spoke up, "How about--Kraut Killer, I kinda like that name?"

Hans laughed then said, "Are you nuts? That would be like putting a target on our backside—ours would be the first tank they would light up, just to prove us wrong. A lot of those Heinie's speak and read English pretty damn well."

Arnold flinched at the thought of a tank on fire, and the tankers didn't miss the look that clouded over his eyes as Hans said, "Aw hell, commander, I apologize. I didn't think about what I was sayin'. Let's go with *Avenger*---that's pretty good."

Miggie piped up, "Come on, Cowboy, you gotta just put all that other stuff behind you and not let it bother you. That's what you gotta do, and better sooner than later, I'd say. No need to take your wrath out on us."

Beads of sweat popped up on his forehead as Commander Kessel stiffened and moved menacingly close to Miggie. Every muscle in his body was on alert as the memories of his tankers from 'Wrath' screamed in his mind. His bloodshot eyes bugged from his blanched face as he grabbed Miggie by the arm and growled, "If one more damn person says that to me, I am not going to be responsible for what I do. Don't push me, dammit---just don't f-----g push me, got that? And, for your information, Wrath was the name of my other tank, you know--the one I lost along with my entire crew!"

The crew was startled by the vehement response by their new commander. Nobody had expected to hear Cowboy use the 'f' word. That was their first clue as to how bad he was hurting. Nobody uttered a sound as Arnold shook his head and slapped his knees with open palms, stood and then moved toward the open hatch, "Okay then, you boys get that name changed; find a few sandbags to throw on the front and sides of our home away from home. I'll be back in an hour or so."

Commander Kessel pulled himself up through the open turret hatch and slipped off the tank hull. He didn't look back, left, or right; he was shaking like a leaf as he made a casual bee line toward a parked half-track at the edge of camp. Once out of sight, he threw his back against the vehicle as gut-wrenching silent sobs erupted from deep within. *How in the hell am I going to pull this off? How am I going to be an aggressive leader and go into battle without all this memory? Help me God, please help m; I miss those men, my boys so damn much! Once we are out there and in battle, I can't be melting down like some prissy little girl. Please Lord give me the strength to lead these men—to keep them and me safe. I know there are things I can't control, but please watch over us. This I ask through Jesus name, Amen.*

As he straightened up and opened his eyes, Arnold felt a particular kind of peace flow over him and he knew God had listened.

Chapter Thirteen

"THE HURTGEN FOREST"[30]

"Blood will have blood!"

Macbeth, by William Shakespeare

The Hurtgen Forest: *"An Allied defeat of the first magnitude".*
19 September – 16 December, 1944.

NOTE: The dark cave-- called the Hurtgenwald Forest (star) is located at the top and to the center of the Ardennes

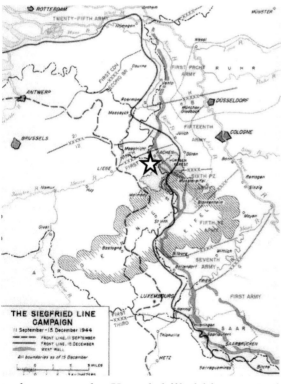

THE SIEGFRIED LINE
CAMPAIGN
11 September – 15 December 1944

Forest--on the Siegfried Line. At this time, portions of the Ninth and First Armies were in heavy battle around Aachen, Germany, directly above the Hurtgen Forest.

The Fifth Armored Division, 81st Tank Battalion, CCB, spent the first part of November gearing up for something; nobody was sure just what it was. They spit and polished their equipment while tank commander Kessel drilled his new tank crew until they were like a unified machine.

Arnold couldn't get the words out of his head, 'Here I am, send me, send me." The Bible verse had become a tormentor to him and he couldn't shake it. On the other hand, Arnold was satisfied and confident that they were ready for anything, and that was a good thing. From 1 Nov. to 10 Nov., the 81st was not involved in any direct conflict. They were in support of their married Infantry and FA (field artillery) securing crossroads. There wasn't a day that went by when they didn't hear some degree of distant thump, thump-thump---shelling. Bobby quipped, "That shelling is getting on my nerves; I guess we don't have much to worry about, just as long as it doesn't get any louder."

Tank 2736, 'Avenger', and five other Sherman tanks stood watch as their Mortar Platoon, attached to the 15th Armored Infantry, formed a six gun battery and pounded the front line at Hoffen, Germany, right smack dab on the Siegfried Line. There was a constant barrage of firing at significant targets. PT yelled, "Give em the whole nine yards boys---see how they like a little of their own medicine!"

The Avenger was among two companies of (28) tanks who were called up to the front line. They used tank dozers to dig them in on the firing line to protect them from enemy artillery as well as attain maximum firing elevation. They rotated every two days and most tankers considered this light duty.

Commander Kessel briefed his crew, "Our troops up north in Aachen are catching hell and they're counting on us to keep these Krauts busy, right here in our sector; they don't need any more Germans up there. High command has pulled an entire GAF infantry division, another separate infantry regiment, a machine gun battalion, as well as several medium and heavy artillery battalions to go in at Aachen. Plus, we got our own problems with a Panzer Brigade as well as a healthy portion of a Panzer Lehr Division---all waiting to have a go around with us. So, we have any questions, Ladies?"

Miggie spoke up, "Yeah, ahhh—so, how many Kraut tanks do you think are over there?"

Arnold replied, "Oh, I'd say there are about 100 German tanks plus infantry! We are gonna have some fighter support in this—those boys are real good at taking out enemy tanks."

17 Nov. 1944: Gloomy, cold autumn rain began to blow around them. The damp chill invaded their uniforms clear to the bone. It was coming down at a steady pace now, falling from the low-hanging slate-colored clouds. The icy rain clung to the low heavy-looming evergreen branches, saturating everything. In the chow tent that evening, Commander Kessel announced, "We just received the orders we've been waiting for---the 81st is heading to Roetgen, Germany, located south/central in the Hurtgen Forest. We bivouac two miles west of the village of Roetgen; any questions?"

Miggie spoke up, "What in the hell are we supposed to do in Roetgen blooming Germany? Twiddle our thumbs?"

Out of patience, Kessel snapped, "We will do what the hell our orders tell us to do, and as of this minute we have orders to go to Roetgen. Move it out!" The column rolled through Weismes, Malmedy, and then Eupen, Belgium; they passed through Raeren before bivouacking just two miles to the west of Roetgen.

At first, this section of the Hurtgen Forest seemed a little warmer than it had been back in Belgium, which—they hoped would be a good thing. But now there were patches of snow on the ground in the forest and it had melted enough to form puddles and thick mud—not such a good thing. The soldiers were forced to cut branches from trees and pile them onto the half-frozen mud and water, then erect their tents on top of that. There was little to no battle action, and so they spent most of their days corduroying (laying cut pine trees across the road base) the roads to create a more secure road for the tanks and heavier vehicles. They maintained their equipment, smoked more cigarettes than was good for them, played a few hands of cards, rolled some dice, and got on each other's nerves.

Commander Kessel addressed the crew, "We are sitting here in reserve. Most of you know a bloody battle has been raging in the Hurtgen since 19 Sept. ----damn near three months and now they are sending us in to mop up. We all know how the Germans come right back into an area we have just cleaned out, so I guess you could say, we have some cleanup work to do. I hear that eventually we are going to be sent to the Roer River which is just under ten miles away from where we are right now, but to get there we have to go through the Hurtgen Forest. Hear say is, the First Army has had over 10,000 soldiers killed in this place already, and what gets my goat is that we will be facing third-string Kraut troops commanded by first-string German officers. Our commanders are adamant about us fighting in this meat-grinder, even with considerable opposition. So, get your guns and shit together because eventually it'll be out turn in that dark icy hell!"

"By the way, for your information, this here Ruhr River --- when it runs through France and Belgium it's called the 'Ruhr' River. When we cross into Germany it will be called the Rur River. I just thought I should mention that so you boys don't get confused when you see signs and stuff. Hell, you know, let's keep it simple and refer to the damn river as the Roer. We can try and pronounce stuff the way the people do over here, but it gets damn confusing. We'll call it something we can remember—so it's the Roer River."

~~~~~~~

Tank Commander Kessel walked across the soft spongy forest bed of needles and decaying leaves. He looked up through the canopy of trees and watched the gray clouds billowing and moving. *Winter? They are sending us into this damn thick forest in the winter---it's going to be a nightmare, I can just feel it. What in the hell are the brass thinking? This isn't tank country. Hell of a thing!*

9 Dec. 1944: The dank forest floor was covered in leaves and pine needles, creating a perfect hiding place for the trip wires of the diabolical 'Schu-mines' (*Schutzenmine*) the Krauts had peppered the forest with. When the trip wires were activated the mines detonated into the air, exploding at crotch height. The American troops soon discovered that a tripped mine alerted the Krauts, of their position and they could expect a barrage of

sporadic mortar and artillery fire. The German shells were designed to shred the tops of the trees, send down a rain of knife-sharp slices of wood as well as metal shrapnel.

Commander Kessel stood in the open hatch as they rolled through the confining woods. *These tanks are in a no win situation. The only thing we are good for is cover for the infantry. We can't turn, can't move like we like—we're sitting ducks, a rolling tin can loaded with a ton of high explosives and just as much gasoline.* Arnold didn't share his thoughts with his crew, his job was to lead and to keep the morale of his crew up, not shoot it down.

Holding their new orders in his hand, Commander Kessel addressed his crew. "This here piece of paper is our one-way ticket through the Hurtgen Forest! It sounds pretty simple—we move through the forest, swing down and take the town of Schmidt, then clear the Monschau (corridor) and advance onto the Ruhr River. We need to protect the Ruhr Dam---if the Krauts take that they'll release all that water downstream and stop us flat from crossing into Germany. The direct route to that dam is through the Hurtgen Forest."

"Intelligence indicates that the fortifications in the forest are manned mostly by old men plus a few younger ones, with a minimum of training. Be very aware that they have the whole area is mined; they are as thick as mushrooms. Follow the man in front of you if you don't want to get blown to pieces. " Cowboy shifted uncomfortably in his tank seat and continued, "It shouldn't be too bad. Hell, like I said, our guys have been in those woods for three months killin' Germans—what can be left for us? Any questions if not, we move out at 0400 hours."

What intelligence didn't pass on was that tanks could only move forward on a limited number of the narrow existing logging roads. The Germans had set the stage, this was their ball game and they called the rules. German artillery was pre-targeted in on those debris-covered roads carpeted with mines set just under the surface as well 50 feet on either side. In some instances, when the roads were impassable, special equipment had to be brought in to doze and blast passages through the dense conifers so the tanks could move through the forest; the hairpin curves and precipitous drop-offs were another matter. It was a known fact that American forces had been fighting and dropping like flies ahead of the task force for a couple of months. It was also obvious that they hadn't taken the time to clean up after themselves as destroyed equipment and debris clogged the passageways. They had been busy fighting for their lives and hadn't taken time to clean up after themselves.

The narrow roads were lethal for tanks whose preferred battle ground is open terrain, not dense forest or narrow mountain roads where they can't turn the tank or the cannon. Because of the thick forest canopy, American fighter planes couldn't see the area below well enough to drop bombs or to strafe German fortifications, so they were no help. The Americans in the Hurtgen Forest were pretty much on their own, left to fight and suffer in their own freezing, dark, and bloody hell with one hand tied behind their backs.

10 Dec. 1944: So far, the forest around Rotgen was still intact with thickly-planted 75 – 100 foot conifers; there were only narrow, haphazardly laid logging roads to maneuver through and around the trees. Commander Kessel and most of the other tankers rode with their hatches open, inhaling the crisp smell of molding leaves, pine needles, and damp wood. They couldn't hear much over the constant growling clank of the Sherman tank treads as they rambled over the mud covered forest road where the sun's rays didn't penetrate the canopy. The army moved in a constant twilight effect that persisted all day, every day. There was no way in hell they were going to accurately shoot artillery through all those trees and they all knew it.

PT wove the Sherman tank around the narrow mountain roads, trying to avoid going over the edge and down into a ravine. Finally with his nerves getting the best of him he growled, "What the hell are we getting ourselves into here? This is crazy---what jackass gave the order to fight in this kind of an area? This isn't tank battle ground, that's for damn sure! I don't like it one little bit---there's nowhere to turn. What the hell do we do if a Tiger comes around that next corner? Say our prayers! It won't matter one bit how much camouflage we have on this tank if we can't swing our cannon or get the hell off the road. Besides, this damn mud is clogging up the treads, it's up to our axles and—and, it's just a gol damn mess. Mountains, forests, roads with hairpin curves---this is no place to be fighting battles with tanks."

PT added, "I don't think we have to expect seeing too many generals or higher-ups in this hell hole. As soon as we were ordered in, they slammed the door and dropped the bar!"

The 81st Tank Battalion's CCB and CCR slogged their way through four miles of mud and tight roads before they called it a day. They pulled off the road in an abandoned logger's clearing where infantry previously cleared it of mines. Bobby opened his hatch and looked around, "Well damn, so far it hasn't been too bad. We haven't even seen a Kraut---they musta heard we was coming and hightailed it outta here!" He jumped off the tank and lit up a cigarette while PT pulled their tank to a stop in a narrow clearing.

Commander Kessel replied, "Don't be too sure of that Bobby---intelligence tells us to be on the watch for Kraut scout teams; they are on the move between 0300 and 0400 most every morning, checking us all out on the QT. If you think you see a

German, before you shoot just make damn sure it's not one of our guys taking a leak."

While they still had light, the soldiers began to dig in for the night, laying pine boughs over the cold wet ground under their tents. Bobby and Miggie elected to sleep out in a tent while Cowboy, PT and Hans took turns sleeping both inside and under the tank. When they turned the tank motors on to warm up, the transmission oil would stay warm for quite a while after the motor had been turned off---thus, it is was usually warmer under the tank than in it. Kessel said, "I don't like turning the tank on any more than we absolutely have to—the Krauts can get a bead on us when they hear our engines. It makes me damn jumpy!"

It was a cold, dark and wet night with a steady drizzle that soon turned to snow. The wind picked up around midnight and became so strong it broke off a pine tree which crashed over onto a company tent killing the two men inside, and that was only the first day. It was just the beginning of the constant bitter cold hell they would fight through.

11 Dec.: Before sunrise the next morning, the 81st was up and ready to get back on the slip and slide path HQ called a road. The predictable clouds were already moving back in as the 15th Infantry moved out on their own, their support tanks were momentarily immobilized. After an hour of maintenance, the tanks jumped off and caught up with the Infantry. When they crested the top of the hill and rounded the curve, they were stunned by the sight that lay in front of them. They'd all heard about the German shells that were rigged to explode at tree top so they'd shatter the

trees and rain down deadly sword-like splinters along with shrapnel—tree bursts.

Silhouetted like black warning skeletons of death against the morning sky. They were surrounded by what was once a dense and beautiful forest. It was one of those eerie moments most never forgot.

Han's eyes followed the haunting landscape as the platoon of tanks inched forward through what was once a beautiful forest. "Hell, it looks like a forest of giant toothpicks. I can't imagine the hell this musta like to be here when those Kraut rounds were going off and exploding those trees; the fellas under them were bombarded with wood splinters and shrapnel. I hope to hell we don't have to go through anything like that!"

Bobby said, "Hey Cowboy, when I jumped off to take a leak a minute ago, I thought I heard tanks rumbling and they weren't ours. Have we heard anything from recon yet as to where the Krauts are exactly?"

Commander Kessel got on the two-way and called the info in then waited for a reply. Turning to his crew he said, "Good job Reb—we DO have Kraut tanks and artillery about a mile up ahead. Our FA is going to shell them for about twenty minutes; in the meantime we keep rolling."

The tanks were moving up to support the 2nd battalion of the 330th Infantry Battalion. They had moved maybe a half mile and were passing through an open spot when out of nowhere their semi-quiet morning erupted into thunderous chaos. German mortar fire had just plowed up the fields around the town and was moving in their direction. A hidden German battalion opened up on them with high velocity artillery. Two tanks went up in flames almost immediately. Kessel shouted, "INSIDE the tank, NOW! Lock UP!" But he didn't need to waste his breath—his crew knew instinctively what to do.

Cowboy yelled, "Up ahead—take cover behind one of those destroyed houses in the village. We can't turn back—too damn many mines so we're between a rock and a hard place. I'm gonna call for air support since we are in the open." By 1300 hours, the American fighter planes had taken care of the Germans and CCB was able to get back on the road.

They hadn't been on the road five minutes when an explosion rocked the 'Avenger' as the tank in front of them hit a mine and was partially blown off the road. After a few minutes, Commander Kessel yelled, "PT---easy does it now—can you push that tank to the side of the road? It's kaput and everyone is out, the rest of us need to pass!"

They moved through the destroyed villages of Gerietere and then Hurtgen. The mortar and artillery fire was increasing as they inched their way through the scarred battle ground. They went about another half mile before coiling and bivouacking to  repair their damaged tanks. From then on, they fought one battle after another, took one foot of ground at a time—all the time, every day.

In the predawn hours the battalion began to stir. Dense fingers of fog invaded the inner sanctum of the dense forest. Hans commented, "Hell we can't see the Krauts in this soup and they can't see us either---don't see how either one of us can move in this stuff. At least we gave as good as we got yesterday, that felt pretty damn good"

The tanks stayed put—while motor pool repaired the damaged equipment; their married infantry was already on the move before dawn. The mail wagon finally caught up to them and they all had a letter or two, even a couple of packages made it through. Commander Kessel wrote to his sweetheart and his family when he could, but lately they had been busy just trying to stay alive. If anyone had written a letter, then they hung on to it until the mail wagon came through; it wasn't like there was a post office on the next corner.

It had snowed another inch or two during the night making it slow going for the married 15th Infantry as the men slogged over the snow and slush, through what was left of the tiny village of Kleinhau. Pockets of menacing fog hung low over the snow-covered valley and they began to see rows of frozen dead soldiers, mostly Americans. Their squads, battalions, outfits had just left the dead bodies there, like carefully cut cord wood, waiting for the Mortuary Wagons to move forward and pick them up. The convenient thing was that they could wait; it wasn't like it was mid-summer—the bodies were frozen stiff. On more than one occasion the dead were overlooked and/or left behind when the 'graves registration or mortuary battalion' simply didn't find them.

Commander Kessel called, "Move out---let's go-go-go! We are jumping on the trail of the 15th—they have made it to some high ground just on the other side of Kleinhau and need our support. They are just tryin' to hold that high ground and keep the damn Germans from infiltrating back in an area they just cleared. Those Krauts are bull-headed persistent SOBs I'll say that for them!" As the daylight faded, the tanks from the 81st rolled into the area where the 15th Infantry was attempting to chop out their foxholes. The earth's snow-packed crust was frozen down to about a foot deep as the infantrymen hacked away at it, trying to get it to open up and give them some protection. Some guys even set small charges in the frozen ground to open it up. Every time they moved to a different area, they had to dig new foxholes and it was frustrating work. Some were successful and some weren't.

PT quipped, "I don't know if it's worth digging those fox holes, they just fill up with ice water and the fellas have to lie in that shit and freeze and get trench foot. Besides that, the damn Germans have booby-trapped some of those old foxholes so when our infantry jump in them, they get blown to bits anyways. This is all just bushwa misery, that's what it is." They were constantly under fire from German artillery and mortars, making it impossible for any 'thin-skinned' vehicles to bring up supplies and ammo or even take the wounded back to the base field hospital.

Cowboy passed on the information he had received over the two-way. "HQ has a couple of light M5 Stuart tanks to act as supply/ammo couriers coming up and ambulances on the way back down. I suppose they'll be making a few trips before morning comes. In the meantime, let's find a place to park this baby and dine on our K-rations! I wish like hell we could light a fire so we could have something hot in our bellies, but that would bring a whole world of hell down on top of us—probably not worth it." He looked off into the fog of the woods and said, "Damn—I would give anything for a hot cup of java; it's been days since we had anything hot or cooked."

WWII – Field Stove

Trying to keep warm inside their steel tank was no small feat. Hans shivered under his blanket and wool overcoat, "Damn, it's cold in here, it feels like an icebox. I don't suppose we could start this baby up and let it run a couple of hours so we get some of that engine heat? If not, then what about firing up that little field stove, you know the one that we heat up our K-rations on--- anything just to get my hands warm?"

Miggie shot back, "WHAT? And, you're always bragging what a hot guy you are!"

Miggie collapsed into a heap of laughter as Hans shot him a drop dead look.

Commander Kessel said, "Wish we could run the tank for a little bit longer, but the Colonel would have my hide—it's tough to get fuel and supplies up to us in this forest and so we'll just have to stay warm the best way we can, at least we aren't out on the ground. Our infantry is taking a beating out there from the Krauts and the weather. I'd like to crank up the portable generator to charge our batteries when we are just sitting, but you guys know that the Krauts hone in on our location and we get shelled. It's the shits--that's what it is."

13 Dec. 1944: Kessel was stunned when he received the Battalion report that next morning and read it off to his crew. "Men, FYI--the 15th Infantry started out with 735 enlisted men and 18 officers--- now they report they have 170 enlisted and 4 officers. What the hell? I didn't realize it was that bad but our tanks can't move in this crap and give them the support we usually do---damn it to hell! By the way, where is Miggie? Did he just vanish?"

Hans looked up from his breakfast of K-rations, "He slipped out through the bottom hatch to take a nature walk—said he just couldn't hold it any longer, his gut was on fire. He's been gone a while now."

PT opened his hatch and stuck his head out just enough to take a look around. PT yelled, "Cowboy, over there, he is behind that tree to the left. Why the hell is he behind a tree?" PT moved his range of vision a little to the right and was stunned at what he saw. "Krauts—coming up the hill through the woods to the right—about twenty of 'em----using trees as cover, they got Miggie pinned down."

They heard the German small arms fire along with the high pitch chatter of a couple of burp guns and the stutter of a machine gun. Bobby jumped on Miggie's machine gun and returned fire as PT tried to maneuver the tank towards the forest. Commander Kessel looked through his periscope and grabbed the two-way, sounding the alarm. "PT, swing this baby to the left about 10 degrees and Hans---give me a HE shell and keep loading and firing until I tell you to stop. FIRE, FIRE, FIRE!" Arnold opened the turret hatch and manned the 50.Caliber machine gun as the rest of the tank battalion and infantry joined in. When the smoke cleared, there was nothing but dead Germans on the slope of the hill, and then they spotted Miggie. He was down.

"Cover me Bobby---Miggie is lying about ten feet to the left, I gotta go get him. Cover me!" Arnold pulled his Colt .45 from his shoulder holster, cocked the hammer and released the safety. He slipped down through the floor hatch and dropped onto the frozen ground below the tank. He wriggled his way out from under the cover of the tank. Standing with his back against the tank's steel hull, he inched his way along; finally turning onto his belly he belly-crawled across the snow to where Miggie was slumped against a tree. "Miggie, Miggie---can you hear me?

Miggie, answer me." Cowboy looked around to make sure there weren't any revived Germans as he rubbed some snow on Miggie's face. "Miggie are you hurt---shot?"

Miggie face contorted in pain as he nodded his head to the affirmative; one word gurgled out, 'Ma-ma'! Blood gushed from his nose and mouth as he grabbed at his own coat, pulling it aside exposing his belly. Arnold looked down; his breath caught in his throat and tears blurred his eyes. Miggie's gut was blown wide open and his innards glistened in the cold morning light. They both knew a gut shot was one of the worst. Arnold pulled the morphine syringe from his vest pocket and jabbed it into Miggie's thigh, then yelled, "MEDIC!" He held Miggie in his arms until a couple of medics crawled up the hill but by then Miggie didn't need any of them. They grabbed his dog tags and moved on to the next wounded man screaming for them.

Arnold looked back down the slope where the German infantry had been advancing and saw them all lying dead in the snow; red patches of fresh blood, limbs, and bodies covered the hill. Arnold reached up and closed Miggie's eyes then grabbed him by the back of the collar. He was consumed with a deep, hot raging anger as he began dragging Miggie towards the tank. Bobby yelled out of the hatch, "Cowboy, what the hell are you doing? "

Momentarily, the weight of the war and the killing and the dying bore down on him as Cowboy turned and puked into the white snow. With tears streaming down his face Commander Kessel replied, "I'm not leaving Miggie here in the woods with all these dead Krauts. He's one of my men and I won't leave him behind, he's coming with us! I don't leave my men behind, no way, ever!" Commander Kessel lashed Miggie's body to the left rear hull flank of their tank. The frigid weather would 'keep him' until they ran into the Graves Registration people; only then would they release Miggie's body.

Dec. 14: It was after sunup when they got their first orders of the day. Kessel shouted, "Move out. We are pushing forward toward Strass on the east edge of the Hurtgen in support of the 330th Regiment. Our combat command along with CCR is assigned to the left flank of the line attacking the village."

It was slow going through the fresh snow, and the tankers let the infantry ride on the tanks when they could; many of the foot soldiers had some form of frostbite or trench foot from the cold and wet conditions. Bobby said, "Those guys perched on our tanks are sitting ducks for some damn Kraut sniper, but I guess it's no different for them when they are on the ground."

Hans began rubbing his arms and complaining, "Damn, I don't even remember what it's like to be warm; being in this tank is like being inside my Momma's icebox. We haven't seen the sun for weeks. Every damn day the sky is cloud-covered and ya know it's really getting to me. How much further do you think we have to go until we are out of this miserable Nazi hell hole?"

Up to that point nobody was really listening to Hans, then, to their amazement, Hans lost it. He began to shake, rant, and scream as he hit the inside walls of the tank. "I can't take this bullshit any longer—what kind of generals send us men into someplace like this. They've hung us boys out to dry, pure and simple. Where are they? They're probably sittin' on their butts in some nice warm office. Day after day, we get no breaks; every damn day we fight for our lives in a battle. When is this all going to end, just tell me? Oh God, I can't do it anymore. I'm done, I'm going to end it my way, not sit and wait for some unexpected bullet." He rose and lurched toward the floor hatch when PT grabbed him and shoved him back in his seat until they could talk him down.

This was a first for the crew of the Avenger but it was a daily wartime occurrence when one or another soldier cracked under the constant danger and pressure. They had all heard about incidents when a soldier defied orders and purposely walked into enemy fire or took a crazy risk that he knew would probably get him killed. They lived with the fact that the odds were against them and when some couldn't take it any longer---they cracked. They were glad Gen. Patton wasn't around, they'd all heard about him slapping a soldier in a hospital who had a nervous breakdown.

Commander Kessel put his cold, cracked and bleeding hand on Han's shoulder. "Come on now, we depend on you, Hans. We all feel the same way, believe me, but we gotta keep going, we just gotta do it. You know the crew and I need you—we're a team and we gotta stick together to make it out of here, we need each other. We've seen a lot of bad, real bad stuff and we're still in it. We all agree that we shouldn't be in this crazy forest; this isn't tank country. But I guess we follow orders and just know that it will all end when enough people die. That's pretty much how it always is." *But what they had seen wouldn't compare to what waited for them ahead, no---not by a long shot.*

~~~~~~~

Commander Kessel lit a 'smoke' and studied the terrain maps. "From what I can tell on this map, it's only a couple of miles or so from Kleinhau to Strass. The question is how much resistance are we going to encounter along the way? That will determine how long it'll take us to get there."

The two companies of Sherman tanks and married infantry moved forward along the treacherous mountain road, pushing destroyed equipment off road when they couldn't pass.

PT hollered, "We're coming to a small village up ahead—looks like ten buildings at the most. I see fresh tracks in the snow and I don't think they're ours. Just 200 yards east of Schafberg the American tanks began taking on sporadic fire from Kraut anti-tank guns. Commander Kessel yelled, "Lock up, here we go!" The crew reacted like a well-oiled machine, locking their hatches and preparing their stations and ammo.

Without warning a screeching volley of German machine pistols filled the forest air. Slamming his hatched shut, PT swore,

"Damn it, I hate the sound of those machine pistols—reminds me of the dentist drill. Where are they---anybody see where those rounds came from?"

Just then a thundering barrage enveloped their convoy. Several Jeeps and a field artillery gun burst into flame, infantry dove for cover under anything close. The tanks stayed put as mortar shells burst high in the trees, sending down the knives of wood and shrapnel. As if that wasn't bad enough, the Krauts sent their Screaming Mimi rockets just to sweeten the mix and enhance the carnage. Tanks were inching forward, trying to find open ground where they could move their cannons in an arc. Commander Kessel shouted, "FIRE, FIRE—keep it up—wherever you see a flash. Move up, keep moving--ATTACK!"

~~~~~~~~~

The night was dark as sin as the task force bivouacked near a burned out village. There were several hot bonfires scattered across the area and the men crowded close in an effort to thaw out or simply feel some rare source of warmth. Arnold watched as one of his married infantrymen sat alone on a rock, staring at the fire. Commander Kessel walked up and offered Johnny Maxfield a cigarette. "Want to talk about it Johnny? I got a feelin' that something pretty bad happened to you out there today. I saw how you infantry guys were diving in those foxholes during the tree bursts and shelling. I remember seeing you and then it was like you disappeared. It was pretty damn intense."

Johnny Maxfield turned and looked at Arnold, his eyes glassed over, his face void of expression. Commander Kessel laid his hand on Johnny's shoulder. "I've got nothing better to do than to listen to how you spent your day, come on---let's have it. It might help to get it out."

Johnny swallowed and took a drag on the cigarette before he was able to gather his thoughts about what was eating at him. "Well, Cowboy, it was pretty much a nightmare—you guys in those tanks don't see and hear what us dogfaces(infantry) on the ground do. It's a whole other existence for damn sure, not exactly the 'life of Riley'! Like today, we was marching along and the next thing we knew, somebody yelled 'Incoming' and the air was sucked from our lungs as explosion after explosion hit the tops of those trees and the ground. I had just walked past this here shallow foxhole between two downed trees and I didn't wait for an invitation---hell, I flew through the air and landed hard on the bottom."

"I plugged my fingers into my ears. When you are in a hole like that and those mortar explosions are hitting the ground—it's just so damn loud—and when the shells hit---the shock—you feel it through your whole body. I don't think there's any way in hell of avoiding that rain of shrapnel and tree bursts coming down other than to be in or under something that takes the brunt of it all—that, and hope to hell you get lucky!"

Johnny lit another cigarette and took a swig from his canteen. "There I was flat on my belly trying to make myself flat, in that next second, something heavy and solid landed on top of me. I was pinned to the bottom of that damn hole and I knew it. I had my face to the ground and so I couldn't see what the hell it was—I just concentrated on breathing—thank God, I'm not claustrophobic—is that the word? Well, I knew I wasn't going anywhere, so I just laid still. I thought maybe a piece of a tree landed on me—that is, until the 'thing' jerked, then screamed, "I'm HIT!"

Arnold's eyes widened and he said, "No shit? There was another guy on top of you?"

Johnny shook his head to the affirmative, "Oh hell, Cowboy, I actually felt his body jerk when that second bullet hit the guy. That's when he whimpered, 'Oh God, I'm gonna die, it hurts. Oh Mother, help me help me!' I couldn't do a damn thing to help him cause like I said, he had me pinned in that hole. Finally the guy musta bled out. Shit--I really began to wonder if I was going to be buried alive in that hole—if anybody would find me and that's when I started to panic."

"I waited a while longer—after the shelling stopped, that's when I started to scream at the top of my lungs for the medic, just anyone to get that guy off me. Hell, I couldn't lift my head or nothing to see if there were even medics around. Then I thought I heard men talking right over my foxhole, I felt them lift the dogface off me and first thing I did was to catch a good deep breath, then I felt their hands on me—asking me if I was shot, if I was hurt. I guess they thought I had been shot because of all the blood." Johnny said, "Can you believe if? I had a dead guy lying on top of me for over an hour."

Johnny continued, "I don't think I will ever forget it. I don't get it---why the other guy got the bullets and I didn't?"

Commander Kessel said, "Johnny, it's that old thing about being in the right or wrong place. It's just the way it is—no better way to explain when something so crazy like that happens. It happens every second of every day in this damn war. Every soldier asks the same question---why me? Why didn't I get shot instead?"

Commander Kessel put his head back and blew the cigarette smoke into the dark of the night. "Not many guys know this about me Johnny, but I had me another tank crew before Hurtgen—when we was crossing the Roer River last fall. I had opened the turret hatch to take a look behind us and that's exactly when a Tiger tank gave us the goods. That explosion shot me out of the turret like a shell and killed all of my crew. So—I'm just saying, that if not now, by the end of the war, all of the living soldiers will more than likely be asking that very question---why didn't I get the bullet? Try to shake it off, okay buddy? Pretty soon you will just feel numb, like me. That's how we are going to get through this hell!"

~~~~~~~~

Back on the road before dawn, tank 2736 was fourth in the column of five tanks; Commander Kessel rode with his head barely out of the open turret, scanning the area ahead with his binoculars. PT swore, "Damn it to hell, there aren't a lot of places where we can coil or even turn off if we need to. Hell of a place to try and fight in a tank; stupid damn big brass that sends down orders like these!"

Without warning, several Panzerfausts erupted from the trees, directed at the column of tanks as Kraut burp guns peppered the tank turrets. Enemy machine guns stuttered and anti-tank artillery shells began to explode around them—they were sittin' ducks! In rapid succession three tanks were hit and two of them burst into flames. The turret of the tank in front of them jammed but that didn't stop the rest of them from firing on the Krauts.

Commander Kessel ordered, "Hans, hose that damn Kraut machine gun nest at 12 o'clock—take 'em out. Bobby, you are gonna have to take Miggie's gun for now, I'll load for Hans. FIRE, FIRE---." Arnold had just shoved another shell into the cannon when a German projectile ripped into their tank's cannon barrel. It sounded like the church bell had been rung. They felt their tank buck from the concussion of the Kraut shell, but nothing happened---no explosion.

The crew of Avenger looked at each other; everyone held his breath, waiting for an explosion that never came. Commander Kessel yelled, "The shell must have hit our cannon then ricocheted off cause now our cannon is jammed but good! I'm going up top and fire the 50.Caliber machine gun; you guys keep firing on anything off road that moves. Hey—Bobby, how many belts of ammo do you have left for that machine gun?"

Without warning, PT screamed, "Sarge, we've got some nutso Kraut soldier advancing on our tank with a luger. He's shooting at our tank with a gol damn pistol—looks like he's out of grenades. If he keeps coming I'm going to run over him—I have nowhere to turn—I can't turn. Son-of-a-bitch, Cowboy, what do I do?"

Cowboy shouted over the growl and roar of the engine and clanking tank treads, "Run over the damn fool—just run the hell right over him!" And, he did! PT and Bobby watched as their tank tread grabbed the German and pulled him under, crushing him into the snow and mud. Cowboy stood high in the turret hatch with his finger on the trigger of his machine gun. He turned and looked once they had passed over the Kraut; there was nothing visible but a boot protruding from the pulverized ground.

Cowboy listened intently to the two-way radio then passed their orders on, "We've only got five tanks left and HQ wants us to pull back to the assembly area near Kleinhau; the 330th Infantry will move forward without tank support." Once back in the bivouacs area, tank mechanics climbed all over the damaged tanks; they couldn't believe what they found in tank 2736's cannon--- fragments of the German shell were embedded in the actual nose of their shell that was in the cannon barrel. The shells had canceled each other out without exploding.

Cowboy started laughing, "Well if that isn't the, damnest thing I've ever seen. I guess it wasn't our time yet, boys—that's a miracle if I ever saw one!"

Dec. 15: Before dawn CCB was back on the road to Strass. Kessel said, "It seems the Germans have trapped the 330th Infantry and those boys are facing annihilation. They've lost four commanders in two days; they're out of food and water and running dangerously low on ammo. Word is that they have to urinate on their rifles to keep them from freezing up. They got wounded in there who need medics, so we are going back and get those boys out. We've got orders to sweep around to the North of Gey and then move back south while CCC comes around from the West. Okay boys—let's go kill us some Germans and get our boys' outta that trap!"

The scene along the snow-covered road between Gey and Strass was an unscripted nightmare. Destroyed Allied and German equipment, horses, and the dead were dumped and left alongside the narrow road. Wide-eyed with horror, Hans remarked, "Holy Mother of God, have mercy on us. I can't believe I am seeing what I am seeing! How do you describe this carnage to someone?"

PT yelled out, "Up ahead, Cowboy, we got trouble—looks like one of our forward tanks got knocked out by a road mine, then some idiot tank retriever went on up to move it off the road and it hit a mine too—it's one hell of a mess. Some jackass tried to use explosives to blow them both off the road which got 'em off the road, but our road is now a huge crater—too big for us to cross and we have nowhere to go."

Commander Kessel stood tall in the open hatch of the turret listening to his two-way. He shouted into the receiver, "Don't do it

McNulty—don't try and jump that crater with your tank. Are you nuts?"

Kessel said, "Hey guys—Commander McNulty is going for it,"—they all watched out of their hatches as the forward tanker stepped on the gas and made a run at the huge crater. There was dead---total silence from the other tankers as McNulty's tank hit the other side of the crater wall and toppled, growling and clawing into the hole. As it turned out, the tank ended up half on its side which wasn't the plan, BUT it worked well, protecting the rest of the tankers from enemy fire. Once McNulty elevated his 75-mechanism to traverse and his traversing mechanism to elevate, they were in perfect position to lob round after round into enemy positions. It was like the 4th of July the way their shells shot up and then exploded just before they fell to earth —on target. The beauty of it was that the Allied tank was relatively protected in a tank-made foxhole.

Engineers were finally called up to bridge the crater and McNulty's trashed tank, so the rest of the column could pass over and around. By this time, the Germans had an idea of what was going on and poured in their heavy artillery and mortar fire on the bridging engineers. Standing in his turret supervising the bridging, Capt. Frank Peters was hit by a German burp gun and had to be evacuated. By 1100 hours, the bridging was complete and Lt. McNulty ordered Sgt. Joe McKinney to drive his tank over the bridge. "Get across that damn bridge and fire on the right flank so the rest of the tankers can get across." It was a fine plan, but McKinney's tank was hit, again blocking the road, and McKinney was hit by sniper fire and had to be evacuated. *So much for that morning!*

The tank column eventually got around the road mess and continued on, to wait even longer for the engineers to come up and clear the road ahead of mines. It was a yard-by-yard advance, and the constant sheer tension did a number on all their nerves. By the end of that day, CCB and CCC were in control of the woods west of Schafberg and had rescued the 330th. Exhausted, they bivouacked for the night but got precious little sleep, knowing that at daybreak, they were heading into another nasty battle at a quarry located southeast of Strass.

Dec. 16: Commander Kessel passed their orders on to his crew, "Intelligence tells us that the Krauts are dug in and waiting for us----NOW that's a surprise! Anyway, they got their usual snipers alerting their artillery to our position. Word is that we are to take Hills 253 and 266 as well as the villages of Berghein and Bilstein. Just before dark yesterday our advance Recons started hitting them with an all-out artillery strike plus an air strike. Thank God, our planes can see this target, even if we are still in the Hurtgen. Here's the plan for today—we jump off at daybreak like always. This time, we're gonna mix it up a little for the Krauts. We know they 'expect' us to follow our normal code of attack. Just over that hill, there are six German antitank guns dug in and supported by infantry, waiting for our traditional artillery fire, followed by our armored attack. That's not what they are going to get. THIS is what we are going to do-----!"

~~~~~~~~

Twenty-eight tanks from Task Force Anderson moved through the sparse woods to within 400 yards of where the Germans were dug in. They paid no attention to the sharp sporadic chatter of the German machine guns or the identifying pings of rifle fire. Without warning, the Sherman tanks broke from the cover of the woods and roared across open ground, gaining speed and firing as they moved.

Commander Kessel screamed, "FIRE, FIRE, FIRE----Let's go, go—move it for hell sake!! EEEiiiieeeehah!"

The wall of approaching American tanks with the large white star on the hull was a frightful sight, firing continuously as they roared toward the stunned Germans. As planned, the flabbergasted enemy hardly had time to react and return fire before the American tanks pulled to a stop, allowing infantry to swarm the quarry and mop up.

Bobby squealed with laughter, "Damn it to hell, now THAT was fun! Where are we going now, Cowboy?"

They received orders to proceed east toward Gorzynski. PT called out, "Cowboy, we got us a house up ahead—looks too pretty, too quiet for my taste." Commander Kessel made a call to the two tanks behind him, advising of the situation. He eased his turret hatch open and moved slowly out, just far enough to put his finger on the trigger of his .50 Caliber machine gun, "Bobby, put a shell in the cannon and then slip over and man Miggie's machine gun—strafe the upper windows when I give the signal!"

Cowboy yelled FIRE and hosed the lower windows of the farm house. Commander Kessel fired continuous short bursts as they moved up. They watched as their bullets smashed into the white-washed house and shattered the windows. Before the dust settled, a German SS officer and ten infantry 'hot-footed' it from the house with their hands in the air. Then, as if by magic, another thirty surrendering Germans slid from the woods on the left AND more on the right. It was as if the forest was puking surrendering Germans.

As the infantry gathered up the POWs, Commander Kessel instructed, "Bobby, why don't you and Hans pull your pistols and take a look/see inside that house—those Germans might have left some food and even better yet, something to drink. I've worked up a powerful thirst."

Ten minutes later, the two tankers emerged from the deserted farm house with big smiles on their faces. Their helmets were filled with eggs, Bobby had a half of a cold roasted chicken stuck under his right arm and Hans carried a basket with strudel and even a couple bottles of wine. They proudly handed the booty up to the crew, "We are gonna eat real good tonight. Too bad we have to wait to drink that wine; I wouldn't mind a quick drag off one of those bottles.

Cowboy stashed the food away inside the tank as he uncorked one of the bottles of wine. "I don't know about you boys, but I'm not tellin'. We deserve a couple swallows off this bottle to wash down the dust from that last battle. We'll save the rest for another time. Good work men---good work!"

PT said, "Say, when are we gonna eat some of those 'cackleberries'? Hell, I could even scramble 'em up in my helmet. I've had a belly full of those gut packings that they call K rations. I'd like to get my hands around the throat of whoever packs that crap up."

Later as tank 2736 and the married infantry herded 187 German prisoners down the road, Commander Kessel had a hard time holding back a smile. "If that wasn't the damnest thing I ever did see. I guess Germans get tired of fighting too. They are smart enough to know when they are whipped. Just goes to show you it's all in a day's work! That's what they get for not inviting us to dinner in the first place."

~~~~~~

Commander Kessel said, "We are going to sit tight here overnight, then we have orders to take Hill 253; that way we'll have the high ground overlooking the Roer River towns of Winden, Untermaubach, and Udingen. When we do that, the northeastern reaches of the Hurtgen Forest will be in American hands. All I have to say to that experience is –this is one damn fine crew! Good work men---that forest was a bushwa assignment but we took it like the soldiers we are; it was pure hell and I'm one thankful man to be outta there! I'm real proud of you boys, real proud!"

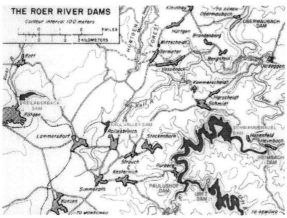

Cowboy leaned up against Avenger's hull, having a smoke and a moment to himself. Suddenly a shaft of moonlight slipped through the thick woods and washed across his tank hull. Cowboy looked at it for a moment and then thought of Miggie, *I miss you man; I miss you real bad and hope you are in a better place.*

That night, sleep eluded the tank commander. Cowboy couldn't shake the image of the faces of infantry who had come out of the Hurtgen Forest alive. Sure, they had all gone through hell, but it was the 'dog faces'---the infantrymen and their staring eyes, like hollow holes in their heads. Most of them were covered with snow, mud, blood, and powder burns. *Some of them men acted like they could hardly put one foot in front of the other – body language. It was like what they called the walking dead, I hope they get them men some R & R real soon like!*

Trying to relax before the next big battle, they all had their heads sticking out of the hatches when a moving-van size military transport rolled past them. It shocked the hell out of them to see it filled to the top with stacks of bodies, both German and American. Hans' face was ashen as he said, "Holy Shit, did you boys just see what I saw? They had those bodies stacked one on the other like you see sardines in a tin. I didn't know they did stuff like that, but I guess them are the boys that come in after a battle and take the dead, no matter who they are. That's a hell of a sick job---having to pick up the dead and then go over their bodies for ID and stuff. Do they save the clothes and boots and stuff, do you think? What about the Lugers and watches, who gets those?"

PT replied, "I don't know for sure Hans, but I suppose anything that is worth keeping, to use again, sure---especially boots. Hell, we take good boots off dead Germans! They send the next of kin the personal stuff, I think. I'm thinking those boys should get something for doing that job!"

Bobby asked, "Commander, not to change the subject, but when do we get a replacement for Miggie? Not that I'm complainin' but I want to do my job as a loader and there are some cases when that is a full time job."

Kessel answered, "I've been asking about that---not a lot of spare men around this area, but HQ promised to have us a new gunner in the next day or two. We're gonna stay put for a couple of days while we wait for replacements for our wounded and dead. Just hope to hell we get a fella who can shoot." Arnold tried to shake the memory of Miggie dying in his arms. *That's another horrible memory that I have to live with--- Mac, Joe, Reb, Hero, Danny Boy, now Miggie---all my buddies, my boys--all dead! Thank you God for getting me and most of my boys out of that Hurtgen Forest alive---Thank you!*

Two days later, the Avenger received its new gunner— Prescott W. Hughes from Madison, Wisconsin.

Arnold took one look at the new assistant driver and the acceptable words of welcome stuck in his throat. "Well I'll be dammed! What is your name boy? How old are YOU? You're your Mother know you are here? Have you had any training at all in being an assistant tank driver? Shit—have you ever been IN a tank?" Commander Kessel slapped the hull of the Sherman tank in frustration. "What the hell, HQ is sending us babies to fill in our tank crews now? You're nothing more than a squirt!"

Private Prescott Hughes stood as tall as his 5'7" bony frame would allow as he replied, "Yes sir; Private Prescott W. Hughes reporting Sir! I am seventeen years old and I signed up to serve. I had a crash course in tanks at Fort Knox, Sir! I have been inside a tank and even driven one."

Kessel took another look at the baby face of Pvt. Hughes and began to laugh in spite of himself, "Hell, we need a man to fill this position and you aren't much more than a kid, for cryin' out loud! Can you shoot straight?"

Pvt. Hughes responded, "I can shoot straight and on target, Sir! I excelled in tank marksmanship, SIR! I can do it, I wanna fight!"

Kessel shook his head as he lit up a cigarette, inhaling he held it for a moment then blew it out, hard. "Well then, I guess we'll give you a try, but you'll go by the call tag of 'Squirt'. This here is PT, Bobby, Hans, and I'm called Cowboy or Commander Kessel. Got that? Oh, and one more thing, I realize you are pretty green but, you don't call me Sir. Call me Cowboy, or Kessel but not sir; I don't intend on taking some Kraut bullet because you nailed my rank by calling me sir, got that?"

It took the crew of the Avenger a while to accept Priv. Prescott W. Hughes—they broke him in with a fair amount of grief, starting with Bobby. "So Squirt---what does the 'W' stand for---wiener or whiner?"

All PT said to the kid was, "Listen Squirt, this here outfit will make a man out of you whether you like it or not so grow the hell up cause you are in it now. You'll have to take a few lumps to prove yourself, but hang in there. If you screw up, you'll have the rest of us to answer to, got that? We nail the screw-ups to the front of the tank hull—just you remember that!" PT looked out of the front hull hatch and shook his head in disbelief, "Hell, at seventeen I was chasing skirt and drinking Coca Cola!"

~~~~~~~~

The American troops moved eastward at a calculated pace, taking one village after another along the banks of the Roer River. CCB got the credit for clearing dangerous pockets of resistance out with their pile-driving armored thrust through the towns of Obermaubach and Untermaubach in the Roer area. They drove the last Kraut from Untermaubach just as a mammoth battle was taking shape to the south of the 5th Armored Division---they called it the [31]Battle of the Bulge!

~~~~~~~

Allied HQ withdrew the majority of American troops from the Hurtgen Forest area, which was no of interest or a military goal. They simply abandoned and forgot the vicious, needless fighting that occurred in that region---suddenly, it wasn't important. Later, military experts and those who critiqued the war would question if the Hurtgen Forest had ever been an important conquest or was simply some officer's pipe dream. After the Hurtgen campaign, Commander Arnold Kessel was awarded his third Bronze Star for leadership and accomplishment in battle which he immediately threw in the bottom of his duffel bag along with the other two medals.

The green, inexperienced American soldiers who were sent into the Hurtgen Forest came out of it, forever changed. They now questioned high authority and became bitter after suffering more humiliating, terror-filled defeats than they could count. They were cold, tired, hungry, and discouraged. Few had winter clothing and what they had been issued had not kept out the cold. Their poorly made boots deter the dampness or eventual trench foot. Their tanks were outnumbered and paralyzed by the terrain; their guns froze and would not fire. They learned how to fight in real cold, in deep snow, in impossible circumstances, and under overwhelming and pre-calculated enemy fire power, strategy, and odds. Those men who walked out of that dark icy hell would never forget it.

In Hurtgen did I lay Thee down
In wintery blustery mire
The only silence was the sound
When death God gave Thee here

The 'Bloody Buckets' they coined us
When they saw us fight and die
Our country longed to forget us
For we brought no victory
Though give our all
We Did and Do and Will
And all for Love
Of Service, Duty, County, God
And Brothers who watch above.

Author Unknown

Chapter Fourteen

"THE ARDENNE FOREST"
"Fear has blinded Reason"

Just one day after the 81st Tank Battalion and married Infantry saw the sunlight emerge on the eastern side of the Hurtgen Forest, 250,000 Germans in their supreme impetus to win the war, attacked a force of 83,000 American troops. The Allied forces were stationed along a thinly held front, twisting some eight miles through mountains and valleys in the southern Ardennes Forest. At the battle's height, the Germans forced a prominent undulating bulge in the American lines almost 60 miles deep. At the same time they thrust decisively to the north in hope of punching through and gaining a direct route to the coveted port of Antwerp—this was, the Battle of the Bulge.

~~~~~~~~

Dec. 21: After the Hurtgen Forest, what was left of the 81st tank battalion was battered and bloody. They'd had precious little time to lick their wounds and morn their dead, but they had their orders and they were ready to go. Commander Kessel turned to address his crew, "We've got orders to pull back and briefly reassemble; those orders include armor and infantry. CCB and CCR have been chosen move out into the northern edge of the Ardennes Forest on a special mission to act as a final wall of tank and artillery power if the Germans punch north through in the Battle of the Bulge. We know their objective is to get to Antwerp and that port, but they will have to go through a corridor, a seven-mile long valley called the Losheim Gap that funnels them directly toward where we will be waiting in ambush in a Ghost Front. Our frontline position will be secured by the 83rd Infantry." Arnold ignored the groans and bitching when he mentioned they were going into a possible battle in another forest. This time the Ardennes!

NOTE: *The press gave this battle, 'Battle of the Bulge'-- its name when it started on December 16th.*

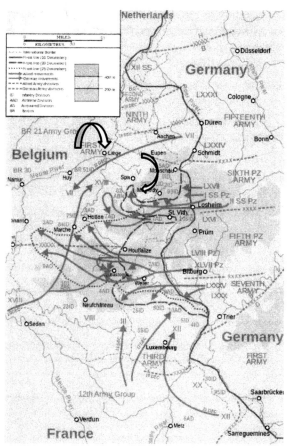

Commander Kessel announced, "Button up, we are moving out for more woods around a place called Liege. Look here on this map, you can all see the northern finger of the bulge sticking up right there. That is where the German I and II SS Panzers are pushing hard toward the Meuse River. Right there at the top where the Meuse and the Ourthe River meet, is Liege---our target area. We'll be right in front of the First Army and the Ninth Armies is to the north of us, on the Allied Line. Our Fifth Division is dug in close to Spa just below where us boys from CCB and CCR will be. They want us to camouflage our tanks with snow and branches and then sit in those woods facing the German line---sit and wait. We are gonna be close enough to the battle that we'll hear it and see it at night. Orders are not to move and aggressively attack unless we get the call to fire, and there may be a time when we are in total silence mode. Are there any questions?"

~~~~~~~~~

Dec. 22: At 1300 hours, CCB and CCR along with their married infantry completed the 30-mile mad dash to a wide-open, snow-covered meadow, skirted with thick conifer and spruce trees on the fringe of where the Battle of the Bulge was raging in full force. Commander Kessel announced, "It looks like we aren't going to get that real Christmas dinner with turkey and the works like the rest of our Battalion---it looks like we are the chosen ones and what we get on Christmas is K-Rations. I'm real sorry guys, just like most of you I was looking forward to going to church services on Christmas Eve and then having a nice hot Christmas dinner. I suppose we should be bustin' our buttons because obviously headquarters knows we are the task force that can stop the damn Krauts if they break through, let's not let them down if presented with the opportunity. If the Krauts reach Liege or Verviers---THEN, they have to go through us—we, make the kill!"

Arnold looked out of the turret periscope and surveyed the area. It kept coming back to him---what he'd read in his Bible the night before and prompted him to say to his crew, "Boys, I'm just saying---whether you believe in God or not, we have a damn lot to be thankful for and it won't hurt any of us to remember to say a prayer or two, thanking God for watching over us and to continue doing the same--that includes you Squirt! Most of you boys know the Battle of the Bulge is in full force as I speak; things could go either way—that's a real decisive battle. The 5th Division will not participate, except for us—the rest of the force is being held in reserve."

The combined 28 tanks from CCB and CCR woke to a fresh blanket of pristine white snow that laid like a white quilt over the expansive mountain meadow. It was so cold it froze the little hairs in the noses of the men and caused them to pull on their wool overcoats which worked well, when dry. Most of the soldiers would never forget the uselessness of their wet wool overcoats and even uniforms in the Hurtgen Forest and how they would end up freezing to their bodies.

They'd all read and re-read the special instructions regarding exiting their tanks during this silent night ambush. Once they exited a tank to take a leak, they had to cover all tracks with the boughs of an evergreen. There should be no sign of troop movement; infantry was dug in.

Around mid-day, Commander Kessel and PT exited the tank together, after attending to business and covering their tracks they met up at the rear of their tank. Reaching out, PT stopped Arnold, "Commander, can I talk to you for a minute. I gotta tell someone and I guess it's gonna be you; stuff has been bothering me. Shit—I can't sleep, I have nightmares—I can't stop thinking about Hurtgen, it's with me every damn day and night." To his utter embarrassment, tears began to roll down his cheeks, his chest heaved and his body shuttered with internal sobs. Cowboy grabbed PT's elbow and shoved him hard against the hull of their tank.

Cowboy ordered, "Snap out of it PT, what you are going through isn't any damn different than the rest of us. Sure, Hurtgen was a special kind of hell and we were the lucky ones, we were strong enough to have made it through that freezing nightmare. You don't have to apologize or explain to me—I've got the same damn problems---we all do, none of us boys are ever gonna forget what we went through, but we have to try. You are my driver and I depend on you. Come on now, it's Christmas---we lived to see another Christmas and Hurtgen was all in a day's work. Let's get back inside our unheated designer vehicle where we have us a bottle of vino waiting." The tank commander gave a little lopsided grin, knowing he probably hadn't helped PT much and frankly he didn't know what to say. He did know that his men each had their own way of dealing with the everyday trauma and horror of the war, of what they did and what they saw. *Maybe PT is just letting his nerves and fears get the best of him--about what awaits us. All I know is that we are all tense with the excitement and dread of what is to come, if and when it comes.*

The two soldiers joined the rest of the crew back inside their camouflage, snow-covered tank, wishing the table was set with turkey, mashed potatoes, corn, and apple pie along with several cups of hot joe instead of the boxes of cold K-Rations. With wide-eyed innocence or ignorance, Squirt said, "Say, those K-Rations aren't so bad, except for that Spam stuff. Is it really made from beef and chicken guts? You were just kidding around again weren't you fellas? What's really in that stuff? It really ain't too bad if you're hungry enough."

PT laughed, "Squirt—you are a quick learner, that's for damn sure, but you can't believe everything you hear, you Nin-com-poop."

Bobby teased, "Say Squirt, what do you want to drink? We could scrape you up some moo juice, maybe even a cold baby's bottle. Or---do you think you'd like to drink like a man startin' now? For entertainment we might just sit and watch you get bokoo soused!"

Squirt responded "I've had about enough of your bushwa. You don't think I've had me a drink before? Why, I think that's just what my system needs to activate all of those 'repeaters' I ate today, just for you Bobby—just for you! I'll be sure to let you have the first whiff, when those beans are coming through---savin' it for Bob-by!" Squirt laughed wickedly as Bobby attempted to box his ears.

The crew passed the bottle of wine around, Squirt made a face every time he took a swallow. Hans kidded him, "Squirt, you know I'd be happy to take care of your share of it—just cause I'm that nice of a guy."

Squirt smiled up at Hans and said with authority, "Nope, it's just right—best vino I've had!"

Unsmiling, Commander Kessel's voice tensed up, "Boys, on a serious note. If this next battle actually comes to us, it ain't gonna be a picnic, we all know that! Just to get you guys up to par, word is that the Jerries' have dropped a bunch of English speaking Krauts dressed in our uniforms, behind our lines in the Battle of the Bulge. As if we didn't have enough grief to think about, we may or may not run into them here in fringes of the Ardennes. HQ doesn't have a bead on them yet, nobody knows for sure where they are. You all know that the password is changed every day and there are a few questions you can ask a stranger if you suspect they aren't who they appear to be. To be on the safe side, remember to ask the 'soldier' in question to pronounce any word with the letter 'J' in it. Like 'jackass' or something similar. Krauts can't pronounce the sound of a 'J'---it comes out 'yo'—like jackass would be yo-kass. So, just saying---be on the alert! Okay, Bobby you are next on watch---let's go! The rest of us are gonna try and catch some shut eye."

The next morning, the entire company remained on virtual alert when they noticed a lone Sherman tank with a white star on the hull, barreling down the forest road toward where they sat in ambush. Before any of the sitting tanks could respond, the lone Sherman tank opened fire on them. With lightening knee-jerk reaction the Avenger returned fire, hitting the rogue Sherman just below the turret. Another Sherman sent a shell into the side hull and the lone tank erupted in a ball of flame. Men on fire jumped from the hatches and began running toward the woods screaming in German. With lightening reaction, Commander Kessel opened the turret hatch and grabbing the machine gun yelled, "They're Krauts--Krauts—FIRE, FIRE!"

Later, after the men were positively identified as Germans, Squirt asked, "Cowboy, how the hell did you know they were Jerries?"

Arnold responded, "Well Squirt—first thing was---one of our tanks firing on us, was a pretty damn big clue. Second, when the tankers ran in the opposite direction of our tanks and I heard them scream in German—I was positive. They were obviously some of those Krauts dressed and acting as Americans who had probably stolen one of our tanks. Well shoot, we didn't get a chance to ask them any questions starting with the letter 'J', oh no--too bad! That is a prime example of why we stay on alert at all times."

~~~~~~~~

The Task Force was in place with the attached/married infantry and another tank battalion standing down with them. There were, give or take--- 40 American tanks from CCB and CCR along with two other complete combat commands dug in at and scattered throughout the edge of dense woods about a half mile from the Meuse River. Sitting just on the outskirts of Liege, they faced east toward the German and American lines on the Battle of the Bulge. The field of battle had been chosen wisely; it was the type of ground, tanks like to fight in---concealed, with freedom to roll out and to move. For now they were at the edge of thick woods with a 15-acre clearing between them and where the Krauts would naturally advance through a corridor. The task force stood ready and waiting. This could be the perfect storm!

24 Dec. 1944: The cold glowing dawn spread across the bird-egg blue sky. Commander Kessel looked out through the periscope and thought, *I hope to hell this is the day because visibility is unlimited and its perfect flying weather for our planes to come in and pulverized those Kraut tanks and troops if they break through.*

The surrounding forest was deathly quiet as it had been for the past twenty-four hours; they were under strict silence orders. They had checked and then checked again their ammo, range finders, sync'd watches, and rubbed cold inflexible fingers until they could bend; all of their throats were dry with tension and tempers were on a short fuse. Camouflaged in ambush, the only reason any of the Allied forces moved was to take a piss; the heavy metal artillery and tanks didn't move at all. The standing down silence order meant no personal chatter, no two- way radios, no unnecessary verbal communication---the airways were to remain

clear until they got HQ orders to open FIRE, if/when the enemy broke through. The tanks and artillery were all positioned at the edge of the forest, partially hidden like a black winding steal snake ready to strike. The cannons were aimed where HQ presumed the

Krauts would emerge from the woods—if /when they broke through the American lines.

Commander Kessel and his crew tried to entertain themselves with non-noise activities; the one bottle of wine hadn't lasted near long enough. They all knew they could have gotten in big trouble for drinking that bottle when waiting in ambush. They all agreed with the excuse *we needed something to settle our nerves; besides, one bottle between five men didn't go very damn far.*

Their ammo and other equipment had been checked and re-checked; now all they had to do was sit tight and wait. Waiting was always the worst part, it was the time that their minds played tricks on them, the time when their emotions got the best of them. Inside the tank they communicated via note and hand signals; there was no belching, farting, coughing, or even whispering. Everyone was on edge because they could tell by the sound of the artillery and explosions that the battle was inching closer. Night time was impressive both visually and audibly, at the same time it was frightening because they all knew there was a hell of a battle going on just a few miles away. The sky lit up like the fourth of July, intense flashes of falling bombs, shelling, and artillery trouncing a target was followed with ominous volleys of thunderous explosion after explosion.

The sights and sounds of the raging Battle of the Bulge crept closer like an enormous staking, threatening animal. During the daylight, they could hear the concussions of the big artillery and witness the day time horizon, strewn with black plumes and clouds of smoke. Distant low level drones from the west turned into high piercing screams as American P-38 Lightening and P-47D Thunderbolts fighter planes zeroed in on their targeted zones. The tankers knew that men were dying just a few miles away. The obvious tension was so prevalent that few could sleep or even catch a cat nap. It was agony---the waiting and wondering. More than one guy had the heebie jeebies and tempers flared!

Commander Kessel peered out of the periscope for a final check before he tried to catch some shuteye. The brilliant moonlight fell across the gleaming white meadow wonderland. *Such a beautiful sight this winter moon gives us. It also makes it a lot easier to spot the Krauts if they decide to come at us during the night. Of course they will be wearing their white snowsuits, but we will know they are coming. That's what trip wires are for, damn right!*

Cowboy received a one-hour alert, there was no doubt, the Germans were advancing—and as suspected they were coming right at the Ghost Front. The crew silently checked and double checked everything inside the tank. Arnold even dropped through the floor hatch and inching around, checked the exterior of his tank. They were ready and right as rain to do battle!

Cowboy looked through his periscope again, at the pristine beauty of the fresh snow on the open field that spread out in front of them, a tanker's dream --open field of battle. Large lacy white flakes of snow continued to flutter to the open ground; it gathered like glittering sugar on the branches of the evergreen trees and covered their tanks with another layer of fresh cover. Arnold thought-- *that is such a beautiful sight, so pure, so clean, so perfect—God's canvas and it is Christmas Eve.*

Kessel had been sitting with the head phones glued to his head. Pain shot up his stiff neck, and he had no feeling in his ears, he decided to remove the headphones for a just a moment. Arnold scratched his head and rubbed his ears and neck. At first he thought he was hearing things because he'd had the headphones on so long. Then, they all recognized---the unmistakable ominous clanking metal on metal grinding sound of German tanks---Tigers and Panthers. At first it sounded like they were all around them, getting louder and louder. Subsequently, the sound settled—it was coming from the woods on the opposite side of where they waited—exactly where their guns were aimed. Commander Kessel quickly put his headphones back on then hit his fist against his open palm, the motion for prepare to attack. Their eyes zeroed in on the strategically positioned field gunnery officer whose arm was raised in hold position. Suddenly, his arm dropped like a stone as the verifying order came across the headset, FIRE! FIRE! FIRE! Adrenalin and fear mixed a potent cocktail of response without reservation or thought as the crew sprang into action. They could see the Germans now, the tanks—wider, lower, and larger than their Shermans—they were marked with the ominous black SS cross.

Up and down the line, every tank cannon and field artillery began to belch a marriage of flame and smoke as their shells erupted, tearing through crisp air and pine trees to hit their mark. The ground and then the trees shook with the explosions causing great mounds of snow to fall in sheets of white from the quivering spruce branches. It was constant----the barrage of firing went on for an hour or more until the cannons were literally hot to the touch. Then the infantry moved out, advancing around and across the meadow then through the trees to slam the white-clad German SS Infantry who merged out of the cover of the forest like eerie, white-sheeted ghosts. They came, thirty to fifty at a time, moving purposely through the deep snow. The crew in tank #2736 never heard the American 51D Mustang and P-38 Lightening fighter planes until they were right on top of them. They felt their tank shutter when the plane's bombs hit their mark and those on the ground were grateful for the help.

"Cease FIRE!" Responding to his orders, Arnold waved his arms and leaned back in his commander's seat, sweat rolled from beneath his leather helmet and down his back, his hands shook and his jaw was sore from clenching his teeth. He lifted his head to peer out of the periscope, to witness the finale of what they'd done. His brain did not believe what his eyes registered--- out there in the meadow, the battlefield. The once virgin primeval ground, covered with frosty glistening snow---was now swathed with smoking and destroyed equipment. Both German and American bodies sprawled in grotesque shapes, body parts freezing where they fell. And, blood---so much blood that the snow-covered meadow was glistening red. It was a scene of utter carnage – one the tank commander would never forget. Arnold thought of something he had heard just a week or two before, something General Patton had said to his men after a great battle. *"Brave rifles, veterans, you have been baptized in fire and blood and have emerged as steel!"*

Arnold couldn't get that quote out of his head, *that's pure bushwa—just another Patton-ism to encourage killing and to make it seem glorious. Killing is not glorious for most of us. Glorious? Hell, it's what we have to do to stay alive, pure and simple. I take no pleasure or feel no gratification in killing.*

In the refuge of his own mind, his own thoughts, Commander Kessel pondered the thought, *in France we fought the Germans as Americans—without hate, because it was the right thing to do for the world. Now, after the hell of the Hurtgen Forest and the Battle of the Bulge, after seeing what atrocities the German soldiers are capable of, we Americans have learned a new lesson from our foes, to hate. Most of us now kill to avenge and we are learning to live with our conscience, with our sins. It appears that most of our enemy kills without mercy or guilt; it's all in the training.*

---

1 Jan. 1945: The 81st Tank Battalion left the battlefield and moved to an appointed safe bivouac area where they received maintenance. Bobby chirped, "Sweet Mother of God, it feels like heaven to finally leave our tank and actually stretch out in sleeping bags even if it's inside a tent for several nights." In the meantime, all tank commanders were ordered on sporadic reconnaissance trips in the vicinity of Aachen to aid in the simulation and formulation of future attacks across the border into Germany. They were moving eastward!

7 Jan. 1945: The fifth Division executed new training exercises near Bilstain, Belgian, in anticipation of a massive crossing of Allied armies over the Roer River---an essential key to a successful invasion onto German soil. The American armies were like a pack of hungry wolves at the gate.

27 Jan. 1945: Another little piece of heaven--it was pure and unadulterated pleasure to actually sleep inside a building/house, instead of being cramped in a tank with four other guys, or trying to get comfortable in a pup tent, sleeping on the ground. That's what they found at Hergenraat, Belgian, and they never forgot it. For most of them it was the first time they slept inside a building since they left England; it lasted only two days.

Commander Kessel announced, "We are movin' out; we have orders to bivouac for an undetermined period at Ubagsberg, Holland. As it was, the Battalion and married infantry were to spend the next of couple weeks---getting some much needed R & R in the friendly Dutch village. They parked their vehicles in between buildings, in barns, or in any available space. Kessel informed his crew, "We are to billet inside the Dutch homes. They have invited us boys in to take a bath in their tubs, to sleep in real beds on real sheets, and to eat hot food they will prepare for us. We are to be their guests for the next two weeks. I expect you boys to mind your manners this is real nice of these folks and I for one am looking forward to sinking up to my neck in a tub of hot water and soap."

The tankers from the Avenger were assigned to billet in the home of Pieter and Emma Meijer. Their five children were grown and had moved away; the older couple welcomed their new American guests with genuine hospitality. Pieter opened the front door wide while Emma stood to the side her hands wrapped coyly in the skirt of her checkered apron; both tried not to stare at the grubby and smelly American soldiers and their nine-day growth of beards. "Velcome to our home, come in, come in. Mama has some cool beer to first help you like our home. She has been cooking for days and we are hoping you like to eat much." He smile widely as his ruddy cheeks glowed with pleasure.

Commander Kessel stepped forward and shook Mr. Meijer's hand. "Sir we are very thankful for the wonderful offer of food, a bath, and a bed with no bombs falling over head."

Pieter laughed as he stepped aside and gestured for the tankers to have a chair out in the cobblestone courtyard of their home. "Also, ve have no more of the German bombs thank you very much to American soldiers and pilots. Ya, but first ve vill sit out here and have a little to eat and drink." Not wishing to appear rude, but barely able to avoid covering his nose from the rank odors coming from the unwashed soldiers, he added, "Mama has already prepared the first hot bath. I understand it has been many weeks since your last one and this would add much to your comfort, ya? You may choose who is first to go—it is in the small room at the top of the stairs."

"The others must sit with me to try Mama's Bitterballen with a cup of cool Dutch beer. zee Bitterballen are little fried battered balls filled with fine mix of chopped beef, broth, butter, herbs, flour and Mama's special spices. I think you will like them best dipped in my hot mustard--YA—they are very good partners with zee beer!" Pieter Meijer glowed with anticipation and good humor. "After your baths, we will go in to Mama's kitchen for the meal, YA"

In the privacy of the small bathroom, Commander Kessel sat his mug of beer on the table before stripping his filthy uniform from his body and as instructed by Mrs. Meijer, put it in a woven grass basket and set it outside the door. Taking his clean clothes from his backpack, he laid them neatly on a nearby wooden stool. Then, without hesitation, he stepped into the steaming water and sank to the bottom of the porcelain tub. The lavender scented water devoured his body, clean up to his chin as he closed his eyes in pleasure as blessed quietness rolled over him. Tears rolled down his cheeks as he soaked in the healing warmth and luxurious sensation of the hot water as it enveloped his battle weary body and soul.

The Meijer's served the soldiers light food and beer outside until each of them excused themselves to bathe upstairs. After the men had soaked the weeks of sweat, blood, and tears from their bodies, they congregated around the massive well-worn wood kitchen table, covered with a soft red and white cloth and set with traditional blue and white Dutch dinner plates. Emma Meijer proudly carried bowl after bowl of steaming Stamppot and other Dutch favorites to the table. The crew thought to themselves *hell, it smells delicious, but it looks like someone puked in the bowl; that big sausage on top looks good to me.*

Arnold looked at Mrs. Meijer's large wooden table and thought of his mother. He could picture her standing at the kitchen table at home, rolling out her extra fine German noodles for the chicken and noodles she was famous for. The wonderful aromas of home cooked food filled his nostrils and snapped him back to reality.

Emma Meijer explained, "I'm most sure most of you have not eaten Dutch food so I explain, ya? This is main bowl is called Stamppot, a very favorite Dutch food. I make it with mashed potatoes, mixed with chopped onions, carrots, and kale. Sometimes I mix it with sauerkraut, but I have this feeling you might not eat that." Her rosy apple cheeks blushed with the humor. "That plate over there is our favorite, tiny raw herring which I have prepared for you. It is tradition to take them by the tail and hold over your mouth and swallow. They are very good for you—ahhh, digestion!

For after the meal I have prepared Koffie Verkeered (café latte) and two Limburgse Vlaai (light crust pie)—one filled with cherries and the other with apricots." Emma took her seat, beaming as the smiling American soldiers eagerly began to dish the steaming food onto their plates. She smiled sweetly as she added, "Please, if you do not like the Dutch food I will not cry---I will try to make you something better you like. Thank you. Now, enjoy, I hope!"

Just to sleep between clean sheets, undisturbed was pure heaven for the tankers. Frankly it took them a few hours to relax and accept their situation. But, in time they all gave into to a peaceful night of undisturbed slumber.

Their time in Ubagsberg passed all too quickly. A few of the tankers choked up when it was time to leave their gracious hosts in the Netherlands. It was equally as hard for the crew of the Avenger to say their goodbyes to their hosts. With heavy hearts they climbed back in their tank as the 81st Battalion rolled out, heading east, leaving the wonderful memories of the Meijers and the Dutch people behind them. They remembered the hard-earned time spent, simply resting, eating, smoking, playing cards, and taking walks along with daily calisthenics and maintenance of equipment. The people of Ubagsberg had been the essence of cleanliness and hospitality; they had treated the American soldiers like they were their own sons, creating a special bond between all the people involved.

~~~~~~~~~

5 Feb. 1945: Commander Kessel reported to his crew, "You will never guess what--- they are sending American forces back through the Hurtgen to rid it of infiltrating Krauts then take the Roar River Dam. The crossing is on the books for **10 Feb.** so that gives us some time to get in position. The other thing is that Task Force Anderson has created a couple of new smaller, more mobile tasks forces—CCB is now with Task Force Guthrie— named after Captain Guthrie, our Company C officer. "

Arnold looked at his terrain map. "I have been instructed to pass on a few items about conduct and the like when we get into Germany. Number one---we are not to fraternize with the Germans, even if they act friendly they might not be and it could be trap. They are the hostile enemy, bottom line! We might feel sorry for some of the civilians especially the women and kids—but just remember the Krauts use their people to get to us too. Reconnaissance tells us that IF the German military learns that particular civilians refuse or are afraid to fight against us, they are most often killed. Also, reports are reminding us that the Heinie's use haystacks to hide tanks, machine guns, artillery, hell--- anything to shoot at us with. So watch out for innocent looking haystacks, barns or anyplace the enemy could be hiding. Remember the grain shocks in France?" As soon as he said it Arnold realized the grain shock incident had been with his first crew, with Danny Boy. He felt his face flush and he quickly wiped his hands over his face which didn't go unnoticed by his crew.

"Just a refresher course, if you run into someone who you suspect might be German in an American uniform—if you think something isn't just right, ask them questions like this, "What's a jelly bean?" Pronounce it! 'Who is Joe DiMaggio? Pronounce it! If they say a 'yelly bean---you've got trouble in river city!"

"Remember that in the German language there is no such sound as our J makes ---they cannot or do not pronounce it like we do. We've got some strong indication that there are still Krauts impersonating American soldiers---remember that Sherman tank in the Ardennes? They are out there so watch it! That is all!"

Chapter Fifteen

"GERMANY"

"War will ultimately hurt everyone involved, and you will carry it for the rest of your life."

Joe Thimm, K Company,
395th Regiment, 99th Infantry Division

American Forces were gathered in force to take the Roar Dam on **10 Feb., 1945.** When the Germans received intelligence informing them of the advancing mass of Allied troops, they immediately put their own plan into effect and blew a huge hole in two of the dams on the Upper Roer. This caused the usually placid river to become a raging, impassable torrent for the next two weeks. The Americans sat in their tanks cooling their heels, waiting for the water to recede, which was exactly what the Germans hoped for. During this waiting period, the 5th Armored Division attached to the Ninth Army under LT General W. H. Simpson to create a more efficient fighting force.

~~~~~~~~

18 Feb. 1945: Commander Kessel had a big grin on his face all day and his crew couldn't figure out what was up? He had requested that his crew assemble in front of their tank at 1900 hours. PT, Bobby, Squirt, and Hans were not late as they squatted down on their haunches in front of the cooking fire. PT said, "So Cowboy, what's up?"

Arnold handed each one of them a tin mug and then explained, "Boys, today is my 21st birthday. I am now old enough to drink and in honor of that, I found us some premium hooch to celebrate with, that is---IF you want to help me celebrate and kill this fifth? One of the cooks even made me up something that might be called a cake, but I don't think I'm gonna mix the two, not tonight. They also fried some thin-cut potato slices so they almost taste like potato chips."

Squirt held his mug high in the air and said, "Here's to Cowboy—the best there is and ever will be. It's an honor to be under your command and with this bunch of old rabble rousers, Happy Birthday!" *That was one unforgettable 21st birthday!*

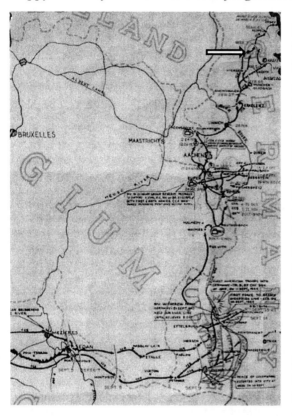

23 Feb.: The Rohr River water table had subsided to the point that the Americans were able to cross. This time CCB was not the first unit to cross into Germany, they moved to Baesweiler, Germany, to await orders to traverse. Under cover of darkness and a dense smoke screen the 81st tank battalion moved out.

26 Feb.: There was a muffled growling clanking sound as six Sherman tanks from CCB crawled around the corner and moved slowly in preparation to cross the Roer River at Linnach. Once across and following orders, they proceeded to the assembly area North of Hottorf to await further orders.

It was no cake walk as they moved forward, routing numerous pockets of fervent but poorly trained Germans. A church's monstrous black bell tower rose above the roof tops of Linnach like a menacing stone guardian over the town. As they passed a residential area, Arnold couldn't help but notice the traditional German manner of decorating the exterior of their homes with 'ginger bread' carving and etching of decorative boards and window frames. Once in a while he would spot a filmy white intricate lace curtain fluttering from a broken window. It reminded him of home and the cherished lace curtains that hung in his Grandmother Katja's dining room.

(**NOTE**: Go to Google – 'Linnich, Germany's Critical Past' and watch the crossing video).

The inky black night sky was illuminated with German artillery flashes aided by a gigantic search light, probing the darkness for any sign of the Americans. At first light and without warning, American P-47D Thunderbolt fighter planes came out of nowhere, swooped down and accomplished their mission. By the time CCB moved forward the next morning, the town of Linnich was a smoking, bombed-out remnant of what it had been. The surrounding woods resembled the Hurtgen Forest battle area--- peppered with matchwood tree bursts; huge craters pockmarked the surrounding farm fields. They passed approximately 80 German POW's marching past with their arms clasped over their heads. Great ghostly hulks of destroyed Sherman, Tiger, and Panther tanks dotted the rubble-strewn village streets. The Task Force knew this was going to be at least a two-day battle as they smashed through the Kraut defenses along the Roer River and their push to the Rhine!

The early morning mist only enhanced the eerie feeling of the completely vacated German village, where an occasional white flag was seen draped over an open door or hanging in a window. It was like something had sucked the breath out of the once bustling town. A bakery on the corner stood dark and empty, its front door splintered and display windows smashed. There was a metal tulip chair lying on its side beside a table. The Americans never got used to seeing the dead maggot-covered bodies of German horses, left in the streets where they fell, to die and bloat. The smell of death and blood filled the air, mixing with the smoke and ash from smoldering buildings.

PT yelled, "Hey guys look at that, someone has torn off the doors and shutters and laid them over bodies in the street." The carnage was bad, real bad. They all had seen some gruesome stuff, but today seemed different. The Mortuary wagons hadn't been through this area yet and the dead lay everywhere. The heads of the crew of the Avenger and its sister tanks could be seen just sticking out of their respective hatches, faces mirroring the carnage, eyes darting to the left and then to the right, not believing what they were seeing. No one had words for the sight.

Later, he would never remember just why, but just then, Arnold glanced to the side of the road and saw something that would haunt him for years. It was a little blond girl, probably nine or ten years old, propped against some sort of netted hedge, just lying there on the street outside a pastry shop. There was a gapping bullet hole between her 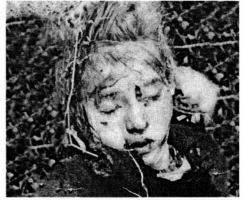 eyes; dried blood clung to her perfect porcelain face. The little girl's long eye lashes lay softly against her cheeks, almost like she was napping; her blond hair was feathered in disarray and her coat was matted with dirt and blood. A piece of grass or straw poked from her blond hair like a feather adornment.

Arnold coughed into his hand, hoping to distract from the emotion he felt the tears that threatened to roll down his face. He couldn't help but turn to stare at her as their tank rolled past. *Oh dear God in heaven, why do the little children have to suffer in this hell, why? I'm just thankful that it must have been a quick death; she probably didn't even know what hit her except it looks like a bloody finger or hand smudge there on her forehead. Whose little girl was she? What was her name?*

A dead American infantry man lay in the ditch, next to his two legs---looked like a shell had severed his body from his legs at the hip area. Another soldier was minus his head which lay a few feet away, intact and eyes open. They'd all seen gut shots, but this one was probably one of the worst. It looked like the fella had been shot, then tried to crawl under a wagon with his guts trailing behind him. He didn't make it. That was all he could take, Squirt began to puke down the front of the tank hull. He was crying as he vomited.

Arnold reached up and squeezed Squirt's shoulder, "You okay Squirt? Don't feel bad, we all do that and I wish I could tell you it gets better, but the hell of it is, it won't!"

Commander Kessel instructed, "I know this is bad boys, but stay vigilant—it might look deserted, but then again it might not be. Just two days ago some of our American tanks were attempting to cross the Rhine and 17 Sherman tanks were blown to pieces by German Tiger 88 shells. We don't have anything that can withstand those Kraut 88 shells—they know it and we know it. I also heard that the 5th is going to spearhead the XIII Corps to cross the Rhine on 30 March. I hope to hell we beat them again---being the first across the mother of German Rivers. Then, it's to the Elbe River and Berlin!"

"Headquarters tells us that our rush to the Rhine cost CCB nine halftracks, twenty tanks disabled, and one jeep 'kaput'. Task Force Anderson lost eight men, thirty-nine wounded—Task Force Dickenson didn't fare quite as bad as we did."

Commander Kessel said, "Just a heads up boys, we are gonna be short a couple of light tanks for a few days. HQ needs them to act as ambulances to take the wounded back to the field hospital. The wheeled vehicles are having a devil of a time getting through this muck."

That night, Squirt asked to speak to his commander. Arnold motioned for him to sit by the fire, "So, what's up? I know that was some rough stuff today. I've seen a lot, but that was rough I have to admit. I don't want you to feel bad about getting sick, Squirt. It happens to us all."

The young kid, looked up and wiped more tears from his cheeks, "It's just that, I'm having nightmares about them Sarge, I try to forget, but I can't. I think the worst ones for me are the guys that have their eyes open. I guess I never knew that you could die with your eyes open."

Commander Kessel stood and gently slapping Squirt on the shoulder, said, "Prescott, we all have nightmares, and even though I'm not a betting man, I would bet that none of us ever will be able to forget what we have seen and did in this damn war. It's just something cach of us has to learn to live with, in our own time and way. Do you believe in God? I've got my little Bible here if you want to read a few verses in Psalms—might help you, it does me. Try to shake it off now and get some sleep."

26 Feb.: HQ chose the village of Hottorf as their assembly area for ammunition, gasoline, food, and water; the service battalions worked out into the field of battle from that point. At 0430 hours, Arnold listened to his two-way and then announced, "Hold up—we just got orders to move out for an attack on four objectives to the east and north of Erkelenz."

The Avenger and five other tanks moved cautiously along the chopped up dirt road. About two miles from the Erkelenz-Rheindalin road, PT suddenly jammed on the brakes and sent Bobby sprawling. "For hell sake PT---give us a little notice, what the hell is up?"

PT answered through his headphones, "We've got us a deep anti-tank ditch across this road, we're gonna have to turn this bag of bolts around and go to the right, around and through a place called Rath. What say commander?" Arnold got on the two-way and the tanks of CCB were soon rolling at top speed toward Rath.

Cowboy, said, "Move out—we are gonna meet up with our Task Force Guthrie and help them take out a half dozen German Panthers outside of Rath." Kessel called for their married infantry to jump on the tanks so they could make better time over the uneven mucky terrain.

Kessel commented, "The terrain where we are going is nice flat open ground—just the kind we like except it's been raining for a couple of days and our half-tracks and wheeled equipment will have a hell of a time getting through there, but we are gonna love it. It will be cake compared to the Hurtgen where we couldn't turn or move. Okay---spread out. Let's go, let's go!"

It was high noon, under rain-laden gray skies when Task Force Guthrie and Tank Force Hedlin crossed the LD (Line of Departure) at 1215. The air was filled with the ominous clatter of tank treads grinding and clanking across German soil as they moved with menacing prowess toward their objectives.

A piper cub (Horsefly) reconnaissance plane with a Time magazine correspondent on board circled the battle field, watching the attack unfold. The correspondent later wrote: *"The tank drive was a thing of the sheerest beauty: First came a long row of throbbing tanks moving like heavy dark beetles over the cabbage fields of Germany in a wide swath---many tanks in a single row abreast. Then a suitable distance behind, came another echelon of tanks even broader, out of which wheeled from their brown mud tracks in the green fields to encircle and smash by fire some stubborn strong point. Behind this came miles of trucks, full of troops maneuvering perfectly to mop up the tough spots which had been by-passed. Then came the field artillery to pound hard knots into submission....."*

"Tigers!" yelled PT. Commander Kessel knew that one Tiger tank was equal to four maybe five Shermans and now they had a whole flock of those damn things coming at them. These tanks were monsters, with the longest cannons they'd ever seen and the unmistakable Black Iron Cross was plastered on the upper turrets.

Cowboy screamed, "FIRE between the wheels, at the engine compartment, hit the ammo rack. FIRE, FIRE, FIRE! The .30-caliber machine gun bullets from Squirt's machine gun bounced off the lead Tiger like a pea shooter. Anti-tank artillery hit the tank and it went up in flames as the Avenger moved full throttle, circled and zeroed in behind another Kraut Tiger tank fired and circled again and again. Cowboy yelled, "Keep it moving PT---circle, MOVE!"

"This is the only way to kill a Tiger---keep it confused, don't give it a stationary target. Move like the other Shermans are, circle—circle and then when you have a shot-take it!"

All twelve Sherman's and tank destroyers took aim and continued to fire, circling and plowing up the meadow and taking out the enemy tanks one by one. They all knew that unless they got lucky, the only thing that could take out a German Panther Tank with one shot was a .105 howitzer. Instinctively, CCB (Task Force Anderson) and their married tank destroyers jumped into the battle with a monstrous barrage of fire, helping to knock out the seven German tanks in a spectacular synchronized fire fight. The Tigers scored one Sherman tank kill.

They were heading back to the bivouac area when a Mark V Panther roared out of the brush right in front of them, obviously loaded for bear! It hesitated and the stunned Sherman tankers watched in numb disbelief as the turret moved ever so slowly first this way and then that, obviously looking and selecting the most advantageous target. There was a fiery orange blast from the monster's cannon as it fired one round at CCB's lead tank. The round hit low, knocking the track off. All of the crew bailed except for the commander and his gunner who stayed put and foolishly tried to finish the Panther off. No such luck as their shells bounced off the steel hull of the Panther like tennis balls off a stone wall. Finally the Panther obviously lost patience and fired a shot that caused the Sherman to 'blaze up' like a kitchen grease fire. Kessel called for air support. The crew of the Shermans watched minutes later, as a P-47 fighter swooped down, caught the Panther in the center of the field outside of Rheindalin and put it out of is misery with one shot---bulls eye and *kaput!*

The remaining crew of the torched Sherman caught rides with CCB tanks back to camp. By the time they hooked up with Task Force Rice and the third platoon, they had already taken Erkelenze. Count was: Forty Germans killed, 250 prisoners, and three 75mm AT guns wiped out, plus a Mark IV tank torched. The Task Force lost three tanks and two more knocked down which the mechanics were able to 'glue' back together.

All of them had the perpetual problem of running low on ammo. Kessel said, "We are going to start carrying 50% more ammo with us. The supply trucks can't keep us stocked on schedule---guess they're having trouble getting across the Roar River fast enough. We've also got a few more changes in procedure from HQ: Married infantry is responsible for destroying all discarded weapons they find—so the Krauts can't come back and use them again. Also, kudos to our speed of attack—it has kept the Heinie's off balance and not given them the time to adjust their guns. HQ also commended us on firing while on a fast attack because it seems to scare the shit out of the Krauts and they either give up or run! Eiiiihah!!"

During the night there was no moon, only a clear sky dotted with millions of bright stars to light the way. By morning, the task force was re-supplied with ammo and supplies by their service battalion and they were ready to roll! Around camp that morning, the scuttlebutt was that a captured German tank officer said he had observed the tank battle which Task Force Anderson (CCB) had been a part of the previous day. The German officer was reported to have said, "*From an untainted strategic point of view, that was one of the finest Panzer (tank) engagements I have ever witnessed. My compliments to your Sherman tankers; they demonstrated expert proficiency and skill in battle today.*"

Commander Kessel announced, "New orders boys. CCB is now under 'TF Guthrie'. We are attacking and blocking all traffic North and South of Erkelenz. Our objectives are the towns of Mauthause, Wockerath, Terheeg, and Mannekrath. We assemble south of Wockerath where we are to aid the 102nd Infantry in taking that village, then support them in clearing the rest of the towns. We also have orders to then move out to protect the left flank of the 29th Infantry Division as they move up from the south to. They are attacking the city on the right flank. Our mission is to block all roads from Wickrath north through Rheydt to Munchengladbach. HQ has called in the Bullshit wagon to convince the villages along this stretch of road to surrender ---or else!" (*Sherman tanks outfitted with loudspeakers demanding unconditional surrender; they were audible from two miles away*).

Hans hooted, "Hey guys—they are sending in the Bullshit wagon—that's just HQ's way of saying, this is your last chance. See, there goes one now; we'll see if the town of Hehn goes with the surrender offer or not. If not, get those white phosphorous shells ready Bobby cause we'll be following up after the 406th Infantry takes care of initial business. Damn Right!"

The Bullshit wagons were sent in with terms of unconditional surrender to the remaining Germans who were determined to defend their towns. Today, their answer was a return volley of small arms, bazooka, and light artillery fire. AT 1400 the 406th Infantry moved up and without opposition searched all houses and surrounding area. It was the same routine with each small village along the road; the BS wagon went up, then infantry and finally, if needed--the tanks fired their white phosphorous shells and burned them out.

On their approach to Munchen-Gladbach which sat approximately twenty miles from the west bank of the Rhine

River, Commander Kessel's crew had every tank hatch open. They were all well aware that five miles to their rear, fire and smoke from at least a half-dozen towns and villages could be seen on the horizon. Commander Kessel commented, "Hell, we gave them a chance to surrender and save their towns, it was their choice and our duty. We did what we had to do and now we are moving on to the next objective."

Munchen-Gladbach, Germany: Again, the bullshit wagon was deployed to this key town to encourage a peaceful surrender from a reported strong German resistance. It was a fact that Hitler was running out of seasoned soldiers, in a dire attempt to boost the military numbers he had ordered and armed German citizens to fight the enemy to their last breath. If and when they refused, they were shot or hung as an example for all to see. The Allied troops witnessed German citizens hanging from trees or quickly erected gallows at the edge of village after village. When they learned of the reason for the hangings, the Allied soldiers grew even angrier.

When the bullshit wagon broadcasted their demand for an enemy surrender, white flags usually appeared out of windows and or hung in doorways. Unfortunately in this particular village, there were numerous die-hard Nazi officials leading insignificant paramilitary units of local older men called Volkssturm or people's army.

Commander Kessel stood in the open hatch as the impressive convoy of tanks moved down the German road toward Munchen-Gladbach. He thought about when they had first landed in France with a complete battalion of 65 light and medium tanks. After everything they had been through, Falaise, Hurtgen, Ardennes, and now into Germany, they had maybe—forty tanks if that. HQ tried their best to replace the destroyed tanks, but a lot of things didn't happen that fast, so they made do.

As Task Force Anderson entered Munchen-Gladbach, CCB Battalion moved ahead unimpeded for perhaps four city blocks. Bobby had a white prosperous shell already positioned in the cannon. PT took the tank slow and easy over the narrow cobblestone streets as CCR paralleled them and the two companies fanned out along the city streets. Locked down inside the tank, Squirt had his eyes glued to the periscope, watching for any sign of trouble, any movement in windows or around buildings. Hans moved the cannon this way and that in a menacing manner. Cowboy also watched for trouble, standing slightly out of the turret hatch with his hand on the trigger of the .50 caliber machine gun. Suddenly small arms fire began to clatter off their tanks like ping pong balls. The attached infantry dove for cover and at the same time Commander Kessel dropped inside the tank.

Squirt yelled, "Sniper to the left, 200 yards, behind that overturned wagon."

Kessel replied, "Take him Squirt--- take him out!" Squirt watched for another movement then strafed the area until the body of a sixty-year old man crumpled into the street. Within seconds, the muzzle of a Panzer Faust (bazooka) slid out of a second story window and fired at their married infantry. Commander Kessel ordered, "Hans, second story window to the right—FIRE!"

The shot was nearly point blank and the entire building exploded in a massive fire ball as the blast sent debris flying through the air. Bobby shouted, "Hell, there was a white flag on that door on the lower floor and we just blew the whole building."

Kessel shouted back, "Damn right we did---Gross Mutter probably hung out the white flag downstairs while her Nazi Opa or son was upstairs with his bazooka! We don't know for sure Bobby, who they are or what they are going to do, and we sure as hell aren't taking any chances. Sometimes we are right and probably now and then we get it wrong, but this is war!!" Proceeding slowly, methodically through the devastated city—the tanks fired deadly white phosphorous shells into upper floors while their married infantry pulled the pin and threw live grenades into cellar windows. They heard and watched the city burn and crumble to the earth around them. Every now and then they would hear the chatter of a 76mm or a .30 caliber machine gun—infantry cleaning up behind the tanks. The mop up infantry reported finding crumpled Nazi flags and smashed pictures of Hitler lying in alley ways. In some of the villages, they came upon German bodies, stuffed into large paper sacks waiting to be collected or burned. Riding with their hatches open, the crew was silenced by the eerie scene---the pile upon pile of rubble, some with part of a piano or a velvet covered chair protruding as if it struggled to escape the destruction. There was usually some evidence of window boxes, some with flowers still clinging to life while others hung by a nail from a partially destroyed house. An entire house might be bombed or burned with only a majestic chimney still standing tall and proud from the rubble.

The tanks moved forward, slowly, carefully testing the waters, while the infantry lagged behind until the tanks cleared the area out, then infantry would move up like always. Infantry liked to cozy up next to the tanks for cover while they mopped up, just in case of a sniper. That's how they worked together, it was swift, it was effective, and it was final. Three task forces remained southwest of Munchen-Gladbach for a couple of days strengthening their position as infantry flushed out remaining Kraut nests from the area.

3 March: PT let out a yell, "Luftwaffe—11 o'clock—two or three of them coming in low. Hang on!" PT wheeled the tank off the road into the woods just as the German fighter planes leveled out and strafed CCB's scattered position. When the dust cleared, Cowboy relayed the info that came across the receiver, "They got a few infantry, but no artillery or tanks. That was a close call."

Small and large Deutschland town after town was overrun as the Allied troops pushed eastward toward the Rhine River, Germany's 'mother river.' It really brought it all to focus when the American soldiers came face to face with the long lines of civilians on the roads, trying to escape with all of the worldly goods they could throw on the car or wagon. There was a noticeable difference between the French and German civilians. The French appreciated the American soldiers and would cheer them; the Germans detested them and didn't hesitate to throw ugly words their way as they passed. After all, it was their country that the Americans were destroying now—after Germany had destroyed half of Europe. Cowboy told his crew, "You can't expect the German people to throw flowers at our feet. They are

a loyal people and their diehard allegiance is with their Fuhrer and their soldiers, no matter what."

~~~~~~~~~~

6 March.: Commander Kessel finished reading the stamped 'Restricted' First Army report. "Boys, we need to have a little chat. It seems that in France and Belgian where we were treated as heroes, the grateful citizens treated us like kings. For the most part, the American and British soldiers acted like Boy Scouts---remembering their manners and treating the French people with respect. Whenever we were invited into their homes, we were on our best behavior. We saw how the people had suffered under the Germans and had very little to share with us as far as food, etc. There were very few rapes and only minor instances of looting reported.

Now that we are in Germany, on enemy soil, it seems everything has changed and the Allied soldiers have shown a change of heart and attitude. Some of our infantry have gone into homes and found luxurious household goods; they've found framed displays of medals from the Third Reich for child bearing. There are crucifixes and Christian symbols hung on the walls, comfortable overstuffed chairs, silver coffee services, fine imported carpets, and lace curtains. They have also reported seeing a faded patch of wallpaper where the picture of the Fuhrer had previously hung."

"I realize we Americans are pissed off and damn angry at the suffering we have seen and experienced at the hands of the Nazi and SS soldiers; we are horrified at the way they treat their own countrymen—the senseless hanging, mass murders, etc. When we find luxurious household things like silver candlesticks, trays, dishes, crosses, and furniture, that's when the looting happens. Headquarters has overlooked this because some feel it's the right of the soldier who's putting his life on the line to take a few of the luxuries left behind. It's an accepted part of war. The looting doesn't bother me as much as the raping of women. In my mind, only an animal rapes—only an animal takes what isn't given. Now, if it's given, then I don't have a problem with that."

Commander Kessel continued, "One last thing. I know lots of you guys want to take home a German Luger or some other weapon as a souvenir. Let me tell you this, if—you are caught by the Germans with a German weapon on you, there will be no questions asked, you will be shot on the spot, capiech? If you want to take that chance, then be my guest."

"I just heard from headquarters and they want us to bivouac in Kolhausen, take a break and get some rest while we wait for more replacements and supplies to catch up. Since the civilians have cleared out, we have permission to go into their homes and find what comforts we can. I want my crew to stick together, so we'll find us a house where we can all bed down, hopefully on real beds! Maybe we'll rig us a basketball hoop and play a little ball. I'd like to see if Hans can really dunk it or if that's all talk. I also have a few skills I haven't disclosed to you boys yet. Be afraid, be very afraid!"

~~~~~~~~

10 March: Commander Kessel announced, "We have spent the last week or more mopping up and billeting in some of the German towns, Kolhausen being the last. We've got new orders. We are traveling black out for approximately ten miles north to a new area east of Oedt, Germany, where we will set up a military government for the surrounding area and maintain checkpoints along the main roads, coordinate civilian traffic, and watch for civilians without proper identification. During this time, maintenance will conduct an intensive motor continuance including painting some of our vehicles. We will catch up to our physical conditioning as well---maybe another game of basketball for the guys who survived the last game you played with me?"

"From what I can tell we will be in the vicinity for about four weeks. Other units will be trying to facilitate an adequate river crossing via an intact bridge. If that mission fails, we will cross the Rhine on pontoon or Bailey Bridges, constructed by our engineers. Are there any questions? If not, then we MOVE OUT!"

On 11 and 12 March, CCB occupied areas in and around the German villages of Vorst and Oedt, where they garrisoned the area and set their military government in motion. Things were changing—the Allied Forces noticed that in the villages they occupied, civilian morale was at a high state due in fact to the fast rate of speed of the Allied invasion. The attitude of the German civilians toward the Americans was improving especially when the German villages were left intact. Everybody---almost everybody just wanted the war to be over!

Commander Kessel announced, "We are sitting tight and all units prepare for imminent orders to move out." He had noticed there were quite a few nice-looking Fräuleins strutting past their bivouac area, and he knew he wasn't the only one who noticed; after all he was---young and male. One evening, Bobby and Hans were quick to offer to walk down to the kitchen truck and pick up a few things for the tank. After about three hours, they came strolling back into camp, both smoking cigarettes, strutting like a couple of roosters, and laughing it up.

Kessel leaned against the tank smoking a Camel. "Well boys, did you have a hard time finding that kitchen truck? You've been gone---." He stopped midsentence, took a drag on his smoke and exhaling said, "Well, I hope you washed your hands and didn't pick up anything that will send you to the medic. You know, these Fräuleins are hoping to get knocked up and get a free ride to America---you boys do know that don't you? I've got me a feelin' you two might have sowed some wild oats and if I were you, I'd be praying for a crop failure!"

Chapter Sixteen

"ACROSS THE RHINE"

"I don't know what I expected, another Mississippi River? This damn river flows 'north' across Germany to empty into the North Sea. It's fed by 150 glaciers in the Swiss Alps and is known as the 'father of waters.' Since time began, it formed a legendary moat against invasion from the west. The Rhine is the world's 15th largest river in volume but is broad and deep. It flows so fast that crossing it, is compared to crossing a narrow sea. There are no fordable areas, even during low water."

U. S. Military Engineer, 1945

Wesel, Germany---24 March, 1945: The Canadian First Army led the carefully regimented massive Allied crossing as they funneled over the bridge on the far left wing. General Simpson of the 9th U.S. Army (CCB and the 5th Armored Division was attached) was not a happy camper because he had to wait for the 'tentative' British forces to cross. They were set to cross on 31 March and they were itching to go.

As CCB was chomping at the bit, along with the rest of the American Divisions and armies, Bobby joked using an English accent about the lackadaisical movement of the British armies, "Them blokes are probably having a cup of tea, before they cross the Rhine!" After the Brits finally got organized enough to make the crossing, over the next week seven allied armies made quick work of crossing the Rhine River over the engineer-constructed pontoon bridges. After their crossing was completed, the 5th Armored Division's orders were to drive across the northern edge of Germany's major industrial region, the infamous *Ruhr Pocket*. Instead of attacking this area, they simply encircled it in a snare of steel and fire power—trapping and strangling the entire area as the main force drove into the heartland of Germany.

30 March: Commander Kessel announced, "CCB headquarters just handed down our orders to constitute our Task Force again. Once we cross the Rhine, we will move to assembly positions just west of Munster in preparation to drive to the Weser River. After that it will be to Hannover, then on east to Berlin!" A cheer went up from the infantry and tankers as Cowboy raised his fist in the air. The Fifth Armored Division was attached to the Ninth Army when they crossed the Rhine River on **31, March, 1945.**

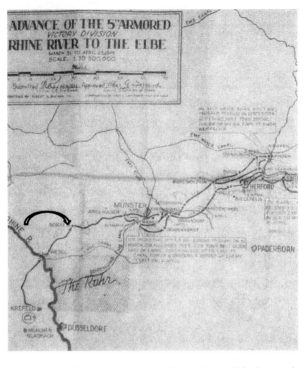

Unfortunately, before the Allied armies could seize them, the Germans managed to blow up almost every substantial bridge spanning the mammoth river, Of course, this caused the engineers precious time setting up the enormous pontoon bridges for the crossings. However, Gen. Patton and the Third Army crossed the Rhine River below Remagen, over one of the last remaining bridges. Their campaign would take them through southern Germany just above Frankfurt, through Nuremberg and on to the Elbe River.

NOTE: *The 5th Division spearheaded 260-miles into enemy territory in just under thirteen days. They had their orders and their goals---nobody slept for long, or ate except on the run. No one did anything but attack and keep rolling forward – attack and 'move out!'*

CCB didn't hang around Wesel after crossing, mostly because there wasn't anything left of the once bustling town. As the column moved, lead tanks fired continuously at woods and  houses, flushing out any lingering Krauts who still had some fight left in them. When they had access to a good German highway, the column was able to race toward their destination at 30 miles an hour. Whatever the conditions of the weather or the roads, they pushed and pushed hard!

Following the map, they moved out eastward racing abreast with CCR to the Weser River. The third member of the Task Force CCA remained behind fighting large clumps of by-passed Krauts in the rear. CCB was on the road of designation toward the German village of Borken while CCR was to their left or to the north. As they were rolling down the dusty dirt road, PT suddenly called out, "Hey Fellas take a look see to the left in that field and the woods---they are covered with what's left of our gliders. Looks like we'll have some super hero airborne boys helping us out or maybe they already did all the hard work for us and we'll just have to mop up!"

The spring day couldn't have been prettier—clear blue skies, sun shining, and the trees were filled with birds. So far, there had been no sign of any Krauts. Still on high alert, the tankers were riding open hatch and enjoying the scenic route to Borken as they entered a thick stand of conifers and deciduous trees that were just beginning to leaf out. Commander Kessel stood high in the turret hatch, smoking a cigarette yet keeping a watchful eye. Some of the infantry were trotting alongside the tanks and down the road, while others took turns riding when they could. Few prisoners were taken as their speedy advance didn't allow anyone to dawdle. Any prisoners taken were quickly encircled with a wire fence and guarded by a few armed soldiers until they could be taken to a more secure compound.

Cowboy, stiffened---something wasn't right, the air smelled differently---there was just—something odd. The boys in the infantry sensed something was up as well, some of them were even holding their hands over their noses. Down the road, Cowboy could see where the trees opened up and there was some sort of structure or group of structures. "Heads up, button up---we've got something up ahead—don't know for sure what it is."

Commander Kessel's turret hatch remained open as he gripped his .50 Caliber machine gun. The overwhelming stench became almost unbearable---like nothing they had ever smelled before; nobody could say for sure what it was. Then they all saw it at once, the 12-foot fenced enclosure with barrack-like structures inside. There was an iron gate with something written in German---ARBEIT MACHT FREI – (*Work Will Make You Free*). What they saw next stunned them all.

Emaciated men, women, and children were clinging to the wire fence; skeletal hands reached through the fence pleading for help for food. Hans and Arnold could make out some of their German words --"Danke Americano, Kommen sie herein, bitte-- bitte." (Thank you, Americans. Come in here, please, please).

Trying not to gag from the stench that filled the air, Arnold looked at one of the prisoners and said, "Vas geschieht?" (What is happening?") "Vas ist los?" (What is this?)

In his best German, Hans asked, "Vo ist das Deutsch Soldat'? The prisoner managed to point down the road and weakly mutter, "Das ist Veg!" *They are gone.* The inmates crowded around the Americans and touched them, crying---some were too weak to move. Hearing that the American troops were advancing, the German guards had simply run away in the night, leaving their prisoners without water for the past six days. The grounds were littered with wasted dead and dying bodies; some buildings were used as holding areas for hundreds of unburied corpses. Those who clung to life didn't have the strength to do anything but stagger or sit and wait to die.

PT and Bobby joined the throngs of other soldiers who couldn't help themselves as they vomited from the horrendous sickly-sweet stench of rotting human flesh, filth, and open excrement. Other American soldiers held their hands over their faces, exposing only their horror-stricken eyes. None of them believed what they were seeing—that something like this was even possible.

Kessel reached for his two-way radio, he called Captain Guthrie and Battalion Commander Anderson, asking them to advance forward quickly. Over the next two hours the men of CCB discovered they had happened upon a small German holding/slave camp called [32]Weseke, Borken. It was a collection point in Northwestern Germany for mainly Jews and other prisoners taken out of the Netherlands. It served as a holding camp until the prisoners could be moved to Bergen Belsen north of Hannover and or then perhaps on to Auschwitz extermination camp. *(It may have been the holding camp that Anne Frank and her family spent a short time in.)*

Germany was peppered with all sorts of prisoner/slave/extermination camps—some small like this one,

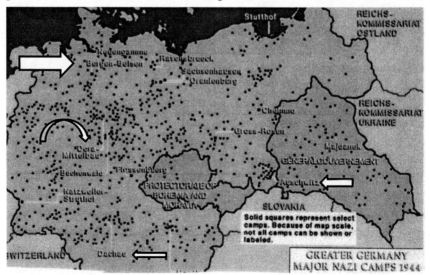

some large like Bergen Belsen. This was only the beginning of the horror and inhuman conditions the Allied soldiers would find as they moved across Germany.

A late afternoon mist clung to the trees and road making it difficult to see very far ahead. CCB received their orders to move out and later to assemble in the area of Applehalsen, Germany, just west of Munster; they were 70 miles closer to the Elbe River in eastern Germany. They knew Task Force Dickenson was somewhere parallel to their own route but in this soup, it was hard to spot them. Commander Kessel passed on their orders to hold their fire unless they were absolutely sure it was an enemy target.

They couldn't get out of the Borken hell area fast enough— every tanker and infantryman had seen all and more than they had ever wanted to see. Squirt said, "Dammit Sarge, we thought what we saw the German SS do to some of their own people was cruel as well as the heinous way they machine-gunned some of the American prisoners they captured. I never in my life, even imagined anything like what we just saw back there. How can people do something that to another human---its pure evil! I mean to shoot someone is bad enough, but to make people suffer like that---who thinks those things up?" None of them had an answer for Squirt's questions they all wondered the same thing.

NOTE: Arnold Kessel never forgot the German concentration camps and prisoners they saw along the roads--- they were the prodigies of his nightmares and 50 years later, he still broke into tears when he tried to tell of this experience. So, he rarely spoke of it at all.

~~~~~~~

April 1, 1945: At 0700 hours, Commander Kessel briefed his crew, "Well boys, I know this is Easter Sunday and some of us were hoping to go to church in camp, but orders are to seize and secure a bridge crossing of the Dortmund- EMS Canal. Combat Command wants us to bypass Munster and make our drive toward Hannover! We are to keep north of the main canal, looking for a passable route and hope to hell we find a damn bridge in tact— we'd be the heroes then!"

With the bridge in sight, the column began shooting as it rolled faster and faster toward the bridge and the defending Germans. PT had the Avenger doing about 20 mph and they were about 300 yards from the bridge when it blew sky high. Commander Kessel swore, "That's the bloody shits! The damn Krauts just blew the only bridge across the canal! HQ is calling in the engineers to lay down pontoon bridges to cross this big ass canal about four kilometers east of Senden."

The Task Force received orders to coil for the night at Venne, on the east side of the canal edged within a small grove of trees. Earlier in the day, they had noticed what looked like a few burned out but once impressive summer homes; the defiant charred remains poked up through the woods. After chow, Arnold felt like stretching his legs and having a bit of time to himself. He lit a cigarette and checked his side arm; after telling the other tankers he was taking a short walk up the hill, he set out on a narrow winding path that lead up through a grove of linden and pine trees at the edge of the camp. Taking his time, Arnold carefully inspected the path and the edges, looking for trip wires that some sick Kraut might have left behind as a final gift. It felt good to work his legs as he hiked the steep rocky incline, away from the main camp. He came to a section of the path that jutted off toward a rocky outcropping. *That big rock up ahead looks like a good place to take a breather and have a smoke.* Lowering his long lanky body, he leaned back against another rock and lit a Camel. Inhaling deeply, he gazed over the lay of the land that spread below the hill top. Arnold began to feel the tension leave his body as he surveyed the scars of war that pockmarked the rolling wooded hills. He closed his eyes and listened to the sounds of nature, letting the quietness envelope his mind.

At first he thought he was hearing things—music—a piano? *I must be going nuts, who would be playing a piano out here, all of these homes and villages have been bombed and burned out---any remaining Germans were taken as POW's or killed weeks ago.*

Arnold stood and began to move in the direction of the lilting melody—it was one he had heard his Grandmother Katja play on her Victrola—something about an Evening Star. Curiosity pulled him toward the music; he had to find out where it was coming from. Cautiously he made his way through another clump of pine and Linden trees and came to an opening where a once magnificent German home had once proudly stood. The vast grounds were strewn with rubble and a burned out half-track sat near the front gate. Parts of the castle-like home were still standing; Arnold could see that most of it had been bombed and burned.

Listening again, he surmised the music was coming from somewhere inside the house. Arnold tossed aside what was left of his cigarette and pulled his Smith and Wesson M1914 from the holster; he released a shell into the chamber and laid his finger on the trigger. Watching where he stepped, he quietly and slowly edged around the side of the house. As he drew near the rear wall, the music became clearer; whoever was playing had a light, lilting touch, it was beautiful. He put his back up against a standing wall which edged a former courtyard with a stone fountain and what had been a lush flower garden. He edged along the wall until he could peer into what was left of a grand room. Shredded, partially burned burgundy velvet window drapery clung to a rod which was hanging by one nail—threatening to join the rubble-cluttered stone floor. Opulent tapestry-covered sofas faced each other in front of a magnificent stone fireplace. Arnold could see only edges, scraps of costly Persian rugs which had once covered the stone floors. *It must have been a beautiful home,* he thought, *probably a rich German's summer home in the hills.*

Arnold froze when he saw a painfully thin young blond German woman sitting at an unscathed dusty black grand piano. She wore a plain soiled black dress that clung to her lean body in all the right places. Her hair was pulled back and coiled into a large golden bun, indicating she had very long hair. Wispy blond strands of hair escaped the bun and curled against her ivory neck. He could only see her profile; her eyes appeared to be closed as she played. Instinctively Arnold could see she was very beautiful.

The woman was immersed in the music she played from memory and was not aware of the American soldier watching her with his gun drawn. Her nimble fingers slid over the keys of the instrument; her high cheek bones and classic features reflected the inner turmoil of sentiment as her thin shoulders arched and moved with the rhythm, the emotion of the music. Arnold became transfixed watching the young woman mentally and physically express and experience the composition. Arnold waited mesmerized until she finished the piece then he inched cautiously into the room. He paused at the edge of the ruins until he was sure she saw him, and then he spoke. "Guten Abend--Bitte Fraulein, Bitte. Sprechen Sie Englicsh? (Good day--please Fraulein, Please, do you speak English?)"

Startled, her ice blue eyes narrowed with loathing as they defiantly rose to meet this intruder, this Ami soldier. "Ya, I speak your English. Look around and be proud of what your American bombs have done to my beloved home? This is all I have left—my family is all dead, my home gone. This piano is all which remains of my once beautiful life. I have nowhere to go, no one left to go to—no one who cares what I do or that I live or die."

Arnold moved closer, "Fraulein, I have seen how many German civilians suffer because of the war and it's not what we wanted, surely you understand that. This war has to stop. We wanted it to stop when we landed at Normandy, but your armies kept fighting and now we are in your country and still they fight. We are as tired of this war and the killing as you are." He paused a moment, still holding his pistol, "What is the name of the song you were playing? I remember hearing it in my Oma's house—she loves classical music."

She looked at the keys of the piano for a moment then sarcastically spat her words, "You are German? Isn't that ironic! Your 'Oma' played this song? How does it feel to kill your brothers---your cousins?"

Arnold blanched and responded with curt truthfulness, "About as good as it feels to them to kill me and my American countrymen who may be their cousins," He rounded the piano, unconsciously wiping dust from the black finish and said, "The song—what is the name, because I have heard it before?"

Defiant eyes blazed as she tilted her head, her eyes flashed with animosity, "It is called "Tannhauser—or Evening Star in English and was written by our German composer, *V*agner! You know of *V*agner?"

Arnold studied the beautiful young woman; momentarily he felt like what he was---a virile young man; he wanted nothing more than to take her into his arms---to experience that feeling again, if only for a moment. But, he knew that would be a mistake perhaps a deadly mistake to even try.

She stood and walk slowly toward him, "Are you going to shoot me with that pistol? You haven't told me your name, Ami soldier."

Arnold said, "My name is Arnold Kessel; surely both of those names sound familiar to your ears. Now, what is your name, Fräulein?"

"My parents baptized me Anastasia Magdalena Kat'therina---my, my last name is not important. Aren't you concerned that I carry a weapon?"

Arnold said, "I am happy to meet you Anastasia. Of course I am concerned you might carry a gun or even a knife, but if you were armed, I am quite sure you would have already shot me. I will put my weapon away, however I must make sure you don't carry a gun or a knife, do you understand?" He stepped forward as she lifted her arms, he took great pleasure in putting his hands on her and patting her down, slowly.

Stoically, she said, "Certainly you must realize my being in the same room with you, and even worse, speaking to you could most certainly get me killed by the SS. You have seen the unfortunate civilians hanging by their necks outside the villages since you crossed the Rhine, Ya?" She didn't wait for an answer. "As civilians we are forbidden to speak or have any contact with the Ami and if we refuse to pick up weapons to fight you---all reasons to be hung or shot. It doesn't matter if my father was important or not---I will be killed if certain authorities discover I even spoke to you—it is treasonous action. But, I don't care, I have nothing left to live for so I speak to you."

She stepped back from Arnold as her eyes narrowed with distrust, "When are you going to rape me? The Volksempfanger has told all German citizens the Ami soldiers, the British, and Russians would soon invade our country to rape, murder, loot, and burn our cities."

Her lithe body swaying ever so slightly as she walked, Anastasia moved slowly to stand in front of what remained of magnificent window where she wistfully gazed at a once beautiful garden. After a moment of silence she said, "The SS took both of my young brothers, 13 and 15 to be in the [33]Jungvolk. The last time I saw them they were marching in uniforms too big, carrying outdated guns that perhaps didn't work or have bullets in them. My mother ran after the Nazi SS general, screaming and pulling at his uniform, trying to get him to release my brothers because of who their father was. He turned and simply shot her in the head. Even though we were Nazi's and---," she paused and turned to face Arnold. "It did not matter to the animal who shot my mother and took my brothers---it did not matter who my father was."

Defiant tears rolled down Anastasia's porcelain cheeks as she continued, "Enraged, the SS general came back to the house, found me where I hid and raped me until I was unconscious. He left me, thinking I was dead or simply because he needed to get on with the business of war. For the last couple of weeks, I have survived by eating what I could find in the house. Before that, I sold my body for food and I've been raped too many times to count. Early in the war, because I was tall and blond, a true Aryan, our mighty Fuhrer Hitler assigned me to his Lebensborn Program which provided comforts to a special league of his elite SS officers. I feel like a piece of stinking meat, I have thought of attempting to find friends or distant family in Stuttgart, I've thought of suicide. Wouldn't that be wonderful not to feel any more, not to hurt, not to be hungry, not to be concerned with tomorrow?"

"I realize going to Stuttgart would be a long and dangerous walk for a woman alone and I probably wouldn't make it if I did try. I don't care one way or the other. I know if I live through this war, being German, will be even worse afterwards. We have very little food now, you have cut all of our supply lines, burned our factories. It's true you have strangled our armies, but also the people, all the innocent people who had no voice, no decision---as cruel as it is, we are now victims of our Fuhrer and of all of the bullets."

Anastasia gazed across the once elegant room, her mind recalling the glamorous evenings spent here entertaining with her family. A life that was --- so long ago. She put her head down and pushed at the rubble of her life which lay at her feet, "The German people only wanted to be strong and powerful again, to have what the rest of the world had. We all went forward hoping for a swift victory for the grand promise of the New Order of Germany, a respected world power. We believed Hitler was the man to give us back our glorious Germany—our pride, because he said he would, he promised us everything. He tricked us, he used us, and now he kills us. Once we realized he was most probably insane, once we realized things weren't right, it was too late---there was nothing we could do. Most of us have seen the cattle cars crammed with Jews, political prisoners, and captives; we also realized anyone who spoke or acted against the Reich disappeared; it didn't take long to figure it out. We did not dare act on what our eyes saw if we wanted to live; many people will say they did not know. We knew--we knew what would happen to us if we spoke up. If we wanted to live, we shut our mouths and our eyes."

"Now, most of our homes, our sons, brothers, husbands, fathers, and even grandfathers are gone. The women and some children are left---how are we going to live, to eat, to continue on in disgrace?" She looked at Arnold, "You would do me a favor if you shot me now; it would end the suffering which certainly lies ahead. I will always be German, so where does that leave me? Where will we be safe when this world of ours no longer exists?"

Arnold studied her beautiful face for a moment then said, "Of course our leaders know what you have said is true. But as one German woman said, *'It was us, it was the Germans who started this war and for that we will now suffer for a long time.'* As a soldier out for a solitary stroll to have a cigarette, I could easily be killed by a lone sniper tonight as I walk back to my tank or tomorrow when my tank turns a blind corner and meets a Tiger or Panther tank. I dream of going home to my parents and my girl, of living my life but I have no assurance that will happen for me. This is war Anastasia, we never know if tomorrow will come for us. Sometimes, it's the right thing to do to live, to live in the moment. Does that make sense to you? I am sorry for all of the personal losses which you suffer. Before I leave you, I will make sure you are taken behind the American lines. At least you will be safe, you will eat, where you will live."

Arnold reached into his pocket for his smokes, taking one from the pack, he offer it to Anastasia. "Would you like a cigarette?"

Her blue eyes twinkled as a smile crept across her face. "Yes, thank you. It has been so long that I have smoked, it will probably make my head spin."

Arnold flipped on his lighter, lit the woman's cigarette then his own. She motioned out to what was once a beautiful garden where a lone wooden bench stood under the remains of a linden tree. "Here, we can sit, if you have time, American tank commander."

Anastasia and Arnold sat together, not saying anything for a few moments, then he said, "Do you mind if I touch the skin on your wrist? I –I, it's been so long since I touched a woman's skin. I am beginning to feel like I am--my tank—a steel killing machine without feeling or emotion wound so tight that I don't remember not feeling like this. Can you understand what it is like for us too? I know you and your people have suffered terribly and it's not over, but I was not born to kill or to hurt people either. Does that make sense to you?"

A single tear slipped from Anastasia's right eye as she turned to face this American soldier. She put her head down and laid her hand on Arnold's forearm. "Yes, I have thought about what you say. We all become someone we do not recognize because of war, it's how we survive, how we do what we have to do. Even I wonder what will be in my future. Will I ever find a man who will treat me with love, will I have children? OR, will I not survive? Sometimes, I think the easier of the two would be not to survive because then all these terrible memories will leave me forever."

Arnold stood, stamped out what was left of his cigarette and holding out his hand to Anastasia he smiled and said, "Will you walk with me? That's all—just, walk to the top of that hill."

~~~~~~~~~

Commander Kessel approached camp just after dark and was immediately stopped by perimeter guards. After examining his identification, they said, "Commander Kessel, we have men out looking for you---where in the hell have you been?" Later, after explaining his 'long' walk to his battalion chief, Arnold slipped into his sleeping bag and fell into a deep sleep, dreaming of a piano, a beautiful blond German girl, and life. At least she would be safe at the VooDoo prisoner camp where he had taken her. Because she was the daughter of a prominent German general, they would see to it that she was kept safe. That's all he could ask for because after his brief intermission, he was back in the tank and back in the war.

2 April: At first light, Task Force Guthrie's company (CCB included) moved out toward Munster. Mid-morning, Bobby commented, "You had a bit of a late night didn't you Sarge?" Before Arnold could respond, Bobby said, "I know, I know---it's none of my damn business. Hell, I have to say that this latest campaign is getting to be a cake walk---almost boring it's so quiet and that makes me antsy—it's too quiet! I don't trust those Krauts---there are still plenty of the SS buggers left!"

Dense fog blanketed the countryside again this morning. It was around 1100 when the fog lifted and the armored column moved into the village of Sassenberg. Lt. Duran was the lead tank in the column—he radioed back that he'd spotted an old black horse pulling an 88 mm. gun through an intersection up ahead, followed by another 75 mm. self-propelled gun mounted on a Mark IV chassis. Without further discourse, Duran's tank opened fire with its 75mm. cannon taking out first one, then the other German gun. Suddenly they encountered a vicious cross-fire as a German Panther tank roared around the corner of a stone building, stopped and began to fire its cannon and machine guns. Duran's tank spun and fired, taking out the first tank, but the tank that followed it hit Duran's tank, wounding his driver and loader. The next two tanks in Duran's column circled and advanced firing on the move, taking out the German tank and the dust finally settled.

They coiled that night with over forty-eight miles of German territory under their belts. Tomorrow they would be on the Berlin-Hannover Autobahn and could make even better time. The plan was to cut this main highway across Germany then the central truck roads into Hannover would fall into CCR hands.

Commander Kessel remarked, "You know, all those sandbags Duran had on his tank—probably saved their butts today. That's why we all have as many sandbags attached to our tanks as we can---kinda evens the score with those big-ass German tanks. All in a day's work boys! Where else are you gonna earn $70 - $80 bucks a month, room and board for getting shot at and risking your life? And, we aren't even mentioning the great food and accommodations!"

Kessel spotted Col. Cole walking across the bivouac area toward him looking none too happy; the colonel motioned for him to walk with him toward a grove of trees. Col. Cole gave his subordinate a friendly, solid slap on the shoulder as he said, "Cowboy, I just heard where you were two nights ago; we just received a report from the POW camp where you took the girl. Do you have any idea who that girl was? I assume she said she lived in the house? Well I won't mince words, you may be damn lucky you lived to tell about it. Anastasia is the only daughter of SS Panzer General Helmut Von Alverheldt who was killed in action a month ago."

Arnold blanched as reality hit him, then he responded, "I didn't know who she was; at the moment I didn't care. I'm getting so tired of this war, of this fight, sir. I know better and it won't happen again. But frankly sir, I did frisk her for a weapon and she had none. I just wanted so damn bad to talk to a pretty young woman. I took her to the VooDoo PW camp after she told me she had no family left and planned to walk to Stuttgart, alone. I knew she wouldn't make it. It won't happen again! Thank you Sir."

~~~~~~~

4 April: The Task Force made their way through flat, rich farmland sprinkled with typical German villages of white houses

and red roofs, surrounded with once immaculate fields, drainage ditches, canals, and precisely groomed woods. It looked like a fairy tale until the men of CCB spotted close to forty emancipated slave laborers walking slowly from a field and lining the road, waving and cheering at the Americans. A few of the virtual skeletons even stood at attention and proudly saluted each liberating armored vehicle that passed in front of them. Cowboy said, "Damn, is this what we are going to see from here to the Elbe; how many of these starving slave people are in this country?" He didn't say any more, he didn't need to because they were all thinking the same thing as they wiped the tears from their eyes and threw some of their rations, chocolate and gum to the people.

Squirt asked, "Sarge, are those people all Jews?"

Kessel replied, "From what I've learned, no they aren't. Some of them are POW's from Poland, France---every country Germany has been in, they take Jews, religious people, political---hell, anyone who defies them and they throw them in these slave, death, or POW camps. Some are even soldiers from France, Poland, Russia, who knows? I don't think our American POW's are in these kinds of camps because of the Geneva Convention rules and all that. But they sure as hell aren't in any Boy Scout camp either---they are probably starving along with the rest of the prisoners. Shoot---Germany can't even feed its own soldiers, much less their people and all the prisoners they have taken."

Joe spoke up, "Hell, the other day this German woman told me that the Gestapo took her husband to a concentration camp just because he didn't want his sons to join up with the Deutsch Jungvolk—the German Young Folk army."

5 April: At the crack of dawn the column moved out in a northeasterly direction, moving through Berhholsen, Nuenkirchen,

Rhemslon, and east toward the town of Bindle. All that morning they had been pestered with a relentless cool spring rain—just enough to muck up the road. PT called out, "Up ahead, Cowboy, looks like we've got two maybe three anti-tank guns that allowed the first three tanks from Battalion's C Company to pass and now they are opening up on the rest of the column." Commander Kessel heard orders coming from his receiver. "Get artillery on that hill. Put assault guns on it, now. Lay in the mortars. Everybody shoot at the targets until HQ tells you to stop!"

Kessel shouted over the roar of the tanks, "Hans get a bead on that target, Bobby stick a HE shell in the cannon and let em have it. FIRE!" Tank machine guns chattered as their cannons boomed, cutting a swath to Anrath. Assault guns, mortars, and artillery pounded the hill as tankers and infantrymen followed behind to cover the targeted area like a blanket. Once in the town, they roused three Kraut gun crews in their billets before they could grab their guns. The town was thick with white surrender flags as American infantry entered the houses where lights burned brightly, fresh German bread baked in the ovens as radios played. Obviously the German civilians left rather quickly! The Americans grabbed the bread and didn't even turn off the lights or the radios as they marched their prisoners down the road.

Commander Kessel no sooner finished with his instructions when Hans said, "I'll be damned---look at that--those Germans just took the hell off and left those guns sitting right there! If that doesn't beat all—I hope that's what the rest of the Krauts are going to do from here on in! I wouldn't mind that one little bit. Infantry said that the Germans were just streaming out of houses and falling over themselves to give up."

Cowboy remarked, "Wow—if our column had been moving slower, they might have wiped us all out---see, again speed saved our butts!"

Bobby said, "Did you guys hear that Hitler just went on the radio and demanded that all Germans---men, women, kids pick up a gun and launch a guerrilla campaign of sabotage against our forces. Shoot, I bet most of those little kids don't even have a clue what their leader is demanding of them. Dammit anyway—making little kids pick up a gun and expecting them to kill for him, for Germany. There's something not right about that. I kinda feel sorry

for the civilians—from what we've seen and can tell, they know it's over and they know that to continue fighting us is just plain crazy, it's suicide. I guess that's why even though one house puts out a white flag, we gotta remember that there might be some nutso Nazi's in the other house that we have to take out. Nothing our tanks can't neutralize in a blink of an eye for damn sure!"

Hans added, "I heard that some of those kids are hiding in the hedgerows and bombed out farm houses to pick off our infantry when they come marching by. A few of our guys have shot those kids and felt real bad, but hell, it's them or us. Just too damn bad when the kids have to pay for what the adults do or tell them to do."

PT called out, "We got us an unidentified column---staying with us to the north. Can you get some info on it Cowboy, ---foe or friend?" Commander Kessel got on the two-way and in a couple minutes reported, "Don't fire for hells sake—that's the Brits---determined to take Minden before we do. I say let em get their butts shot at----better them than us!"

8 April: CCB stayed in the middle position of the main Task Force as they moved forward closer to Minden and the Dortmund – EMS Canal which fed into the major German city of Hannover. The bridge across the canal at Minden was still intact but so far, the town refused to surrender. A Bullshit wagon was called in and issued an unconditional surrender message across the loud speaker. Commander Kessel said, "CCB and the infantry have received orders to sit tight during the night until HQ finds out if Minden is going to surrender. Then we will know what they want us to do, so grab a bite or a nap, whichever you need the most 'cause we are sittin' right here."

A relentless rain fell throughout the night and the next morning washing the soot from the ruins and rinsing what it could from the village cobblestone streets. Cowboy opened the turret hatch and stuck his head out, breathing in the fresh, crisp morning air. "That was a good rain we had, but now we are going to deal with the damn mud!"

That night as they coiled, the tankers sat around having a smoke after chow when one of them started talking about the Bob Hope USO show was touring through Germany. "Hell, he has Francis Langford, Patty Thomas, and Jerry Colonna with him. Scuttlebutt is that it's a hell of-a-show. I guess he was makin' all sorts of jokes about the village of 'Bad Kissingen,' *"The name of the town is not a description of a girl with a weak pucker!"* The tanker continued, "I hear Patty Thomas is a real looker and some dancer---great gams. I wish we'd get near enough to see one of those shows, but Hope is sticking pretty close to central Germany---not coming south or east where we are. They say that normally there are like 5000 soldiers sittin on the grass, hanging from the trees, up on tanks and trucks—watching his show! That's swell of him to come over here like that!"

PT asked, "Hey Cowboy, have you heard anything? Are they sending us into Hannover? I'd sure like to see that after our bombers finished with it; I heard it's just a pile of bricks."

Commander Kessel raised his goggles and looked at his map. "Nope PT, I know we are only about 9 miles from Hannover, but CCR has plans of its own for the city. They are cutting it off and letting what's left to wither on the vine. Our orders are to stay on course—directly east all the way to the Elbe River!"

~~~~~~~~

Cowboy stood at attention when Colonel Anderson approached their camp fire, the colonel motioned for Arnold to walk with him. "I have something to tell you and wanted to give you a moment alone to deal with the news."

Arnold paled and stiffened, and then he said, "Is it from home? Did something happen to my folks?"

Col. Anderson turned to face him, "No, it's nothing like that. I know you shared with me the time you spent in the hospital in Paris; I remember stopping by to see how you were doing. I know how you appreciated the doctors and the way they worked with you, got you back in shape and back in your tank. Hell Arnold, there's no easy way to say this, a Red Cross Hospital tent outside of Borken took a direct hit yesterday. Dr. Renee Markham was in that tent—working with some of the fellas. She didn't make it. I'm sorry to have to be the one to tell you; I know how special she was to you. She was one hell of a doctor; we lost a bunch of good people yesterday."

Anderson put his hand on Arnold's shoulder and said, "I'll let you have some time alone. Word is that none of them suffered—it was over in seconds."

Arnold felt numb. He wasn't aware of the other tankers staring at him as he made a beeline for the woods that flanked their camp. Once in the solitude and under the cover of the trees and brush, he dropped to his knees and put his face in his hands as sobs wracked his body. *Why did such a good woman, a great doctor have to die? She did nothing but help other people in his damn war. I never could have dealt with the loss of my men, with me living through it and not them. She helped me—she was the one who got me to climb back into a damn tank. I remember that night when she told me that 'this is war—we never know when our time will come. I could be killed crossing a street in Paris. Now, she was dead because she had ventured out to a Red Cross field hospital to help the wounded.*

Grim-faced, Commander Kessel walked back through camp and toward his crew. They had all watched him walk with the colonel and knew he was getting some bad news, but they didn't know what. Now they watched him walk toward them and slowly lower his body onto a log by the fire. His face was pale and somber as he tried to find the right words. "I know you heard part of what the colonel said, it's just that I got some terrible news. It's not my family or nothing like that, it's—ahhh, it's just that the psych. doctor from the hospital in Paris, the one who helped me get my head around losing my crew and all that bullshit---she's dead. She was in a Red Cross Hospital tent outside of Borken, yesterday---the tent took a direct hit."

Arnold looked away as his eyes filled with tears again. "I just need some time boys, time to wrap my head around this. She was a special person to me---I wouldn't be here without her."

The next morning, as red, coral, gold, and mauve rays streaked across the blue morning sky, a Horsefly spotter plane swooped low, making several passes then radioed in the exact position of a pesky German battery of six 88mm guns. CCB called for the P-47's to help them out. In a matter of moments the Thunderbolts were overhead strafing and bombing the wooded area neutralizing the irritating sporadic German ground fire. The 47th Armored Field Artillery Battalion went to work on the position and finished up what the Thunderbolts hadn't hit on the high ridges. The 120th Infantry Division came in around noon and scoured the area. CCB bivouacked on the west bank of the river and spent the next two days helping infantry round up 1,060 POW's from the surrounding woods.

The 5th Armored Division had set up the VooDoo Prisoners of War Cage where most of the POW's or 'Kriegsgefangener' were taken and corralled or held with only 'one wire' surrounding them. Often those in charge would do a head count at night and get a count like, 877 prisoners. By the next morning's headcount, they might have 934. Germans were sneaking out of the woods and sliding under the single wire—surrendering without a shot! One guard complained, "This is nuts, we have German prisoners like some people have mice, they just keep coming and multiplying!

Squirt said, "Shoot, the Germans know this war is over, I wish to hell someone would tell Herr Hitler! Squirt laughed at his own joke then said, "Did you guys hear what their word for surrender is---'kapit-u-lation,' that's right, crazy huh? They are kaput alright!"

By the end of the day, Minden was just another town crossed out on the road to Berlin! The crew of the Avenger stuck their heads out of their tank hatches and watched the parade of German POW's. Squirt said, "Infantry musta been working all night—they corralled themselves a lot of prisoners or else the Krauts are surrendering as soon as they see an American with a gun. They look like they are as tired of this war as we are!"

April 9: CCB garrisoned outside of Minden until that night. After chow, Commander Kessel gave his crew the news, grinning ear to ear, "Boys, we've got ourselves some new orders--- "C Company/CCB" has been chosen to move to Division Headquarters and act as their advance guard. How do you like those apples? The rest of the Task Force will move out in a southeasterly direction crossing the Weser River at Hamelin. Before you know it we'll be at the Elbe River, then Berlin!"

Squirt piped up, "Hey Cowboy, what does the word Minen mean. I keep seeing it posted on the fences, buildings—all those places?"

Commander Kessel laughed out loud then responded, "Think about it—a lot of German words are similar to ours, just take the 'n' off their word and what do you have? 'MINE,' you knucklehead!"

Commander Kessel commented, "You know the 5th Armored Division is lucky in that we haven't had any major encounters with large SS Divisions or fanatical German armies. The scuttlebutt is that Patton and his boys are getting into it with some ass-kickin' battles down around Nuremburg; you gotta know that's Hitler's favorite city and those Krauts are defending the hell out of it. We're just getting the stray platoons who want to harass and challenge us—nothing major and that suits me just fine and dandy! We've mixed it up a few times and lost some tanks and trucks, even got some of our guys killed, but nothing like back in Belgium and France."

Squirt asked, "Hey Cowboy is it true that the Krauts haven't been using their 88mm anti-aircraft guns ever since we crossed the Rhine? Why is that, do you suppose?"

Kessel replied, "Probably because they have more tanks coming at them than planes. From what I hear, they discovered that by lowering the barrels of those cannons to a horizontal position, they make a hell of an anti-tank weapon! That's the shits for us boys in the tanks!"

April 11: After traveling over 103 miles, CCB coiled with the column at Deine for a couple of hours to regroup, dish up a hot meal, and grab a quick nap. Houses lined the road and the tankers noticed the fire trenches. They took their time now as the columm

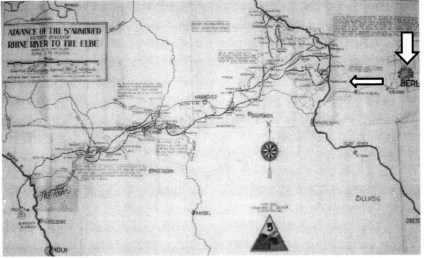

crawled—infantrymen walked along next to the tanks, taking out Kraut bazooka men from their foxholes and blasting Germans out of their basement hideouts. It was a house to house search/fight. Everyone stayed on alert, frequent Kraut artillery rained down on the columm causing enough casualties to keep them on their toes. Without further incidence, CCB moved through four more villages in parallel forked formation with CCR and CCA—towards the Elbe River. One infantry platoon was dropped off at each small village they passed through to search for enemy stragglers and to make sure none infiltrated back through their rear. PT quipped, "Commander, you know once we got on this side of the Rhine, it was like we broke through the main gate and had the Krauts on the runout the back door. We breached his frontal positions and now we are having us a real, gen-uine Rat Race to the Elbe"

Cowboy laughed, "This is like France all over again, it's the way we like to fight a war---fast and furious. No one eats or sleeps, nothing but fight and move out, attack and push hard. Now the white surrender flags are flying from German houses instead of their country's flag. Just for your information, our division has spear-headed 260 miles into Germany in about 13 days—how do you like that for blitzkrieg?

At the final village for the day, Cowboy spotted a couple of American infantrymen running out of the edge of town waving their arms. "Hey, you guys, hold up—you gotta come and see what we found, you won't believe it, you damn well will not believe this!" Bobby wheeled the tank around and headed for the village center. They pulled up next to huge mound of dirt and the infantrymen motioned for them to shift into park and come take a look. Commander Kessel and his men climbed out and jumped over the edge of the tank, they walked about 50 feet to where the men were pointing down at the ground. It was a grave, a mass grave with probably thirty bodies inside; next to the hole were more bodies of German military dead that had been laid out in a long neat row, ready for burial. Squirt said, "Someone obviously collected the bodies of the dead soldiers we killed back in them there towns we just cleared out and brought them here." From the green SS uniforms, they could tell that they had stumbled upon a SS Panzer burial; they were all young, so very young—too young to fight and die in any darn war.

Hans remarked, "Look over there; I'll be a monkey's uncle if that isn't a damn Nazi Panzer Training School. That's why them Germans put up such a fight in those little villages—they were fanatical baby Panzer soldiers. Damn, most of them can't be over fifteen—a couple look like they might be ten. Hell of a thing, hell of a thing."

The next night CCB bivouacked at Grussendorf where their Task Force (C Company) was released from guard duty at Headquarters.

Kessel listened to the radio and then responded, "Well that's the shits! 2nd Armored Division just radioed in—they are on the west side of the Elbe River at Schonebeck!" The next day, 50 miles downstream, CCA from the 9th Army's 5th Armored Division took Tangermunde on the Elbe.

12 April, 1945: That morning after chow, the crew watched as their tank commander walked across the bivouac area towards them. He seemed tense, even more serious than usual.

Squirt called out to his sergeant, "Hey Sarge, what gives, you look like you just lost your best friend, just saying!"

Tank Commander Kessel waited until he was beside his crew, "We just got word boys that our President has died. President Roosevelt is dead and Truman will take the reins! I wouldn't worry any, nothing has changed in policy or this war--- his dying won't affect anything that we have to do with; business as usual! I guess it's just that he was loved and respected—he's the one who got us out of the Great Depression and all."

~~~~~~~~

Allied armor continued the push toward the Elbe River. CCR reached the Elbe in the northern part of the division zone at Peine, while CCA dropped down to come in at Tangermunde. CCB's orders had them reaching the Elbe at a third point, Sandau, between CCR and CCA.

Commander Kessel's C Company (CCB) was straining at the bit---as they raced for the Elbe, reaching it at 1300 hours on **April 13th**. That night around the camp, word came down that Lt. Pearce's tank platoon had come upon a wagon load of American POW's. Squirt laughed when he relayed the story, "Yeah, I guess those boys were pretty damn happy to see the stars on the sides of our trucks and tanks. And, get this—a ways up the road, they came upon a cage full of Russian prisoners; our guys blew the lock and opened the door. Two hours later, the Russians were still inside the cage---cause they didn't know what to do or where to go! Doesn't that beat all?"

Late on April 13th, when CCB rolled into Sandau, Germany, on the west banks of the Elbe River, they had a surprise. PT yelled, "Cowboy, look up ahead at the river's edge. Just look at em' lined up; it looks like we got us about sixty Kraut trucks all loaded and waiting for that ferry to take them across to the east side. I think there are a couple of German guards on this side, over there by that truck to the left—can you get a bead on them? Hans sighted in on the guards, stopped and turned to his commander. "Sarge, those guards---are kids—little boys in uniform. I can't shoot them."

Kessel replied, "Well, just sit tight on this side, they aren't shooting at us. Go ahead and take care of the Krauts on the other side, the ones who can't decide whether or not to aim that artillery gun at us. We need to drop them right there. Go ahead and solve their problem for them!"

Kessel commanded, "Bobby get a shell in that cannon— Hans, you got that ferry sighted in? Let's hit that first, and then go after the trucks across the river. FIRE, FIRE again—keep firing until there's nothing left!" Columns of black smoke rose in the morning air as the enemy vehicles were put out of their misery and decision to cross the river.

Commander Kessel climbed down from the tank as Squirt covered him, just in case. Their married infantry was coming up the road as the two young German boys dropped their guns and lifted their hands in the air. They were frightened to death with tears streaming down their faces. The ten-year old lad to the right said, "Ubergabe---Ubergabe Ami, Bitte, Bitte!"

Kessel almost lost it himself as he looked into the boy's face. Freckles dotted his sallow cheeks and his brown eyes were filled with terror, fear, and tears. He was shaking so hard, Arnold didn't know how much longer the boy was going to be able to stand up. The tank commander said, "Sprechen Sie Englicsh?"

The boy shook his head to the affirmative, "Yah—I do, sir. I surrender. Bitte, do not shoot me, Bitte."

Commander Kessel said, "Do you have a gun or a bomb on your body?"

The boys quickly replied, "Oh, Nein, Nein—no explosive, no bullets, no guns. We don't want to fight; do you have food, Sir? Water? Me and Jurgen haven't eaten for three days; we just want to go home Sir, Bitte!"

Against his better judgement Arnold held out his k-rations to the boy as Bobby approached the other German lad. The brown-eyed boy fell to his knees with the K-ration in his hands, tearing frantically at the box. Before he ate, he reached over and kissed the pant leg of Commander Kessels uniform. "Danke, Danke Amerikaner. Will you take us to the prisoner camp now?"

Arnold reached down and pulled the boy to his feet; he wrapped his arms around the frail young German boy and hugged him to him. "It's okay, we won't hurt you. Here is some chocolate and more rations for later. Those soldiers there will take you back to a prisoner's camp. Nobody will hurt you now and soon you will go back home."

The boy turned as he was taken away by the infantry and waved at Commander Kessel, "Danke Amerikaner, Danke."

Arnold was near tears, trying to get his head around what that kid had seen and done to survive. *Damn this war and damn those who started it---and for what? It's not right that kids like that and innocent people, the civilians are caught up in something so terrible and they have no choice but to do what they have to do to survive.*

<center>~~~~~~~~</center>

During the next three days, the Fifth Battalion was busy securing a corridor six miles wide establishing a main supply route from Osterburg to the Elbe. Squirt asked the million dollar question, "Hey Cowboy, what do you think our next move will be. Hell, I hope we get the order to jump the river and head the fifty miles to Berlin. That's what we've been fighting for isn't it? Damn---I hope we are the first ones in---wouldn't that be something? Do you think there are some Kraut armies still in Berlin? Do you think he know how damn close we are to Berlin?"

PT maneuvered the tank around the hordes of civilians on the narrow road. "Where the hell are these people all going? Obviously they have no homes left; it looks to me like they are all headed to the west where I suppose they hope they will be safe, at least away from the Russians. Who is going to feed all these people?"

Commander Kessel rubbed his two-day beard and replied, "I can't answer that PT. I suppose the Allies will set up some sort of camps for them. Hopefully some of them know people to the

west where they can stay, but they've got nothing but the clothes on their backs and a few things in their wagons. They are caught right in the middle of it all. I don't expect there is too much love left for Herr Hitler about now."

He paused to light up another cigarette, "I'm pretty damn sure that there's at least a division of Nazi German SS just waitin' for us or the Russians to come into their capital but I haven't heard anything like that. I'm not countin' on anything right now. Some are saying we might get orders to go north along the Elbe to Denmark. All I know for sure is that the Russians are coming and coming fast—they want Berlin probably worse than we do. It all depends on what headquarters decides and I got a feeling that right now they are playing political footsy!"

~~~~~~~

Berlin: That night, 50 feet underground Berlin's streets, a phone rang in Adolph Hitler's fortress/bunker---60 miles from where CCB sat in their Sherman tanks. Herr Hitler was informed that the Americans were as close as 50 miles from Berlin and grouping in strength to attack the city. As reported later, Hitler went into an expected rage upon hearing the news, threatening to have several of his generals killed, then he realized that his biggest problem lay on the Eastern Front where a much larger Russian Army was preparing to cross the Oder River and attack Berlin. If Hitler hated and feared anything, it was the Russians----much more than the contemptuous Americans who he referred to racial mongrels. "They have no pure Aryan blood coursing through their veins as do our German master race!"

The next day, CCB moved to the west bank of the Elbe River area above Magdeburg, south of Wittenberg, Germany.

Chapter Seventeen

³⁴BERLIN

General William Hood Simpson, commander of the American 9ᵗʰ Army (attached to the 5ᵗʰ Armored Division) took the phone call from his superior, Gen. Omar Bradley, expecting to hear orders for the invasion of Berlin. Simpson listened to the voice on the other end of the line, "Simp. we need to see you in Wiesbaden immediately. I'm sending a plane for you. We have news regarding Berlin, which I expect you have been waiting for." Simpson was on the plane within the hour and flew to Wiesbaden where Gen. Bradley stood waiting for Simpson on the tarmac.

General Simpson climbed nimbly down the steps of the light aircraft and shook Gen. Bradley's hand. Back in Bradley office, he didn't waste any time getting down to brass tacks. Gen. Bradley said, "In a nut shell, orders are—you are to stop at the Elbe. You are not to go any further in the direction of Berlin. I didn't want to give you this news over a damn phone, I'm sorry Simp., but there it is!"

Simpson stared. He looked as if someone had just slapped him and he sure as hell didn't believe what he had just heard---not after everything his men had been through with the prize of Berlin right in front of them. "Where the hell did you get this?"

Gen. Bradley looked him in the eye and replied tartly, "From Ike!"

~~~~~~~~~

April 15 – 23, 1945: Commander Kessel addressed his troops, "First thing this morning, General Oliver wants us to swing by some village called Gardelegen. Some of our guys from the 5ᵗʰ Armored stumbled upon this massacre and the general wants every one of us to see it, to remind us of why we're in this fight. For all I know it happened two days ago; a train load of prisoners from a central German concentration camp called Dora-Mittlebau were being taken to Bergen Belsen for extermination. The train was sabotaged and the Krauts herded the prisoners out and into this huge barn that had been doused with gasoline. They locked the doors and torched the place; over 1100 people burned to death. When our troops caught up with them, the Heinies had pulled half of the bodies out and were attempting to bury them. From the word that comes down, this is going to be the worst thing we've seen to date, so brace yourselves."

No one spoke inside the tanks after they left the site of the massacre. The long empty dirt road stretched across the valley as Arnold stared out of his periscope. He couldn't help but notice the onset of springtime over the war torn country side; birds were busy building nests, colorful flowers pushed through the ground and spread over hillsides, and a baby calf was having its lunch. He thought to himself, *this is all insanity, pure craziness. What the hell? I will never, as long as I live, understand what makes people do such things. They said that there were even some of Hitler's youth---kids from 8 - 18, helping with that massacre, probably because they didn't have a choice.*

Arnold rode in the open turret hatch, wanting—needing to be alone with his thoughts. *I get it that the world has changed and now Germany has changed in a way most civilians did not contemplate. I don't think any one man is good or bad just because he is American or German, or Catholic or Lutheran. It's the way things go---there are rich/poor, master/slave, man/woman, good/evil, right/wrong—beautiful/ugly. We live the life that we are given the best way we can, we all do what we have to do to survive and live another day. This life of mine is not something I ever take for granted.*

~~~~~~~~~

All was not quiet on the eastern front as the Russian and Ukrainian army groups began to close in on Berlin. Commander Kessel noticed that first reports stated----*strong German forces moving in from the north toward the Elbe.* Acting on this intelligence, the 5th Armored Division, including CCB turned and raced fifty-five miles to the rear hoping to intercept and destroy the advancing German army. Kessel listened to the radio—to his orders. "Boys, us and the 15th Infantry are being deployed to

Winterfield. From what we hear, Col. Cole reports that a convoy of our trucks was ambushed near Ehra. The Avenger and five other tanks are being sent on a reconnaissance mission north, between Ehra and Klotze to smoke out the Krauts."

The morning of the 16th, six of CCB's Shermans and married infantry combed the woods and all roads in the area then set up roadblocks along a twenty-five mile front from Wittingen to Ruhrberg. They thought they had come up empty-handed—it was like the Krauts had disappeared!

April 17th: Kessel stood in the open turret hatch, with his right hand on the trigger of his .50 cal. machine gun, at the same time enjoying a smoke. He heard the Piper Cub Horsefly reconnaissance plane coming in low over the woods then circle back around a particular area. It wasn't two minutes later that they got a read on twelve Kraut vehicles, including five tanks entering the woods just up ahead. CCB and CCC sped to the woods, surrounding the area. The Piper Cub returned and radioed instructions for the tanks to deliver their direct fire onto the Germans. From a range of about 1000 yards, they took out a Panther tank and a half-track. By the time they actually reached the area, all they found was empty Kraut equipment, out of gas.

April 18th: Arnold Kessel rose before dawn and climbed up on his tank to sit and have a smoke as the sun came up. It promised to be a clear spring day as the sky over eastern Germany was pierced with glorious shades of mauve, gold, pink, orange, and just the tiniest bit of red. Arnold felt his throat grow tight as he thought of his home and mostly his mother. *My Mom---my Mom had a dress with all those colors in it; that dress was one of her favorites and I remember how pretty she looked when she wore it. Maybe next year at this time, I'll be home and remember this morning, when I had a little bit of homesickness.* Commander Kessel smiled as he hopped down from the tank and walked over to the line in front of the chow truck.

The 81st Tank Battalion finally had a new heavy tank of their own---one of the M-26 General Pershing tanks that was on equal terms with the German Panther. Arnold said, "We'll follow that beast into the woods up ahead, wish we were in it, but behind is just as good I guess. Man, that's a beaut! I can't wait to see it in action. They say it can take a Panther in one shot. I wish to hell the engineers had come up with it about a year or two ago. Their timing is pretty much the shits!"

They eased into the woods around Jutar where they got word there were enemy vehicles sighted. PT followed right on the track of the new M-26 as it growled and bucked over the road. Suddenly it's canon belched fire and smoke, it picked up speed and kept firing as it went. Bobby loaded a shell into their canon and Hans was ready to fire if and when he spotted something the M-26 had missed. Squirt complained, "Man, I sure do miss having those P-47's at our beck and call. If we hadn't spearheaded the 9th Army's advance into Germany so fast, they could have kept up--- miss that fire power they gave us."

The column continued along the heavily wooded road with the M-26 in the lead. Commander Kessel and the other tankers heard the sound of small arms fire up ahead and the infantry platoon dismounted the tanks and hit the ground running. Captain Boyson in the lead tank called in Horsefly for more eyes in the sky. He received some welcome news which he passed on.

Commander Kessel shouted out, "I just got word that we've got some of our P-47's in the air and they are looking for something to do---Capt. Boyson invited them on over here. Now we've gotta get our infantry out of those woods, pronto!"

In another minute, the sky was filled with three flights of four Thunderbolts each. Commander Kessel and his crew just watched with delight out of their open hatches. Bobby squealed, "Look at those babies swoop down with their .50 caliber guns blazing and dropping their bombs like candy out of Santa's bag." When the planes sent tracers blazing to the ground---it looked like 4th of July but it sounded like the end of the world! The Thunderbolts ended all hope that the Krauts might have had, by totally destroying three Panther tanks, five half-tracks, three trucks, and a jeep-like vehicle. By the time the Allied tank and infantry column advanced onto the scene to mop up, there was nothing moving. Every German who could run did just that or died where he fell!

CCB received orders to double step it 55 miles to the rear to aid in a trap that was being set for the Von Clausewitz Division. CCA and CCR stayed abreast of each other as they circled around to form the trap for the Kraut Division.

PT shouted over the growl of the tank treads, "Cowboy, it looks like there's a pretty damn big Panzer column coming right at us from the north. I can't tell for sure, but I think it might be ours—there are three American half-tracks in the lead. Commander Kessel got on the two-way with their married infantry, "Echo – 6- Bravo; Echo -6 – Bravo. Need Scout ahead on column approaching to determine if foe or ours. Get on it! OUT!

Five minutes later, Kessel listened intently as infantry reported, "Sir, they are Krauts. We thought they were ours---got some of our equipment, but we listened to em speak English—got a distinct German guttural ring to it. They ARE Krauts –the whole damn lot of em! Dressed up like Americans—what the hell do they think this is –Halloween? Let's show em' what's in our bag of tricks!"

Kessel passed on the reconnaissance info and the armor set up roadblocks at Lindorf and Ohrdorf, while infantry headed for the woods to outflank the column. Artillery got their guns into place then sat back and waited! Some of CCB's tanks were camouflaged in the woods while others were out in plain sight blocking the road. The Avenger had drawn a short straw and they were sitting out in plain sight. CCB was about to engage in its most decisive engagement.

Commander Kessel shouted, "Button UP!" The stutter of machine gun fire filled the air, followed by the thump K-thump of mortars in the distance. It didn't take long for the Krauts to realize that their charade was up and the Americans knew they were German, and then all hell broke loose. PT screamed, "A Mark IV just came out of the woods heading straight for us."

Cowboy, yelled, "FIRE, FIRE—keep hitting it with those HE shells! Keep moving PT, circle and FIRE!" With the fifth shot the Mark IV swerved to the left and literally bucked as the track fell off. Smoke poured from the hatches as the crew began to bail.

Commander Kessel yelled, 'Get ready boys, Bobby stick a HE shell in the cannon—you got your sights on something Hans? PT---start moving this thing around, we don't want to be a sitting duck today! Give 'em hell Squirt---work those bastards over. FIRE, FIRE!

Cowboy shouted, "Dammit, we are butting heads with Von Clausewitz's Panzer Division---remember, we just heard about them two days ago. It's one of the last big groupings of fanatical SS Nazi's and we are enlisted to give them the heave ho!" CCB trapped two task forces of the Von Clausewitz Panzers, backing them up against a stone ridge.

Hold tight, I see something." With that Commander Kessel slipped off the side of the tank and ran to the right through the woods, with this Colt 45 drawn. Minutes later he returned with his gun pointed at the head of a German Corporal. "Get Lt. Col. Anderson on the two-way, he's gotta hear what this guy has to say!"

Commander Kessel walked behind the German prisoner as they headed for interrogation. Once inside the command center at the rear of the operation, the Nazi soldier didn't need much encouragement to spill his guts. Speaking German, Kessel instructed the prisoner to answer his questions as directed by Battalion Commander Anderson.

"It will go easier for you if you tell us the truth the first time and don't try and hand us any bullshit. All that will get you, is a bullet---JA? Identify your force, strength, mission and operational plan and do it now! That will get you into the POW camp and you might get out of this war alive."

Nervously, the prisoner looked around the room at the armed American soldiers. He didn't miss the intensity or loathing in the commander's eyes as he said, "Ve are the newly organized Von Clausewitz SS Panzer Division, consisting of three task forces and approximately 3000 men. Each task force of 1000 men has one Mark V tank, two Panther tanks with 75mm. guns, one Mark IV tank, a tank destroyer with an 88mm gun, 25 half- tracks, four 105mm self-propelled Howitzers, three tractor-towed 105mm. guns, many captured American trucks, Jeeps, half-tracks, uniforms, and many more German trucks. We are led by the last of Germany's elite SS Nazi Panzer commanders. For us there is no surrender."

The prisoner asked for water, after he drank he continued, "Our mission is to push hard to the south from the Veser-Elbe Canal heading for the Hartz Mountains in the heart of Germany, vhere ve vill make a last stand to the death if necessary."

All that afternoon the Task Force artillery and tanks continued to crush the bottled-up vehicles of Von Clausewitz's Division.

By the next morning all of the German armor and troops which attempted to bash through their lines had been annihilated. CCB counted 5 of their own men killed, two wounded, and two still missing in action. They added to the number of Germans they had captured since April first; their count was now 3,150 Kraut PW's! In this decisive battle, the American task force had wounded around 790 Germans, killed over 800 and had smashed 75 various assault guns, 12 tanks, and over 120 German vehicles. They also captured a crucial trainload of ammunition meant for Von Clausewitz.

April 19th: Commander Kessel relayed his orders to the crew of the Avenger. "We got orders to leave the Klotze Forest and move out to the west. That's all I've got for now." For all intense purposes, that was to be their last major combat order. For them the war in Europe was all but over. The Fifth Division would go down in the history books as carving out one of the most accomplished combat records of any other American division in the war in Europe. *NOTE: See Endnotes for all of the Fifth Divisions--- 'First' accomplishments.*

BERLIN, April 20, 1945: There was a constant stream of well-wishing Nazi party officials and generals entering Hitler's underground bunker on his 56th birthday. Clicking their heels as they lifted their glasses, shouting 'Heil Hitler,' the first Russian artillery shell exploded a block from the entrance to the Fuhrerbunker! A momentary hush fell over the well-wishers as Hitler laughed, breaking the tension with, "No need to worry; obviously the Russians have only captured one of our large railroad guns. They are over twenty miles away from Berlin."

Approximately 50 miles from Berlin, in the darkest part of the early morning on April 20th, American sentries heard the gargling metallic growl of numerous enemy vehicles starting their engines in close proximity. The American camp came alive as they were rousted from their sleeping bags or wherever it was they had slept that night. Commander Kessel barked, "Sounds to me like they are north of Ohrdorf, in those woods. We need to jump into positon to block the roads and stop them once they start to move. However, we sit tight until we get some orders from Col. Anderson, no need to jump off in different directions; we need a plan."

PT said, "It's blacker than black out there. Why the hell are the Krauts pulling out in the middle of the night? They have to know we are sittin' here and we're going to fire at anything moving down that damn road!"

CCB and the rest of the 81st were in position, peering into the darkness, trying to see anything that appeared to move. Suddenly Squirt said in a loud whisper, "Cowboy, I think I see em'—it's the glow of exhausts over there on that road to the east---watch. SEE---there---that's the Germans, I'm pretty damn sure."

Commander Kessel got the go ahead and passed it on to his crew, 'We are to fire on anything that moves out there. Hans, sight that Nazi Dummkopf column in and FIRE. Keep firing---you all fire on anything that even wiggles until it stops wiggling, got that?"

A call was forwarded to the 71st Artillery to fire on the German column but it was too close to the battery site for them to use their indirect fire. Just as the sun crawled up into the blue morning sky, the 71st was able to rain heavy unforgiving artillery fire on the German division. CCB was joined by five more tanks as they moved from Ohrdorf into Lindhof, seizing the villages of Haselhorst and finally Lindhof.

"Hallelujah! Here come our P-47's with guns blazing! Go get em boys---have at those sneaking Krauts!" Bobby yelled at the top of his voice. They watched as the American planes swooped in with guns blazing, bombing and strafing the enemy column as they tried to hightail it out of Hinchof.

After the 15th Infantry recaptured all of the villages and secured them it was all pretty much over—as was the 13-day flash and sizzle of the glorious Von Clausewitz Division and their final mission to defend the motherland. It was all but virtually destroyed

and the entire army and staff captured in less than two weeks-----
Kaput!

Commander Kessel commented that night after chow,
"Now what? We sit and wait for our orders to cross the Elbe and
move on Berlin. Are we ready boys? Are we, ready or not?" The
crew and every tanker within earshot yelled and waved their fists
into the German night sky. They could hardly wait for the
opportunity---for that moment they had fought for since they
landed on Normandy!

~~~~~~~~

Berlin, April 30, 1945: Hitler's underground bunker was
stifling with uneasy generals and their jumpy aides-de-camp who
were curious and at the same time alarmed by the close proximity
of the Russians. They all saw/understood the writing on the wall
even if there leader did not. Now, they wanted to see what brilliant
plan their great Fuhrer was going to introduce to them next. Hitler
seemed oddly detached and unconcerned about the Russians or
even the advancing American armies.

An aide bent to whisper into the Fuhrer's ear. "Mein
Fuhrer, reports are the Russians are outside the city limits---just a
few miles from here." Hitler abruptly dismissed his entourage` and
moved on to his final plan; he found his long-time lover and new
wife Eva Braun, gave her a cyanide capsule and a glass of water.
When that was completed as planned he pulled out his luger and
shot himself---three days before Germany surrendered,
unconditionally.

Outside of the Third Reich's headquarters the Battle of
Berlin was in its early throes as eight Soviet armies rapidly
converged on the opulent grandeur of the hated German capital
city. A cold-blooded rampage of longstanding incensed hatred
between the Germans and Russians promised to come to a head in
the days ahead, in an attempt to even a score that would never be
evened! The long and bloody Battle of Berlin took place from
April 16th and lasted until May 2nd, 1945. All the while, German
civilians huddled in burned out buildings, in basements, cellars,
and makeshift shelters, praying and hoping the Russians or one of

their bombs didn't find them. They were caught in the middle, just trying to survive a hideous war and a barbarous foe.

On the west side of the Elbe River, civilians fleeing the region with horse-drawn wagons and carts were relieved of their horses by bands of German soldiers who simply confiscated the animals to pull their wagons and artillery guns into Berlin. Civilians were left along the road with carts and wagons heaped  with all of their earthly belongings and no way to pull them out of harm's way. Arnold was certain that the people had not put up a fight for their horses—if their soldiers needed them more, then they took them. Even in these dire straits the civilian's eyes and body language burned with defiance and fervent hatred as they glared at the advancing American army.

~~~~~~~~

VooDoo – 5th Armored Division had set up another single-wire strung POW camp enclosure near Ohrdorf, guarded by carbine carrying, bored-stiff guards. It was a mighty popular destination, in fact the Allies had so many POW camps they were losing count. Inside the tank, PT quipped, "Hell, you'd think that it was the Waldorf the way them Germans are scratching to get in. I walked by there the other day and this here guard told me that some private with one gun, was ordered to take 60 prisoners to the POW camp and by the time he got there he had 800. He said that young, old, arrogant SS soldiers, pot-bellied reservists, fuzz-faced Hitler youth, monocle Prussians are all willing inmates. There are German female nurses and even some wives and girlfriends who tried to join the POW's.

The American guards watched them sit around, playing sad songs on their accordions, reminiscing about the glory days and their heroic feats in battle. The POW's scavenged the grounds f or discarded cigarette butts and in their spare time plucked abundant lice from what was left of their field-gray and black German uniforms. They eagerly ate the same basic rations as the U.S. troops and were thankful for them and the fact that for them, the war was over.

The American Task Force tanks thundered into the outskirts of Tangermunde which lay on the eastern side of the Elbe River. Suddenly the town's sirens began to scream---a signal for the Germans to begin shooting with everything they had. Still smarting from the fact that they were denied access to march on Berlin, Commander Kessel and his fellow tankers stood on the Western banks of the Elbe and watched another battle on the Eastern side to which they were not invited. Tank commander Kessel listened to the sound of machine gun chatter off in the distance and thought of when he was a kid.

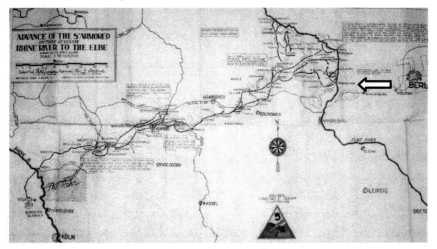

Tangermunde, Germany, May 6, 1945:
The final battle of WWII

"Hey PT, doesn't that sound like when we used to take a playing card and attached it to the wheel spokes on our bikes with a clothes pin?"

PT laughed and replied, "It sure does—also remember how it sounded when we'd take a stick and drag it along a picket fence---that same rat-a-tat sound!"

On the Eastern side of the Elbe River under a piebald-gray sky, a mammoth Russian army descended on what was left of the defiant German Twelfth Army. American soldiers sat across the river on the west side, as mere spectators. It was a final strangulated attempt to make a difference in the European holocaust---a war which in all actuality had ended months before. To protect themselves, the Americans sent up flares so the Soviets would know their position and not fire on them. The Americans couldn't fire on the Germans for fear of hitting a Ruskie—so all they could do was sit tight and watch.

CCB and married infantry park themselves at the edge of a flat four-mile square meadow near a partially destroyed railway bridge which crossed the Elbe River. They had been watching thousands of German soldiers and civilians crowding the bridge and the banks of the river, waiting for days--hoping to get a turn, a chance to get across and away from 'Ivan.' Suddenly the Ruskies began to shell the railroad bridge and again the Americans sent up flares to show their position. Most of the German soldiers escaped into the woods but the civilians became hysterical and a full-fledged mob developed, rushing the partially destroyed bridge. Men, women, and children were seen balancing across and clinging to the railroad tracks. People were trampled, crowded, or pushed off into the river—all frantic to escape from the Russians.

Commander Kessel didn't believe what he was seeing as several young German girls stripped and jumping into the river and began to swim across. Other people on the far banks threw anything that could float into the water and tried to float across or at least down river away from the Soviets. The Germans were insanely

afraid of the Russians, so much so that all common sense left them as they committed acts of desperation in their attempt to escape Ivan.

Then the unbelievable happened on that bridge---German soldiers began to ambush the advancing Russians from behind the bridge piers. When Ivan drew back, the German soldiers stampeded over the top and through their own civilians as they crossed the bridge to safety, obviously amused at their clever ruse. The Americans who waited for them on the other side were not smiling.

Hans shouted with outraged, "Those Nazi bastards---is there no amount of decency left, even for their own countrymen--- their women and children? Let's go get those shitheads, come on!"

The German civilians had all heard how the Russian soldiers savagely rampaged through the streets and German homes after the Battle of Berlin. The Russians, on the other hand felt they had the right to loot Berlin, they had not forgotten what the Germans had done to their people in Stalingrad---now it was payback. If a Russian soldier spoke the words, "Frau Komm," it struck terror into German women because they knew it was the Russian prelude to rape. Young, old, pretty, homely, dirty, clean--- the Ruskies didn't care. They didn't make excuses, they were crazed with power and lust and hate!

~~~~~~~~

Earlier that very morning, **May 7th, 1945, at 0800** the command post of the 81St Tank Battalion received a telegram from General Eisenhower's headquarters. *"The mission of this Allied force was fulfilled at 0241, local time, May 7, 1945. The German High Command has signed the unconditional surrender document at Rheims, France."* The war was over! Germany was divided into four major sectors---American, British, French, and Russian.

During the months of May and June, many Germans caught in the Russian Sector were imprisoned for five years after the end of the war. German reunification did not take place until March 15, 1991, when the *Treaty on the Final Settlement, With Respect to Germany* was signed by the four powers as well as the two reigning German governments.

The Nuremberg War Trials were held to prosecute particular Nazi SS German officers and commandants of concentration camps for war crimes.

Chapter Eighteen

"IT'S OVER!"

On V-E Day, May 8, 1945, Gen. Dwight Eisenhower commanded 61 Allied Divisions with over 1,625,000 soldiers in the country of Germany. Now that the shooting had ended, those troops became occupation forces, charged with establishing a military presence and maintaining law and order. The objective was to transition and control the defeated population, suppressing any and all pockets of resistance. Allied Divisions were positioned in areas across the country while Battalions were separately assigned to distinct locations.

As one might expect, this all took time, for everyone to receive their orders and to establish the military occupation. Two weeks after VE day the 81st Battalion received their occupation orders. Commander Kessel said, "Well boys, we are pulling out of Barwedel and moving to a place called [35]Bleicherode, just south of the central Hartz Mountains. We'll be in charge of 50 square miles of German territory. Nobody is going home just yet!" It was a sight to behold as CCB and the 81st Tank Battalion moved westward on the autobahn toward Bleicherode.

The center of the intricate German highway system was filled for miles with the defeated German army, marching toward detention, a long process of interrogation, and finally dispensation before they were released to return to their homes or what was left of them. They all walked, even the officers. They did not ride in their tanks, or their command cars, half-tracks, or antitank carriers; there were no 88 artillery pieces or soldiers on motorcycles or horses.

PT commented, "Look at their faces; hell, some of them look downright relieved, others look ashamed at being defeated, and then there are still those with hatred and defiance written all over their faces. Did you see those German words on the fences, what do they mean Cowboy, can you make it out?"

Arnold looked at the words 'Aus der Traum.' He thought for a moment then said, "I think it says something like 'the dream

is over.' I would say that pretty much nails it on the head, wouldn't you? Herr Hitler's Volkskrieg or people's war didn't go quite like he planned it. Jawohl! (Yes sir)"

Standing tall out of his turret hatch, Commander Kessel responded, "Hell PT, they'll probably get to go home before we do. That's the damn shits for sure!"

May 11, 1945: Nobody had even speculated about where they were going or what they would find when they got there. Hans questioned, "Where the hell is this town and why are they

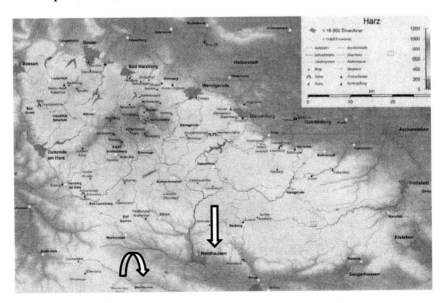

sending us there? I guess I don't mind being sent to central Germany---anywhere, where we don't have to have anything to do with the Russians.

Commander Kessel's face blanched as he listened to their orders, then turned to his crew, "It's to the south of Nordhausen in the woods. Boys, take a deep breath because this is going to be damn hard. We are rolling right into the middle of a major slave labor or concentration camp called, Mittelbau-Dora with a previous barely-living population of 23,000 civilians and prisoners of war. According to HQ, the upright prisoners have been 'employed' at one of the two underground factories in the area and have been dying at a rate of around 150 per week. Over 9000 of the inmates have serious illness and 1000 have tuberculosis." Kessel paused trying to regain composure before continuing. "That's not the worst thing—that would be the fact that we have to bury over 3000 rotting bodies and prepare for at least another 2000 – 3000 that will most likely die before we can transport them someplace else. You can bet your sweet ass that we will be getting the German civilians from the towns around there to bring in their shovels, 'cause they are the ones who are going to be doing the digging and burying!'"

German villagers digging burial pits for Dora -Mittelbau POW dead

"We'd have more prisoners to deal with but the Germans forced over 2,000 of them on death marches to other extermination camps like Bergen-Belsen and Ravensbrueck."

"Remember a month ago, all those concentration camp prisoners that the Krauts torched in that building? They were from this camp! HQ instructs us that after we get those bodies buried, we are to burn the disease-infested barracks. Hell, we might even bulldoze the crematorium. This is probably gonna be the worst thing any of us have seen and I doubt we'll ever forget it!"

Commander Kessel smiled when he conveyed the next past of their orders, "Headquarters also has told the German civilians in the towns to get the hell out of their houses the surviving camp slaves are moving into them. Seems right to me---what do you boys think?"

~~~~~~

"Was konnen wir tun?" (*What could we do?*) So many Germans were indignant with their response to why they didn't know or do something about the concentration camps. Day after day they had seen the starving skeletons walk by their towns on the way to the mines or the fields, yet they did nothing to help the prisoners. From Werner von Braun the German rocket scientist, to the village street sweeper---their response to the question was always, "Was Konnen wir tun"?

In all truth, those who did speak up against the Reich, against Hitler, against the brutality of the SS, joined the ranks of the concentration camps. So, perhaps in an attempt to survive within a system, in a country such as Nazi Germany----to survive---there was not a lot they could do if they wanted to survive, other than to ignore what was happening. Most German civilians who dug the graves did so willingly with tears and guilt flooding their faces. Many had wished to help, but knew better than to put themselves or their families in the same plight. After the war ended, many Germans continued to hesitate to help with voluntary offers of food, clothing or medical aid. It is a fact that they were deeply ashamed, humiliated, and actually unsure and afraid to act without being told to do so. We understand many were traumatized by living under the iron grip of Nazi rule. German history was not taught in their schools for ten years after the war, it was not an era of pride for the once proud German people.

A week later, at precisely 0600 hours, the 81st Tank Battalion received new orders concerning the destroyed entrance to the Bleicherode mines where the slaves had worked. Commander Kessel addressed his crew, "Headquarters isn't saying just what it is, but they have received word there is something very valuable in

those mines, but first we have to uncover the entrance. The tanks with dozer heads on them are working on the rubble now along with infantry with shovels. Once we find what we think is in there, we have orders to put it on those there rail cars and trucks, and getting it the heck out of here before the Russians get their hands on it. This town and those mines are in the Russian Occupation zone, or so they say. I'll be damned if I know what the head mucky mucks are after but its top priority. I guess we'll find out soon enough."

PT looked at his commander with disbelief, "The hell you say? We are loading V-2 Rocket parts and equipment. That was supposed to be Hitler's secret weapon that he was gonna win the war with, right? Holy shit, is this a lucky grab or what?"

Kessel grinned as he lifted another box into the rail car. "Right as rain---that's exactly what we got our hands on and the sooner we can get it out of here and onto our ships sittin' in Antwerp, the better. I guess HQ is sorta just overlooking the fact that the great German scientist, Werner von Braun, used slave labor to build his rockets."

A second company of infantry was transferred in to help get the 'merchandise' loaded. When they weren't loading something or another into railcars and transporting it via what was left of the Reichsbahn or German railway system, the 81st Tank Battalion was kept busy guarding their intelligence areas as well as trying to aid a displaced population. They had a system of check and balances whereby they tried to keep track of the German civilians, help them with food and lodging as much as possible, and disarm a few fanatical Nazi's  that continued to pop up here and there. The ominous battalion tanks stood guard, but only the machine guns were manned and that seemed to be enough of a deterrent to a people who had seen enough of war.

One night after chow, Arnold sat down around a camp fire where a bunch of fellas from the 78th Lightening Infantry Division were sitting. They got to talking like guys do, about stuff like where are you from and what did you do before the war? Arnold sat down next to this great hunk of a soldier who was intent on eating his chow. Arnold reached forward and pulled a stick from the fire to light his cigarette before he spoke. "So, what is your name buddy and where are you from?"

The soldier looked over at Arnold with the bluest piercing eyes Arnold had ever seen. With a slow easy drawl he said, "I'm Private Elmer Gernant, my friends call me Pete; I'm from a small farming area in northwestern Wyoming!"

Arnold coughed on the smoke he had just inhaled, "You're from Wyoming? Northwest Wyoming? What farming area?"

Pete looked off into the inky darkness of the woods and said, "A place they call Emblem; settled by a bunch of German Lutherans around the turn of the century. Me and my four brothers farm around the area, but right now we're all in the war, either here or in the Pacific. What about you, where are you from?"

Commander Kessel slapped the private on the back and said, "Well son-of-a-gun, it looks like we were neighbors, I grew up in the Lovell – Cowley area. My family is also German Lutheran---belong to St. John's church there in Lovell. My sister and brother-in-law live in Emblem. I'll be damned, here we are half way around the world and we run into each other." Arnold paused then asked, "So Pete, when did you get into this mess over here?"

Pete looked up and replied, "Well, I landed at Normandy, after D-Day—in the winter, and we was all loaded onto a truck to take us up to the Battle of the Bulge. It was cold, real cold in the back of that truck and my feet froze, so they left me off in Paris at this here hospital. When my feet healed up, they were right there with another truck. I guess I was damn lucky or the good Lord was watching over me and kept me outta that Battle of the Bulge. Anyways, I rejoined my outfit, the 78th Infantry--- we was the infantry that crossed over the Ludendorff Bridge or better known as the Bridge at Remagen." Pete turned to look at Arnold, "You heard of that bridge across the Rhine? Well me and about two dozen of our infantry was the first Americans to cross that there railroad bridge that was wired to blow but the connections were all messed up and we got across; the rest is history, so they say."

Arnold stared at Pete with disbelief, "Well, that's a story to tell your grandchildren for sure. That was one damn important bridge for sure. Good job soldier."

Pete looked up at Arnold, "Thanks, but you didn't tell me what outfit you are with, what you do."

Kessel looked back at Pete as he rose from his seat, "I'm with CCB of the 81st Tank Battalion—I'm a tanker. Commander Arnold Kessel at your service! It was great talkin' to you Pete; hope to run into you when we both get back to Wyoming, maybe I'll see you in church! God's speed my friend!"

~~~~~~~

PT slapped Arnold on the back and said, "Hey Cowboy, a few of us are going to take a stroll into the village later today. There's supposed to be a beer garden open and somebody said they have damn good bratwurst and sausages too, wanna come along?"

As the crew from Avenger made their way through the rubble-strewn streets of the village, they were surprised to see crews of German women out in the streets, using their bare bleeding hands along with several shovels to clear the streets or bricks and rubble. They picked up the unbroken bricks, brushed, scraped, and washed them off as best they could, and then stack them in neat order. They were followed by other women with brooms who swept the street until it was thoroughly clean. It was their new normal!

Arnold smiled as he commented, "They don't change---it's the same at home, any way with my Mom and grandmothers. They are always cleaning, cleaning and then cooking! I can't wait to taste some of the bratwurst and sauerkraut at that beer garden--- washed down with a good beer!"

Spring in Germany, 1945: The roads, paths, waterways, and rubble-clogged streets of Germany were congested with people of every age, shape, color, origin, race, gender, and financial status, struggling to find food, stay alive, and get home or make a new home. When the war ended in early May, over 5.2 million people were on the move with a desire to get somewhere else but where they were, and mostly it was home. Most of the travelers were lucky if they had a suitcase or a bag strapped to their backs with a few belongings inside. Most military, soldiers, and former POW's wore the same ragged uniform they had on when they were taken prisoner or when they joined the army years before.

Squirt remarked to his commander, "How come those people seem almost happy, they don't have shit to their name and who knows if they will make it to their homes or what is left of their homes? Yet, look at em', some of them are even singing and smiling as they trudge along."

Arnold responded, "Well I suppose it's all relative; most of them are just plain happy the war is over, they survived and they are on their way toward home. I did hear that there has been some looting by these folks, but who can blame them."

Most of the American troops were billeted in Quonset huts or some large confiscated German building. That night after chow, Arnold took out his pen and found a few sheets of paper. I haven't written to my folks in a while, I know they get most of the dope from the news and they've been swell with the letters and goody boxes.

Hartz Mountains, Central Germany, 1945
Dear Mom and Dad;
   First I want to apologize for not writing to you more often,
I guess I can use the excuse that I was busy just staying alive,
which isn't far from the truth. Now that the war is over, I have a
little more time to myself; at least nobody is shooting at us. I don't
know how long they are going to keep us here with this occupation,
I guess until they establish some sort of local law and order.
   I don't know if either of you remembers what a beautiful
country this is. We are close to Bavaria/Austria and the Danube
River. It's probably one of the most fertile and green places I've
ever seen; now I know why Grandma Kessel missed
Austria/Hungary so much when she moved to Wyoming. It's odd
that out in the countryside, I see farmers working their fields with
horses, women putting in gardens, chickens, cows, etc. Every once
in a while you see a farm house destroyed, but it's nothing like the
cities. When we come to a large village or a city, it's a whole
different sight; because they used those phosphorous bombs that
burn so hot, there isn't much left but dust. It's a rare sight to even
see one wall of a house standing. That must have been pure hell to
have been in one of those cities when our bombs were dropping.
   I talked to this one German lady the other day, nice lady
too. She had her scarf on her head and she was picking up bricks
and cleaning them off. I told her I was sorry that we had to bomb
them and so many people died. She turned to me with tears
running down her cheeks and said, "We started the whole thing,
now didn't we? This is what we did to London, to Russian cities.
This is the wrath of God which rained down on us. We thought
Hitler was God---we believed his promises to make Germany great
and this is what we got.' She stopped crying when she said, 'And
he put a bullet through his brains instead of facing the end like the
rest of us have to!'
   I can't tell you how many people there are trying to walk
back to their homes—thousands. The good news is that our guys
have caught thousands of prominent Nazis who are going to have
to pay for their war crimes. I can't tell you what our crew is doing
now—top secret stuff and all that, but someday I will be able and
proud to tell you what we did.

I may get to come home before some of the other guys because of a new system of points accumulated during the war. I think I have about 70 points but they add on to that for decorations and I have four Bronze Stars for courage during battle. If I was married, I'd get more points. Anyway, it's looking like I might get out of here sooner, which would suit me just fine. Thanks again for all the boxes of baked goods, the cards, and letters. I can never tell you how much that all meant to me---it just plain kept me going.

Until I see you in Wyoming, your son, Arnold

~~~~~~

The 81st Tank Battalion had cleared the mines of the valuable rocket parts and information in less than a month, just in time to turn the Bleicherode area over to Russian occupation. PT commented, "This occupation stuff hasn't been a cake walk, that's for damn sure. I guess I can understand a little of what these Germans are feeling---they just want us the hell out of their country now and I think's that's exactly what we want as well. But, we all know it's not going to be that easy or happen that quickly. The German people have years of reconstruction left, financed mostly by the American government at first anyway. They are hardworking people and I don't expect it will take them long to get their country shipshape."

Commander Kessel looked up from his written orders, "Well boys, tomorrow we take that first step in going home. That's right we are jumping south to Eschwege where we'll billet in the fields around Vierbach. That's where we turn in our tank and all the other vehicles and equipment. I think that might be sorta bitter sweet. We spent some memorable days and nights in that can of bolts!"

Squirt jumped up and down near to tears, "Then are they going to ship us back home, Sarge---are they huh?"

Arnold replied, "I don't see that down on paper yet so don't start packing your jock strap until we find out what the brass has up their sleeve. All I know is that on the order sheet it says we are to prepare for redeployment, period!"

Right after chow the next morning, there was a call for a general assembly. General Lundsford Oliver addressed the 81st Tank Battalion and their married Infantry and Service groups.

"Gentlemen, I couldn't be prouder of the record of the 81st Battalion and the 5th Armored Division. I realize that all you want to hear right now is when you are going home, so what I have to tell you is very difficult for me. Orders from Allied Headquarters state that, going by the point system, if you have not accumulated a total of at least 85 points, you will not be released from the Army at this time. A lot of you boys are going to receive orders for Okinawa to train for the invasion of Japan. Those who have points totaling over 85 will be released from the Army and sent back to the states. As you will recall, points are added up for each month in military service, each month overseas, each decoration or metal, and if you are the parent of a child."

An outraged soldier called out from the assembly, "Why do we have to go fight another damn war? We won ours---that stinks, it really stinks!"

The general stopped before he left the staging area, "I realize the order stinks men, I feel your disappointment and frustration because this includes me as well. We are the 5th Armored Division and we go where we are needed and called, that is all! Dis--missed!"

Morale among the troops really hit rock bottom---they had counted on going home, now that they beat the Germans and a bullet with their name on it. Each soldier was busy adding up his individual collective points. Most of the guys that landed on Normandy with Commander Kessel had just over 70 points. What put Staff Sgt. Arnold Kessel over the top of the 85 points were the four Bronze Stars he received and several other military awards that merited points.

Because morale was so low during June and July, maintaining discipline proved to be a daunting task and not just in the 81st Battalion. Over 1,000,000 pissed off soldiers were waiting for their redeployment to Japan; the lucky ones were waiting for their orders back to the states. Officers were kept plenty busy with discipline problems which ranged from drunk and disorderly to AWOL.

Staff Sgt. Kessel pulled his former crew together one evening, "Fellas, I know these new orders are damn unfair and the delay to ship out is getting to us all, but don't make it harder on yourselves by getting stupid and not following orders. Getting drunk and fraternizing with a German girl comes with a stiff fine and maybe even brig time; let's face it, you aren't making a bunch of money as it is. Hell, who knows, we can always hope that our boys over in the Pacific might just win that war before we get final orders and are shipped over there."

~~~~~~

August 6, 1945: An American B-29 bomber dropped the first atomic bomb on Hiroshima, Japan; three days later another was dropped on Nagasaki. An unconditional surrender was signed by Japan on August 15, 1945. EVERYBODY WAS GOING HOME – THE WAR WAS OVER!

~~~~~~

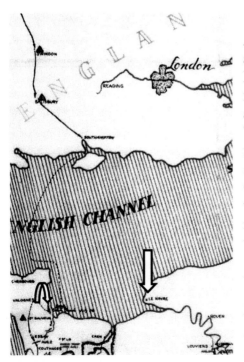

Before the 5th Armored Division disbanded and left Germany, General Lunsford Oliver called for a final 'division' general assembly, including the 81st Tank Battalion. Arnold was impressed as was every soldier there that their General made the effort and took the time to shake every man's hand, saying a few words to him regarding his service. Bobby said, "That was damn good of the general, he didn't have to do that, but he did and I now every man in there appreciated it."

The day before they had orders to turn in their tank, Arnold called his crew together. "Well guys, this is it." He blinked away the tears that were building in his eyes and tried to swallow the lump in his throat. "We've been through hell and back and I want to tell you that—that you've been one of the finest damn fighting crews and I feel blessed to have been your commander. I also feel blessed that we made it through and now we are going home to America." Arnold stood and went from one to the other, shaking their hands, "and hey, when you get home, let's keep in touch!"

~~~~~~~~

Staff Sgt. Kessel relayed the latest orders to his crew, "We are leaving for the port of Le Havre, France where we will be assigned to a ship that will take us home. What did I tell you guys?" He paused a moment, looking off in the distance, "It's kinda weird that port of Le Havre is on the eastern side of the Normandy Beaches---directly across from where we landed in July of 1944. How ironic is that?"

By mid-September they waved goodbye to Eschwege, Germany and hopped aboard a train bound for France. The American soldiers packed themselves into forty passenger cars and eight box cars amidst cheers and a few tears of relief that they were leaving Germany. Once across the border into France, French civilians lined the tracks and train stations waving hankies, flags, and assorted bloomers at the passing trains. Their American liberators who hadn't given their lives in the war, were leaving Europe----going home. Once they arrived at the French coast, they had to wait at Camp Twenty Grand for a couple of weeks for an available ship assigned to their Battalion.

As day broke on Sept. 30, 1945, the 1,925 soldiers from the 81st Tank Battalion along with men from the 5th Armored Division; 15th Armored Infantry Battalion—minus their equipment--were thrilled to see a less than posh refitted freighter, the 'India Victory' waiting in dock for them. Seven days after a smooth voyage from the shores of France, they docked in Boston harbor. In the paper the next day they read that their ship was among the eight other transport ships that brought more than 11,000 American men home on Sept. 7, 1945.

Sept. 9, 1945: LTC LeRoy H. Anderson issued orders inactivating the 81st Tank Battalion. The men stuffed their honorable discharges in their bags and headed for the nearest train depot that

would take them HOME! In the bottom of Staff Sgt. Arnold Kessel's duffel bag lay **four** BRONZE STARS; the EAMF Theater Ribbon; a red ribbon 'Conduct Metal' for Efficiency, Honor, and Fidelity; and a green-ribbon medal for Military Merit/Victory Medal for WWII.

NOTE: Staff Sergeant Arnold W. Korell was decorated with FOUR, Bronze Star Medals31. He never boasted or cared to talk about his medals or his experiences in World War II. Talking about it only brought the horrific memories back to the surface of the current life he was trying to live; he struggled every day to forget the horrors of war.

PART TWO

Chapter Nineteen

"JUST FORGET THE WAR"

Lovell, Wyoming, September 30, 1945: Arnold had not told his parents when he would be back in Wyoming or even Lovell, frankly he didn't know exactly when he would get home. Travel all depended on the luck of being able to catch a ride on a plane, train, or hitch hiking. Most GI's didn't have the spare cash to buy a ticket and so they were forced to wait on military standby or take advantage of the generosity of some civilian. Many civilians were happy to give up their seats so a GI could make it back home sooner.

A south bound train from Billings, Montana, pulled into the Lovell train station around 2000 hours, or 8 p.m. Arnold didn't even wait for the train to come to a complete stop before he grabbed his duffel and jumped from the car. He stood for a moment, inhaling the familiar scent of his home town, the sugar beet factory, the falling leaves, the last roses of the summer in the city's famous rose beds—it was all there. Other soldiers, airmen, and sailors, were moving toward a crowd of milling people, parked cars, and Main Street. Since Arnold hadn't told anyone when he was getting into Lovell, nobody was waiting for him and he liked it that way. It gave him time to gather his emotions, besides he loved these kinds of surprises.

Picking up his worn duffel bag, he squared his shoulders and headed for Main Street; after all it was a Saturday night and there should be some action. *Maybe I'll see somebody I know from the old crowd.* As he rounded the corner near the Busy Corner Rexall Drug, he noticed part of the street was roped off and a large crowd was pushing in from all sides. *WOW, they've got a good band and everything. I wonder what the big occasion is for them to decorate the place like this for a dance. It's too early for Octoberfest. I just gotta stop and take a quick look, see if I recognize anybody.*

Arnold stood at the edge of the crowd. That's when he saw her, out on the street, dancing with some tall swell who was trying his best to put the moves on Norrie. He left his duffel bag with an old couple who said they'd watch it for him. Arnold didn't waste another minute as he pushed his way out onto the dance floor.

The band was playing "It's Only a Paper Moon"—the group had a great 'toe-tappin' beat. Norrie had her back toward him as Arnold reached slowly around and tapped the swell on the shoulder, "Mind if I cut in?"

Norrie's ears picked up the familiar voice. She whirled and screamed; she forgot all about the slick swell, as she flew into Arnold's arms. Flinging her arms around his thin shoulders, all she could think about was kissing him and how good he felt. Her 'soldier' was home, right here in her arms, and she wasn't letting go any time soon!

Not taking their eyes off each other, Arnold and Norrie made their way out past the crowd. He reached for his duffel bag and thanked the older couple who smiled and remarked "Looks like you found what you was lookin' for; welcome home son!"

Arnold and Norrie started walking down the street; suddenly he stopped walking, turned and pushed Norrie up against a parked car; he kissed her again, long and hard. He felt like he was drowning in her---"Oh Baby, how I missed you. I love you, I love you. I can't believe I'm here and you're here. I'm home to stay and we need to get on with the rest of our lives---how does that sound to you?"

Her answer was another long, slow kiss as she wove her fingers through his blond hair and pulled his face to hers.

Norrie offered to drive him home so he could see his folks. "Just let me off here on Shoshone Avenue by Winterhollar's Grocery Store, I want to walk the rest of the way. If I'm right, the folks will be sitting out on the front porch cause it's a nice night. I'll call you tomorrow, maybe we can catch a movie tomorrow night---is it a date?" He leaned in the open car window and kissed her one more time before he turned and headed south.

Arnold glanced in the window at the familiar neighborhood grocery store where he remembered buying penny candy as a kid. Then he hastened his step past Lovell High School and the Elementary school. Some things had changed as he had expected they would, but for the most part the town was as he left it. The sidewalk was covered with fallen leaves that crunched under his feet as he walked. He'd always loved this tree-lined street where the little yellow and white Lutheran church sat with a candle in the window. He stopped and looked at the church, "That's where I am going to marry Norrie, but I guess I have to ask her first!"

Arnold saw his folks sitting out on the front porch; his Dad was having a smoke and his Mom was rocking slowly in her chair--just like he remembered them doing. Taking deliberate steps and staying in the shadows, he moved closer to the house.

Rosie turned to Jake as she bent to pick up her empty glass, "I guess it's about time to go inside, it's getting pretty dark." She paused and was about to comment on that man walking down the sidewalk at this time of night---then she froze. "J-Ja-Jake, is that--- is that man, Arnold? LOOK, over there on the sidewalk in front of Lynn's house. Oh dear Lord, it's our boy, our boy is home."

Rosie couldn't stop crying from happiness; even Jake shed a few tears of relief and thanksgiving that their only son was home safe and in one piece from the war. "Come on in the house, but be quiet; Grandpa Karl is sleeping in the front bedroom. You can have the couch for tonight." They sat around the kitchen table until almost midnight talking and hugging. Rosie had to fix Arnold something to eat, "I gotta put some meat back on your bones, you're way too skinny!"

That first night back, in his parent's home, sleeping on the couch was surreal. Around two in the morning, Arnold woke drenched in sweat and hoped to hell he hadn't yelled out. The dreams hadn't left him, and he had a gut feeling they didn't intend on leaving any time soon. Arnold ran his fingers through his thinning hair and sat up on the couch; he reached for his pack of Camels, pulled one out, and put a light to it. He inhaled deeply, hoping to relax and forget the damn dream.

I gotta concentrate on remembering what it was like to just be me---the life of the party, good ole Arnie Kessel! I've dreamed of this very moment—of being back home in one piece —dreamed about home from day one in Europe, when I realized I was actually going to war. Sure, I look good on the outside, but they can't see what is on the inside. I know it'll be a day by day thing—trying to forget and trying to get on with my life. He closed his eyes and said a prayer, *Dear God, thank you for bringing me back home. Please heal me inside, give me strength and courage to live the rest of this life you've given me. And, God—make the nightmares leave me in peace. This I ask in Jesus' name. Amen.*

~~~~~~~~

Norrie came for supper at the Kessels that next night, and afterwards she and Arnold left for their date to see the new movie "Tall in the Saddle" with John Wayne.

After the movie, they sat in Jake's car for a long time and talked about the future. Norrie laid her head on Arnold's shoulder as they talked. She said, "You know I have another year of nursing school at the university up in Bozeman. I want---I need to get that diploma first; the government is paying for me to go to nursing school and it's a great break for me. They need nurses or they did need nurses because of the war. Regardless, it will be a good career---there is always a need for nurses and I intend on working after I'm married. While I'm up there finishing up my degree, you can take some time to go fishing and then figure out what you want to do for a job."

Arnold lit a Camel and said, "I just about forgot about you still going to college. When do you have to go back to school--- soon?"

Norrie smiled, "This is my last year; I just came home for the weekend to see Mom and then you popped in so I am taking a few more days off classes. I really need to take the bus back up to Bozeman the day after tomorrow." Norrie turned and smiled as she said, "Just for your information, I will graduate in May."

Norrie's soft grey eyes sparkled as she smiled up at him and said, "We have time to make plans, but we need to take this slow and make sure. I am certainly not rushing you or me into a long-term relationship the moment you get home!" She took his face in her hands and pulled him toward her, "Arnold Kessel, I love you and I'm pretty sure I want to make a life with you but we both have some things we have to do first. By the way, do you have any ideas about what you want to do---work, I mean?"

Arnold leaned back, "Naw---haven't thought about it much but I will now, I sure will now!" He felt a sudden gloom come over him as he said, "You know Norrie, I've been feeling like I lost that kid I was, you know, like---I lost that freedom of youth, fresh outta high school and all. Hell, I shoulda been dragging the streets of Lovell, going to dances, flirting with the girls—instead I was in a tank, killing Germans—doing and seeing things I will never forget. I didn't have the leisure of time, to grow up and figure out what I wanted to be or do. I'm pretty sure I wouldn't have gone on to school like you did, I never liked school that much."

Norrie stroked his cheek, "I've thought about that too Arnold, that's why we need to take this relationship slow—to give you time to adjust and figure it all out. I'm not going anyplace, I know what I want!"

Living space was at a premium after the war, but Arnold lucked out and found a small studio apartment. It was a couple of blocks to the north, half way between his parents and the apartment where Norrie lived with her mother above the Elite Ladies Dress Shop on Main Street. Arnold heard that a lot of vets were taking anything they could find to live in like barns, trailers, old streetcars, those Quonset huts, and even cars.

Arnold had a problem---none of the civilian clothes he'd left at home fit him now. When he went to shop for new clothes, he discovered another problem---there was a shortage of civilian clothes for men because all the returning soldiers needed new clothes, the demand was high. What was available was pretty darn expensive and he didn't have that kind of money to blow on a lot of new clothes. He and his mother drove to Billings one Saturday; Arnold came home with four shirts, three pairs of pants, a couple of sweaters, some brown loafers, socks, and underwear for a start.

~~~~~~~~

Arnold was honorably discharged from the Army and he was ready to begin a new chapter in his life. Everybody was looking for a job—there was a glut of men fresh out of the war and most of them wanted to work. Arnold got lucky in Lovell and found a job as a mechanic at the Ford garage. He loved to tinker and was good at mechanics even though he hadn't been to school for it. With Norrie away at nursing school at Montana State University---Arnold had plenty of time to catch up with his high school buddies who were still single or had survived the war. They played a few hands of cards, shot some baskets, went to a few dances, saw some movies, shot pool, and drank too many beers. He borrowed his Dad's car and went to Bozeman a couple of times to see Norrie; other than that his phone bill was pretty high. They were both looking forward to her Christmas vacation when she would be home for two weeks before starting her final semester.

Christmas Eve, Jake and Raisa invited Norrie and her mother Ethel for a special Christmas Eve Dinner after church. Their pregnant daughter Beth and Jimmy were there with Karlie who insisted on sitting on Norrie's lap. They attended early services in the little yellow and white clapboard Lutheran Church on Shoshone Ave., just down the street from their house. Raisa had been cooking for weeks and the house was filled with the smell of roasted chicken and Christmas.

After church they gathered in the dining room, found their places at the lavishly appointed table as Raisa carried in numerous bowls and platters of steaming food. Arnold dug in with the rest of them and they were laughing and having a wonderful time when suddenly he pushed his chair back and stood, his face pale and drawn. "Excuse me for a minute, I-I ahhh I need some air." With that he rushed from the room. He grabbed the door knob and twisted it hard; he was out the front door before anyone could respond.

Stunned, they all sat there looking at each other as Jake stood, "You all go ahead and eat, I'll go see what's the matter."

Jake found his son out on the front porch, leaning against the roof support and smoking a cigarette, his hands were shaking. He reached up and laid a hand on Arnold's shoulder, "Did somebody say something to upset you? Wanna talk about it son?"

Arnold turned and in the light of the street lamp, Jake could see the reflection of dampness on his son's face.

Arnold wiped angrily at the tears and in a low voice said, "Just---memories--it's just that—last year at this time, I was sitting in a tank in the Ardennes Forest, waiting for perhaps the biggest battle we'd see yet. We were freezing our asses off, eating cold K-rations, on blackout and absolute silence, waiting, waiting for the Krauts to break through in the Battle of the Bulge." He stubbed his cigarette out, "Now, a year later, here I am-- back with all my arms and legs, back home like I never left, except for my head. Dad, my head is filled with it all and I'm scared to death it will never leave.

I can't even tell you some of the things I saw and things I did. It's like it happened to someone else---it's so horrible, it's like it was all a real bad dream. I'll never be that kid I was when I left, that smart aleck high school kid, Arnie Kessel from Lovell, Wyoming---he's gone forever."

Before Jake could respond, Arnold continued, "What about those poor saps who came home with missing limbs, with burns, with wounds they will carry for a lifetime? Why did I live and another guy beside me didn't? WHY, Dad, WHY? What about my crew who died in that tank and I was blown out and lived? I feel damn guilty, that's it! I don't understand what I did or didn't do that I should have the privilege of making it through. Sometimes at night when the nightmares come, I wish to hell I had died over there, at least I wouldn't have to live with these damn dreams and the guilt of living!"

Shocked, Jake grabbed Arnold's arm, "Son, I can't say I know what it was like, only those who have been in a war know that. All I can say is that we love you and we are so grateful you are home in one piece. We're so very thankful you are home and I'm sorry for what you had to go through son. I'm sure you saw and did things no man should have to do, just like my brother, being in that Bataan Death March and then dying on that Jap slave ship in the Sea of Japan. Let's give it time Arnold, give it time and try to pick up your new life. That's all you can do. Have you thought about seeing Dr. Horsley---maybe he can give you something to help you get some sleep."

Arnold embraced his father and to his horror, broke down again, "It was so bad, Dad, so unbelievably bad---you can't know. I never in my life imagined anything like that, ever. I'll try to forget, I'll try, that's all I can do." They opened the door to the house and went back to their Christmas dinner, nobody said a word---they all suspected Arnold remembered something from the war and it probably wouldn't be the last time.

As a family tradition, after dinner they each choose a gift with their name on it from under the tree. Everyone had a gift except Norrie. Suddenly Arnold stood in front of her, his blue eyes twinkled as he smiled and dropped to one knee. Taking her hand in his, he said, "Noreen Fisk, I love you and I am asking you to be my wife." He opened a small blue velvet box and held it up to her.

Norrie squealed as she jumped to her feet and threw her arms around Arnold, knocking the ring to the floor. Arnold laughed and asked, "Is that a yes or a no?"

~~~~~~~

Arnold drove Norrie back to her mother's apartment that night. They sat outside, parked on Main Street and talked for a long time about their future. She looked out the car window, "Say kid, you don't have a problem with me working after we're married do you? Like I see it, we'll have two incomes and that will help us get ahead quicker. I'll take time off to have your babies, but Arnold, I love nursing and I want to keep on doing it."

Arnold looked down the nearly empty city street, "Norrie, I'm so proud of you, graduating from college and that you have found something you really like to do. I don't have a problem with you working after we're married. But, I guess that means I better agree to push the vacuum and wash a few dishes then too, huh?"

Arnold wrapped his arms around her, "I have an idea---I

could stay home, take care of the kids and cook while you go off to the hospital and work. Sounds good to me and I am sure my mother would be thrilled with that!" He laughed as he winked at her with his twinkling ice blue eyes.

That next week they made an appointment at Jansen Studio to have their picture taken for the newspaper announcement of their engagement. Norrie insisted that Arnold wear his uniform because he looked so handsome in it.

~~~~~~~

Noreen Fisk graduated with honors from Nursing School at Montana State University in Bozeman in May. After that, she was ready to concentrate on her wedding. Arnold and Norrie had decided on an August 1st wedding in the little Lutheran Church in Lovell. She had taken instruction in the Lutheran religion and was now a member of the church---something they both wanted, to have the same religion and go to church together. They choose their groomsmen and bridesmaids; Norrie chose her nephew Lanning as ring bearer and Arnold's niece Karlie as her flower girl. Norrie said, "You know Arnold, since my father has passed away, do you think people would talk if I asked my mother to walk me down the aisle?"

Arnold's eyes lit up as he replied, "I think that's a great idea. She raised you after your Dad died and I think that's a really nice tribute!"

It was a hot and humid August day in Lovell when Noreen Fisk became the bride of Staff Sergeant Arnold Kessel! As she and her mother walked slowly down the aisle toward the altar, Arnold's blue eyes misted over and he had a huge lump in his throat. His bride was absolutely stunning in her white lace wedding

dress, carrying a bouquet of deep pink roses. He couldn't believe that in the next hour this beautiful woman was going to become his wife!

After the wedding and pictures, they had a large reception in the basement of the church. Tables were filled with gifts and food. They cut their wedding cake and Arnold thanked their guests for attending the wedding and for their generous gifts. "I think most of you know that Norrie is working at the hospital and we only have a few days for our honeymoon. But, you can bet your bottom dollar that when we get back, we'll have a Dutch-hop dance to celebrate! But folks---in my book, the honeymoon comes first, just hope you understand!"

The newlyweds exited the church in a hail of rice and cat calls from Arnold's buddies as the couple climbed into the waiting Ford coupe. Since Arnold didn't have a car of his own yet, his brother-in-law Jimmy loaned them his car for their wedding trip to Yellowstone Park. The car was all decorated---complete with crepe paper streamers, tin cans rattling behind, and Just MARRIED! written in white shoe polish all over the hood and trunk. Jimmy commented, "I hope that white polish comes off, I don't want to be driving around Emblem with Just Married on my car, people would sure talk."

As luck would have it, just out of Cody, they had a flat tire. Arnold threw his coat and tie in the back seat and dug out the spare tire. Norrie stood leaning against the car looking gorgeous in a teal blue dress and hat. "Hey, husband, how long is that going to take. I can't wait all day to start this honeymoon you know!"

Arnold grinned wickedly and leaped to his feet; dusting his pants off, he scooped his bride up, throwing her over his shoulder and headed for the woods. Norrie laughed and kicked her high heels as she squealed, "Arnold Kessel, you put me down right this minute, what-- what in the world do you think you are doing? A bed of pine needles is not what I had in mind. Just you get busy with that tire." As they walked back to the flat tire, they both giggled at the thought of a honeymoon in the woods.

Arnold winked as he said, "Now, wife, I expect you to stand there and look pretty and don't talk to me so I can get this dang thing changed. We need to get back on the road to that cabin up in Yellowstone and get our honeymoon started!"

That night was the first night in a long time that he didn't have a nightmare, but he didn't expect it would stay that way. The horrors of war, the memories promised to take their toll on his sleep, his life, and his marriage.

~~~~~

Feb. 13, 1947: The newlyweds moved into a small apartment in Lovell, not far from the hospital where Norrie was working. They'd been married about six months and Arnold had found a job as a driver and rig helper with the Ohio Oil Company in Byron. He didn't bring home as much as she did and that grated on his ego, so he went ahead without asking her and did it.

That night after supper, Arnold got up his nerve. "Norrie, pure and simple--we need more money. We have expenses, like the rent, food, and we need a car to get around in. I'm not bringing in nothing but peanuts and so I signed up for the National Guard." He watched her face blanch and quickly added, "Now, Norrie---just listen to me, I don't have to do much at all—just a few drills and two weeks at camp once a year. There are other guys signing up. We don't think the world is going to hop right into another big war, besides the extra money will help out a lot when we go shopping for a car."

~~~~~~~

Norrie had tried to deal with Arnold's persistent nightmares, souvenirs of his experiences in the war, but the frequent episodes were beginning to wear on her. Religiously she attended the monthly meetings of veteran's wives, where they shared how they each were coping with their husband's military experiences, but nothing seemed to help. It became quite clear that Norrie Kessel wasn't the only wife of a serviceman who was still fighting the war.

A spring thunder storm was brewing to the east when Arnold and Norrie went to bed that night. The storm was distant and low at first, then a sudden crack of lightening was followed by a crashing volley of thunder that rolled across the Shoshone River valley. It brought Arnold to a sitting position, his eyes were open and sweat beaded on his forehead as he screamed frantically. "IN COMING; Button up. We got mortars. Coil, PT, coil. Stick a damn shell in that cannon and FIRE, FIRE. Gol-damn-it, there's a Tiger tank coming-left flank, left flank. Spin it PT, keep moving and fire one up that Tiger's ass---NOW, PT—FIRE!"

Norrie laid her had gently on Arnold shoulder and squeezed. Even though his eyes were open, she knew he was asleep and dreaming; she also knew better than to try and wake him suddenly. It was like when someone walked in their sleep--- they were IN whatever was happening and to physically try and alter that dream was not a good idea.

Arnold slapped at her hand, "I said, get the damn shell in that cannon and FIRE!" Suddenly, Arnold's eyes closed and opened quickly as he came out of it. The first thing he saw was his wife cowering to the far side of their bed. She flinched when he reached for her. Another volley of lightning and thunder rolled across the night sky as the storm increased.

"Norrie, Norrie----what? Did I hurt you? Why are you looking at me like that?" She moved toward him and he took her into his arms as she began to cry. "Baby, I am sorry; I wish to hell I didn't do this, it's just the shits I know! I've talked to lots of guys---it's the same with them. I try Honey, I really try, but there's something embedded in my head---it all comes back and I am fighting to save my life, my crew all over again! The damn battles, they were---they were so tense, so frightening. I had to make the right decision for my men."

Norrie eyes filled with tears as she said, "Your voice, Arnold—it didn't even sound like you. I've never heard you like that. It scared me, it really scared me. Can you see a doctor? Is there something, someone who can help you get over these dreams?"

Sometimes weeks, months went by without an episode but whenever it happened, it was always upsetting to both of them. He wanted to leave the memories behind but he didn't know how; Norrie felt helpless to help her husband. His folks didn't help much either—his dad expected him to just forget the war and get on with his life and his mother babied him until Norrie felt sick to her stomach. Norrie knew she and Arnold weren't alone in their experiences with war nightmares—the wives talked amongst themselves and they all had the same story. Nobody knew what to do or how to help. Norrie decided to start with her mother-in-law because she wasn't helping the situation, maybe if she understood what she was doing by coddling Arnold.

"Mom, you've got to let Arnold work through these nightmares and his life in his own way. You are not helping him by making such a fuss over it all. This is something that happens to

95% of the men who saw terrible combat and those concentration camps---your son isn't the only man this is happening to. I am going to meetings where other wives and professionals work with us to do what we can in our homes." Norrie paused and thought, *okay, now is as good a time as any.* "Another thing Mom, you and Dad can't expect us to come to dinner every Sunday after church. We have our own life and our own plans sometimes. We appreciate everything you do for us and I know you missed your son, but he is married now; please let us have time to ourselves. I don't mean to hurt your feelings, I just want you to try and understand."

It did not go as planned or hoped.

~~~~~~~~

Norrie opened the door to their apartment after working the night shift at the Lovell Hospital. Arnold was sitting at the kitchen table, with some papers spread out over the surface. He jumped up when she came in and pulled out a chair for her. "I got coffee made; can I fry you an egg –or make toast?"

After he poured two cups of Folger's coffee, he spilled the beans. "Norrie, I think I might have found something that I can sink my teeth into. You know how I like to tinker---I'm not a book guy, I'm not going to go to a university like you did. I've found this refrigeration/air-conditioning school, but here's the kicker—it's in Minneapolis. It's for like a year and I'm not going without you—so, we'd have to move there." Arnold paused just long enough to catch a breath. "My GI benefits will pay for most of it---it's a Yellow Ribbon College which means that what the government GI Bill doesn't cover the school gets us financial assistance. It sounds good honey, what do you think?"

Norrie took a long sip of her black coffee and then lit a cigarette. Arnold waited with baited breath, waited for an answer. Norrie looked at the papers on the table, took a long drag from her cigarette and looking her husband in the eye said, "Well, it sounds like a good idea—but wait, NO, I don't think I can stand the thought of leaving all this behind." She smiled out of the corner of her mouth as she said, "Actually, I think it's a great idea. When can we leave?"

Arnold looked at the papers, "I think I can get in with the fall class; I'll check on that right away. The other thing is apartments—the rent is sky high even if we can find a place it'd probably be a dump. I know this might sound crazy, but number one, we love to camp, number two we need a place to live in Minneapolis, and then we'll need a place wherever we move after I graduate from the tech school. SOOO, I was thinking of seeing if my Dad would co-sign on a trailer house---you know one of those slick Air Stream ones. I'm not thinking of a big one, just big enough for the two of us? What do you think? I'm gonna see if he wants to go fishing this next weekend—I'll ask him then."

Norrie, said, "Not one good idea, but TWO! I love it---I think that would be a great investment and we'd be saving rent, sort of like buying our own place that moves with us. Who knows where we are going to end up---this is the nomad time of our married life."

<center>~~~~~~~~</center>

August 1, 1947: Jake and Arnold rode in the truck up the winding Big Horn Mountain road to a special place where Jake liked to fish. "Just you wait until I show you this hole, nobody else knows about it that I know of."

Arnold cleared his throat and broached the subject of a co-sign on an Air-Stream trailer. "Say Dad, I think I want to go to Refrigeration School out in Minneapolis this fall. Norrie and I think that the best thing to do---to, ahhh, save on rent and just have us a place to live until I get myself a good job, would be to invest in one of those mid-sized Air Stream trailers. That way, we'd be putting our money in on something we could live in and then have for vacations later on—not dumping it down the drain in a rental place. The problem is that I need a co-signer and was hoping you would do that for me. I would sure appreciate it Dad and I promise I won't let you down."

They hashed over the details, cost, payments, etc. for a few minutes and Jake slapped Arnold on the back and said, "Son, I think that sounds like a good solid plan. You are darn-tootin' I'll sign for you. I'm happy you have settled on something that interests you. It sounds like its right up your alley too—I know how you have always liked mechanical things and to tinker with motors and stuff, just like I do."

It wasn't long before Jake pulled off the highway onto what looked like some grassy cow path. He carefully maneuvered the old truck over the ruts and rocks until they dropped down beside a slow-running meandering creek. He pulled up under a mountain ash tree and killed the engine. "This looks like the place. You are gonna like this place son, it's a humdinger of a fishing hole."

They stood beside the truck, each attaching one of Jake's special-tied flies to the end of their hooks and then headed in opposite directions. After a couple of hours and with a full creel of trout, Jake walked upstream to where the truck was parked. He stopped short, seeing Arnold sitting out in the middle of the creek minus his fishing pole. Jake stood still, just watching his son who wasn't moving, wasn't doing anything but sitting on the rock, staring at the water.

Jake put his fish in the cooler in the back of the truck and walked slowly toward the creek. He stood on the bank and said, "Are you all fished out son? Ready to head down the mountain, are you?"

Arnold turned, "Yeah Dad, I really couldn't get into fishing today, sorry." Jake watched as Arnold hopped from rock to rock towards the grassy bank of the stream. Jake put his arm out and stopped his son, "What's up with you Arnold? Is there something else on your mind? You always liked to fish and I thought you'd enjoy coming up here today—just you and me. Relax like we used to, just the two of us."

Arnold squatted down beside the creek and began to toss skippers across the surface of the water. "Ahhh, Dad, I-uhh, I just can't seem to get into it. I can't relax like that anymore."

To Jake's utter confusion and surprise, tears began to roll down his son's cheeks, "Dad---ahhh---Dad, nothing I do seems like it used to. Nobody is the same as when I left for Germany. You and Mom, my sister and her family, even my friends—you all feel like strangers, like I don't know you anymore. Nothing is like I left it—like I dreamed of it. I am messed up, Dad—I can't seem to figure anything out. This is like a totally different life with different people, a different town, even this country. I am struggling to find something any damn thing, that feels normal and I can't find it, Dad, I can't find it!"

Jake squatted down beside his son, "Arnold, I know you have heard this before, but it all takes time. Things will fall back into place after a while, people and things around you will start to feel normal again after you have lived with us, in this town, this country---after you start living the life you want. You have to have a little patience son, for things to right themselves. Believe it or not, you are different to us too. You went away a kid right out of high school and returned a man from war. We know you went through hell over there and saw some things we only read about in the papers. No, we don't understand everything you have inside you—everything you saw and did over there. We don't know how to help you, what to say to you son to steady the boat! We see your anger, your short temper, your nerves—being so jumpy and all, and we don't know what to say or how to act."

Arnold said, "I know I'm different too Dad, I know I've changed but now I'm am trying to do the normal stuff, like get a job, go to church, get married. The worst of it is, Dad, that I feel numb. I am really trying to 'feel' emotion again, to feel love, to relax and enjoy a day just fishing. But if truth be had, Dad, I am scared to feel, to love, to care about anything because in the war— in the damn war, most everyone I cared about was killed, and I saw them die. That wasn't like watching a parent die here in the hospital or something. These deaths were brutal, bloody, painful and final. It's what we faced every damn day for two years. So, is it going to take me two, maybe three years to forget that, to accept that, to be normal again? I don't have any answers either and it's making me nuts!"

Arnold stood up and kicked the stump of a dead tree, "I think that over there, after a while most of us guys just stopped feeling, stopping caring about things, about people---we just became numb to it all. I'm going through the motions of living, Dad—nothing around me feels normal, feels real. I do love Norrie, I do---and that scares me every second of every day. I don't know how to deal with that---I think I'm just plain scared to care about anything and I feel like I'm walking around waiting for someone else I love to die. I know I've been home almost a year now and the only thing that feels real to me is still that damn war and the buddies I lost over there. This is hell Dad---it was bad overseas and now it's even worse that I'm home. I thought it would be different, that everything would be great again, but it's not!"

Jake pulled a pack of cigarettes from his pocket and handed one to Arnold. He flicked his lighter on and lit both their smokes. Taking a deep drag, Jake blew the smoke out into the crisp mountain air and said, "Arnold, I hear what you are saying and I'm trying like hell to understand what it must be like for you, but I was never in your shoes son. Have you thought about talking to your commander, to a doctor? There must be help for you guys and I know for damn sure you aren't the only one going through this. Maybe it just takes more time than you've given it, maybe when you get to Minneapolis and get enrolled in school, things will get better. Pray son, pray for strength and courage to face this new battle and remember that Mom and I love you. You got a wife now and have a plan for a future, try and think about the good things, not the bad memories!"

~~~~~~~

August 10, 1947: Arnold and Norrie celebrated their first anniversary pulling their new Air Stream trailer home to Minneapolis, MN. He'd managed a double loan, for the trailer and also for a second-hand maroon Ford coupe. The trip from Lovell to Minneapolis had been uneventful except for their anniversary celebration. Leaving Lovell and his mother's tears hadn't been a good scene, but at least his Dad understood.

At the Shady Lanes trailer park in Minneapolis, with Norrie guiding him, Arnold backed their Air Stream into spot #118. He cut the engine, hopped out and slid blocks behind the trailer wheels. He unhooked the trailer from their Ford and said, "Okay, wife, we are here. Damn it's hot and muggy. Bet there are lots of bugs too—this is the kind of weather they like. You know we are going to need groceries, but how about grabbing a burger and a beer someplace close. Tomorrow morning we can go grocery shopping and check out the school later."

After a couple months of school, Arnold was getting bored and antsy with the regimented class schedule. He found a second job selling Rex Air Vacuums. It was a new idea in vacuums where it sucked the dirt in and then blew it into a tray of water. "It cuts down on the dust and those filthy bags. You just empty the tray and put clean water in when you want to use it again, it's a heck of an idea." He sold one to everyone he knew and a few he didn't.

"I guess I'm like my Dad, I like to tinker, I like machines, and I think I'm pretty good at selling although I don't like it as much as tinkering!" Norrie wrapped her arms around her husband, "I know I'm probably prejudiced, but I think you are good at lots of things!"

Arnold stuck it out at the refrigeration school until March and then he threw in the towel. "Honestly Norrie, I hate going to school. I'm not a book-type fella. I'm a hands-on---I want to get into what I'm doing."

Norrie sat across the breakfast table from her husband and smoked a cigarette with her morning coffee. "Well, you aren't telling me anything new, that's for sure. So, what now? I will have to give my notice at the hospital here before we leave. Do you have any ideas about what you want to do or where we are moving?"

Arnold leaned across the table and grinned at his wife, "How about you and me grab a bite to eat tonight? We could go have a few drinks and listen to that great little band they have at the Swank Club?" Norrie got all dolled up in a little red number and put her hair up on her head, just the way Arnold liked it.

After dinner, they settled into a corner booth at the Swank Club to listen to the popular band. Arnold liked this kind of upbeat music, it lifted his spirits. They both tossed back a few whiskey sours and, out of the blue, the band changed tempo and began to play a slow song, Danny Boy. Norrie had been people watching and tapping her fingers to the music when she turned to say something to Arnold. She stopped dead in her tracks. He was sitting straight as a board, rigid in the seat with his tightly clenched fists lying on the table. There were tears rolling down his cheeks and his face was contorted into an agonized grimace as he struggled to control himself.

Norrie leaned in toward her husband, "Arnold, Arnold---what is the matter, what happened to upset you so?"

Arnold turned slowly to look into her eyes as a tormented whisper crawled out of his throat, "Danny Boy---why the hell did they have to play that song—Danny Boy?"

Norrie moved in closer and put her arm across his shoulders, "Why does that song bother you, Arnold?"

He looked up at her as a sob broke from deep within, "He was, he was my gunner in the first crew. Danny was a hell of a kid, kinda like the little brother I never had; I called him Danny Boy all the time. He died when our tank went up in flames---after it blasted me out of the hatch. All my guys died but me! He was special to me, Norrie, real special. He was a real good kid who never had much luck in life." He laid his head down on the table and sobbed.

Norrie looked at the couples in the next booth who couldn't help but notice; she explained in a whisper, "The war, he lost a buddy named Danny, sorry about this."

It took Arnold a bit to get a hold of his memories. The two couples next to them stood up to leave. They stopped at the table where Arnold and Norrie sat and the men extended their hands. "Just want to say thank you for your service, we were both in the Pacific and we know buddy, we damn well know. Hope the rest of your evening is better. Hope you have a good night!"

~~~~~~

Lovell, Wyoming – Spring, 1948: They rented a trailer space at the Lovell Trailer Court that sat back in a grove of trees down by the Shoshone River. Arnold looked up everyone he knew in Lovell and sold them a Rex Air Vacuum and then the bottom fell out of that.

Raisa commented, "You are just like your Dad, when we was in Port Huron. He tried lots of different jobs, but nothing seemed to work for him. Maybe he should try and get you on at Marathon or Ohio Oil again?"

That night in their cozy little trailer, Arnold and Norrie talked about their future. Norrie admitted, "I don't think it's good for us to stay around here---around your folks and my mother. We need to have our own home, away from all the interfering. We can't sneeze and there are family comments and frankly, I'm getting damn tired of them always butting in our business."

Arnold sipped his can of beer and took a drag on his Camel, "Yeah, I have to agree with you, Honey. I don't know how that will work with me being in the National Guard with the 300th

Armored Field Artillery Battalion, if we move out of town and all. I know you can get a job pretty much any place---the problem is mine. Working for Ohio Oil is okay, but I don't see me getting anywhere with what they have me doing."

The next week, Arnold found out he was being moved into the National Guard Reserves and he only had to report for duty two weeks out of every year. It would stay that way indefinitely or until another war broke out. They stuck it out in Lovell for the next year and half, Norrie worked at the Lovell Hospital and Arnold was with the Ohio Oil Company doing whatever they needed him to do. He hated his job, he hated the nightmares, and he was beginning to hate living in Lovell. He thought to himself, *I guess I have my Dad's wanderlust, I want to try a bigger town or city. I didn't like Minneapolis—too damn hot and buggy. I know I want to stay close to the mountains—the fishing and camping. Norrie and I sorta like Billings, MT. ---that would be far enough away from our folks, and there'd be more job options for me. I just wish I could settle down and like what I am getting paid for doing. I don't know what the good Lord has in store for me, but I hope it happens soon!*

July 30, 1950: Norrie tried to keep herself busy while Arnold was away at the National Guard Reserves camp for a few days. *I think I'll take a walk down by the river after I have a bite to eat later today. A short walk will do me good, help clear my head and settle my stomach. I need to lose some of this weight any way so the exercise will do me good. I just haven't felt very good for a while; I'm going to see Dr. Craft tomorrow morning and get a checkup.*

Arnold drove up in their Ford that next afternoon around four p.m., he was early. He parked the car and sat behind the wheel for a bit, his hands gripping the steering wheel. Norrie watched him through the window and thought he acted a little off. *Something must have happened at the Guard, I'll open a cold beer for him and we can have a little chat---yeah, that's what we will have, a little chat! What I have to tell him won't take that long.*

Arnold and Norrie sat at their tiny kitchen table. The air was tense and neither of them was eager to spill the beans. Norrie spoke first, "Here's a cold beer. I don't know what happened at the Guard, but I can tell you are upset, so let's have it, I can take it."

Arnold's face was pale and his large tanned hand squeezed the cold can of beer. "I hope to hell you can take this, Norrie, because I don't know if I can?"

Norrie sat up straighter, with one hand in her lap, "Come on Kid, you are talking to me—your wife. So, give it to me straight. Did they demote you or something?"

Arnold stood and paced the small trailer; he wasn't smiling when he turned and said in a low voice, "The National Guard, the 300th Armored Field Battalion is being activated—we are going to ship out to Korea. I am going to have to fight in another damn war---that's the truth of it and it's the total shits! Those nightmares I have—well, they are going to be my real life all over again. The brass is calling the Guard from Cody, Powell, Lovell, Thermopolis, Worland, and Sheridan, along with a few fellas from some smaller towns."

Norrie's face went absolutely white as she stood so fast she knocked over the kitchen chair and barely made it to the small sink before she vomited, not once but twice.

Arnold rushed to her side and handed her a paper towel, "Norrie, you okay? What's wrong with you, did you pick up a bu-----?" He stopped in midsentence as the truth of it exploded white hot in his brain.

Arnold wrapped her in his arms as tears rolled down his cheeks, "Aw, no, Baby, no---you aren't pregnant are you? Is that it? No, you can't be pregnant now. The timing of this whole thing is the shits! Talk to me."

Norrie looked up at him, her face was ashen as tears spilled over her cheeks, "I'm due around the middle of December. I saw Dr. Craft yesterday and was waiting until you got home. I've had some weight gain and felt a little queasy. I'm not regular so I couldn't tell from that. I thought that maybe I had picked up a bug. I guess you could say I picked up one of your bugs!" She stood at the window for a moment, collecting herself, "When is this all going to happen Arnold, do you know for sure when the guard is leaving Lovell?"

Arnold ran his hands through his thinning blond hair and replied "We are to report for active duty by August 19th; then we will begin our full-time training. Hell, some of these guys are as green as apples. There are only a handful of us who are WWII vets the rest are right out of high school or under twenty including my cousin Jimmy."

He gazed out the tiny trailer window, "Fighting the Germans was one thing; hell, I don't even know where Korea is except it's next to China and the communists are trying to take over the whole country." He laughed, "We are going in there to save the South Koreans from it all!"

16 Aug. 1950: Arnold hadn't told his parents about the 300th being called up—just wasn't prepared for the 'water works' and the hysteria. Of course they knew Norrie was expecting and were thrilled. That day, Norrie and her mother had taken an overnight shopping trip to Billings and so Arnold decided to make a night of it. Later in the afternoon, he and a few of the guys from the 300th met at the local pool hall for a couple of beers and a few games of pool. A couple of beers turned into, too many beers and at 2 a.m., the bartender called Jake to come down and pick his son up.

Jake reached under Arnold's arm and darn near drug his inebriated son out to his parked car and literally stuffed him into the passenger seat. Walking around to the other side, Jake slapped the rear fender in frustration. He opened the car door, slid behind the wheel and started the engine; he made a sharp U-turn on Main Street and headed for their house back down Shoshone Drive. Suddenly he pulled the Mercury over to the curb.

Jake turned in the seat to glare at his son, "Arnold, you have got to get ahold of yourself. What the hell is wrong with you that you can't go have a few beers without gettin' drunk? You'd better straighten the hell up----grow up and be a man."

Bleary-eyed, Arnold cocked his head to the side as he turned to face his father, "Well, Da-Dad, I have to t-tell you, I needed a few too mannnny be-errs tonight. I'm gonna have another cha---chance to grow up, in---in Kor-rea!"

Jake's face lost color as his eyes bugged out, "What the hell did you just say? Korea---what about Korea? What the hell are you talking about, Korea?" Arnold's head bobbed around as his eyes fought to focus in on something, "We---ll Dad, juss got news thaat the 300th Baaa-ttal-ion is shipping out, to Kor—reaa! I get the thrill of getting shot, shot at again, Dad. Annnnd—I probably won't be here en aur baby's born. Now, thasss reason to celebrate juss a little, donnnna ya th-ink?" Arnold paused and then added, "Oh and be - be a sss-port and tell Mom for me. I c-can't handle her reaction to this right now." And with that, he passed out.

The Lovell, Wyoming, 300th Armored Field Battalion – 1950

Chapter Twenty

"Back in Hell - Again!"
[36]Korea: 'The Forgotten War'

August 19, 1950: The Lovell High School band gathered at the train station and played a rousing rendition of patriotic songs as a send-off for the Lovell 300th Armored Field Battalion! Half the town showed up, dressed in their Sunday Best for the historical event. Lovell's streets and alleys were jammed with hundreds of parked cars as people pushed in around the little train depot, showing their support. Nobody wanted to miss this day, it was a big deal---sixty-five of Lovell's best young men were shipping out for Korea!

Jake and Raisa held on to each other as they stood next to Arnold and Norrie. Jake said in a low voice, "This is nuts—seems like we just did this a couple years back and here we are again. It's not right, no it isn't, but our boy has to do what he has to do and that's the end of it." Raisa's face was a mask of anguish as she struggled to control her emotions. Jake had urged her to take a pill before they left, hoping it would help her get through the morning.

The steam engine blew its whistle as it rounded the curve at the east end of Lovell. The troop train consisted of several Pullman cars, a baggage, a diner car, and the caboose. It had just picked up the Thermopolis and Worland boys, now Lovell, and after that they'd load on the men from Cody with a stop in Frannie. The train was headed for Billings where they would meet up with the Guard from the other side of the Big Horns, from Sheridan. Once the entire Wyoming Guard was on the train it would head northwest to Ft. Lewis, Washington, for further training as a unit.

Jake and Raisa went ahead and said their goodbyes, leaving Arnold and his wife to have a few private moments before he had to board the train. Arnold noticed that his father practically had to drag his mother to the car; she was crying so hard she could hardly stand up.

Arnold took Norrie in his arms; she laid her head on his shoulder as the tears began again. Her pregnancy was obvious and he could feel their baby bump as he held her close. He said, "Honey, I think I might still be state-side in early December when our baby is due. If we are in Ft. Lewis or state-side, I think I can get special leave to catch a flight home for a few days so I can be with you when our little bundle of joy arrives, that is if you have some idea of when that will be."

Norrie wiped at the tears and looked up at her husband through red, swollen eyes and replied, "I already talked to Dr. Craft and he told me when I am close to being ready and the baby is a good weight, there are a few things they can do to hurry the process along. So, I guess we just wait and pray everything turns out. You know I want you here if at all possible."

It was all they could do, to tear themselves apart. This wasn't supposed to happen like this. They both held on to the slim chance he could still be present for the birth, they just had to pray it would all work out. Earlier in the week, the 300th loaded their respective guard equipment onto a special train that would take it to Ft. Lewis; after training in Washington, the equipment would be loaded onto a ship headed for Korea.

Norrie stood with the other wives and girlfriends as 65 of their husbands and boyfriends boarded the train for Ft. Lewis, WA. *This is all so surreal, like playing the same record all over again. When he left for WWII, we were just beginning our love story, and now I carry his child and he has to leave me and our life to fight in another war. Please dear Lord, bring Arnold home for the birth of our baby and keep him safe so we can live this life together. Bring him back to me, again. Amen!*

Arnold watched and waved from the train's window until the image of Norrie standing on the station platform was just a memory. His hands were shaking as he flipped a cigarette from the package of Camels and struck a match to one. Arnold inhaled deeply, letting the nicotine smooth his ragged nerves. *Well, this is it—I'm back--here we go again. It's the same old prayer, Lord, 'Keep me safe and if not, then let it be quick'! Amen! Oh and Lord, protect Norrie and our baby. Thank you.*

Arnold looked around the troop train and felt the spasm of fear and resentment in his gut. *Most of these guys are kids right out of high school, like his cousin Jim Larson. Only me, Bob Baird, and two others are veterans from WWII and have some inkling of what is coming. The rest of these guys are clueless.* Arnold looked out the window at the passing scenery. *Well, they'll learn fast enough just like we did, or they will die real quick.*

The 12-car troop train slowed as it neared the little Wyoming burg of Frannie to pick up the Cody guard; John Zwemer and his wife were waiting at the station. They had permission to board the train and hand out paper cups of hot coffee and some of Mrs. Zwemer's famous cinnamon rolls. Arnold knew the couple from his church and wasn't the only one who was thankful for the kindness. *That coffee and those warm rolls sure did hit the spot, that's for sure. It's going to be a long ride to Washington. One thing about this group that's good and bad— we're mostly friends and neighbors; it isn't like we are all strangers. But if somebody doesn't make it, then it's going to hurt more, I know too much about getting attached to a guy and then watching him die---I've had a gut full of that.* Every man there knew that having your friends around you when so far away from home was a good thing; they would all be watching each other's back---the 300th from Wyoming was special like that!

The size of the troop train increased daily as they made their way across Montana, Idaho, and then into Washington. The trip took longer than expected because a freight train had priority; the troop train was instructed to pull over to a side track and wait for the freight to pass. To help pass the time, the soldiers read, slept, and played cards; when it came time to stop at a town, most of the gung ho young men hung out the windows. At the majority of the stops there would be women and girls waiting on the station platform, loaded down with home baked goods and just plain good food for the soldiers. Some of the guys even managed a quick kiss or two from a pretty girl!

Ft. Lewis, Washington: The 300th Armored Field Battalion was stationed at an advanced training camp where they became more proficient with their equipment and each other. They slept in barracks equipped with army-issue cots from September through the end of December and drilled over and over again. Arnold watched with dismay, all of the green recruits as they learned the ropes. *"They don't really have a clue what they are up against. Hell, I don't either because this is a whole different war, but I know the sights and sounds and memories of battles, that never changes or goes away.*

The first thing Warrant Officer Arnold Kessel did was to put in for maternity leave around the first of December. Upon learning the reason for the request for leave, his superiors signed the papers without hesitation. Whenever Norrie called with news of the imminent delivery of their child, Arnold was set to fly home.

Arnold was just sitting down to chow when a private tapped him on the shoulder, "Sir, you have a phone call, you can take it over there in that office."

For the last few weeks Arnold had been jittery, knowing Norrie's time was near. He picked up the phone and felt his legs go rubbery when he heard her voice. "Hi, Honey, Dr. Craft said that you better get on a plane—everything is ready—this baby wants to be born and I am SO ready for this pregnancy to be over. Come home as soon as you can catch a flight. Your Dad said he would meet the plane in Billings and drive you to Lovell. I love you honey—we are about to be parents."

December 6, 1950: The waiting room and halls of the Lovell Hospital were quiet at 11 at night as Arnold and his folks hurried through the double front doors. Making an exception to the rule, a nurse ushered Arnold to the labor room where Norrie lay in the hospital bed. She reached for him with tears running down her porcelain skin. "Oh, dear Lord, Thank YOU. You made it--you really made it in time, Arnold. I don't think it's going to be long now, I can't keep my legs crossed forever, you know!" She gave a little laugh then suddenly Norrie's grip on his hand got much tighter and she gritted her teeth; she began to pant and blow out air. "You better stand back because I might take a swing at you for putting me in this situation!" Arnold was relieved that Norrie smiled when she said that and also relieved when the doctor told him to go back to the waiting room and---wait!

Arnold smoked about a pack of cigarettes and wore a path on the floor with his pacing. Finally around 4 a.m. a nurse came out, "It's all over, congratulations, you are now a daddy! Dr. Craft will be out in a minute to talk to you, just have a seat."

Arnold stood and chased after the disappearing nurse, "Wait, you didn't tell me what we have---boy or girl?" Just then Dr. Craft appeared wiping his hands on a towel. "I think I can answer that—you have a fine, healthy son!"

Jake and Raisa squealed with delight---a Kessel heir. Arnold's legs felt rubbery all over again and suddenly all he wanted to do was to see Norrie and his son. Dr. Craft took him back to the room where Norrie lay in bed, looking flushed and gorgeous. She was holding a small bundle wrapped tightly in a blue blanket. Grinning ear to ear, Arnold cupped her face in his hands and kissed her. "Norrie, thank you, for going through all of that and giving us a son. Does he have all his fingers and toes?" Arnold stopped and said, "Say, do you realize what day this is--- what day our son was born on? It's December 7th, Pearl Harbor Day---now that is, crazy."

Norrie looked down at her son; stroking his tiny red face, she said, "I would like to name him Terrill William, what do you think of that name? Terrill is an English name and of course he will have the same middle name as you."

~~~~~

January 25, 1951: The 300th, nicknamed the "Three Double-Nothings, sailed south from Seattle, Washington, to San Francisco, California, where they docked for a couple of days, taking on fresh water and food. The soldiers were allowed to disembark and do some sightseeing, but few had any extra money to spend. Arnold got permission to leave the ship and look up his mother's sister, Amelia, and she treated him to dinner then he had to report back to the ship.

Before sunrise the next morning, the huge convoy, including two aircraft carriers set sail for Japan. The upper decks were packed with men, gazing at the glittering lights of San Francisco. They cheered as the ship slipped under the famous Golden Gate Bridge and out into open water. The trip across the

Pacific took just over three weeks, with the troop ships bobbing like corks on the ocean surface while the heavy aircraft carriers looked as though they were gliding across the water.

For the handful of WWII veterans like Arnold this was nothing new, but for the green guys, seeing this much water was obviously daunting. Arnold patted his cousin, Jimmy Larson, on the back as Jimmy hung his head over the side of the rocking ship. "It gets better when you get your sea legs under you, anyway I hope it does. Some guys are sick the whole way!" Arnold grinned wickedly as Jim gave him a single finger salute!

Yokohama, Japan: Arnold and a couple thousand American soldiers stood on deck gazing at the impressive Japanese city. Someone shouted "Hey look at all those beautiful Jap girls, maybe they'd like some chocolate and cigarettes." They had been anchored just offshore for two hours and now had pulled anchor and were moving out of the harbor. "What the hell, I thought we were going to stop off here and continue training for a month? Now the military has obviously changed plans and they are sending us on to Pusan, Korea, to train? That's the shits---I'd rather hold up here but they didn't ask me! I guess McArthur gets to make all the rules in this war."

On February 15th, the convoy of troop ships slid into the harbor at Pusan, Korea. Those men up on deck smelled the city before they saw it. People seemed to be running everywhere—like a million ants. The soldiers on board crowded the decks to watch as filthy pigs, scrawny dogs, and humans stopped wherever they were and did their 'business' in

The Korean peninsula

the streets. The little kids had slits in their pants so they could take a poop whenever they needed to. There were no houses to speak of, along the wharf. The majority of the people there obviously lived in the mangled assortment of cardboard and corrugated tin huts that were crammed together along the water.

Baskets and barrels of rotting fish and vegetables lined the piers; the smell was so bad those on board could hardly breathe. Arnold quipped, "I hope to hell it gets better when we get off the ship and start moving inland. This place is the shits!"

Wes Meeks elbowed Arnold and said, "Come on 'Chief,' they got the local band out for us playing "If I Knew You Were Coming, I'd Baked a Cake." What more can we ask than that? Look at those people just waiting for us to walk off this ship with our cigarettes and chocolate bars. Someone said we might get one of those girls to follow the camp and wash our clothes. That would be darn swell; I'll see if I can arrange that!"

~~~~~~~

KOREA: February 1951: The 300[37] Armored Field Battalion was initially affiliated with the USA 2nd Division along with two South Korean (SK) divisions. After they disembarked from the troop ship, the Army moved to a camp along the coast. The Division remained there for a month, huddled inside their tents, trying to acclimate to the terrain, weather, and country and simply survive what was left of the brutal winter weather. This kind of mountainous winter cold was nothing new for the men from Wyoming; using 'rural' ingenuity a couple of the men took the spent shell casings and made a super chimney out of them. That little stove they rigged up made their tents the warmest in the camp and they had lots of visitors. The soldiers kept busy with equipment maintenance, paperwork, and on clear days the greenhorns took the binoculars and scanned the nearby hills for signs of the North Koreans (NK).

Arnold said, "According to HQ, the NKs are farther north, hooking up with all the Chinese that came across the border. I'm not worried about the NK army—but if we have to mix it up with those Chinks, we're going to have our work cut out for us."

His nephew asked, "How the hell do you tell them apart? Those Gooks all look alike to me."

Arnold laughed and replied, "The Chinese will be the ones leading the attack, dressed in moss green quilted jackets and hats with ear flaps. They know how to fight; hell, that's about all they do---fight wars. They are more fanatical and disciplined than the NKs or even SKs; they don't retreat, they just keep coming at you."

~~~~~~~

After two months of waiting, the battalion had word the ship with most of their equipment had finally docked in Pusan. The M-7 tanks, 105 Howitzers (could shoot 5 miles and weighed 100

pounds each), 45-caliber machine guns, and a mountain of cases of ammo were loaded onto a train. No one could predict when that train would arrive. It was moving at a snail's pace northward on the fickle Korean railroads. Word was that sometime in the next couple of weeks they hoped to unload in Wonju, closer to their camps. In the meantime, the 300th mostly sat and twiddled their thumbs until they were finally reunited with their equipment. They manned a few roadblocks—stopping the civilians who pushed against the barriers. These Koreans were only a part of the constant flow of refugees that oozed out of the north, heading for the UN Red Cross tents where they could get something to eat and maybe a blanket. Most were poor farmers with families, wrinkled mama-sans, and scrawny half-dressed kids. HQ's orders were to stop and search every one. They knew the Communists often infiltrated and blended in with the peasants to slip across the UN lines. The civilians smelled like rancid cooking grease combined with the foul odor of unwashed bodies rank which permeated the rags they wore. It was the kids that got to the Americans the most, boney brown-eyed innocents that pulled at the soldiers' coats, begging for anything. Their dirty emaciated faces with those hollow, black eyes---pleading for candy, gum, food, help, and safety, were hard to ignore or forget about.

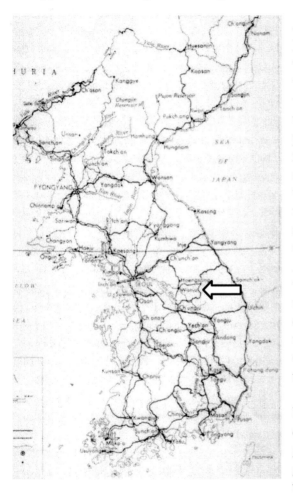

May 14, 1951 - Wonju, Korea: Men from the 300th were at the railhead with wheeled vehicles, waiting for their 105mm self-propelled Howitzers mounted on a tank chassis, service trucks, and the rest of their equipment to arrive from Pusan. Chief Warrant Officer Arnold Kessel was with them after they unloaded their equipment, formed up under the control of X Corps, and headed for the front lines.

The 300th barely had time to check the oil and gas gauges before they got a taste of what they came here for, war! As soon as possible and without much sleep they began pushing hard toward the 38th parallel. The flatter coastal topography turned abruptly into steep, rugged, wooded mountains. Sharp outcroppings of jagged rock pocked the hillsides. It was perfect ambush terrain and they were put on constant alert. Arnold knew what it was like to fight in the enemy's country---it was never good because they knew it and you didn't—simple as that.

They knew the advantage points, where to dig in and where to attack.

Arnold watched the faces of the green draftees as they passed smoldering Chinese and Korean equipment and piles of rubble. The real shock came when they came upon a mound of semi-naked Korean dead—stacked like cordwood with identity tags around their big toes. Arnold knew that scene would get the 'greenies'---and it did. They were all surprised at how mountainous Korea was and by an occasional wild persistent mountain spring flower that pushed its colorful head up through the inhospitable rocky terrain.

Because the boys from Lovell/300th guard were in a service battery, they were always moving, always following the front-line fighting. They had to be close to 'service' the fighting troops with resupply of ammo, food, and medical services. Their job was to be at the beck and call of the guys on the frontlines even if it put their path in harm's way. They knew how to dig a foxhole and fire a weapon, but that wasn't their main job.

Arnold shivered in his army-issued winter overcoat and hat, the cold and humidity biting straight through the wool. "This place gets damn cold in February, that's for sure—feels like Wyoming but it doesn't smell like Wyoming! I didn't even think about it being this hilly and mountainous; that is going to make for a few headaches when it comes to fighting." He knew he wouldn't be with these hometown guys for long—he already had his first reattachment to another battalion, serving as a technical artillery advisor, the role that most warrant officers played. HQ would hand him around where he was needed and he never had much heads up as to when and where that would be.

NOTE: *Warrant Officers weren't considered enlisted nor officers but former highly accomplished enlisted men, whom everyone trusted.*

Before they camped that night, their convoy traveled across a high ridge. They could see a rugged valley below; the valley floor was dotted with obvious campfires. Arnold heard some of the guys asking what/who was down in that valley and the reply was--- "Chinese, you duffas! They are probably training a whole division of North Koreans, right down there."

The 300th plodded up the narrow mountain road in single file, they were unbathed and unshaven and some were limping from blisters. They marched to the  right and paused, letting the stretcher bearers pass. Their lieutenant asked, "You got a jeep down here? We need a jeep real bad, got wounded coming off those slopes to the west and we need to get em' down the mountain. You boys better get ready cause you got some real bad shit up ahead."

Reaching their destination, the convoy joined up with the 2nd U.S. Infantry Division. The troops grabbed some chow and a little sack time until daybreak. At this camp they had cots to sleep on, they all heard that what waited for them up ahead didn't include sleeping in a tent on cots.

Chief Officer Kessel checking on green sentries.

Arnold left his post and walked down to where a couple of new guys were keeping watch. "Just keep your eyes and ears open for any movement out there and don't take your hand off that machine gun."

May 15 - 20, 1951--The Battle of Soyang: Arnold got the news along with the rest of the group in the mess tent the next morning. They would be reinforcing the 23rd Regiment, 37th Field Artillery, as well as the 2nd Division – they were going to Chaun-ni!

The 300th had their orders and Chief Warrant Officer Kessel had his. They were headed in opposite directions. On the east coast of Korea, the boys from Wyoming would be part of a spearhead from Chaun-ni through Inje to Kansong. During the morning briefing their commander told them, "We think we have around 10,000 Chinese just sittin'–where we can move around and get them in a trap. *We are moving* out along a long valley next to the Soyang River."

^{38}**"COWBOY ARTILLERY AT SOYANG"**
– Hongchon, Korea
Heritage Series Painting - May 18, 1951
--- Compliments of the National Guard

Early in the next morning---on the 16^{th,} the 300th was up before daybreak and headed for the Soyang River when suddenly one of their spotter planes buzzed the convoy. It came back around, flying in low enough to drop a message---"*Chinese in regiment strength, in front of you!*"

In less than two minutes the 'horsefly' was back with another message, "*Looks like it might be two divisions of Chinks and NKs!*"

The 300th was packing up the camp when the plane came in low a third time, "*There is no end to the number of Chinese coming at you.*"

"*That was when our guys started to spot them. It was shocking—hundreds of Chinese and North Korean troops— crawling over the hills like ants. It was obvious they weren't interested in our small group---they were after bigger cheese. We could hear their guns down the valley, the sound of big guns that thundered and rolled up the walls of that valley---barrage after barrage as they moved past us, to the west.*" (Taken from veteran's interview)

~~~~~~~

Ken Black was driving the last ammo truck in the service battery convoy on the way to Soyang. It was raining cats and dogs and he was having a heck of a time holding the loaded truck on the narrow muddy mountain road. The entire column was just inching along while infantry and mortar crews struggled with the steep angles of trying to fire at the Chinese they knew were up on the ridge. It was a three-ring circus!

UN soldiers staggered down the hill, passing the infantry column going up. The 300th looked into the faces, the eyes of the battle-weary men. They all bore the telltale signs of battle fatigue—the bloodshot stare of sleeplessness, of deafness from grenades and mortars. Ragged bloody makeshift bandages threatened to fall to the road as the soldiers stumbled past, down the hill to safety from screaming mortars and a continuous barrage of bullets.

Now, they could hear the distant boom boom of Howitzers from the Marines who were dug in, straight up in front of them. They saw the telltale plumes of smoke rise from a shell hitting a target---or not. Arnold thought about that past night when he had talked to a couple of new recruits about keeping their guns from freezing up. "In Germany, some of our attached infantry used hair tonic instead of the regular gun oil to keep their guns from freezing up. Worked like a charm." Arnold laughed to himself because little tips like that were exactly why those enlisted guys loved warrant officers.

Ken's fingers gripped the steering wheel as he tried to avoid running over the dead Chinese bodies that littered the road and hillsides. "I've never seen anything like this---do the Chinks ever come and pick up their dead or do they just leave them there?" Somebody remarked, "We don't know what they do, we never stuck around that long!"

They finally bivouacked for the night in a clump of trees next to the river where they saw even more dead Chinese bodies floating down the river—that was why they all added two or more purifying pills to the water they took from the river. They dug their foxholes and cut trees to cover the tops of them or drove their tru:ks over the holes—anything to keep the deadly shrapnel off themselves. Ken was in a fox hole next to another Lovell guy when the shelling started that night. WHAP, WHAP—somebody screamed, Incoming!"

The next morning Ken asked his buddy, "What the heck were you thinking when those shells were coming in—jumping out of your foxhole like that?"

Rex flushed and laughed, "Aww, well, I aaah—all I heard WAS---Incoming---and I was thinking of incoming MAIL! And then---I heard the shells hitting. Guess I was darn lucky."

The infantry got their orders that morning, "We are going into a quiet zone—that means secure grenades, canteens, and helmets.

Attach bayonets and remember that our pass word for the day is Marilyn! The point man will be shadowed by the sharpshooter's rifle squad. Mortars are next in line, then the Howitzers followed by another mortar group. Everyone stays in order, stay tight and dig in when we stop." The LT turned back, "One more thing, the Chinks will wait us out, they are great warriors, got discipline—it takes a lot to panic them. And, you don't want to be taken prisoner by them Gooks, trust me on that."

Kessel in a mountain foxhole w/troops

The wind was blowing like a banshee on the top of the ridge; it was their friend and enemy at the same time---it was muffling their movement towards the Chinese, but would also muffle the enemy's movements. The thermometer dropped like a hammer making and the relentless wind felt like it was cutting straight like knives through their winter gear. Small bands of panicked South Korean troops stumbled past them as quickly; a look of terror and flight filled their faces, their eyes.

Arnold heard some low mumbling, "Whatever is waiting for us in those hills up ahead has got those Gooks on the run back to Pusan and Mama-san." Now they moved off the road onto some sort of trail, a trail that had been recently used by a multitude of feet. They saw other signs along the road like fresh fox holes and big gun pits that had been scraped out of the mountain. All abandoned!

All hell broke loose at midnight when the UN troops were attacked by 120,000 Chinese Communist troops--so much for trapping 10,000 Chinese. It didn't take long before two ROK divisions were in full retreat. HQ ordered the 300th to cover the gap in the line by realigning their fire 90 degrees. The battalion spearheaded time and time again; on the edge of being overrun, they continually fell back with the infantry. The enemy was dropping like flies as the fighting raged day and night, but they just kept coming. In one 24-hour slot, two batteries fired 7,200 rounds with their 12 Howitzers. Rather than off- service trucks just backed loading all the ammo, the up to the guys on the front lines firing the Howitzers.

Chief Advisor Kessel sighting in a machine gun

They stayed there unloading ammo until the truck was empty then turned around and took off down the mountain for another load. A full truck was always waiting to move up to supply the front lines. The boys in the empty trucks hauled ass back down the mountain and reloaded more ammo like their pants were on fire.

The 1st Marine Division was on their left flank as A and C Batteries retreated 50 kilometers to the rear. "We gotta take Myong Rock Road—it's critical for the UN forces." The Chinese wanted that road as well and launched a heavy attack trying desperately to cut the road and trap the UN troops. A Battery and HQ Battery made it out of there while C Battery remained, firing at the enemy until late night.

Kessel advising the front armor

In the black of night, driving closely together without headlights, the two batteries formed a tight column through a long gorge road cut into the side of a steep hill. The road was narrow with a river running through the gorge about 30 feet below on the right and steep cliffs to the left. They were sitting ducks and they knew it—it was just something they were trying to keep from the Chinese. The men could hear the whistles and bugles from the Chinese troops as they swarmed the hills. The UN boys had their fingers crossed, hoping the Chinese heard the formidable rumble the tank chassis were making and would not fire on them because they knew their mortars would not be a deterrent. In the cover of darkness their plan worked as they slipped through without losing another man.

May 18, 1951: Arnold was back at the ammo depot when the service trucks came barreling down the mountain road, pulling up for a quick refill of shells. He pitched in and handed off the shells to the drivers. Arnold said, "How goes it up there? Sure are making a racket."

One of the drivers replied through gritted teeth, "Those 105mm Howitzers are amazing. Hell, they have such a high rate of fire that they can fire at targets 10,000 yards away and keep it up until those remaining enemy are as close as 2,000 yards. The beauty of them is that they have the mobility to get the heck out of there before they are under small arms fire. I watched them blast away---directly and indirectly at this here road block while our infantry jumped around to infiltrate the roadblock. They are something, I'll say that!"

~~~~~~~

Chief Warrant Officer Kessel didn't have too much to do when he was back with his outfit for short periods. He had a few technical assignments with the 300th, but not many. At chow one day he was chewing the fat with some of the Lovell guys. Sgt. Ken Black and Hank

Arnold Kessel on the far left with 300th buddies

Emmett were talking about how the Chinks kept bombing the American air strips at night and our boys would get up the next morning and rebuild them. "Shoot, they fire tracer bullets at them all night long, but them Chinks are slippery and determined, they just keep coming back like a bad dream!"

Being in a service battalion was no cushy job. Their trucks were required to drive through thick and thin to get to the American and UN troops who were fighting on the frontlines. They carried machine guns which they put to good use more than a few times. It was their job to service those forward troops with supplies like food and ammunition and sometimes there would be times when they were dodging enemy bullets and mortars to get to the men on the front lines.

**Chief Warrant Officer
Arnold Kessel – 1951**

The 300th was on the move again. As the convoy headed north they were slowed and then stopped after about a mile. Arnold and another WWII vet, were in a jeep with a .30-caliber heavy machine gun (HMG) mounted on the back. They pulled up next to one of the service trucks and asked, "What the hell is going on? Why are we stopped here?" Motor Sergeant Bob Baird replied, "Ahhh—we've got some knucklehead Goomba truck driver from Brooklyn up there who never drove a truck in his life and he crashed head-on into a duck (amphibious vehicle). So we gotta wait while they clean it up."

Kessel said, "I don't know why they let these city dudes do anything –they can barely tie their own shoelaces! We all know that us Wyoming boys know a heck of a lot more about shooting guns and driving trucks than those city boys ever will."

When Arnold joined up with the 300th in Lovell, because of his decorated combat service in WWII he had been promoted to [39]Chief Warrant Officer. His duties included being a technical and tactical armored military advisor and he would be in the thick of things, meaning in combat again if and when the situation arose. He knew that meant he would be transferred around to different batteries where he was needed at the time—not always serving with the 300th from Wyoming.

They'd been on the road for over a week—heading farther north to the frontlines. When they set up camp, it was in tents with no real heat. Those little stoves they had rigged using fired shells for the chimney, worked slicker than snot! When the weather broke the next day, they were close to a river---some of the young bloods jumped in the water in their long underwear. Arnold watched from the bank, "I think them boys got a case of spring fever. I guess I think that water still looks a little chilly---think I'll stick to a warm bird bath for now!"

Arnold noticed that every time they set up their 300th Armored Battalion camp, there was a road sign, 'Entering Wyoming' stuck in the ground at the edge of their compound. He was curious about the sign and asked his cousin Jim Larson. Jim laughed and said, "Oh, some of them guys confiscated that sign on the way out of Sheridan, they wanted to bring a little something from Wyoming with em' to Korea---sorta makes the place feel like home now, doesn't it?"

The next day the road turned narrow and the long convoy with the familiar 'bucking horse/cowboy' markings on all the equipment, made the slow grind up a steep and primitive mountain road that resembled a crude path in areas. Some of the guys from back east couldn't stand to look over the edge that dropped straight down to a small stream at the bottom. Arnold heard one of the younger guys ask, "What is down in that valley?"

Arnold replied, "More Chinese – thousands of Chinese are down in that steep valley, watching what we do and where we go---they are everywhere and don't you forget it!"

The fellows from Wyoming had no problem navigating those roads—it was just like driving over the Big Horn Mountains back home! Later that afternoon, they passed by a 'regular army' wrecking yard that held a whole slew of parts and even a completely good Caterpillar tractor. Sgt. Bob Baird and Wes Meeks eyed it and mentally remembered that yard! As luck would have it, up the road a mile or so, one of their service trucks broke down, and that night when the guys tried to dig foxholes the ground was so frozen they couldn't get a shovel in it. Somebody had to do something!

Wes slapped Bob on the shoulder and in a low voice said, "Hey, I guess it's up to us to solve these here problems. Why don't you grab another guy and we'll just take a short stroll back to that wrecking yard and 'requisition' us some truck springs and ---say, that Cat would make it a heck of a lot easier digging some nice deep fox holes." *Yip---those Wyoming boys made do with what was available and it paid off every time!*

The farther north they moved, the thicker the Chinese were. That next morning they got word from a spotter plane that it had picked up on a Chinese convoy that was keeping up with them, right across the river. All it took was to fire a couple rounds from the Howitzers at them and they took off like jackrabbits! But the soldiers in the 300th knew they weren't far away, they'd be back—that was certain!

That night the camp MPs set up trip wires attached to flares—if the Chinks tried to sneak up on them, they'd trip a wire and the Americans would know the Chinese were trying to move in on them or just out there. The UN troops knew that the Chinks wouldn't hesitate to slit somebody's throat and that they liked to move around in the cover of darkness! They also had portable mortars which were deadly.

The ammo service trucks were getting busier now that they were nearing the front lines where the Marines were dug in. Unlike the war in Europe, the war in Korea was more of an artillery war with both sides dug in, slugging it out. The ammo trucks were running day and night; most of the trucks had .50-caliber machine guns attached, but the guys still felt like sitting ducks and stayed close to each other and/or made the deliveries then got the heck out of there.

Arnold was with the 300th for the next month—advising the Howitzer's that were mounted on tank chassis. He had a lot of combat and tank knowledge from Germany, but then again, this country, this fight was a whole new animal! They were just finishing up chow when Arnold heard an all too familiar sound and screamed, "INCOMING – Hit the dirt!" The mortar hit about 200 feet away.

The handful of WWII vets knew darn well what an incoming round sounded like and their split-second reactions saved more than a few men from their graves.

**Chief Warrant Officer Kessel
manning machine gun**

Chapter Twenty-One

"SPRING - 1951"

Chief Warrant Officer Arnold Kessel was finally back with the 300th after weeks of being transferred from one battalion to another—going where they needed his expertise. He noticed that this camp along with most others had stopped using search lights at night because it gave the Chinese easy targets. This war was a whole different dog and they were learning as they went. The guys in the ammo trucks kept moving them on the hour from one spot to another to avoid being targeted.

Chief Warrant Officer Kessel leaning on a jeep

Arnold stopped by the chow tent to say 'Hi' to their cook---Hawkeye! "Hey buddy, what's cookin'?" Hawkeye turned around and immediately threw his beefy arms around Kessel's thin shoulders. "Well son-of-a-gun, aren't you a sight for sore eyes. You take that hat off in my kitchen and then we can talk about where you been now, man."

Arnold laughed, took his cap off and slipped onto a bench, "I had to come back to you, Hawkeye—nobody makes hot biscuits with jelly and butter like you do, not even my Mama. I was getting pretty damn hungry for some if I do say so! Don't want you gettin' no big head or nothin', but you could make an Army boot taste good!"

Hawkeye went to the back and brought out a plate of his biscuits and jelly, along with two cups of hot coffee. "You been behaving yourself, Kessel? Personally I'm just damn glad that the Korean winter is over. They say it was a bad winter, even for this place. It was bad as any winter I ever spent in Wyoming, that's for sure! I'm just glad we weren't here for the whole thing."

Hawkeye watched Arnold scarf down the food and then said, "Did you hear about those twelve Dutch guys that wandered into our camp a week or so ago? It was the damnest thing—they just came out of nowhere, limping down the road there. We could hardly understand what they were saying—none of us guys speak Dutch, but we could tell they were in a bad way. We finally made out that they got separated from their unit and were trying like hell to find them. I put some hot food in their bellies and the commander tried to get them to spend the night cause those hills were crawling with Chinks—we knew it. We even gestured to them what the Chinese would do to them if they found them—you know, slit their throats. But them fellas were hell-bent-for-leather that they were gonna find their unit and so they set out in the dark, mind you! Well, it's bad—the next morning a squad found them down by the river, their throats all cut and the bodies stripped down to nothing but their skivvies!"

Arnold stopped eating and took a sip of hot coffee, "Holy cow---that's just the shits. Why the hell didn't they listen to you guys—that's nuts!"

Hawkeye cleared his throat, there was more to the story, "Then about two days later one of our patrols came upon this Chinese kid, musta been about 15 – 16---had his foot blown off and bleeding like a stuck hog. Our medics were doing what they could for him when one of our officers came over and grabbed him by the hair and held a butcher knife to the kid's throat.

Come to find out, he was pissed off about the Chinks cutting those Dutchmen up and he was bent hell for leather to take out his revenge on this kid. About that time the Colonel walked in and when he saw that, he went off his ladder---that's right. He grabbed this officer and bounced him around for a bit and told him if he touched that Korean kid again he was going to write him up. Well, that's about all the excitement we've had in the last seven days!"

While Arnold was talking to Hawkeye, he had been watching him mix up a batch of Hot Chocolate for some of the guys waiting for a cup over at another table. Hawkeye was searching high and low for a large spoon to stir the stuff with when he suddenly threw his hands in the air in frustration. He stuck his left hand up to the elbow in the pot of cocoa and stirred it up. One of the guys saw this and yelled, "Hey, Hawkeye, what the hell are you doing—your hand is dirty and you just stirred our cocoa with it?"

Hawkeye laughed and held up his hand, "See---no dirt now and you can't even see it in the cocoa either, now can you? Gooooood Cocoa!"

Arnold noticed an ammo truck pull up outside the mess tent; there was a bunch of commotion, so he pushed open the flap and went out to see what was going on. He recognized Bob Baird, a fellow WWII vet from Lovell as he jumped from the ammo truck. "Hey, Bob, how goes it?"

Bob turned, his face was ashen and he was shaking like a leaf. "Boy, if we didn't run onto something on this last run. We got another call eight hours ago from the 101st Marines that they needed more ammo so we headed up there just before daybreak, got there around 5 a.m.; all hell broke loose with constant, and I do mean constant, shelling from the Chinks, it was brutal. Those boys have been under fire for the last ten days---we can barely keep them in shells with our trucks running day and night. Some of those 101 guys were trapped in there and we dropped off ammo and supplies to them as close as we could. We could hear the wounded yelling, from out in the field and the corpsman or medics were trying to get through the hail of bullets to get to those guys and load them up with morphine---the ones that morphine would help. It was a terrible sight, unbearable."

"We've been delivering those 100 pound shells as fast as they can shoot them. Wes already called headquarters asking for more ammo trucks. Yesterday HQ sent up eight, maybe ten, trucks loaded with ammo and we sent them straight away up there to the line. About the same time, down the road came these walking wounded from those battles—they were weak, scared out of their minds, and staggering like they were drunk. They just kept muttering, "I can't do it any more, just can't do it! Don't make me go back up there, please don't make me!" There was even a kid, and I mean he was sixteen, if he was a day—who knows how he crawled under the fence to join up with our Army, but he was outta his head blubbering with fear for his mother. We sent him back down the road to headquarters and I'm sure they put him on a boat back to the states."

Bob grabbed a cup of coffee and sat down, trying to get a grip on himself. "I'm telling you if I hadn't seen it with my own eyes, I wouldn't have believed it, but those hills around where the Marines were dug in were absolutely crawling with Chinks---like swarming ants—gave me the 'willies' just to see it. Man, those Gooks just kept coming and coming in waves after wave. Our guys called in for air support and a couple of our B26 planes flew in and bombed the hell out of the Chinese while our guys made a run for it. I never seen anything like that!"

Bob looked at Hawkeye, ready to give him some grief---"So, big cook, what's up with you—anything exciting happen while I was risking my life for this country?"

Hawkeye flipped Bob's hat backwards off his head and said, "So glad you asked—yes—we had us some excitement while you were driving around the countryside making deliveries. You remember Joe Mallard, the gunner? Well it seems he and his platoon was trying to send some fire down on this Chinese camp. He was working from some coordinates and info on just where this camp was and all that bushwa—well, he made the adjustments and hit the FIRE button---the shell went straight up and drifted a bit then fell straight down---not into the target camp, but into a Chinese ammo dump that he didn't know was there. That thing was sittin' right under our noses and boy did she blow sky high---it was the damdest thing I ever saw!"

~~~~~~~~~

It was their turn--Arnold and some of the guys got a five-day R & R to Kobe, Japan. It was everything they dreamed of and missed---steak, ice cream, hot showers, a hot bath in a tub—all of it. They spent their leave going out on the town, seeing the sights, dancing with beautiful girls. Arnold saw a few of the guys who had a little too much fun and ended up in the brig, same old reason---a fight over a girl!

Then it was back to Korea and the war, not that every day was spent in a battle, but pretty darn close. Being guys, they tried to take time out for fun too, like getting up a basketball game when they could find a bushel basket to use as a basket; some of the guys just liked to watch movies, play board games or a couple hands of cards. They were always on the watch for Care boxes from home---most guys shared what they got because it was such a treat!

The minute Arnold got back from leave, Hawkeye couldn't wait to tell him about the latest fiasco. "This whole battalion was in convoy coming down the mountain into this here river valley over yonder. They hadn't seen any Chinks for a couple days and so they let up their guard. It was a pretty nice day—sun was warm and right in front of them was this lake with a long beach. They radioed up front and got the lead jeep to stop for a break; at least half of them guys stripped butt-naked and jumped into the lake. They were having one hell of a time diving and splashing---washing the dirt off, when all of a sudden the surface of the lake was peppered with small arms fire and about four rounds of enemy artillery hit near the area. So picture this---1000 naked, white butts running out of that lake and diving for cover under the nearest truck or bush." Hawkeye laughed so hard he had to brush the tears from his eyes. "I bet the Chinks were laughing themselves silly. Anyways, they suddenly stopped and it was all over. Nobody got hurt—those boys just got the crap scared out of them, that's all!"

~~~~~~~

Arnold started making his way across the muddy camp area toward his tent when suddenly the sky was filled with the ear-splitting scream of American B24s and B 51 planes, flying so low over the camp you could see the pilots smiling! Arnold hit the deck as a reflex and laughed when he spotted some of the other guys cussing and throwing rocks at the low flying American planes.

He heard one of the guys yell at the pilots, "You sons-of-bitches, go drop some bombs on the Chinks and quit scaring the hell out of us down here, this isn't some damn game!"

~~~~~~~~

It was about a month later when they were bivouacked on a ridge close to the front. The 300th service trucks had been running night and day. Just before lunch, they spotted a Navy plane coming in low over their camp. Some of the guys just stood there watching it while others dove for cover. The pilot lowered his landing gear, like he was going to set it down, but they all knew that wasn't possible in that terrain. Then he dropped his flaps and started firing his cannon in short spurts, trying to get their attention. He made two more passes over the camp, wagged his wings and roared off into the wild blue yonder.

At one point, a couple of the guys had even grabbed their rifles and began to fire back, "What the hell was that crazy fool doing, he had to know we are Americans? We're gettin' damn tired of those flyboys buzzing us." About that time the message center began to chatter with a CSBO---which is different than a CSMO---close station move out. They were ordered to close station and BUG OUT! *"Entire Division of Chinese on left flank. Get artillery and men out of there, NOW!"*

~~~~~~~~

Chief Warrant Officer Kessel looked at his orders for his next assignment. He was leaving for a place called Inge, Korea as a technical assistant to the 300th, Battery B from Worland, WY. Arnold packed his bag and hitched a ride that caught him up with B Battery. The first guy he met was young kid, a tank gunner by the name of Fox. The former tank commander asked the young soldier, "Can you shoot straight?" Arnold grinned and continued, "I was in a tank in Germany, had two great gunners under my command—that takes a special kinda guy!"

The Company commander slapped Arnold on the back and smiled, "We know about you Kessel, I hear you're here to help us position and move our tanks and Howitzers. Good to have you aboard, the word is we move into position tonight, under the cover of darkness."

The Lovell 300th Service Battery didn't hear from Chief Warrant Officer Kessel for three weeks when one day, out of the blue, he drove up in a jeep, parked it and headed for the mess tent. Hawkeye spotted him and without waiting, brought Arnold a cup of hot coffee and some biscuits and jelly.

Arnold's face was raw as hamburger from the high altitude elements and his lips were so chapped and split that he couldn't smile without grimacing. He looked up at Hawkeye through red rimmed, hollow eyes that were glazed over from lack of sleep and whatever it was he just went though.

Arnold muttered in a low voice, "Ya got a cigarette, Hawkeye, do ya, huh?"

Hawkeye dug inside his shirt and produced a Camel. "Here ya go, boy. You don't look so good—been through some rough stuff out there?" Arnold just nodded; his hands trembled as he tried to light the cigarette. He inhaled on the smoke and reached for the hot cup of coffee.

Hawkeye continued, "So where you been, out in the mountains and valleys showing the boys how to shoot those tanks and artillery at the Chinks?"

Arnold looked up from his cup of coffee and he didn't need to say a word. Hawkeye knew it was bad, knew the guy had been through something pretty damn bad. He laid his big hands on the table, "So, talk to me---where you been?"

Arnold mumbled, "Been in In-ge----been trapped by the Chinks and North Koreans for three weeks in some god-forsaken place called In-ge." Arnold looked out the window, "I went in with this 300th B Battery from Worland—went in a convoy of tanks and Howitzers—you know, all the big guns and infantry too. Well, we was no sooner making camp then the Chinese and North Koreans surrounded us and started to squeeze in. We'd clear them out in one direction and they'd push in on another. It was pretty damn obvious that they wanted to wipe us out!"

"We were at the top of this hill. We had good position and good visuals, but they surrounded us and then started climbing up the mountain to get to us. We'd roll live grenades down on them and blow the shit out of them in one direction and another wave of them Chinks would start up in the opposite side. They kept coming back, like a bad dream—they were trying to wipe us off the map and we knew it. Hell, Hawk---I have no idea how many of them

Gooks we killed---they were stacked up at the bottom and all over that hillside—pure crazy shit."

"I advised setting up double lines of fire and double weapons for the men. Those men set up a field of fire the Chinks couldn't possibly breach, but the sons-a-bitches kept trying, kept coming and coming and coming. Three weeks of pure hell, not knowing if we was going to get out of there or not."

"We ran out of everything and thank God, those C119s, you know, the flying box cars, dropped us what we needed or the Chinks woulda had their way with us! You wouldn't believe the way those Chinese shot us up with mortars. We never knew where one was going to land cause they'd shoot one long, then two short—you know mixed it up to where we never knew. We couldn't put up tents, they were just targets—had to sleep in the damn water-filled fox holes---it was the shits! Needless to say, there wasn't any hot food either. In the end, we only lost one G.I. and had 24 wounded. The North Koreans and Chinks lost over 1,000. I'm thinking I like those numbers!" Arnold wrapped his shaking hands around the warm cup of coffee and looked up, "Ya know, Hawk---being in a battle like that one, brought the Hurtgen Forest shit all back to me. It's when you find yourself in a situation, a hopeless situation when you'd almost give up, just to have it all stop, for it to end."

Hawkeye listened to Arnold talk and then asked, "So did you win another one of those bronze medals by rescuing somebody or stuff?"

Arnold looked up with blood-shot eyes, 'No Hawk—they tell me I got two Bronze Stars with this one!"

Hawkeye straightened and leaned in, "TWO Bronze Stars? What the hell did you do, rescue the General or something?"

Arnold finished off the coffee and laid his hands on the edge of the table, "Yeah, it was ahhh-something alright, it was sure as hell something. I'm not talking about what I had to do; I don't like getting awards for having to kill another man, even if he is trying to kill me, and that's all she wrote!"

Arnold sat for a moment longer and with his head down he said, "Ya know Hawk—MacArthur put us in a hell of a spot, put a noose of Chinese around our necks. You don't see 'his' behind any wheres close around here, do you? He's got some big ideas and no damn sense a-toll! I guarantee those Chinese will take a bunch of us with them before this whole thing is over. Damn shame, senseless damn shame!" With that he stood, put on his cap on, and walked out of the tent then turned, "Thanks for the coffee and biscuits!"

Hawkeye watched Chief Warrant Officer Kessel walk across the compound, the setting sun bathed him and everything around in a buttery soft golden light, and then he was gone.

Arnold had one of his nightmares that night and it took two guys to get him awake before he hurt himself or someone else. They woke to hear Kessel shouting, softly at first and then at the top of his lungs. He was sitting up in his sleeping bag, eyes wide with fear, but he wasn't in there. Hell, he looked awake, but they knew he was asleep.

"Here they come, here they come---up the right flank, in that gulley—grenades, fire that Howitzer, fire fire fire fi---re! Damn Chinks, know every inch of these hills, know it all--- thousands of them crawling up the hill, coming for us---they are coming for us!"

~~~~~~~~

Chief Warrant Officer Arnold Kessel didn't let the mud dry on his boots---his orders took him from one battery, one camp, one battalion to another as technical artillery advisor. He had a few close calls, but he didn't see the same kind of action here, that he saw in Europe five years earlier when he was a tank commander. *I gotta keep movin', not think about the killing, the dead, the wounded, the hills crawling with endless Chinks. I never saw anything like them in Europe---the Krauts were persistent, ruthless, and smart, but these Chinese are another story. They don't even need guns, they overwhelm the enemy just by their numbers and spooky screaming that we are gonna die, gonna die.*

It was around the end of September when Arnold began to notice he was feeling kinda weak, not up-to-par, he'd lost his appetite, was dizzy, and felt tired all the time. That morning he had spotted some weird purple looking things like bruises on his legs and arms, he'd had two bad nose bleeds in the past two weeks, and yesterday he'd coughed up blood.

After he passed out at chow, the medic took one look at him and called for transportation outta the camp. Late that afternoon, he was in a Red Cross vehicle, on his way to Pusan and an American field hospital.

In Pusan, Arnold lay in the Army hospital. The room was spinning and he was spitting up more blood. Weakly, he propped himself up on one elbow, "What's up doc? You took some blood tests and samples of every sort of body fluid you could get, now what is wrong with me 'cause I feel like the shits! Is it the flu?"

The doctor looked over the top of his spectacles, "Not good news I'm afraid. We can't help you much here so we are sending you by air to Yokohama, to a bigger hospital there. We think you have what is called Hemorrhagic Fever and it's serious. You might need a complete blood transfusion and around-the-clock supervision."

Arnold's face was ashen, "Could I die from this Hemorrhagic Fever stuff? How did I get it?"

The doctor said, "I think they will be able to help you Arnold. We need to get your infected blood out of you and give you some fresh stuff that will be able to fight the fever along with some big gun antibiotics. We don't know too much about this disease except you could have been bitten by an infected rodent or consumed contaminated food or water that was fouled with this nasty virus. Either way, we have to get you out of here and someplace where they have the facilities to treat you, STAT!"

~~~~~~~~

Oct. 22 to Dec. 10, 1951--American Hospital, Japan: Chief Warrant Officer Arnold Kessel was a patient in ICU for about 6 weeks. For the first couple of weeks, he was completely out of it, not realizing where he was, or what was happening. The military sent telegrams to his wife and also his parents advising them of the seriousness of his illness and tentative prognosis. Hemorrhagic Fever was one of those rare illness/viruses the doctors didn't know much about other than treatment and recovery was based on the physical condition of the patient and how he responded to the limited, known treatments.

~~~~~~~~

Norrie Kessel: Norrie called the hospital in Japan and asked to speak to the head of ICU. "My husband, Warrant Officer Arnold Kessel is a patient in your hospital and I understand from the telegram that you have diagnosed him with Hemorrhagic Fever. I am a registered nurse and so I do understand medical procedure and treatment. My question is this, what do you propose doing for my husband to hasten his recovery? Also, do you have any clear idea how he was infected with this virus?"

The American doctor on the other end of the line responded, "Yes, Mrs. Kessel, although this is a rare disease we do have a newly-developed vaccine which we started him on upon admittance, as well as an anti-viral drug called Ribavirin. We hope he responds within a week to ten days, if not then we will conduct a total plasma replacement. We have no other method of treating his disease other than what we are doing." The doctor took advantage of the silence on the other end of the line and continued, "We think this virus is the result of contact with contaminated fecal matter, saliva, urine, or other body excretions from infected rodents. He may have even have drunk contaminated water without using his chlorine pills. It's almost impossible to tell exactly how and where your husband contacted this disease. The sanitary condition of Korea is not, shall we say, up to our standards. We will most certainly keep you updated on your husband's condition and expected recovery."

Norrie responded with a few appreciative words and slowly replaced the phone in the cradle. Filled with a thousand thoughts and concerns, she rose and walked to stand in front of the window facing the street. *Arnold can't die this way, not in some Japanese hospital bed after everything he has gone through. Please dear God, please help the doctors heal his body. Please bring him home to me and our son.*

Norrie and their son Terrill were living with her mother above the dress shop in Lovell. On November 18th, Norrie received a telegram stating that the doctors had finally given Arnold Kessel a complete blood transfusion and they were quite happy with the way he was responding to the other drugs. The Hemorrhagic Fever was leaving his body and they believed Warrant Officer Kessel

was on the road to complete recovery! If all went as predicted he
would be on his way home by the end of December.

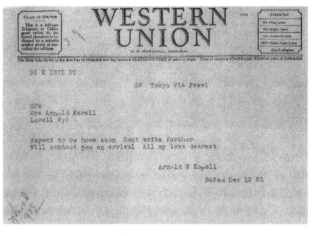

Norrie
was determined
to delay their
son from
walking until
his daddy came
home from the
war. She kept
the wriggling
little boy
confined to a
walker, trying
to postpone his
walking on his own the best she could. It was her dream to watch
their son walk, for the first time, to his Father when he got off the
plane in Billings. It looked like it would be just a couple more
weeks before that happened.

Norrie knew she had another problem. In Arnold's absence,
Terrill had become very attached to Jake, Arnold's father. Of
course, Jake doted on his grandson; the little boy took the place of
his son, just as Jake took the place of the boy's father. This
bothered Norrie, *I don't want to deny Jake the joy of his grandson,
but at the same time I want Terrill to know and want his own father
and I think that may be confusing to our little guy after Arnold gets
home. I will have to talk to Jake alone, and explain why I think it's
best that he back off and let Arnold assume the father role.* It was a
good plan, but would it work?

Chapter Twenty-Two

'HOME'

"Must you have battle in your heart forever? The bloody toil of combat?"

'Homer'

On December 18th, Chief Warrant Officer Arnold Kessel left Japan on a ship, arriving in San Francisco on December 31st, 1951. He was released from active duty before his tour of duty was up, due to acute illness. He was issued a thirty-day leave once he arrived in the states. Chief Warrant Officer Kessel left the war in Korea before his unit, the 300th Armored Field Artillery Battalion, who remained in Korea[40] fighting until the end of the war. When his ship landed in San Francisco, Arnold caught a taxi and went directly to the airport to catch the next flight to Denver, Colorado, then finally to Billings, Montana.

Chief Warrant Officer Kessel was on a plane headed for Billings on New Year's Day 1952. He hadn't held his wife in his arms for over a year and had not seen his son since he was born. Of course Norrie had faithfully sent photos of Terrill with her letters, but to finally see and hold his son would be an emotional reunion. He had missed the entire first year of his son's life.

Arnold sent Norrie the long awaited telegram, stating the time and date he would be landing at the airport in Billings. What he didn't tell her was that he was expected to report back to Ft. Hood on Feb. 9th and remain there until May 2, 1952 when he was scheduled to be released from active military duty. For now, it was better that she didn't know he had to go back to Ft. Hood for a couple more months.

~~~~~~~

The twin-prop Western Airlines flight from Denver circled the Billings airport once before setting down on the icy tarmac. Arnold pressed his face against the small window of the plane peering into the stormy night. He struggled to find his wife and son in the crowd that gathered at the fence. Large white flakes of snow drifted from the sky and the ground was covered in a mantle of white. Arnold could see where the runway crew had cleared an area near the fence so passengers could walk to the terminal without stepping in snow.

Norrie wanted to meet Arnold's plane alone with their son, but Jake and Raisa insisted on being there too. They promised to stand back and let the little family have their reunion when their son stepped from the plane. Norrie had stayed inside the terminal as long as possible, not wanting to take Terrill out in the bitter cold Montana night. She began to bundle the squirming toddler up when the plane landed on the runway. Jake and Raisa pushed open the door for her as they all went out to stand together, pressed against the fence.

Norrie was glad she had the 8 x 10 photo of Arnold which she showed to her son several times a day. She always said, "That's Daddy, say Daddy, Daddy!" Norrie whispered now into Terrill's ear, "There is your Daddy, Daddy' is home, son. You are going to walk out to meet him, aren't you?" Norrie had a tight grip on the wriggling child's hand; her knees felt like 'Jell-O' from the long anticipation of this very moment. They watched as the plane rolled to a stop and the pilot cut the engines. The runway attendants pushed the portable stairs up to the plane door and set the brake. Suddenly the door opened and the stewardess stood to the side as the first passenger stepped from the plane; it was Arnold!

Raisa gasped at the sight of her son, "Oh my stars, look how thin he is—even worse than when he came home from Germany."

Nothing in the world existed at that moment for Norrie except her husband. She pushed toward the gate, "Please let me through, that's my husband, please let us through!" She reached the restraining gate just as Arnold arrived at the bottom of the portable stairs and began to walk toward them. They made eye contact and both were crying as the attendant opened the gate and Norrie put Terrill down. She pointed toward Arnold, "There's your Daddy, walk to your Daddy, Terrill, walk!"

Freedom at last---holding his arms out to the sides for balance, Terrill took first one step then two wobbly steps forward. Upon his fourth step, he was in the arms of his father. To everyone's surprise, the little boy laid his head on his father's shoulder. Norrie put her arms around both her men as she reached up and kissed her husband. She hooked her arm in his as they walked toward the gated area and his waiting parents.

~~~~~~~~

Jake and Raisa gave the little family a few days to themselves. They realized it was important that Arnold have time alone to bond with his son and reunite with his wife. They were content in the knowledge that he was alive after another harrowing war-time experience and, by the grace of God, he was home for good.

Norrie had moved out of her mother's upstairs apartment a month before and had found a new place for her and Arnold. It wasn't much, a basement apartment, but it was theirs and they settled in. That is until Arnold told Norrie that he was home on a 30-day leave and then had to go back to Ft. Hood for a couple of months before he was released from active duty. Norrie was not happy about that news; she had big plans for them.

"Hell Norrie, I have a whole month, let's not ruin it by fighting. It is what it is and I want to enjoy this time I have with you and our son. I also need some time to recuperate from that disease that damn near killed me. I really thought I wasn't going to make it, it was the shits."

Norrie was alarmed at how thin and pale Arnold was, how weak he seemed. She knew it was going to take a while before he was his old self. She couldn't help but notice how uneasy/jumpy he seemed especially when all the family was around, like he couldn't wait to be alone. He was so restless, always wanting to take a drive, a walk, go to the pool hall, and he was so impatient with his son. Sometimes he'd leave the house saying he just needed to stretch his legs and when he returned an hour or so later, Norrie asked, "Where did you walk?" Arnold would remark, "Ahhh, just around town."

That next Sunday, they went to church, then over to Arnold's parent's house for Sunday dinner. The minute they walked in the door and the toddler saw his grandfather he made a beeline for him, leaving his father standing at the door. Norrie could tell that Arnold was not happy with the situation, but they had talked about it. It really wasn't anybody's fault—Jake and Raisa had both been wonderful to Norrie and her son during Arnold's absence, but now that relationship had to take a back seat and it looked like it wasn't going to be easy.

At the dinner table, Raisa put Terrill in the highchair between his father and grandfather—just to keep the peace. Arnold tried to feed Terrill some mashed potatoes and gravy and he pushed the spoon away. Jake picked up the spoon filled with the potatoes and Terrill opened his mouth. Arnold stood up, threw his napkin in the chair and headed for the back door, "Well if that isn't the shits!"

Norrie was furious with Jake. "Dad, we had our talk and you know that you cannot upstage Arnold like that with his son. Terrill has to learn who his father is and I thought you agreed to back off, and there you go, outdoing your son again. If that is how it's going to be, then I am afraid we won't be spending as much time over here until Terrill learns who his father is! It's very confusing to our baby and frustrating for Arnold."

Norrie and Arnold left early that day as the atmosphere had definitely frosted. They agreed later that they would limit their time with Arnold's parents at least until Terrill had a chance to accept Arnold as his father. Before they realized it, his short leave was over and it was time for Arnold to fly back to Ft. Hood for the duration of his active duty. It would be for just under two months. He was due to fly back to Billings on May 2nd, and then they would make plans for their future. Norrie and Arnold had already talked briefly about moving out of Lovell---finding a hometown of their own to start fresh in, but it all depended on where he could find work.

While Arnold was back at Ft. Hood, Norrie faithfully attended the military wives club meetings. The wives of the 300th Battalion were wonderful support for each other. Most of their husbands were still in Korea and would be for a few more months, until the war ended. Norrie confided in them that Arnold seemed so different, so stressed. One of the women suggested an article that she had read in a well-known housekeeping magazine. The next day Norrie went to the Busy Corner Rexall Drug and bought a copy. That night after she put Terrill to bed, she sat on the couch and read.

The best advice I can give you is to give him and yourself a chance. That takes time---lots of it, probably years and years. Of course most men come back changed, but you probably seem very different to him as well. He has his own adjustments to make, probably much greater than yours. The years ahead are going to be full of problems that will call for two of life's greatest lessons: patience and compromise. Remember that you are the woman he came back to, you are the one he dreamed of, he's yours. In heaven's name, stick with him, reinvent your marriage and your relationship.

Norrie laid the magazine on the coffee table and put her face into her hands and cried. She knew deep inside that the young, devil-may-care man she had married did not exist now, and it looked like it was going to be mostly up to her to take the bull by the horns and make her marriage work. She also knew that she loved her husband and now they had a wonderful little son together. *He's going to have a hell of a time getting rid of me cause I married him for better or for worse, and if we are going to have some worse, then I'll do my best to weather the storm and make things better!*

On May 3rd, 1952, Arnold Kessel officially became a civilian. He showed his wife and his parents his discharge certificate and put it along with his 300th Armored Field Artillery Battalion and 5th Armored Battalion membership cards in a drawer. Norrie noticed he put another small box in

the drawer and closed it. One night when Arnold was at the pool hall, Norrie opened the drawer and inside the box she found several Citations from the Korea Army and the Eighth United States Army – Korea. She read a few of his meritorious citations: *"Chief Warrant Officer Kessel is cited for meritorious service in Korea. Serving as Chief Warrant Officer for his Service Battalion, he was responsible for supervising the numerous intricate administrative details incident to his position; he consistently carried out his many duties in an exemplary manner. His sound judgement, outstanding professional ability and constant attention to duty earned him the deep respect and admiration of all those with whom he worked and contributed immeasurable, to the success achieved by his battalion in accomplishing its vital mission. This award reflects great credit on Officer Kessel and his military service."*

Norrie was shaking when she put the medals and citations back into the bottom of Arnold's drawer. *Oh dear Lord, what terrible things did he see and have to do over there. As if Germany wasn't bad enough, now our marriage has another war to fight, the war of memories and nightmares-----over and over again. Give me the strength, the patience, and love to do what I have to do for my husband and our family. How many of his men died in his arms like Danny Boy? How many friends did he lose, and then those concentration camps in Germany. He won't or can't talk about it and it's all still giving him nightmares; I don't expect them to stop soon if ever. I simply can't imagine what he went through. I wish I could so I could understand, but he won't tell me and I know why.*

Chapter Twenty-Three

"OUR NEW LIFE"

"Whatever took place psychologically or maybe even physically in your body didn't just go away. We didn't say anything. We thought it was normal."

Clayton Chipman, USMC

North Park Mobile Court, 802 Yellowstone River Drive #28, Billings, Montana: Several months after Arnold was discharged from the National Guard, they made the big decision to leave Lovell and move 100 miles north, to Billings. They needed a fresh start, away from their hometown, from family and old friends---they needed a new beginning. Loading up the Air Stream trailer with all their worldly goods, Arnold hitched it to the '48' Ford and they headed north.

With the addition of a baby, the trailer was more than cozy—it was darn right crowded, but it would have to do for the time being as housing and their budget, were both tight. Arnold went to work for Dyson Refrigeration but was actively looking for something better. His father tried to get him on at Marathon Oil but they didn't have any openings. Then he thought of Exxon Refinery in Billings where Norrie's brother-in-law was a bigwig, surely Arnold would have a better chance there.

Arnold made an appointment to go in and talk to his brother-in-law. He dressed up in his one and only suit that hung on his thin frame like a sack; he drove to the refinery on the outskirts of Billings. He knew the minute he walked into Jim Hines's office that he was toast. He sat patiently and listened to Norrie's brother-in-law use all the big words he had in his vocabulary to tell him – no dice! Between clenched teeth, Arnold thanked Jim for his time, stood, and walked to the door where he paused, turned and said, "See you at Thanksgiving Dinner next month, brother-in-law, thanks for your time!"

Jake was furious when he found out how Jim Hines had treated his son---Arnold's own brother-in-law. When Jake got a bee under his bonnet, there was going to be trouble---most knew to steer clear of Jake when he was mad, but obviously Jim Hines hadn't considered that scenario.

Jake hopped in his Mercury the next day and made a beeline up to Billings; he walked into Jim's fancy Exxon office unannounced. "Hines, I have a bone to pick with you, and no, I don't have no damn appointment! I hear that my son Arnold, your own brother-in-law, came to see you asking for a job here at Exxon and you treated him like something you had stepped in. Now you listen here, that man has laid his life on the damn line in two wars for this country, he has gone through pure hell twice and now all he needs is a job, a damn job in your refinery and you slam the door on him. I thought you was a better man than that, Hines, you just lost any respect I ever had for you, which wasn't a hell of a lot to begin with. What the hell was you thinkin'?"

Jake wasn't finished, "I've heard you don't like Arnold, never have—that you think he's a mama's boy. Well, I'll tell you this, you jackass, he's no mama's boy, he's a war veteran with six Bronze Stars, he's family, and he needs a damn job. I think you better do the right thing or else I'll get Norrie's other sister, your wife, and her mother after your hide and it won't be pretty!"

Jake stood, put his Fedora hat on his bald head, buttoned his coat and paused at the door, "Arnold will be expectin' to hear from you, Jim, and soon, real soon!"

Arnold Kessel started work at the Exxon Refinery shortly before Jim Hines was transferred to Huston, Texas. It was a great job, taking stock of Arnold's mechanical abilities and high work ethic---and it paid damn well, well enough that he and Norrie started checking into the G.I. Bill and looking for a house.

A month later Norrie and Arnold sat at the tiny kitchen table in the Air Stream trailer looking at house plans. "I've found us the cutest house out on Custer Avenue, clear at the west end of Billings. They are building out that way like crazy—a whole new development. The house has two bedrooms, bath, living room and kitchen, with an attached garage and a huge backyard. It's my dream house---not large by any means, but it will be just right for us when our second baby arrives in May!"

Arnold, Norrie, and Terrill moved into their brand new white cookie-cutter house on Custer Avenue the end of February.

They were a little short on furniture for a while but they had the essentials and all the room in the world compared to the Air Stream trailer. Terrill loved the big backyard and Arnold made plans to plant it in grass and fence it once the frost went out of the ground. Norrie was blooming with her second pregnancy but planned to continue working at Deaconess Hospital as a registered nurse until a month before her due date. She dropped Terrill off at her sister's day care on the days when she was on staff. Arnold worked shift work at the refinery and their bank account was growing. Life was good!

Arnold's sister Beth and Jimmy and their two girls drove to Billings every couple of months to visit and do some shopping. Beth had loaned Norrie some of her smocks to wear during her pregnancy. Over a cup of coffee at the kitchen table, Beth asked Norrie, "Have you and Arnold come up with any names for the baby? Are you hoping for a girl or another boy?"

Norrie smiled and said, "You might think this is crazy but I want something different when it comes to a name. If it's a girl I'd like to combine our two names---Arneen Yvonne, what do you think of that?"

Beth's eyes opened wide and she stuttered, "Well, that is different, but you know—I like the sound of it."

Arneen Yvonne Kessel was born on May 5, 1953, with the sweetest little face and her father's blue eyes. Norrie stayed in the hospital for the required five days and then brought their new daughter home. She took a few months off work while she learned to manage a new born and a rambunctious 2 ½-year old.

Norrie noticed that Arnold seemed more uptight now that they had two little ones. It seemed that any big changes in their routine threw him off and the dreams increased, he showed some symptoms of depression, and his temper was unpredictable. He still had very little patience with their son especially when the little guy ran screaming through the house or threw a temper tantrum. Loud noises upset Arnold, and of course their son was all boy with a high-pitched cry that sent Arnold into a frenzy. Norrie thought Arnold was too rough on him, and then there was the potty-training issue. She was trying to get Terrill out of diapers and he just wasn't ready. Every time he would have an accident Arnold would blame

Norrie. Tension was high and not getting any better as their fights grew more frequent. His moods went up and down like a Yo-yo.

For the most part Arnold actively tried to ignore the lingering torment of war, it's what society expected, *'forget about the war and get on with your life.'* The returning military were the 'silent generation,' most learned how to cope with their wartime experiences and few sought treatment. Instead of treatment, they drank, smoked, fought, and got divorces, all in an effort to cope with their wartime issues. When the military vets got together or were around each other, they avoided talking about the bad stuff they'd experienced. Instead, they joked about the stupid-ass pranks they'd pulled and some of the goof-ball things they had done on leave. It was an unspoken code not to bring up the horror, the suffering, and the dying they had all witnessed. To do so would merely bring it back to the surface, and none of them needed or wanted that. They'd all witnessed enough to last a lifetime.

Arnold was determined to shake it, to bury the memories, but he wasn't winning and he knew it. It was always right there beneath the surface waiting to explode, waiting to haunt his dreams. There were nights when he delayed climbing into bed. Yet Arnold performed the necessary man-of-the-house tasks, he mowed the lawn, fixed stuff, and painted the fence. He did his job at the refinery, he attended church, he tried to be a good husband, father, son, and brother—but something was always missing. Several times a week Norrie was forced to wake him from his nightmares—the dreams that caused him to shout out frantic orders, desperate fighting words came from deep within--things he didn't speak of when he was awake.

After one especially terrible dream, Norrie asked him to tell her about it. "Arnold, maybe, just maybe, if you tell me about the dream then it won't lie so heavy on you. We can share it—let me help carry some of your burden. I love you Arnold, and I want to help you in any way I can. Talk to me."

Arnold put his face into his hands then ran his fingers back through his hair, trying to push the images out of his head. "I don't want you to know what I know, honey. There are things that are beyond horrible—things you don't need to know."

Norrie persisted, "Try me. Tell me about this dream—I know there was bazooka fire coming at you from the high ground, the high ground you kept screaming. They hit some other tank, Frazier's tank and it exploded with the crew inside. What else, Arnold, tell me about the dream." She reached over and pulled a cigarette from the pack on the nightstand, lit it, took a drag and handed it to Arnold.

Inhaling, drawing the smoke deep into his lungs, Arnold stared across the dimly lit room. "We had our orders to clear out this German village up ahead. There were four Shermans, mine was third in line that day. From out of nowhere, the Krauts were there, firing at us from high on a ridge, behind the town. We had nowhere to hide, they were out of our range, we were like sitting ducks. Behind us the earth exploded and we swung the turret and saw a Tiger tank hauling ass towards us. I yelled at our driver to go left, while the tank behind us went to the right. *"Get behind the Tiger and put a shell up his ass! Fire – Fire - Fire!"* We were all moving, spinning, turning fast and firing; that was the only way to kill a Tiger tank—the only way. The Tiger's cannon belched smoke and it sent an 88 shell into our lead tank and blew it to kingdom come. I kept screaming to get behind the SOB---and suddenly the Tiger erupted in a ball of flame, the crew opened the hatches and ran from the tank, their clothes on fire. They were screaming and screaming. They ran toward our tank and Squirt machine gunned them. I guess it was a good thing, put them out of their misery!"

"That's when I saw two of our tank destroyers come out of the village and proceeded to knock out the other two Tigers up on the hill." Arnold took another drag on the cigarette and passed it to Norrie. "Is that what you wanted to know? When I have these dreams, Norrie, I'm back there in Germany and sometimes in Korea at Inge with Chinese crawling over those hills like a million ants. I never know which war it will be that comes to haunt my sleep."

That next Tuesday when Arnold walked in the back door after work, Norrie was sitting at the kitchen table with a letter in her hand. She wasn't smiling as she asked, "Who is Anastasia?"

The question hit Arnold like a bag of bricks and instantly brought back all sorts of memories and images. Without saying a word, he put his lunchbox on the kitchen counter, pulled his Camels from his shirt pocket and lit a smoke. His hand shook as he grab hold of a kitchen chair and slid it out away from the Formica kitchen table, then he reached for the letter.

Norrie pulled the letter back, "You aren't getting this letter until you tell me who this Anastasia is?"

Arnold inhaled deeply on his cigarette and blew the smoke out. He looked out the kitchen window at their back yard, the garden, the clothesline. Reaching across the table he took Norrie's hand in his and looked her in the eyes. "It's a long story Norrie--- Anastasia, was the abandoned, orphaned daughter of a high mucky muck German SS General."

Arnold told Norrie the whole story of how he had met Anastasia by accident, and how he had taken her to the safety of an American POW camp. "I never knew what happened to her or if this letter is from the same young woman. Let me have it Norrie, let me see if it is from her. I will let you read it if you want, I have nothing to hide from you, nothing."

Dear Staff Sergeant Kessel;

If you are not the American tank commander I met in the war, I apologize for this letter. However if you are the man I first met at my family home in Germany when I was playing the piano, then I am very happy I have found you.

Perhaps you do not remember me---my name was Anastasia Von Alvetheldt, daughter of SS Panzer General Helmut Von Alvetheldt. You took me to the safety of the American POW camp before rejoining your unit. I am very grateful for that deed because it most certainly saved my life.

I met a very handsome, kind American captain at the camp who took special interest and care of me. We got to know each other and we married before the war ended. I suppose you Americans might say it was love at first sight. Captain Jacob Werner (he is German/American) brought me to America were we have lived for the past twelve years. We have four beautiful children and live in the country in Virginia.

I do not mean to intrude into your life, but I have often wondered about the kind American tank commander who befriended me. If it were not for that chance meeting, for your friendship, I am quite sure I would not have survived. Now, I am a very happy American wife and mother. I hope your life has turned

*out as well as mine because you are very deserving. May God
Bless and Keep you---*
    Your friend, Anastasia
    *PS: I never found my two young brothers after the war. I
am quite sure they did not survive.*

    Arnold laid the letter from Anastasia on the kitchen table
and looked up at Norrie. They both had tears in their eyes. She
stood and went to the side of the table and pulled her husband to
his feet, wrapped her arms around him and held him while he
cried. Norrie whispered into his hair, "Arnold, I am so sorry, you
never told me about her---I didn't know, I had no idea who she
was. Now, we both know what happened to her and that she is
alive and happy, all because of what you did."

<center>~~~~~~</center>

    The one place where Arnold could relax and escape his
demons was when he was standing in a fast-running mountain
stream, casting his fishing rod. Both the Hurtgen and Ardennes
Forests held horrible memories. Arnold heard that many WWII
veterans who had fought in those forests wanted nothing to do with
another evergreen tree, forest, or the mountains. There were a
handful of vets who didn't even want a Christmas tree because it
reminded them of the horrendous battles in those forests.
    When Arnold was in the familiar surroundings of his
mountains, he experienced peace and solitude. He felt a familiar
safety in the forests and allowed that to envelope him as he sank
into comforting contentment. At least every other weekend he
would pack his fishing gear and leaving his family home, he would
head for the mountains. It got to the point where Norrie was
beginning to resent his leaving them behind. Heated arguments
arose regarding his obvious preference to leave his family behind
while he went off fishing, of not spending time with them.
    One night after they put their two kids to bed, they got into
a terrible argument about the fact that he was going to go fishing
again on Saturday afternoon. Arnold yelled, "I'll mow the damn
grass when I get home from work on Friday. Why do you always

have to ruin my time off, the one damn place where I can relax—you have to bitch about it?"

Norrie's resentment fueled her anger; she raised her voice and replied, "I'm not bitching, I'm asking. I want to know why you can't spend more time with me and the kids. Why did we have children anyway, why did you even marry me—sometimes you act like you don't want to be around us?"

Arnold turned and went to the garage, seconds later he stomped into the living room with two fly rods in his hands. Holding them with both hands he broke them over his knee in a violent downward thrust. He threw the broken fishing rods against the living room wall and bellowed, "Are you satisfied now, does that make you happy now?"

Norrie stepped back, her face ashen, as she managed to stammer, "W-why did you come back? I thought this family, this life was what we both dreamed about. Why did you ask me to marry you—why did you want a family if this is all we mean to you?"

Arnold grabbed his coat and pack of cigarettes, "I will never know why I came back and others didn't. That's a $64,000 question----why did I come back?"

Lights came on in their neighbor's house and a dog barked next-door. Hearing a sound, they both turned to see their son standing in the doorway to the hall. He was clinging to his blanket and crying. "Why are you mad? You woke me up; I don't want you to fight."

Arnold opened the front door and slammed it behind him. Cutting across the lawn he took long strides out to the sidewalk skirting the street and turned west where he began to jog. He didn't know where he was going, only that he had to get out of the house before he did something he would really regret.

Norrie picked Terrill up in her arms and tucked him back into bed. By the time she stumbled to the kitchen and sat at the table, she was crying, crying hard. She fumbled with a lighter and lit a cigarette. She sat there in the dark, smoking and crying, and wondering how long she could stand this life—live with this stranger, her husband who seemed so angry all the time, so messed up.

"Damn the wars, damn the Germans and the Koreans, damn the bombs, the cruelty, the inhumanity, the suffering. It didn't end when the wars were over; the men who fought in those wars, the men who killed other men they didn't even know, carry the experience the horror inside them and most probably will forever. How are us wives and our kids supposed to deal with this? It's not fair---it's like we now have to fight our own war."

The years went by, Arnold and Norrie stuck it out. They often hitched the Air Stream to the station wagon and went to the mountains for the weekend or summer vacation. Arnold taught Terrill how to fish but preferred to fish alone. Those were the good memories. Things would be going along smooth and then out of the blue something would set Arnold off and there would be another screaming match. Once the neighbors called the police and the kids watched the cops talking to their dad out in the street. They could see the neighbors peeking out from behind their curtains.

Arnold agreed to see a counselor, their pastor, anything that might help. He thought he had dealt with the wounds, the memories, the horror of the war, but he kept discovering he had not. They lingered, they waited, they plotted, and then they exposed their torment of the horror, the loss, the injustice, the cruelty that he had somehow lived through when others had not.

More than once Norrie asked Arnold to just talk to her, tell her about the war, but he couldn't, he just couldn't do that time and time again. If he talked about the war, then it became too real, too vivid. By now he knew what the trip wires were to his nightmares. Fourth of July and the fireworks; thunder and lightning storms; people sneaking up on him and scaring him; any loud unexpected noises; even something like when the kids spilled milk at the table or got into a loud screaming fight. He was jumpy as a cat on a hot tin roof and there was nothing, nothing he could do about it. Once he lost his temper and he went down that road, there was no turning back until his rage was spent.

Arnold was particularly hard on his son, expecting perfection and it galled him that Terrill still enjoyed his grandfather's company more than his father's. He knew he was hurting his son, driving the boy away but he couldn't help it. His kids wondered why their dad wasn't like other dads, why he couldn't have fun all the time like other dads. They grew up not understanding why.

~~~~~~~

On February 18, 1958, Norrie gave birth to their third child, a daughter—Arnold wanted to name her Renee. Norrie had other ideas for their baby's name but Arnold was adamant, "I want to name her Renee."

One night after Norrie had finished feeding Renee, she said to her husband, "When are you going to tell me why you like the name Renee so much. Where did that name come from, Arnold? Did you know someone named Renee? Was there someone in the war you aren't telling me about like Anastasia?"

Arnold lit a smoke and stood in front of the plate glass window; slowly, he turned and moved across the living room to where Norrie sat curled up on the sofa. Arnold's eyes darted from side to side as he struggled to find the right words. "She, she was my doctor in Paris, after I was blown out of that tank. When I came to, I was half crazy with guilt that I survived and all my guys, my crew died. She helped me deal with that, Norrie; she was the one who helped me climb back in a tank, take on another crew. I had dinner with her the last night I was in Paris. That's all Norrie, just dinner. I wanted to thank her—she was wonderful, she was 10 years older than me—there was nothing other than I wanted to thank her and spend my final evening in her company. I guess I felt safe with her, like finally someone really understood what I was going through. That's why the name Renee is so special to me!" Arnold paused, looked out the window and added, "She was killed in a direct hit on a Red Cross Tent, three months before the war ended."

~~~~~~~~~

The years were flying by. As a family, they took more vacations to the mountains in the Air Stream or stayed at Norrie's sister's cabin up near Red Lodge. They drove down to Beth and Jimmy's farm for holiday dinners, sometimes they sent the kids down for a week or two in the summer to ride horses, swim in the canal, and gather chicken eggs. Once in a blue-moon, they'd drive

down to Lovell and drop the kids off at Jake and Raisa's then go out dancing with Beth and Jimmy. Those were good times, they made good memories. But, the monkey never left Arnold's back and continued to haunt their lives, and every now and then he would leave for a while, only to return, uninvited.

~~~~~~~~~

The forest is shrouded in a dense gloomy fog, concealing the evil enemy that lurks in the deep darkness of the trees. Unspeakable agony, explosions, screams, and death wait with outstretched hands at every corner. They all know that every turn the road takes, could be their last. Commander Kessel checks the terrain maps again and again, the compasses, the ammo, his job, his orders---what am I missing, can't make any mistakes, protect my men, my tank. My hands are cold, so cold. No heat in the tank. Can't make any noise; the Krauts will know we are here. I can't control this shaking and I know it isn't coming from the cold; I feel like I am going to implode and something in me wishes I would."

"The Krauts, I hear the damn growling Panzers, listen, they are coming like the CO said they would, coming for us." My neck is killing me, so stiff with tension; my eyes hurt from looking in that damn periscope. He felt the sweat trickles down his forehead and down his back. We all know damn well that it only takes one perfect shot from the Panzer's 88mm shells to blow our Sherman tanks to kingdom come. He felt his belly roll and tighten-- he feels like his bowels will loosen—"oh dear God, not that, please, not that. My men, I gotta protect my crew. Be alert, check everything, the ammo, watch---watch for the Krauts, lock the hatches." He freezes—listens. "There was a noise, listen, there-- there, there they are---to the left, left flank, "PT---swing left, full power, go for the bastards. Danny Boy, feed the whole nine yards, everything you have into your damn machine gun---keep shoving those HE shells into the cannon, FIRE, FIRE, FIRE, FIRE, FIRE,—FI----." Arnold feels the pressure of a hand on his shoulder—not one of his men but a soft hand, gentle hand, and suddenly he awakes.

"Norrie? Oh dear God, Norrie, I thought I was back in the Ardennes Forest. Oh Norrie, not again! When is the bullshit going to leave me? Sometimes, I feel like I am going crazy." Arnold was drenched in sweat and his heart was pounding so hard he thought it might be visible. Norrie held him in her arms as he tried to forget that it was just another terrible dream.

After Arnold calmed down, they lay in bed smoking a cigarette and quietly talked about what had just happened again. Norrie said, "I think we need a change. I know we built Terrill that room above the garage and the girls share the other bedroom, but they are getting bigger now, they need their own rooms and we need more space it's feeling crowded in this house. Especially when your family visits and we have big holiday dinners and things. I saw a house on Glee Place for sale. We have the money, let's go look at it. It has space for a nice big garden like you want and a basketball hoop in the driveway."

All week, Arnold had been working the graveyard shift at the refinery. That afternoon he lay down on the couch to try and catch a nap. He'd been asleep for about a half hour when Terrill came in from the backyard and spotted his father asleep on the couch. Terrill walked slowly over to where his father lay and stood quietly watching him. Getting up his courage, he reached out and gently tapped his father on the shoulder. In one startling and fluid motion, Arnold came off the couch, grabbing Terrill's wrist. "What the hell are you doing? You NEVER wake me up by touching me, NEVER, do you understand? You are just lucky I didn't slap you from here to kingdom come."

Terrill's face was ashen as he backed slowly away from his father. He managed to stammer, "I-I'm sorry Daddy, I just wanted you to throw me some balls in the backyard. I wanted to try my new mitt out. I didn't mean to make you mad, I'm sorry." With that explanation, the little boy's lip began to quiver and big tears rolled down his red cheeks.

Arnold reached out for his son. "Terrill I am sorry. It's just that when I was in the war, I---. It's because of the war son, I am just jumpy and I scare easy, so just don't wake me up like that. Maybe call my name or something. I'm sorry, it's just the way I am now."

~~~~~~~

They moved to the bigger house in 1969 and lived there while their children went to junior high school, then high school, and finally Terrill left for college. In two years Arneen moved to California with her aunt, fell in love and married. Soon Arnold and Norrie were grandparents, a baby girl named Stephanie. Terrill graduated from college, became a high school teacher in Grass Valley, CA. and married Velma. Renee was a Billings West High School cheerleader—where she met her future husband, Tim. They didn't marry until they'd both finished college in Montana. Arneen had moved back to Billings and remarried. By now the Kessels had four grandchildren and there were more to come.

~~~~~~~

Arnold and Norrie were sitting out on their big patio, relaxing in the cool of the evening while sipping cold beers and watching the sun set. Out of the blue, Arnold said, "You know what I'd like to do? I'd like to sell this big house and build a log cabin up in the foothills to the south of Billings. Let's take a drive up there on Saturday and have a look-see. We've always loved the mountains, and if we built something up there, we wouldn't be that far from Billings, the conveniences and all that, but we'd be out of the traffic and hub-bub! We'd have some solitude and peace and quiet."

Chapter Twenty-Four

"THE LAST YEARS"

"The past is never dead. It isn't even past!"
William Faulkner, *Requiem for a Nun*

In 1978 Arnold and Norrie embarked on a great adventure, moving into their modest log home in the solitude of the pine-covered hills south of Billings. Norrie retired from her nursing career and at first it was great living up in Emerald Hills. In his free time, Arnold kept busy with the outside work and tinkering in an oversized garage. Their kids visited often and spent a night or two and then they were gone again. Some people thought they were nuts to live clear out there, but what did that matter, it was their life by damn, and they were going to do what they wanted. It was soon after they moved that Norrie started to show definite signs of inherited family heart trouble, and it worried Arnold.

Everything was going great for the first few months, and then all hell broke loose. Arnold seemed to have one episode after another including a dramatic increase in his nightmares. His abrupt behavior was apparent and seemed to come out of the blue. Like last Sunday when he got up during church and walked out to the car where he sat like a stone with his hands gripping the steering wheel. Then, there was the family barbeque over at Grant and Connie's where he disagreed with Grant about some little thing and took a swing at him. His behavior was like a growing pimple, one day it came to a head.

Norrie had asked Arnold several times to fix the railing on the back stairs and nothing happened, so she reminded him a fifth time.

Arnold threw the newspaper across the room and broke a lamp. "Damn it to hell—I guess I will fix that damn railing when I feel like it. Today I don't feel like it so stay out of my face. You are always bitching at me—do this, do that, don't do this. Leave me the hell alone!"

Norrie picked up her purse and car keys, "That will be my pleasure." She walked out, climbed in the car and left. She didn't return home until around nine that night. The house was dark when she drove into the garage and cut the engine. Norrie got out of the car and walked to the back door, unlocked it and went in.

There was total silence, total darkness. She flipped on a light in the living room and there was Arnold, sitting in his chair in the dark. He moved and blinked his eyes when she turned on the light. Norrie stopped in her tracks when saw his face. His eyes were swollen and red, his skin was blotchy, and he was just sitting there in the dark. She had never seen him like that, ever.

Norrie walked slowly to the chair where he sat, "Arnold, Arnold, what in the world have you been doing all day? You don't look so good, kid—are you feeling alright? Is there something I can do?"

Arnold just sat there with his head down, "I'm at the bottom of this dark pit, Norrie, I can't pull myself out of the memories, the wars, and losing my guys, especially Danny Boy. I don't know what to do any more. And, and my eyes—I can't see good. I didn't want to mention anything to you, you know, worry you and stuff, but I can hardly see. I think I am going blind! I can't live being blind, Norrie, I just can't."

She never understood how, but she got him up and into bed for the night. With her medical background, Norrie knew trouble when it was right in front of her, she knew her husband was severely depressed and needed professional help. But, she was more worried about his eyes, he went to the eye doctor last year and got new glasses, but that was something people their age did. Maybe he is getting cataracts? He never told her how bad it was until now—now that he was scared.

After a good night's sleep, they sat around the breakfast table and Arnold told Norrie about his eyes. "I've been really scared by what is happening to my sight, I know something is seriously wrong with my eyes. I've noticed weird things like—a straight line appears wavy, or some objects appear smaller or farther away than they are. There's also something screwy going on right in the middle of where I'm looking. I see things to the side, but not in the center and bright lights really bother me."

"Norrie, it's like there is a dark blob in the middle of my eye. You said the other day that a color was bright yellow and to me it looked pale gold or even beige. My symptoms aren't getting any better in fact they are getting worse."

Now, Norrie was really alarmed, she knew the symptoms of macular degeneration, but she didn't know very much about it other than it was -- bad! "I am going to make an appointment with the eye doctor as soon as possible. Don't worry about it honey, it's probably just some sort of infection or something simple like a cataract." She had a strong feeling it was not simple, but didn't want him to stress out over the possible scenarios of what she thought was going on.

After the eye doctor examined Arnold's eyes he asked them to come into his office. Dr. Miller laid his hands on an open medical book on his desk as he looked across at his patient and his wife. "I wish I had better news for you, Mr. Kessel, but I am afraid there is no question that you have what we call wet macular degeneration. Is there any of this in your family medical history?"

Arnold's face was pale as he responded, "My, ahhh, my mother has trouble with her eyes but she is diabetic. What can you do for me doctor? What sort of treatment is there to stop this or correct it—you got some drops or something?"

The doctor moved his glasses up on his nose then said, "If you are going to have macular degeneration, then wet is much better than dry. We have some treatments for the wet version, not the dry. All we can hope is that we can slow the progression of the disease and reduce the amount of vision you have already lost. Worst case scenario is that you will become blind."

Norrie interjected, "Dr. Miller, I'm an RN and I've been reading up on this. There are some treatments that have been tried to some success, like medications to stop the growth of the abnormal blood vessels that are distorting his vision. I've also read where you can use light or laser to actually destroy the abnormal growth of blood vessels under the macula."

Dr. Miller nodded his head and said, "You are exactly correct Mrs. Kessel. The laser therapy uses a high-energy laser beam to shrink and destroy the invasive blood vessels that are leaking and distorting the vision. Because you have come in and we have diagnosed this condition early, your chances are good of recovering at least partial vision, depending on the severity of damage to the macula part of the eye. I don't want to hesitate to move you through the system stat and get started with that treatment. Here is the name of a specialist that I want you to see tomorrow. I have already called him and taken it upon myself to make an appointment for you with him. It's imperative to move quickly and hope for the best. Please let me know how things go."

In four days Arnold and Norrie sat in front of Dr. Thornton, another eye specialist in Salt Lake City, at the University of Utah Medical Center. "The good news is that we have realized greater success in this condition than before with a new drug and a new laser procedure. This is what we are going to try first—we will inject a medication called Visudyne into a vein on your forearm which will travel directly to your eyes. You will be sedated in a chair in our ophthalmology surgical room. We will be watching your eyes and can see exactly when the medication arrives and how it begins to affect the blood vessels. That is when we will shine a special laser beam at the abnormal vessels to activate the medication. If all goes as planned, the medication then cause the blood vessels in your eye to narrow and finally to close off which will stop the leakage. It will take about 24 hours to know if we succeeded in our treatment." The doctor smiled as he said, "We hope for the best. We'd like you to remain in Salt Lake City for three days for further evaluation. We will be able to tell almost immediately if the treatment is successful."

The specialist stood, indicating he was finished with the explanation, "This treatment doesn't always work, but we are going to concentrate on the 66% success ratio and hope for the best. How does next Wednesday sound to you—we'd want you to arrive around seven in the morning, and after the treatment you must wear dark glasses for two weeks to ensure the procedure is a success. After you are in the clear, Mr. Kessel, we advise you to wear tinted glasses at all times to avoid bright lights and prolonged exposure to bright sunlight. No reading or watching television for the first three days, after that, in moderation."

Arnold and Norrie walked through the airport terminal and boarded their flight back to Billings. Norrie noticed that Arnold was unusually quiet as he stared out the window of the airplane. Suddenly, he bowed his head and dabbed at his eyes with his handkerchief. Norrie reached over and put her arm across his shaking shoulders. "Arnold, you are going to be okay, the treatment worked, you won't go blind. Why, for Pete's sake, are you upset?"

Arnold turned to face his wife, "Because, Norrie, I dodged another bullet that was meant for me. I don't know why God keeps doing this for me, I try, but I'm not his most devout man."

Norrie reached over and kissed his damp cheek, "The heck you aren't, kid. That man upstairs likes you for some crazy reason!"

~~~~~

A few weeks after they returned from Salt Lake City, Arnold seemed to be going through another bout of depression. Norrie tried to talk him through it but nothing was working. One evening as they sat on the front porch, Arnold said, "You remember me telling you about Dr. Renee Markham, the psychologist I saw in the hospital in Paris; she talked to me a lot and she really helped me." He looked out over the rolling grass-covered hills below them and said, "I think I want to find another good doctor, Norrie--somebody who can help me get out of this depression."

The following Tuesday, Arnold and Norrie sat in the office of Dr. Alfred Riley. He said, "Do you prefer to be called Arnold, Mr. Kessel, or Commander?" At the word 'commander' Arnold stiffened in his seat and his eyes glazed over. Taking his cue, the doctor continued looking at the charts, "Arnold, I see from the information sheet that you have frequent nightmares, temper episodes, depression, and flashbacks. How long have you suffered with these symptoms? Since you came back from the two wars or only recently?"

Norrie was surprised when Arnold straightened in the chair and replied, "I've always had them, first when I was actually in the war, then when I came home from Germany, and they got even worse when I got back from Korea. I know certain things trigger them like thunder and lightning storms, 4th of July, loud sudden unexpected noises, you know, stuff like that. You tell me how I'm supposed to avoid all that—hell that's just plain life." He straightened in his chair and added, "Lately, though, it's been worse. I had a real scare with some stuff called 'wet' macular degeneration and for a while I thought I was going to go blind. I got really down in this damn depression pit---you know, filled with the memories. It's like once you get down in that black slimy pit, you can hardly get yourself out, it's horrible. The eye doctors really helped me with that problem and got my sight back so now, why am I still depressed? My family doctor suggested that maybe I to talk to a doctor like you."

The doctor tilted his head and said, "Okay--other than the scare with your eyesight, have you had any big lifestyle changes in the past year? Perhaps something may have changed in how you have lived for the past thirty, forty years?"

Arnold seemed sharper now, more alert, "Well, yeah, a couple years ago we moved from the house where we raised our kids in, out to the hills south of Billings—built a new house up there in Emerald Hills. We always wanted us a nice log home out there—a place to retire in." Arnold thought for a moment then added, "My wife retired, she was a nurse at Deaconess Hospital and I still work part-time at Exxon."

The doctor folded his hands on top of his stack of papers and looked over his eye glasses, "Well, if I were a betting man, I would say that you have experienced two major changes in your normal lifestyle that have perhaps caused you to lose a sense of security and familiarity. Quite often this seems to cause a chain reaction in a lot of our vets—sending them back deeper into the memories and all that comes with that."

Arnold replied, "Yeah, that might be it, doc. I don't know why I am feeling like this; I don't have much hope or can't seem to take joy in things any more. For a while, like I said, I was depressed about going blind. Now, it's the memories--they seem to come at me more often and I can't control any of it. Do you have some pills or something that will help me?"

The doctor stiffened in his black leather chair, "In the last few years, we've learned a lot more about the internal or psychological injuries that you soldiers come back from wars with, we now call it PTSD—Post Traumatic Stress Disorder. Most of the time, guys can handle the symptoms. Of course we have some medication that can help—you know antidepressant meds. We aren't going to dope you up like they used to do, no—we have some new meds called selective serotonin reuptake inhibitors or SSRIs. They simply help you to feel less worried and sad. Your doctor will want to experiment with the different meds to see which seem to help you the most---it's a search-and-destroy mission, if that makes sense."

The doctor stood and walked around the desk and sat on the lip of it. "We've also found it extremely helpful for you to have several sessions with a therapist who will help you understand and change how you think about the trauma you have been through---it's called cognitive behavioral therapy. You will learn how to replace your thoughts, your memories, with more accurate, less distressing thoughts and actions. They will help you learn to cope with the feelings of guilt, anger, fear, and rage, Mr. Kessel."

Dr. Riley continued, "Have you ever been in strict therapy? If so, was it successful at the time?"

Arnold gazed out the window as memories flooded his mind, slowly he responded, "Yes, Doc—back in France when my tank was hit by a Panzer 88 shell and exploded—blew me out of the hatch and killed by entire crew. I was sent to a hospital in Paris, and when I came to, there was this shrink, Dr. Rene Markham— she worked with me and got me back in a tank with a new crew. She was great and I'll never forget her."

The doctor said, "That is wonderful news---that, you responded to help. That makes me think that this other therapy, called exposure therapy will also benefit you. It is based on the fact that most people experience a response to their thoughts, feelings, and situations occurring that remind you of a past traumatic episode---for instance, a thunder and lightning storm. This desensitization therapy allows you to process the bad memories, a few at a time."

"Does this sound like something you would be willing to try, Mr. Kessel?"

Arnold said, "Sure doc, I'm willing to give anything a try. You know for a long time I blamed my Dad and his father for my bad temper, my short fuse, my rage. I thought I had just inherited it, but that was just an excuse. I say, let's do it—I'll try anything."

In the years to come, both Norrie and Arnold looked back on the next few months and their sessions with the therapist as the turning point. Sometimes he went alone and other times, he wanted Norrie there, to hear it all. Arnold's anxiety and symptoms were knocked down to a level where he could function, could enjoy his life again.

1983: Arnold pulled the mail out of their mail box and leafed through it. His eye caught what looked like an invitation from the 300th Armored in Lovell. Some of the guys had organized a reunion during Lovell's Mustang Days--the last weekend in June; they planned to build a float and ride in the parade, then have a family picnic at City Park. It would be like the good ole days.

Arnold in front row, waving with The 300th Armored

Arnold and Norrie hopped into the car and drove down to Lovell on Friday, June 24th for the 30th reunion of Arnold's 300th Armored Field Artillery Battalion that had served in Korea in the early 1950s. Norrie couldn't help but notice Arnold was in high spirits. "Gosh, it's great to see all the guys. Nobody has changed too much, some have lost a little hair and others turned gray, maybe a few of us have gotten a little thick around the middle. It's just like we was all together yesterday. Where does the time go?"

Norrie enjoyed visiting with the wives who had formed a club during the Korean War and supported each other while their husbands were deployed. They were all grandparents now and delighted in talking about their grandchildren, exchanging pictures and stories. Nobody mentioned the hard times, the nightmares, the depression that most of the wives had gone through with their husbands---those who had stuck it out.

On the drive back to Billings, Arnold mentioned, "I really enjoyed that but wish more of the fellas had made the trip, I'm sure they would have liked the reunion. We went through a lot together and it was great seeing them again."

~~~~~

There was no denying it---Norrie's heart was definitely getting worse, her weight fluctuated like a Yoyo and, she was having great difficulty catching her breath. She went to doctor after doctor, hoping somebody had a miracle for her. The doctors told her that heredity and smoking were catching up to her and there wasn't much they could do. She tried to cut back on her activity and lose a little weight; she noticed she felt better when she was down in the city, rather than up in the hills where they lived.

~~~~~

1985: Arnold decided it was time to fully retire from his job as processor at the Exxon Refinery. He's given them thirty-three years and now it was time to call it a day. He continued to heal from his eye treatments, faithfully wore the tinted glasses and avoided bright light. His PTSD therapy had been successful and he seemed like a different person. They next few twilight years slipped by as they enjoyed their retirement home in Emerald Hills.

Everything seemed to be settling down, except for Norrie's heart problems. Her heart wasn't showing the improvement they had hoped for. After a short talk about their future, they decided to sell their home in Emerald Hills in late 1989. They decided it was best to try and find something less expensive and maintenance-free like what they found in tree-lined Casa Village in Billings. They bought a lovely spacious, double-wide modular home, and their kids pitched in to help them make the move.

The first night, Arnold sat in his chair by the fireplace, looking around the room and smoking. He turned to Norrie, "Well, if this isn't the craziest thing—we've come full circle—back in a trailer!" They had a good laugh over that one and Norrie commented, "Only it's quite a bit bigger than that Air Stream. It's a good thing we were newlyweds because that was really tight quarters."

1995: Arneen stopped by late in the day after work; she had called earlier and said she wanted to talk to her parents. When she walked through the door, she was beaming. Norrie commented, "You must have had a good day, what's up?"

Arneen sat down on the sofa and stuck her left hand out for her parents to see her engagement ring. Arnold said, "Well, it's about time, when is the big day?"

Arneen smiled and said, "We've decided on an August wedding and Dad, I want to know if you will give me away? We aren't going to have anything big, just family---I also think it would be a good opportunity to have another family photo taken. We haven't had one in a while."

Everything went off like clockwork the first week in August. Arneen and Jack were married and she got her wish— an updated family photo.

Terrill, Arneen, Norrie, Arnold, and Renee

1996: It was the first part of July when Norrie finally made an appointment with a prominent Billings heart specialist. That night when Arnold came home from fishing out on the Yellowstone River, she was sitting in her chair in the partial darkness. He knew the minute he walked in and saw her sitting like that, something was wrong.

Norrie said, "Sit down Arnold, I have something to tell you. I've been to the heart doctor today and he thinks I need surgery."

Arnold switched on a light so he could see her face, "What do you mean he 'thinks' you need surgery? What exactly is wrong with your heart? When does he think this is going to happen?"

Norrie dabbed at her eyes with a tissue and said, "Well kid, I told him that our 50th wedding anniversary is coming up and our kids have planned a big party for us. I want to wait until we have that and then I will consider having the open heart surgery. He was pretty straight forward with me, Arnold--I have some serious valve problems and narrowing of the arteries, this surgery is most likely my last chance. That's why I've been so tired, so out of breath and of course he wants me to stop smoking. I told him I think it's a little late for that!"

On August 1, 1996, Arnold and Norrie Kessel celebrated fifty years of marriage with their three married children, and nine grandchildren. All of their surviving immediate family attended

Norrie & Arnold's
50th Wedding Anniversary

and it was a lovely day. Norrie looked radiant and beautiful in a pale pink georgette suit and corsage of petal pink roses. Even Arnold tolerated the noise and excitement of the day as they posed for pictures and cut a symbolic wedding cake. They had made it—fifty years, some great years and some not so great, but they had stuck it out and stayed with each other even though sometimes they both wanted to throw in the towel. There were times when Norrie didn't think she could go on living that way—always on guard, always trying to protect her husband from the world, never knowing when he was going to have a bad day. And now—they were celebrating fifty years together.

"I wish our parents could have been there today, especially your mother. I don't think any of them thought we'd make it to fifty years, but we showed them, kid, didn't we?"

Arnold wrapped his arms around her and said, "Thanks for sticking with me Norrie. I know I didn't make it easy on you with all of my war demons. I could always count on you to be there at my side. So, kid -- what is next?"

Norrie looked up at him and said, "I have to face the elephant in the room now, my heart. Arnold, I think my only chance is to have that surgery."

Norrie was scheduled to have open heart surgery on December 27, 1996 in Billings. She wanted to wait until after Christmas---what might be her last Christmas with her family. The doctors assured her that if everything went well, she would come through it just fine. They didn't beat around the bush though, it was a rough surgery and they were concerned with her lifetime of smoking, her family medical history, and her weight—all strikes against her.

Norrie didn't tell anyone what she was thinking, she knew the doctors were white-washing a pretty dim scenario. They weren't kidding her, with all of their 'rah-rah' stuff, she was a R.N. and she knew more than they were giving her credit for, she knew the odds. In the recesses of her mind she considered it all. *I don't have much choice than to give the surgery a try. I've nursed some heart surgery patients and it's horrible. Maybe I'll luck out and die on the table---naw, that would be too easy for this kid.*

The last Sunday of the month they went to church and took communion. The days passed and before they knew it, it was the night before the surgery Norrie was getting ready for bed when Arnold came in to give her a good night kiss. "Arnold, I want you to make me a promise. Tomorrow, if the surgery doesn't go well and they are keeping me alive with tubes----any artificial means, I want you to promise me that you and the kids will let me go. I DO NOT want to be a vegetable; I don't want to be kept alive by monitors and machines. Let me go. Promise me damn it, now!!"

On the 27th of December, Arnold, Terrill, Arneen, and Renee sat in the surgery waiting room of the Billings hospital. After six hours of delicate surgery, the doctor walked into the waiting room. "It went as well as we could expect. The next few days will be touch-and-go; it's going to be a rough recovery if she makes it that far. Norrie's heart was one of the worst I've seen in a while and we did all we could to repair it. The rest is up to her and the man upstairs. She will have round-the-clock nursing and I expect her to be in ICU for a week or more."

Arnold and the kids looked at each other, horrified that she would be in ICU for a week plus. Terrill said, "We just have to wait, pray, and see what happens. I have to go back to my classes at the end of the week, that's all the time the school would give me off."

Arneen and Renee assured Arnold that they would stay as long as it took. Renee was staying at the house with her father; none of them wanted him to be alone. The next day when Norrie started to come out of the anesthesia was a dark day. She was in excruciating pain, every breath hurt because of the sternum the doctors broke to get to her heart. She couldn't move without unbearable pain that shot through her body and she wasn't comfortable in any position. It was so bad it brought tears to her eyes and her face contorted in a mask of agony every time she moved.

On January 3rd, 1997, Terrill had to go back to California and his teaching job; he hated leaving his sisters and father, but he needed to keep his job. Day after day the girls tried to make their mother comfortable, tried to reassure her even though they were not reassured. It was so hard to see her in this kind of pain. When they left her side, they went into the hall and cried in each other's arms. Finally, desperate, they pulled their father aside, "Dad, Mom told us she really thought she would die on the table, that she doesn't want this, all this pain. The doctors don't have much hope and nothing is getting better. Daddy, we can't let her suffer like this, isn't there something we can do?"

Arnold wrapped his arms around his daughters and said, "When the time comes, if the doctors tell us that she isn't making progress, then we know what she wanted."

On January 6, Norrie's birthday, with her daughters and husband by her bedside she took her last breath and peacefully passed away. Arnold sat by her bedside stroking her lifeless hand until they took her body away. It was over, the incredible woman who had stuck with him through all those years of craziness, who had given him three wonderful children, was gone and he was alone. He had never really thought Norrie would go first—he always thought it would be him. He dreaded what was ahead for him—living without her, he'd watched what it did to his father living without his mother.

I am seventy three years old and I am so used to having Norrie always at my side, always there for me. What, now—how am I going to pull this one off? This feels, I feel--like a ship without a rudder, a fishing pole without a hook---it's the shits!

Norrie's funeral was just as she had planned it, along with a soloist playing the guitar and singing a haunting rendition of Amazing Grace! When the chips were down, Arnold was a rock, when he needed to be there for his family, he stood tall. He reassured all of them, "Norrie knew where she was going when she died. She believed in Jesus Christ as her savior and she is now in the comfort and peace of his arms. She told me once that coming to know Christ as her savior was the best thing that ever happened to her, except for me, of course!"

After the funeral and after everyone went home, back to their lives. Arnold had to reinvent his own life, this new life alone. The first few months Arneen spent a lot of time with her father, helping to sort through the last of Norrie's things. When that was over with, Arnold drove down to Emblem to spend a few days with his sister Beth and Jimmy on the farm. He took long solitary walks out in the fields and down the country roads. Beth was a good cook and took special effort to make sure her only brother was well-fed. She packed up any extras for him to take with him back to Billings.

Arnold was never much of a cook and so found he was going to the senior center or eating out almost every day. Of course his daughter had room at her table whenever Arnold wanted to come by but he didn't want to be a bother. After a couple of years at Casa Village, Arnold started looking into more convenient options, like the assisted-living facilities in Billings. There was a brand new service with all the amenities, Aspen View, at the west end of Billings and they were filling up fast. That next Sunday he and Arneen took a drive out to have a look around.

The woman at the desk was only too happy to show him the apartments and explain the meal system and cleaning arrangements. "Mr. Kessel, this one-bedroom apartment is really very nice. It opens onto its own patio on the north side where you can have your privacy and sit in the cool of the warm days or walk around the gardens. You have your own little kitchenette where you can prepare your breakfast and any other cooking you might want to do. We serve a full lunch and a light dinner if you want to sign up for that. The noon meal comes with the price of the apartment but the evening meal does not, that is extra. We will come in once a week and change your sheets and linens, vacuum and dust, if you want that service."

Arnold looked around, "What about pets? I see some folks here have cats or small dogs. I have a little black poodle, Nokka, who I can't live without. She's a lot of company, you know."

In the fall of 1998 Arnold moved into his new apartment with just a few pieces of familiar furniture and things he wanted from the home he'd shared with Norrie. His kids had helped sort through things and make the final decisions that threw him for a loop. They took care of it all, and after Terrill and Renee went back to their homes in California and Texas, it was just him and Arneen.

It was during one of those Sunday afternoons when Arneen came to visit that she pulled his old Army uniform out of the back closet. "Dad, can you still get into your army coat?"

Arnold looked at the coat and said, "I probably can, but I really don't want to put it on—brings back too many memories for me." Arneen replied, "Okay with me Dad, but for your grandkids, what about me pinning some of your medals on it and then you stand beside it for a photo, so they can see you and the coat you wore when you served in the army. Will you do that for them?" Arnold nodded his head and then added, "Sure, sure—but don't put all of those Bronze Stars on the coat, that will look like I'm bragging or something. I never did like those things— didn't believe that I should be awarded something for doing my job even if it was killing the enemy."

The Tank Commander – Arnold Kessel with his Army coat/medals. – 2002

Arnold's daughter was great company and help ---taking his laundry once a week, helping him shop for a few groceries; they made a point of going out to dinner at least every week or two. He flew to Texas and California to visit his other two children and, of course, down to visit with his sister Beth and Jimmy who had moved to Powell, Wyoming. Jimmy wasn't doing very well— after several serious back surgeries and a couple of small strokes, he was having a tough time of it. Arnold tried to do what he could to help his sister, but she had her hands full.

2002: The long shadows of the late summer evening stretched across the grass in the rear garden at the assisted living home in Billings. Arnold was sitting out on his patio, enjoying the evening when he heard the phone ring inside his apartment. He lifted Nokka off his lap, opened the sliding screen door and picked up the phone.

"Hi Dad, I just wanted to invite you to Thanksgiving dinner. Janet is going to cook—everyone will be there. I'll pick you up around 11 if that suits you?"

Arnold smiled as he hung up the phone. *I'm thankful for my kids and especially for all that Arneen does for me, making sure I'm included in family dinners and all. The week doesn't go by that I don't hear from my other two kids. I'm a lucky guy.*

Arnold and his sister spent as much time together as they could manage, considering their age. It was hard to realize that Beth had just turned 82 and he was 78 almost 79. *I remember when we was kids back in Michigan, picking rags and me getting so sick with that Rickets and all. I remember when she was dating Jimmy, Mom always said he looked like Robert Taylor the movie actor. We sure had fun at dances. Beth and Jimmy, me and Norrie—we knew how to kick up our heels and stay till the party was over. Those were the days. Then all the terrific family dinners at the farm—that big table, all of us sitting around there, eating and then playing pinochle—those were the days, yip---those were the days.*

A week before Thanksgiving, Arnold called Beth, "Hi sis, just wondering what you are doing for Thanksgiving. I know you don't want to leave Powell, what with Jimmy at the nursing home and all. Are your girls coming home? What are your plans?"

Beth smiled and said, "Laura, Linda and Wayne, and Karlie and Mike are coming. Sharleen will be staying in Tennessee with her daughter. I think we are cooking dinner at Laura's then taking it over to have Thanksgiving Dinner with Jimmy at the home— there in the hospital dining room. They make it real nice. What are you doing? Are they having a Thanksgiving meal there at Aspen View?"

Arnold replied, "Well they are, but Arneen is picking me up and we are going over to Janet's for a big family dinner. It should be real nice. Well, I'd better run, you have a good Thanksgiving with your family. Maybe we can get together for Christmas—I might even come down to Powell if the roads are

decent. Well, I guess that's all for now. You take care of yourself
and remember--- I Love you Beth. Bye!"

Thanksgiving went as planned and they all ate too much.
Mike and Karlie were staying at Beth's house and it was late in the
day, around ten o'clock. Beth had gone to bed earlier—it'd been a
big day for everyone. Suddenly the shrill ring of the phone broke
the silence of the house. It rang twice before Beth picked it up in
her bedroom. Karlie was washing her face when she heard her
mother scream. She and Mike ran down the hall toward her
mother's bedroom.

Beth was sitting straight up in bed, the phone in one hand,
her other hand over her mouth. Karlie said, "Mom, what is it, what
happened?"

Beth stammered, "It's---it's my brother, it's Arnold. He
died! They found him on the floor of his apartment. Arneen
called—she said it was a massive heart attack. She said they had a
really nice Thanksgiving day, she dropped Arnold off at the
Assisted Living a few hours ago because he said he was tired and
wanted to go to bed. She tried to call him to say goodnight and
didn't get an answer so she called the front desk." Beth paused to
wipe her eyes.

"They, they found his little dog beside him." Beth thought
for a moment then she said, "You know he always told me that
during the war, his one prayer—the one thing he asked God for
was that when it was his time, that it be quick." She smiled as the
tears ran over her cheeks, "I guess God answered his prayer. He
got through two wars, but in the end, when it was his time, God
took him quickly. For that I am grateful."

After Beth settled down a bit, Mike sat with her while
Karlie fixed her some tea. Beth continued to weep, "My brother
Arnold, oh Arnold. My only, brother—he had such a hard time
with Germany and then Korea. He never would talk about the
things he did and saw, so I don't know what it was, all I know is
that he saw some horrible things and they stayed with him until
now. Now, he is finally rid of the memories."

Karlie said, "You know, Mom, I'm glad he didn't pass
away yesterday, on your birthday. That would have been even
more terrible. I think I should sleep beside you tonight Mom, I
don't want you to be alone. Is that alright with you?"

Arnold Kessel – 78 years of age

Between tears, Beth managed to reply, "I thought of that too. Sure honey, that would be fine, I don't want to be alone."

Beth reached for the picture of her brother that she kept beside her bed, "This is the last picture I have of my brother Arnold." She gazed at it for a while and then said, "I talked to him last week on the phone and the last thing he said to me was that he loved me."

Funeral services were held on Thursday, December 5th at Mount Olive Lutheran Church in Billings. His three children were seated in the front rows along with his grandchildren; Rachael, Josselyn, Chelsea, Stephanie, Kevin, Erica, Alyssa, Jake and Oliva. His children gave their father's faithful little black poodle, Nokka to his sister knowing that would have been his request. They hoped that the little dog would fill her days as it had filled their fathers. Nokka grieved for her master for several months, riding in the car was the hardest time for her. She spent the next ten years with her new master, Beth, giving her love and companionship as she had Arnold Kessel, TANK COMMANDER.

SOURCES:

As a writer of historical fiction, I rely on numerous historical sources for inspiration and concise information when compiling my historical research:

Images and maps seen in this novel are either the property of the author or have been taken from free image sites on the Internet/Google. The 50-year time frame for the Statutes of Limitations has expired; no permission is needed for use of most war information or images. *Those marked restricted were not used in this book.*

Previously stamped Restricted - **Daily Log and After Action Reports of the 81st Tank Battalion Task Force**: Used under expiration of Statutes of Limitations -- Combined Army Reserved Library; Digital Library: 81st Tank Battalion, 5th Armored Division----8/1944 thru 1/1945

Google Web Sites: Free Images of WWII, Korea, Tanks, Howitzers, Civilians, Concentration Camps, Battles, & Devastation. Used after expiration of Statutes of Limitations.

Author Interviews with WWII & Korean War Veterans:

Robert Baird; Kenneth Blackburn; William F. Fink; Robert Doerr; Elmer "Pete' Gernant; John Gibler; Meryl Gibson; Wes Meeker; & Bill Shumway.

Newspapers: Lovell Chronicle & Greybull Standard.

Magazine: TIME magazine article - 1945

Reviewed WWII Movies: *Fury* with Brad Pitt; *Saving Private Ryan* with Tom Hanks; *Band of Brothers; Pork Chop Hill* (Korea)

Novels: Lone Sentry; The Road to Germany; The Story of the 5th Armored Division;

The Rising Tide; No Less Than Victory; & The Steel Wave by author Jeff Shara

Stones from the River - Ursula Heggi; The Far Reaches – Homer Hickam; The Book Thief;

Schindler's List – Thomas Kenealey; The Battle of the Bulge - John Toland; The Historical Atlas of WWII; Bloody Roads to Germany – William Meller; & The Baker's Daughter.

ENDNOTES:

[1] **US 5th Armored Division**: This division was initially part of the Third Army and later assigned or attached to the First Army; it was known as the Victory Division. **Facts:** In 1943, it was first organized under the new and revised flexible command concept which streamlined the division into three combat command headquarters to which other divisions, other infantry, and other combat battalions could be attached for a particular campaign. Combat Command A, CCA and Combat Command B-- CCB and CCR were the three designated armored battalions, known as a task force of the 81st Tank Battalion headquarters. Arnold Korell was a tank commander in CCB with LTC LeRoy H. Anderson – Battalion Commander who kept and recorded the daily log for the 81st Tank Battalion!

It was committed to warfare on August 2, 1944 as part of Patton's Third Army - XV (15th) Corps. The 5th Armored Division **was the first** division to reach the Seine River in France. It was **one of the first** divisions to cross the border into Belgian. It **was the first** division to reach Luxembourg. It **was the first** division to fight on German soil. It **was the first** division to break through the Siegfried Line. It was the American division which ended up **closest to Berlin** after the blitz through Germany. It was stopped at the Elbe River, 45 miles from Berlin, not by any German forces but by orders from the Allied Supreme Commander General Dwight Eisenhower. The Russians wanted to take and inflict severe punishment on Berlin and its people—thus our Allied forces were denied something they had fought for.

Even with its impressive and aggressive combat record, the Fifth Armored Division came through with one of the lowest casualty rates. It was known for its speed, efficiency, courage, and hardiness of its soldiers. The men of the Fifth Armored Division had great trust and respect for their leader, Major General Lunsford E. Oliver. This courageous Division was often lost in the throes of other divisions' accomplishments; it was the Ninth Army Spearhead and the First Army's armored Wedge.

Between 1944 and when the war ended in 1945, the 5th Armored Division's losses included 570 killed; 2,450 wounded in action, and 150 soldiers who later died of their wounds. The 5th Armored Division returned to the United States in October 1945 and was then deactivated at Camp Kilmer, New Jersey, on 11 October, 1945.

[2] **Fort Warren, Wyoming**: Formerly, this was a cavalry facility called Fort Russell; the last cavalry units left the Fort in 1927. In 1930 the facility was renamed after Francis R. Warren, Wyoming's territorial and first state governor. During WWII, Fort Warren was the site of induction for the state's new recruits. It was also the training center for over 20,000 Quartermaster Corps personnel. One of the most memorable facts about the facility was that its 280 wooden buildings were constructed without insulation and interior walls which were neither comfortable, nor warm during the severe Wyoming winters. Ft. Warren also housed a prisoner of war camp during WWII.

[3] **Fort Carson, Colorado**: Named after legendary Army scout, Kit Carson, this training facility (boot camp) was completed in January of 1942. It contained facilities for over 35,175 enlisted men, 1,820 officers, and 600 nurses. Most of the buildings were of the mobilization type (Quonset Huts) except for the hospital which was constructed of concrete block. During WWII over 100,000 soldiers trained at Camp Carson and it was home to nine divisions. During the war the camp also housed 9,000 Axis prisoners of war.

[4] **Fort Knox, Kentucky**: A long time military establishment, it was renamed in 1943 from the Armored Force Replacement Training Center to the Armored Replacement Training Center (ARTC). Soldiers who were sent here received a seventeen week intensive course or instruction for various arms, tank driving and maintenance, big tank guns, chemical warfare, anti-tank weapons etc. As a final test of skills, the men underwent war games on hills named Misery, Agony, and Heartbreak. After surviving this training they graduated and were then sent on to

additional training, assigned to a division, and/or sent to the various theaters of war.

Between 1944 and June 1946, Fort Knox was also the site of a main POW camp—the first prisoners were Italian. After WWII, there were approximately sixteen armored divisions and sixty-six tank battalions attached to Fort Knox. These units participated in every major battle in the European and Pacific theaters of war. Fort Knox was deactivated in October 1945 and reestablished one year later.

[5] **Married:** It was an innovative and progressive new combat strategy devised by the Allied Command during WWII, promoting a more cohesive attack group including the units of a tank battalion, its companies, and the supporting infantry. Once married, the units usually stayed with each other for the duration unless they were called to reattach to another division, etc. Reasoning had it that if the men knew and could depend on what each supporting unit could and would do during battle, the more interconnected and reliable the fighting unit would become—they would react and fight as one large force rather than separate and undetermined factions. During specialty training, the onetime separate squads, platoons, companies, and battalions became 'married' and/or attached to each other in daily purpose and duty. It was exactly this close-knit factor that enabled the Fifth Division to move with unprecedented swiftness and precision over the German lines of defense in France. A column of tanks was usually interspersed with infantry-filled trucks and halftracks. During battle, one or the other would advance depending on the situation, followed by the 2nd in support. Other divisions took note and soon adopted the same strategy to rapidly and forcefully push through France and then Germany.

[6] **Rommel's Hedgehogs: In early 1944,** General Rommel ordered over a million wooden poles (6 – 12 inches in diameter and 8 – 12 feet long) set in the flat lands and farm fields of Normandy in order to cause potential damage to landing gliders and paratroopers. Originally he wanted wires strung from pole to

pole but that was not cost-or time-efficient. These same defense measures were put into effect on the invasion beaches of France. Here, they were buried at protruding angles toward the sea and landing vehicles. Because of effective reconnaissance, glider pilots and paratroopers were aware of these defensive barriers.

Most were easily destroyed with a Heller Mine or the Allied troops used hydraulic methods to pull the poles from the beaches. More effective were the HEDGEHOG devices—a wooden or iron structure that looked like a kid's giant jack. Rommel had expected IF and When the Allied Forces attacked, they would come in at high tide so the Hedgehogs were designed to rip open the bottom of their boats. The Allied Forces landed at low tide, thus exposing the lethal Hedgehogs and Hemmbalken (buried poles).

[7] **Quonset Huts**: First devised by the Navy in 1941, these sixteen foot diameter steel hut buildings were inexpensive to build, ship, and set up. They could be packed in twelve crates and put up by ten men in a day. The half round structures were made of corrugated sheets of steel without windows. The ends were made of plywood with a door in the middle of two mullioned windows. The insides of the buildings were insulated and the walls were covered with pressed wood lining; floors consisted of one to-one-half inch plywood. These buildings might be assembled directly on the ground or on a concrete foundation. They ranged in size from the original structure which was sixteen by thirty-six feet to later models which stood twenty by forty-eight feet. After WWII, Butler Huts and other similar Quonset Huts were sold as homes to veterans and/or anyone who needed a shelter.

[8] **Balls to the Wall**: On Early aircraft, the throttle had a ball on the end for an easier grip. When circumstance arose to accelerate, the pilot had to shove the throttle forward quickly. Hence, the saying for going fast became---*Balls to the wall.*

Origins for other sayings which came out of WWII: "*I gave them the whole nine yards*"—U.S. aircraft were armed with belts of bullets for machine guns. Those ammo belts measured twenty-seven feet or nine yards. When returning from a mission, pilots would boast, "I gave them the whole nine yards!"

"Okay, but it'll cost you an arm and a leg." Because hands, arms and legs take more time to paint, early painters (1700-1800) would price out their paintings by how many limbs they had to paint. Frequently they would position their subjects behind one another or another feature, to cut the cost of the painting.

[9] **Sherman Tanks:** Officially named a medium tank. This 30-ton M4 was the workhorse of the Allied Forces. The British modified the Sherman with their version called the Firefly which was retrofitted with a 17-pounder anti-tank gun. The British tank was the only Sherman tank which was capable of successfully engaging German Panther and Tiger tanks.

The Sherman M4 originally was powered by a four-speed, 470 horsepower, thirty- cylinder Chrysler engine. Top speed on a good road was thirty MPH and its operational range was 120 miles at 1.4 miles to the gallon. Between 1942 and 1946, Americans built close to 50,000 tanks—approximately four times as many as the enemy. Each tank cost a mere $33,000 in 1942.

Early model Sherman Tanks had a 75mm main cannon and single, hatch-mounted .50-caliber machine gun, along with two light .30 caliber guns positioned in the turret and forward hull. These guns were later upgraded to a more powerful 76mm. anti-tank gun that could send a 15-pound shell 2,600 feet per second (this new gun was comparable to the Firefly's 17-pounder). The Sherman tank was most recognized by its system of boggie wheels, sloping front armor and two-inch thick hull, giving the tank a high profile turret.

Not all Sherman tanks were merely tanks; there was the Zippo or mounted flamethrower tank; tanks fitted with bulldozers designed to clear minefields; tanks retrofitted with large protruding blades used to cut through the French hedgerows. During amphibious landings, some tanks were fitted with floatation devices called Wading Kits which sometimes worked and sometimes did not.

A full crew in a Sherman tank consisted of: a driver, hull machine-gunner/radio operator, main gunner, loader (big shells), and the tank commander. Most crew knew how to execute each other's responsibilities in case of emergency. The driver does not steer the tank with a steering wheel but with two lateral sticks/levers, each controlling a track. Pushing the sticks forward and pressing on the gas would cause the tank to move forward. Pulling back evenly on the sticks put on the brakes. To make a left or right turn, the driver would pull back on the left lever to turn it left, and on the right lever to go right.

Between D-day and VE Day, approximately 4,300 Shermans were lost—around thirteen a day for eleven months. Its downsides were that it had a comparatively thin skin (less armor) and had a tendency to catch fire easily. Simply, the large number of M4 tanks made up for its lack of power or survivability against the more powerful armored German tanks; it was extremely effective when working in groups deep behind enemy lines to sow destruction. When they had the option, the Sherman tanks left the Panzers killing to M-10 and M-36 tank destroyers or anti-tank guns.

[10] **The Panther IV:** *This favorite German tank is a medium tank weighing 25 tons and measures nineteen feet five inches by twenty-three feet.* It is equipped with four twin-wheel boggy wheels. It carries a crew of five men. Armor on the front hull is three inches thick, compared to .79 inches in the rear. It carries a noticeably long 75 mm L/43 dual-purpose gun that can penetrate 80mm of armor at 1800 meters and is accompanied by one or two MG34 machine guns. It carries only 120 gallons of gasoline and gets, at best, one mile to the gallon. On road, top speed is twenty-six mph on a good road, and off-road, maybe nine or ten mph. The German engineers added more main armor as well as a spacer and skirt armor to protect against anti-tank weapons. They also came up with a Zimmerit paste to prevent magnetic charges from attaching underneath. Most German Panzer or tank battalions consisted of three medium Panzers and one heavy Panzer IV.

[11] **Goldbrickers**: Anyone who avoids their assignment or duties.

[12] **Live Fire Exercises:** Live-fire exercises are conducted within a military base with 'real' ammunition. All types of guns are tested and fired from small arms, assault rifles, artillery, tank cannons, and anti-tank guns. This is an opportunity to test new guns and rounds under all types of weather conditions in order to experience how the weapon will perform. During Live Fire exercises soldiers became comfortable and confident in what their specific weapon could and would do. Most live fire exercises are performed against abandoned/ruined equipment and/or structures in an area devoid of people. These exercises are usually observed by instructors and superiors using binoculars or other long-range devices.

[13] **Blue 88:** A military force-issued sleeping pill.

[14] **Coiling:** This new defensive tactic was beneficial in more than one way. First it kept the roads clear for other vehicles to move forward rapidly if needed for support---for instance, if the forward vehicles needed anti-tank guns etc. It also gave the rear column time to regroup, resupply, and rest. Also one part of the column may be engaged in a fight and the 2nd wave of the column might advance to fight in a different area. Finally, by not having a large column of military vehicles and personnel on a road in a column formation, an enemy plane was prevented from a convenient devastating air strike.

[15] **Bridgeheads**: Infantry worked first to cross a river in small assault boats and were often first to engage and take out the enemy on the other side. Next, the Engineer Battalions would come in and construct some sort of bridge or bridgeheads across a ravine, a river, or whatever they needed to cross. Floating bridges were as follows: (1) Light Pontoon (rubber) Bridge: a floating one-way bridge that carried up to 10-ton traffic. (2) Heavy Pontoon Bridge: similar to a light pontoon bridge but could support a 25-ton

vehicle. (3) Steel Treadway Bridge: this one would support medium tanks; it utilized special rubber pontoon boats. The steel tread ways were mounted in place by cranes and then the bridge was ready for tank regiments and other heavy equipment to cross the water.

When there was more time, the engineers constructed the Light Portable Steel Bridge, a Simple Stringer Bridge, and/or the most famous—The Bailey Bridge which accommodated spans up to 120 feet and could support up to 70 tons. When they were in a forest of sturdy pine trees and needed to put down a passable road in hours over deep mud, they would cut down the pine trees, strip them and lay them side by side over the ground to form the Corduroy Bridge—which resembled the fabric corduroy.

[16] During WWII, the **USO – United Service Organization** was one of the most popular home front war relief efforts. Towns and cities near military bases found themselves with a serious problem—how to deal with servicemen who were on leave, had time on their hands and steam to blow. Most had raging hormones and were looking for a good time; many found it in the movies, bars, and other less wholesome pursuits. As a result, President Roosevelt requested the private sector to provide some sort of entertainment—a home away from home.

The USO did not provide alcoholic beverages, instead they served the military men and women favorite food served in most American kitchens; cake, coffee, cookies, doughnuts, an occasional birthday cake, and even Thanksgiving and Christmas dinner.

There were different types of clubs catering to specific military personnel needs. One might specialize in daycare for the wives and children of soldiers stationed nearby. The type which was most popular was the Dawn Patrol Clubs. Round–the-clock dances with a live band. The volunteer hostesses would decorate the clubs and wear pretty dresses. These girls had gone through particular training of charm and deportment as well as how to handle a soldier who had too much to drink. They knew how to sew a button and/or sergeant stripes onto uniforms. They not only danced but played chess, ping pong, wrote letters and cards and a few of them sang with the band. They were all volunteers!

As the war progressed, big name stars hopped on the USO wagon and went on tour overseas. Hollywood stars like Bob Hope, the Andrews Sisters, Bill Gilbert, Martha Raye, Rita Hayworth, Betty Grable, and many more volunteered to entertain the troops on their own dime.

[17] The troop ship **Edmund B. Alexander** (photo courtesy of D. Cooper) was originally a German-built ship called the AMERIKA. She was seized in Boston in 1917 before WWI and converted to an American troopship renamed AMERICA. For several years after WWI the ship was a trans-Atlantic passenger ship until 1940 when she was rehabilitated yet again by Bethlehem Steel Co. as a floating barracks for 1,200 troops, her name was again changed to the Edmund B. Alexander. A 21,329 ton coal-burning ship, she could only do 10 knots. In 1942 she was again reworked in Baltimore, converting her to oil fuel which increased her speed to 17 knots. At this point, she was able to carry 5,000 troops and 151,685 cubic feet of cargo. At the end and after the war she continued to carry military dependents until 1949. She was scrapped in 1957.

[18] **D-DAY, June 6, 1944:** On the morning of June 5th, the largest amphibious military operation in history, over 5,500 ships---landing craft, and various vessels pulled their anchors and sailed from the southern ports in England. Nine battleships, twenty-three cruisers, one hundred and four destroyers, and seventy-one large landing craft as well as mine sweepers, troop transports, and merchant marine vessels, carrying over 175,000 troops (half American) gathered off the coast of Normandy, France. OPERATION NEPTUNE (landing) was in full effect. The code name for the actual invasion was OPERATION OVERLORD!

On the night of June 5th, 822 aircraft flew over France, filled with parachutists heading for pre-destined drop zones. Bad weather forced the actual delay of the invasion until the next morning at dawn on July 6th; the parachutists were already in the air and on the way. They dropped into France earlier than planned. Initiating the invasion, naval battleships unleashed their punishing big guns at 0550 hours, to detonate large fields of mines buried on the beaches. The second target was the known German defensive bunkers and machine gun nests reported along the upper portions of the beaches. The deafening noise of the battleship's guns and the subsequent explosions were unworldly---a Biblical hell. After the big guns did what they could, nearly 100,000 men landed in one of the most epic invasions in history. Over 13,000 aircraft filled the skies to provide air cover and fire-power for the invading troops on the ground.

Code names for the five beaches of Normandy were: **Utah:** American- casualties 197/23,000), this invading force pressed inland rather easily linking up with the 502nd and 506th Parachute Infantry. Later in the day they linked up with the 101st Infantry. ***Omaha:** Heaviest enemy fortified—Allied tank survival was two out of sixteen. Every sergeant and officer was wounded or killed. When the smoke finally settled, the odor of cordite, fresh blood and burned flesh was punctuated by the screams of the wounded and dying. Medics did what they could but were overwhelmed with the sheer number of casualties. The surf was filled with the bobbing bodies of the dead. **Gold:** High casualties reported because the 'swimming' DD Sherman tanks were delayed in landing. **Juno:** Canadian forces—first wave suffered 50% casualties. The landing of armor before infantry helped clear the path. **Sword:** British –successfully landed DD tanks. Major objective was Caen which they failed to take until mid-July. It took until the middle of August for all the divisions and troops to land at Normandy. There were ninety divisions/4.5 million military personnel on European soil compared to one million Germans.

[19] **Operation Bodyguard**: *General George S. Patton WAS in England where he was keeping a low profile and acting as a decoy to the German war plan, tying up the German Fifth Panzer Army at Pas de Calais where they expected him to lead the main invasion. Patton would not take part in the actual D-Day Invasion.*

He was there to perform another sort of deception to throw the Germans off. The masterminds of Allied forces created a ghost army consisting of blown-up, full size versions of the Sherman tank, anti-aircraft guns, troop trucks, fake radio traffic, jeeps, planes, and ships. They looked so real from a distance that some English civilians thought they were the actual thing; German air reconnaissance was convinced it was a true massing of Allied troops and equipment.

Patton's Third Army did not receive their orders to land on Utah Beach until the first part of August, 1944. Gen. Patton's Third Army and Courtney Hodge's First Army were under the direction of Gen. Omar Bradley once they were on the ground in France. His Ghost Army regrouped under other command and secretly continued to cause much disruption and confusion for the Germans during the war with their fake equipment and sound effects. See: Ghost Army.

[20] **LST or Landing Ships – Tank,** were naval assault landing craft, specially designed to land tanks on beaches. First used by the British in WWII, they were quickly adopted by the United States to use on the beaches of France and also in the Pacific.

[21] **Operation OverLord**: This was the code name for the initial D-Day invasion of Normandy in northern France. It was a big success, partly due to the fact that at least half of the German forces were massed and waiting at Pas de Calais for a massive invasion there. Once the Allied forces were on land in Normandy they pushed fast and hard against the Germans. Canadian and British forces were under General B. Montgomery and American forces under General Omar Bradley, led the execution of Operation Overlord in an attempt to break through the undulating German lines which had been pushed back from the beaches. German forces were later reinforced with divisions from Pas de Calais, including the Seventh Army.

In the meantime, the American forces had another plan up their sleeves. They took advantage of the fact that the British and

American forces were keeping the main body of the German defense busy in Normandy. They used this fact as a divergent, a smokescreen, allowing Patton and Oliver's newly landed divisions to mobilize and slip undetected down the western coast. They squeaked past/around the weakened and distorted German front line at Mortain/Avranches. The Allied forces then swept south around and *behind* the massed German frontlines in Normandy, encircling and trapping over 150,000 Germans.

[22] **Operation Cobra:** The major land campaign was engineered around the capability of the Americans to break out of Normandy. Large aerial and artillery bombardments preceded the actual attacks, dropping over 170,000 bombs on the Germans. The Allied armies coordinated and hit the German forces and pockets of resistance which were attempting to defend the important deep-water French ports of Cherbourg and Caen; Cherbourg was successfully captured on June 27th. These ports were instrumental for landing Allied supplies, fuel, and equipment for the war effort.

The next campaign, **Operation Goodwood,** began on July 18th and was preceded by an enormous artillery and aerial bombardment. Because a large number of German forces were engaged in the attempted defense of Caen, Gen. Bradley's forces faced only 200 German tanks. On the other hand, Bradley commanded over 2,251 tanks, and 65% of these tanks were outfitted with a saw-toothed scoop that easily bit through the hedgerows or bocages. German tanks weren't retrofitted with these and were forced to stick to the maneuverable roads. Utilizing the saw-toothed cutters, American tanks were now able to utilize the entire countryside without the disadvantage of sticking only to the roads which paralleled the hedgerows.

General Omar Bradley turned over the command of the First Army to General Courtney Hodges while Gen. Patton took the Third Army. Gen. Bradley took command of the Twelfth Army as the Canadians and British, continued to pound and push hard from the north against a struggling and depleted German force. If truth were told, Courtney Hodges was most probably the true Patton of the victorious Allied Forces in Europe. He was not the showboat or media-hungry soldier that Patton was; instead he seemed to have an aversion to self-promotion. He was a reserved and thoughtful soldier's soldier who cared about his men as a way to dictate the outcome of the battle or what the press said about him.

[23] **German Tiger Tank:** Heavily armed with a powerful 88mm artillery gun, this 45-ton beast was the most-feared German tank. A major problem with this tank was its tracks were highly vulnerable to weather. Because of its mammoth size, few bridges could support its weight even though most Tiger tanks were outfitted with a snorkel which allowed them to cross water to a depth of four feet. The tank is easily identified not only by its sheer size, but by the obvious flat sections of heavy armor plate which gave it a menacing square look. These tanks were fuel eaters, and in the end that is what weakened their threat. The only Allied tank that could match a Tiger was the British version of the Sherman, called a Firefly tank. It had a 17-pounder super-velocity gun which was more deadly than the Tiger's 88mm AND it could penetrate the Tiger's armor. It was slow but deadly and could fire while moving. Standard Shermans avoided engaging a Tiger unless they had a rear end shot.

[24] The new **Ford GAA tank engine** featured twin NA-Y5-G carburetors, dual magnetos and twin spark plugs creating a cross-flow induction and a full dual-ignition system. It had an all-aluminum, 32-valve DOHC, and a 60-degree V8 engine produced by the Ford Motor Co. especially for the Sherman tanks. Maximum rated horsepower was 535 @2800 rpm; most models were rated at 450 horsepower.

[25] **Piper Cub Reconnaissance planes:** Nicknamed The Horsefly, the infantry and armored forces utilized the small Piper Cub airplane to fly over enemy territory and pinpoint potential targets. They would spot something and radio the location back to the tanks and big guns; artillery would then compute the distance and take the enemy fortification out. Another lethal air support

weapon-assistance was the **P-47 Thunderbolt Fighter Plane.** Even though the plane had a huge appetite for fuel and a relatively short flying range, it could carry rocket-launchers or 2500 pounds of bombs during one run.

[26] **Task Force Anderson:** This elite tank group was named for its Commander LT. Col. Anderson and was made up of 81st Tank Battalion; "B" Co. Tank Bn.; 15th A.I. Bn. – married; "C" Co. 81st Tank Bn.; "C" Co. 15th A.I. Bn. – married; Service Co. 81st Tank Bn.

"D" Company was under direct command of Combat Command "B". These infantry and tank companies worked in close support of each other and were called 'married companies'. A half-track followed each tank in a company and was often filled with infantry. General Oliver conceived this idea of these groups working so closely and constantly, it was like they were married. It was a brilliant and successful arrangement.

[27] **SIEGFRIED LINE:** The Siegfried Line was five to ten miles deep with 'Pill Boxes' arranged in such a manner that they protected each other along the line. Each Pill Box was constructed of reinforced concrete 4 – 5 feet thick. The line was originally built during WWI—also referred to as the *Westwall.* An impressive 390 mile-long line of defensive forts, large concrete Regelbau bunkers, smaller machinegun Pill Boxes, and the famous Dragon's Teeth tank traps which were pointed concrete formations. They were arranged with small ones in the front of the line and larger ones at the back to prevent tanks from rolling over them. The Germans also used the Czech hedgehog which was made by welding steel bars together to cause a barrier to tanks. Where the land was flat, water-filled ditches became tank traps.

Extending from Kleve on the border of the Netherlands to Weil and Rhein on the border to Switzerland, the Siegfried Line contained over 18,000 bunkers, tank traps, and tunnels. The line was beefed up during 1938 – 1940 in anticipation of war. The 'Todt Organization' and its huge number of civilian workers were mainly responsible for building this impressive defensive line.

[28] **HOMELITE:** Known as Little Joe, the Sherman tanks were outfitted with a 24-volt DC electrical system. It had a power take-off from the main tank engine; it had a 24 volt, 50 amp main generator. When the main engine couldn't be run the main system had to be supplemented by another auxiliary generator—a 30 Volt, 1,500-watt generator driven by a one-cylinder, fuel-fired engine located inside the tank. The men hated the thing because it belched smoke and made an ungodly racket. The Germans often used its sound as means to locate a parked Sherman tank.

[29] **BRONZE STAR MEDAL:** Staff Sergeant Arnold Korell (Kessel) was awarded FOUR Bronze Star Medals during his campaign in the European Theatre of WWII. A Bronze Star is the 4th highest individual military award, awarded for the following: acts of heroism; meritorious service in a combat zone; acts of merit. The V-device denotes heroism in combat, sometimes referred to as a Combat V.

Tank Commander Kessel (Korell) received numerous other outstanding awards during his time in combat which he never spoke of. He put them in a drawer and forgot about them because he didn't think he should be awarded for doing what he was ordered to do—what was his duty to do during WWII.

[30] **HURTGEN FOREST:** *Hurtgenwald--- The battle in the Hurtgen forest was the longest battle on German soil during WWII as well as the longest single battle any U.S. Army has ever fought.* East of the Belgian-German border in a heavily forested area approximately 50 square miles, the battle began on 19 September 1944 and ended on 16 December, 1944.

The Americans committed 120,000 troops plus reinforcements to the battle, compared to 80,000 Germans. This battle alone claimed over 33,000 Allied casualties while Germans forces numbered 28,000; it was recorded as a German victory. Initially the Allied goal was to hold down the German Forces in that area, preventing them from reinforcing the German troops in the Battle of Aachen.

The Germans defended this patch of woods for two reasons; (1) it was a staging area for plans already in motion for their mid-December offensive, Watch on the Rhine or the Battle of the Bulge. (2) The mountains commanded access to the Ruhr Dam/Reservoir. If the dam was opened, it would flood the low-lying areas and deny Allied crossing of the river into Germany.

The U. S. First Army took the brunt of this battle, with Generals Courtney Hodges, Omar Bradley, Gerow, Collins, and Cota calling the shots. General Walter Model was the supreme German commander; it was his intention to bring the Allied push to a standstill or at least slow their progress and to inflict heavy casualties. This battle was so detrimental it was later called an Allied defeat of the first magnitude.

According to historians and military experts, this was a battle which should never have been fought. It was fought on maps by senior staff officers in the rear. Obviously, they were not aware that battles are never won or lost on maps. The Germans were intimately familiar with this forest and had pre-wired it to their advantage with preset road mines on and off the narrow logging roads; hidden machine gun and artillery were pre-sighted onto the road and spaced through the length of the forest. The Germans 'knew' this forest; they knew how to camouflage and hide pillboxes. All in all this battle was completely unnecessary and did nothing to gain the cause—except lose 33,000 American lives. Those soldiers would have been better utilized in the Battle of the Bulge. Gen. Eisenhower, in defense of his approval of this campaign, said—"The enemy could have used this area as an avenue of attack." This was an attitude not appreciated by those who fought in that freezing hell.

One reason why Hitler initially chose to fight in the Hurtgen Forest was because his intelligence reported there were lots of green inexperienced American troops stationed in the perimeter. He thought the Germans had a better chance of breaking through at that point than if they attacked veteran units like the 5th Armored Division. That is why the 5th didn't get into the Hurtgen until later---they were held in reserve because they were veterans.

When those who survived returned from fighting in the Hurtgen, many of them crouched in their vehicles and stared off into the distance---completely traumatized. Most soldiers commented that it became so unbearable that they didn't care if they lived or died. Most of them who lived or went to their graves hated everything about a forest—the spongy ground, the smell of pine, the collection of pine needles on the floor of the forest, and the strong smell of a pine wood fire. They hated the canopy of trees, narrow trapping roads, endless freezing cold and dampness. One man said, *"I smell death when I smell a pine tree. I would never have a Christmas tree after I came home, because it brought the war all back."*

[31] **BATTLE OF THE BULGE:** Under the utmost secrecy, minimizing radio traffic and moving equipment and troops at night, a massive offensive known as *Unternehmen Wacht am Rhein* (Operation Watch on the Rhine) was planned and executed by the Germans. Attacking a portion of the weakly-defended Allied line and using adverse weather conditions to their advantage, the Germans attacked in force.

The Ardennes Counteroffensive or Battle of the Bulge took place from 16 December, 1944, to 25 January, 1945. Catching the Allied Forces completely off guard, the partial surprise attack and subsequent deadly fighting took place in the densely forested Ardennes region of France. Allied forces knew the Germans were planning something—but they didn't realize the extent of the campaign.

The Germans never captured the key city of Bastogne, France, although their forces surrounded it. They came within a few miles of crossing the Meuse River—they were stopped by several American divisions. In early January, the Ardennes Offensive came to a halt as German forces were held off by a stronger American defense. . It was the intention of Germany to cut the British and Allied forces in half AND gain control of Antwerp, Belguim and a critical supply port for the Allied forces. German armored forces were severely depleted, something they were never able to overcome. They sustained great personnel and Luftwaffe aircraft losses.

The Germans initially attacked with 200,000 men, 340 tanks, and 290 armored vehicles---when the dust settled, they lost between 68,000 to 100,000 men—missing, wounded, or killed.

The Americans countered with 610,000 men---89,000 were casualties with 19,000 killed. It was agreeably the bloodiest battle fought in World War II but not the longest. The Battle of the Hurtgen Forest was the longest, most costly battle in the war.

Things the common soldier learned: choose oversized boots and stuff them with paper to act as an insulator; wear two wool shirts instead of a big overcoat—easier to fight in; don't rub snow on fingers and toes—just rub them to start the circulation and put hands in arms pits to warm them up; don't eat snow—it'll make you colder; camouflage yourself in the snow by throw a white sheet over your uniform; heat food over a flambeau---a gas-filled wine bottle with a twisted rag for a wick. Most soldiers learned these survival tricks the hard way—by the seat of their pants!

[32] **Weseke, Borken:** According to Hanna Frank, step sister of Dutch author Anne Frank, Borken was the camp where Anne, her sister Marga, and father were taken after being arrested in Holland. Located between the two major German cities of Hamburg and Hannover, Borken served as a holding camp for Jewish prisoners; they were later transferred to the larger Bergen-Belsen concentration camp. Tens-of-thousands prisoners from other extermination and slave camps in East Germany were forced to march – death marches – to camps like Bergen Belsen.

When built in 1940, Borken was a prisoner-of-war camp for French and Belgian, prisoners. In 1941 it was renamed Stalag 311, and over 20,000 Russian prisoners were added. It was designed to hold 10,000 prisoners, but by the end of the war it held 60,000. Borken didn't contain any gas chambers, but over 35,000 prisoners died of overwork, disease, brutality, starvation, and sadistic medical experiments.

[33] **Jungvolk – Hitler Youth:** Membership for this compulsory group was 7,287,470 in 1939 and most obviously went up during the height of World War II The 'Boys' Jungvolk Oath read: *In the presence of this blood banner which represents our Fuhrer, I swear to devote all my energies and my strength to the savior of our country, Adolf Hitler. I am ready and willing to give my life for him, so help me God.*

Mottos for boys were: "Live Faithfully, Fight Bravely, and Die Laughing!" "We were born to die for Germany!" Motto for girls was: "Be Faithful, Be Pure, Be German."

Hitler was quoted as saying that *"the older German is rotten to the marrow, cowardly, and sentimental. With the young men and boys, I can make a whole new world."*

[34] **BERLIN: Feb. 4 – 11, 1945**, Prime Minister Churchill, President Roosevelt, and Soviet Premier Stalin met in Yalta for talks. Stalin realized the Brits and Americans were still reeling from the unexpected fight they had in the Battle of the Bulge, and were softened for the rest of his plan. The United States was nailed down on Iwo Jima by the Japanese and things didn't look good. By Feb. 2nd the Russians had moved to the west bank of the Oder River---43 miles from Berlin. Stalin knew the British had used up the majority of their resources, and Roosevelt was a very sick man. Stalin had the upper hand and he was ready to play his ace.

In return for Russia's agreement to enter the war against Japan three months after the war with Germany ended, Stalin wanted: Russian occupation of Berlin, although particular sectors would be designated as French, British, Russian, and American. Stalin also wanted the Russian Occupation Zone to extend all the way to the Weser River in NW Germany which was the area that the 5th Armored Division had just fought for in the month of April.

Everyone was getting tired of the war and wanted a quick end to it all so previous guards were let down, especially on the American and British sides. Eisenhower had a belly-full of Field Marshall Montgomery and was increasingly frustrated with Churchill, as well. Gen Eisenhower also saw the writing on the wall in regard to taking Berlin. Looking at it from a military viewpoint, it could be taken, surrounded, and then left to wither on the vine. The fanatical die-hard Nazis were moving in for a final battle of Berlin with plans of holding out against the Allies for months if not years.

As it was---Eisenhower messaged Stalin stating that Allied Forces would be stopped at the Elbe, bypassing Berlin. Stalin went along with the words agreeing that Berlin itself was not important at the time. In secret, he ordered his generals to beef up their forces and prepare for an all-out attack on Berlin; they wanted to make the Germans pay for what they had done when they attacked Russia and the siege of Stalingrad.

The battered German Twelfth Army prepared to fight to the last man against the expected American attack. Around 400,000 Germans dug in east of Berlin ready to defend the city. What was left in the German forces were men who had previously served in the navy or air force as well as men as old as 75 and boys as young as 12.

For three agonizing days, the German army managed to hold off the determined Russians. Typically, Hitler threw the blame for the advancing Russian army on Wehrmacht generals and fired them all replacing them with good Nazis from the Waffen-SS, as commanders of all German armies in the East. Realizing it would be a massive Russian assault on Berlin, Hitler appointed Gen. Gotthard Heinrici as leader of the Deutschland army who was expected to meet and hold off Russian General Zukov. Hours before the Russians attacked, Hitler summoned General Henrici to his bunker deep underground in Berlin. "The German army will stand in place in EVERY sector of Berlin---never retreat a single foot. There will be SS troops behind your Wehrmacht troops to insure that no soldier retreats from his post or he will be shot on the spot."

Ironically, Joseph Stalin was issuing almost the identical orders to his generals---there would be no defeat. Berlin would fall to the Russian Army; there would be 'hell-to-pay' if Russian troops were not in Berlin by May 1st, 1945!"

[35] **Bleicherode, Germany:** In January of 1945, Wernher von Braun was the head munitions scientist of Germany's top secret new weapon---rocket research at Peenemunde. As the tide of the war shifted, von Braun was instructed to arm his scientists to protect their work at all costs, even if it meant their own death. Hitler issued at least five different threatening orders stating that if the scientists and engineers quit working at Peenemunde, they would be shot by a firing squad. Finally, von Braun received orders, to move their rocket work to the Mittelwerk factory, deep underground in central Germany. Sensing an unstable and perhaps ominous end to his work he decided to secretly select and catalogue, their most important notes which were placed in boxes, shipped to Bleicherode, and hidden deep in an extensive mine system of tunnels.

Wernher von Braun and his technical corps were only working at the Bleicherode mines for less than a month when SS General Kammler decided to move them yet again to Oberammergau in the Bavarian Alps. Their precious papers were purposely and secretly left behind, deep in the abandoned mines near Bleicherode, and the entrances were dynamited shut.

On May 2, 1945, through a series of almost amusing events, Magnus von Braun, Wernher's brother, tried to surrender to the Americans in the Austrian town of Reutte. Not realizing at first WHOM they were talking to, the Americans continued to hand von Braun's brother through a series of officers who were finally convinced these were extremely valuable men, who wanted to surrender to them.

Donny Bone was an Army recruit at this time & he missed h[...] kept to Korea & staid in Japan 2 weeks, laying on the beach & dancing with pretty women. A ship became available to take him to Hawaii & then home, to this home.

[36] **The Korean Conflict---The Forgotten War:** June 25, 1950; 75,000 North Korean troops entered South Korea, at the 38th parallel boundary, turning the previously cold war into a full-fledged invasion. Fearing this was a first step in a communist campaign to take over the world, the United Nations responded with a police action against the aggressors. Over 5.7 million Americans served in Korea; more than 54,000 died, 103,000 were wounded, 7,000 POWs, and 8,000 MIA. The American and UN troops scrambled to contain the fast-moving communist troops.

Luckily, the United States had a strong, modern reserve of fairly new battleships, aircraft, ground equipment, and a strong infrastructure of production potential.

In mid-September of 1950, a successful invasion at Inchon cracked the North Korean efforts as the UN troops pushed hard up through North Korea until the Chinese openly intervened, aided by subtle Soviet assistance. The UN troops were tossed back into mid-South Korea; early in 1951, the Chinese Army suffered several defeats, forcing it to retreat. By mid-1951, the situation was almost where it had begun. President Truman threatened to use the Atomic Bomb.

Negotiations went on for two more years---nothing was settled and the conflict continued until 27 July, 1953, when fighting ended and a truce was reached. The Cold War continued in full force. Washington has tried ever since to wean South Korea from its dependence on U.S. military, but it continues to be pushed back.

Over all 5 million soldiers and civilians were killed during the war. More than half of this number, about 10% of Korea's prewar civilian population died.

[37] **The 300th Armored Field Battalion, Cowboy Cannoneers:** This group of Wyoming National Guard units entered the Korean War on August 19, 1950. It was composed of a Headquarters Battery from Sheridan, A Battery/Thermopolis; B Battery/Cody; C Battery/Worland; and Service Battery/Lovell.

They applied the Wyoming Bucking Horse on all of their equipment, identifying their units. This Battalion became the most decorated Wyoming National Guard unit of any war. Citations included: The Battle of Soyang; the Second Presidential Unit Citation for the Battle of Kumsong; the First Republic of Korea Presidential Unit Citation for the Battle of Soyang, and the Battle of Kumsong and a meritorious Unit Commendation.

Between May 16 and 22, 1951, the 300th Battalion was cited for extraordinary heroism and outstanding performance of duty in action in the area of Hongchon, Korea. They defended a critical portion of the 2nd Infantry Division and the Eighth Army as they were attacked by 12 Chinese Communist Divisions---equaling around 120,000 men. Wave after wave of the enemy was intent on annihilating the UN Troops who were not to be defeated as they demonstrated superb battlefield knowledge, discipline, and courage in the face of extraordinary odds.

The Battalion's major weapons were 18 Howitzers, mounted on a Sherman tank chassis which supported the infantry. In 805 days of combat, the 105mm cannon fired over 514,036 rounds. Eleven soldiers from the 300th died on the battlefield and 173 men were wounded in action. There were no casualties from the Lovell Service Battalion.

[38] **"Cowboy Artillery at Soyang":** One in a series of National Guard Paintings, this painting depicts the Wyoming Cowboy Canoneers in Hongchon, South Korea, May 18, 1951. *The 300th attached to the 2nd Division during the Battle of Soyang delivered devastating artillery fire for seven days inflicting thousands of enemy casualties. During the morning of May 18 the battalion was given the mission of destroying an enemy roadblock; pouring both direct and indirect fire on the roadblock allowing retreating UN forces to fall back to secure positions. For its gallantry in action, the battalion was awarded the Presidential Unit Citation."* (taken from the Cowboy Cannoneers in the Korean War, the 300th Armored Field Artillery Battalion book.)

Men depicted in painting are: Bill Whitt, Chief of Section/Thermopolis; Bob Heron, Gunner/Worland; Kenny Boyer, Driver/Thermopolis; Denzel Blake, asst. Gunner/St. George, UT.; Ed Johnson, Cannoneer/Casper; & Dick Campbell, Cannoneer/Bell Flower, CA.

[39] **Chief Warrant Officer:** An Army Chief Warrant Officer's grade is rated as officer above the senior enlisted ranks. His primary task is as a leader to serve in a technical aspect, providing skills, guidance, and expertise to field commanders in their field. They are highly skilled, single-track specialty officers who can and do command detachments, units, activities, aircraft,

armored vehicles; they also coach, train, counsel, and coach subordinates.

[40] **End of The Korean War:** The conflict in Korea ended on 7 July, 1953. The members of the 300th Armored Field Artillery Battalion were taken off-line and loaded onto a train which had all the windows blown out--it was a breezy ride to Pusan. As the vets tell it, they were lucky to have survived the train ride. At one point the train stopped in a tunnel because of mortar fire. The diesel fumes almost gassed them to death before one of the officers made his way to the engine, stuck his pistol in the engineer's mouth and told him to get that damn train out of the tunnel. They boarded a ship to the states, traveling for thirteen days from Korea to Japan, then on to San Francisco where they were met by cheering Americans who lined the dock.

On September 27, 1954, the 300th Battalion – The Cowboy Cannoneers unit was disbanded and the men assimilated back into civilian life. During their tour in Korea they fired over 440,000 rounds, half of that during their first four months in battle. They inflicted over 19,500 enemy casualties. Members of the battalion received 9 Silver Stars, 45 Bronze Stars for valor, and 101 Purple Heart medals for wounds resulting from enemy fire.

ABOUT THE AUTHOR:

Karen Wamhoff Schutte is the first born daughter of Beata and the late Arnold Wamhoff of Emblem, Wyoming. She was born and raised in a German Lutheran farming community in the Big Horn Basin of Wyoming. She attended the first eight grades in a two-room school house, later graduating from Greybull High School and earning a bachelor degree in Design Marketing at the University of Wyoming.

Karen and Mike Schutte were married in 1962 and are the parents of four grown sons and ten grandchildren. After raising her family, Karen owned and operated her own interior design firm as an ASID professional designer for the next twenty-five years. She is member of the Rocky Mountain Fiction Writers; Colorado Independent Publishers; Independent Book Publishing Association; The Wyoming Historical Society; The American Historical Society of Germans from Russia, A.S.I.D. American Society of Interior Design (retired). She is a former Soroptimist and participated in numerous community groups.

Upon retirement in 2000, Karen began to think about simply documenting her knowledge of her family's immigration and all the stories she heard at the feet of her grandparents. As a first born grand-daughter and great grand-daughter she felt compelled to create a record of these family stories, not realizing she had just opened Pandora's Box. Documenting, the historical research, and the family stories consumed her as she began to write.

"When I write a book, a story of life, I am there, it is happening to me as I visualize the entire scene, the dialogue, the drama and conflict. I feel like I am leaving a legacy through my books as well as loving the journey of this new purpose in life. Before I begin a new novel, I go through my files and organize everything I have collected about the subject. I make a mental chronological path for the story as I immerse myself in other books of the same genre. This prepares me—gets me in the mood of the time and the scenarios about which I am about to craft. It was never my dream to become a writer, or to write a novel, but this book is my fourth and I'm not finished yet. I have two more on the back burner—just simmering. Becoming a writer means being creative enough to find time in your life for writing. It's become my passion, my purpose!

TANK COMMANDER is the finale to the trilogy on my mother's side of the family. It revolves around my godfather, my uncle Arnold who served in WWII as a tank commander for Generals Patton and Hodges in the European theatre. After the surviving and returning home after the war, he remained in the National Guard only to be called to serve in the Korean War. He never spoke freely or openly about his horrific experiences but I know they continued to haunt his entire life and relationships. Especially disturbing to him were the concentration camps and the unbelievable extent of human suffering and cruelty. As his son Terrill said, "He is my hero!"

Schutte's fifth historical novel, THE GERMAN YANKEE, begins when her German great-grandfather, Johnann Westhoff secures passage on a ship to America in 1860. He settled in Indiana, just in time for the Civil War; he was a member of the Missouri Calvary. Thanks to all of my readers for your continued support and interest in my writings.

Schutte's novels have been awarded two 'Best in Historical Fiction' by the Wyoming Historical Society in 2010 & 2014; a finalist in the Indie Book Awards; 2013 The PEN Award from the Rocky Mountain Fiction Writers; 2015 Best in Cover & Best in Historical Fiction Finalist USA National Book Awards. Schutte lives in Fort Collins, Colorado with her husband, Mike.

If you enjoyed the
TANK COMMANDER

Don't miss
THE GERMAN YANKEE
Coming in 2019

Karen Schutte weaves a tumultuous true story about an ambitious young German man who elects to immigrate to America, hoping to escape five more years of German military service. Johann arrives in America, in rural Indiana—just in time to join up with the Missouri Cavalry as a Yankee, fighting in a bloody Civil War. Will he survive the brutality of the war? Will Johann eventually find peace, love, and make a new life for himself in the country he barely knows? Will the circumstances of his untimely arrival in America be detrimental to his success? He holds on to all of his dreams for a better future in a country he is willing to die for.

CPSIA information can be obtained
at www.ICGtesting.com
Printed in the USA
FSOW01n0958120816
23557FS

9 780990 409595